GARRY DOUGLAS KILWORTH was raised in South Yemen, the son of an RAF sergeant and has a BA (Hons) in English from King's College London in which his special subject was American Literature. Later he served 15 years in the RAF himself. More recently he was with the British Army in Hong Kong (1988–91), where he wrote for *The South China Morning Post*. He now divides his time between Suffolk and Spain, writing full time. He has won many awards for both his children's and adult's novels.

Other titles available in the 'Fancy Jack' Crossman series:

SOLDIERS IN THE MIST

SERGEANT JACK CROSSMAN AND
THE FIGHT FOR SHELL HILL

Garry Douglas Kilworth

ROBINSON
London

Constable & Robinson Ltd
55-56 Russell Square
London WC1B 4HP
www.constablerobinson.com

First published by HarperCollins 1999

This paperback edition published by Robinson,
an imprint of Constable & Robinson Ltd, 2011

A copy of the British Library Cataloguing in
Publication Data is available from the British Library

ISBN 978-1-78033-257-4

Printed and bound in the EU

13 5 7 9 10 8 6 4 2

This one is for an old soldier:
my stepfather, Edward Shaw

Author's Note

I wish to acknowledge a debt of gratitude to the following works, authors and publishers:

The Russian Army of the Crimean War 1854–56, Robert H. G. Thomas and Richard Scollins, Osprey Military.

The British Army on Campaign: 2 The Crimea 1854–56, Michael Barthorp and Pierre Turner, Osprey Military.

Uniforms and Weapons of the Crimean War, Robert Wilkinson-Latham, B. T. Batsford Ltd.

Battles of the Crimean War, W. Baring Pemberton, B. T. Batsford Ltd. (A wonderful volume!)

The Crimean Campaign with the Connaught Rangers 1854–56, Lieutenant-Colonel N. Steevens, Griffith and Farren.

Rifle Green in the Crimea, George Caldwell and Robert Cooper, Bugle Horn Publications.

The Crimean War, Denis Judd, Granada Publishing Ltd.

1854–1856 Crimea (The War with Russia from Contemporary Photographs), Lawrence James, Hayes Kennedy Ltd.

Heroes of the Crimea, Michael Barthorp, Blandford.

The Thin Red Line, John Selby, Hamish Hamilton Ltd.

George Lawson – Surgeon in the Crimea, edited letters explained by Victor Bonham-Carter, Constable and Co. Ltd.

The Invasion of the Crimea (Vol VI), A. W. Kinglake, William Blackwood and Sons.

The Reason Why, Cecil Woodham-Smith, Constable and Co. Ltd.

Thanks go yet again to David Cliff of the Crimean War Research Society, Major John Spiers (Retired) and David Greenwood.

List of Characters

The following are the names of real people additional to those used in Books 1 and 2 of this series:

Private Patrick McGuire
Mrs Nell Butler, regiment wife
General Soimonoff
General Pauloff
General Liprandi
General Dannenberg
Lieutenant Riley
Captain Crosse
Major Maxwell
Colonel Rose
Colonel Jeffreys
Colonel Mauleverer
Henry Clifford
General Bourbaki
Captain Astley
Lieutenant Acton
Captain Haines
General Strangways
Colonel Gordon
Colonel Somerset
Colonel Ayde

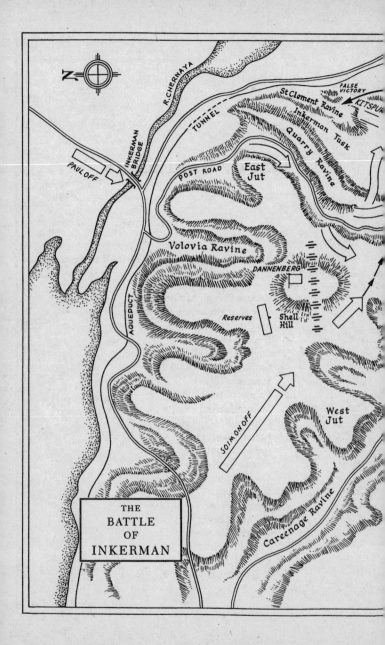

THE
BATTLE
OF
INKERMAN

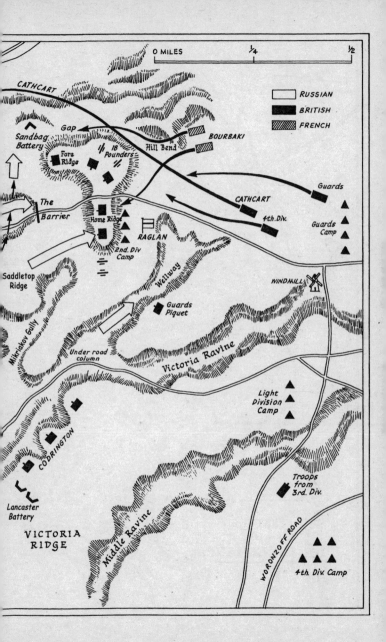

O MILES   ¼   ½

RUSSIAN
BRITISH
FRENCH

CATHCART

Sandbag
Battery

Gap

BOURBAKI

Fore
Ridge

18
Pounders

Hill Bend

Guards

The
Barrier

Home Ridge

RAGLAN

CATHCART

4th. Div.

Guards
Camp

Saddletop
Ridge

2nd. Div
Camp

WINDMILL

Wellway

Mikriakov Gully

Guards
Piquet

Under road
column

Victoria Ravine

Light
Division
Camp

CODRINGTON

Troops
from
3rd. Div.

Lancaster
Battery

VICTORIA
RIDGE

Middle Ravine

WORONZOFF ROAD

4th. Div. Camp

1

'There is a traitor in our midst,' said Major Lovelace, 'and we must remove him with all expediency.'

Sergeant Crossman and the major were sitting on gunpowder barrels just inside the lower room of a hovel. These were quarters shared by Crossman and his four men. The major also stayed there from time to time, when he was not out on one of his spying missions. These expeditions were called 'fox hunts' by General Buller, who was responsible for their formation.

The hovel itself was situated in Kadikoi village, just north of Balaclava harbour, the scene of the gallant stand by the 93rd Sutherland Highlanders against the Russian cavalry just a few days previously.

On a recent mission Crossman had captured a quantity of silver coins – Maria Theresa dollars – from a Russian caravan. The booty was to be shared between all those involved. It would make each of them considerably richer. Prize money was held in abeyance until the end of the campaign however, or men would be buying themselves out of the army right, left and centre. Crossman and the others would have to wait for their cash.

Major Lovelace suspected that the money had been destined for the pockets of a traitor to the allied cause.

'You seem convinced of that fact, sir?'

Lovelace nodded. The major was a slim blond man in his early thirties. An officer on General Buller's staff, he was one of the modern-thinking new men emerging in a post-Wellingtonian army run by old men. Although he had purchased a captaincy in the Royal Horse Artillery, he had nothing against those who rose from the ranks or received field promotions. He had recently been promoted by Lord Raglan at General Buller's request.

Major Lovelace believed in espionage and sabotage as acceptable methods of conducting a war. Lord Raglan and many of the older staff officers did not. Lord Raglan was under the impression that Lovelace had done something on the battlefield to impress Buller, but in fact he had earned his promotion by what Lord Raglan would describe as 'skulking and sneaking'.

Sergeant Crossman had been recruited by Lovelace, not altogether voluntarily, into this new branch of special duties which crossed through ranks and regiments and was in many ways a leveller of class. He too was now a spy and saboteur with a Russian price on his head. The job did not come to him as naturally as it came to his superior officer, however. Certain rather unsavoury acts were carried out reluctantly by the young Scot.

On the other hand, although Crossman had not witnessed Lovelace in action, there was something in the cold blue eyes of the English officer which told the sergeant that, in the major's thinking, expediency overruled scruples. Crossman had no doubt that Major Lovelace was a student of Machiavelli and believed that the end always justified the means. Major Lovelace's next remark confirmed this view.

'Utterly convinced of it. We must seek him out and eliminate him.'

'Bring him to trial you mean, sir?' said Crossman, with more hope than conviction.

'Good Lord, no, man. We must assassinate the beggar

2

before he does any more harm. He's been passing the Russians information on the disposition of our battalions and the positions of our guns. We must kill him.'

Sergeant Crossman puffed on the long curved Turkish chibouque which was his constant companion. Taking the stem from between his lips he said quietly, 'That sounds like murder to me, sir. What if we get the wrong man?'

Major Lovelace sighed and unbuttoned his tunic.

'We must make sure we get the *right* man. Work like this requires precision. Think how it would look to those back home if the culprit were British! His regiment, his parents and his friends, his comrades – they would all die of shame. Think of what the war correspondent William Russell would make of it – headlines across the front of *The Times*.'

'And if the traitor's not British?'

'Then it hardly matters, does it?'

Crossman frowned. He was not sure he liked that answer. He was not one of those who believed in the superiority of the British as a race. Lovelace however saw the frown and interpreted it correctly.

'I think you misunderstand me, sergeant. I meant if he's not British – say he's French or Turkish, or some mercenary from another nation entirely – we should have the dickens of a job to bring him to trial. My feeling is that he would slide out of it somehow and end up laughing at us on the shores of some unreachable country. No, we must shoot him dead and be done with it.'

'And,' asked Crossman with a sinking feeling, 'who is to do this unpalatable deed?'

Lovelace smiled humourlessly with those cold blue eyes.

'Why, you of course, sergeant.'

The pipe came out of the mouth.

'Me?'

'Would I be telling you all this if it were not you? This must remain strictly between the two of us. No other person in the world must know of it.'

'I'm glad to hear that part,' said Crossman. 'If it's to be done I would prefer it to remain a secret to everyone else but myself. Even two of us is one too many.'

'Your wish will be granted in full. I do not know who the traitor is. A Greek informant out of Sebastopol tells us only that he will be in a certain place at a certain time. It is all he knew of the matter himself. He will arrive at Mackenzies Farm at around six a.m. tomorrow morning. You will be there to put a bullet in his heart. On your return you will not need to tell me his name – all I wish to hear is that the mission has been a success. This is not one of the fox hunts I would have chosen for you, Sergeant Crossman, but there is no alternative.'

'Why me?'

'Because I have to be elsewhere and I trust no one else but you to carry this out successfully.'

Crossman puffed on the dregs of his tobacco, muttering, 'I suppose I should take that as a compliment.'

'Yes and no,' said the major, smiling. 'One of the aspects of this business I am certain of is that you are not the traitor – and that makes you entirely eligible to be the assassin.'

At that moment the door opened and Major Lovelace looked up sharply. The noise of the guns along the siege line around Sebastopol could be heard quite plainly through the open doorway. Those Russian batteries replying to the bombardment were slightly fainter, but the eerie sound of 'Whistling Dicks' – large Russian shells which made a peculiar whirring noise – could be heard above all. The two sides had been pounding at one another since the British had repelled an attack a few days previously on the ruins of Inkerman to the north of the city.

Into the room stepped a lieutenant from the Rifle Brigade. Crossman recognised Dalton-James, a member of the old school, and not a modern-thinking soldier like Lovelace. He believed sergeants, whether they came from good families or not, should be seen and not heard. Dalton-James had not been on any fox hunts. He worked more in the role of coordinator of missions for General Buller

Lieutenant Dalton-James looked shocked as he approached the pair of them. Crossman guessed it was because Lovelace was casually sipping at a glass of rum, his tunic unbuttoned and his hat on the table beside him. Crossman himself was in a similar state of undress, puffing away on his chibouque. The major and the sergeant looked like drinking chums enjoying a chitchat in an inn.

'Sir?' said Dalton-James, coming stiffly to attention before the major. 'You sent for me?'

'Ah, yes, lieutenant. The sergeant here will be going out on a fox hunt. He will be going alone. See that he is provided with enough rations for two days in the field.'

'Yes, sir,' replied the lieutenant.

Clearly Dalton-James did not like to be called forth to supply a mere sergeant with his field rations. Immaculate in his Rifle Greens, the lieutenant looked as if he were going to a ball. A ship had recently arrived at Balaclava carrying a trunk of new uniforms solely for him.

Crossman, in comparison, was dressed in rags.

The majority of British soldiers walking around the Crimean landscape were attired similarly to Crossman. After almost a year in the only uniform they possessed they looked like scarecrows. They slept in trenches half-filled with water, they waded through rivers, through thorny brakes, down into dust bowls and up over rocky escarpments – all in the same uniform. Their tents, ancient and threadbare even before being unpacked, were also in tatters. It was a raggedy army which besieged the city of Sebastopol, an army of red-eyed, weary men, attacked by sickness and undernourished.

It was rumoured that there were uniforms, and blankets, and other such riches, thick with mould and rotting in the boats and warehouses of Balaclava harbour. This sorely-needed equipment never reached the men: no one dared take the responsibility for issuing them. The Commissariat 'Purveyors' awaited certificates from England, granting permission to open crates and issue clothing. Such certificates took an age to arrive, after being signed by several government departments, and even when approved were often lost in transit. Soldiers died of exposure not because there were no warm clothes, but because of red tape. Families and the general public in Britain were appalled by the stories coming back from the front and there had been much castigation of the Commissariat in the press.

Winter was coming on, and though a few had managed to take coats and boots from Russian corpses, most were still in desperate need of kit. Crossman had purchased an issue sheepskin coat from French soldiers who were better provisioned. This hid his threadbare coatee which had weathered from its original red into a faded purple hue. He had sheepskin leggings, held in place by leather thongs criss-crossed up his calves. On his head he wore a fur hat, taken from a dead Russian.

Once Crossman had been provisioned, he set off to the north-west, to find the Mackenzie place. The farm, once owned by a Scottish expatriate, was situated not far from the Inkerman ruins, just above the Old City Heights. It was a good ten miles from Kadikoi village over dangerous country. The sergeant travelled light: his Tranter revolver with its two triggers – one for cocking the weapon and the other for firing – and his German hunting knife. Not for him the normal 58 lb weight of equipment carried by a British soldier, most of which that soldier had to purchase himself out of his own pay.

The farm was outside the limits of the siege. In fact, Crossman reflected as he walked, it could hardly be called a siege. Supplies and fresh men were still getting through to the troops and citizens of Sebastopol. The Russians, though soundly beaten at the Alma and held at Balaclava now had the initiative.

Retaining some of the redoubts in the hills, the Russians blocked the Woronzoff Road, thus denying the British a proper supply route from Balaclava to the siege line, and confining them to a small difficult track over the Sapouné Ridge. They also held the coast along the Heights of Inkerman, north of Sebastopol, thus allowing a safe passage in and out of the city. Reinforcements and supplies were transported over the Sea of Azov to the towns of Yenikale and Kerch on the east of the Crimea, and from there overland westwards to Sebastopol.

It appeared to Crossman that men were fighting bravely and dying for no gain. Lord Raglan seemed to be a most ineffectual commander-in-chief, though there were one or two competent generals below him. Raglan was a mere presence on the battlefield, but little else. The one time he had made a decisive order, it had resulted in the destruction of the Light Brigade.

It had been an early dawn of mist and rain when Crossman set out from Kadikoi, passing hovels and tents where British wives took in washing. It was a good time to travel. One could see one's path, yet the shadows of the twilight chased each other across the landscape and disguised movement. One man flitting between rocks and through bushes might avoid detection.

As the morning wore on however, the mists cleared and the rain ceased. It became brighter and more dangerous to travel. Crossman climbed a ridge, found himself a rock hang and decided to get some rest. He had recently been quite ill and was not yet thoroughly fit.

On waking, Sergeant Crossman scratched at his throat, feeling something irritating him in that spot. He thought it was an insect, until he opened his eyes and looked up the shining length of a sabre. Thence along an arm which culminated in the smiling face of a young Russian lieutenant. The point of the lieutenant's sword was pricking the hollow below Crossman's Adam's apple.

'Good day to you,' said the Russian in his own language.

Crossman, who spoke both German and French, and understood a little Russian, nodded without opening his mouth. He glanced to the right and left and saw he was surrounded by Russian soldiers. Unlike their officer they were not smiling. They simply stared, a semicircle of long bayonets at the ready. Their round faces revealed no curiosity. They looked as if they belonged behind a plough, much like the lads who served under British officers.

Crossman now spoke. 'Good day, lieutenant – I was just having a nap.'

'You do not speak my language at all well. What nationality are you?'

'*Je suis français*,' replied Crossman, without hesitation, seeing some Cossacks in the background. 'A corporal in the Zouaves. I'm – I'm running away. I've had enough and my father is sick in a Marseille hospital. I need to get home.'

Since his arrival in the Crimea and his recruitment into General Buller's group of espionage agents and saboteurs, Crossman had been pursued by certain Cossacks. He had killed a number of the blue warriors in the course of his duties. A Greek spy for the Russians had given his name and rank to them, as the perpetrator of these deaths. Now they were looking for a Sergeant Crossman in the 88th Foot, the Connaught Rangers. It was better to be French.

The Russian lieutenant switched easily to the French language.

'A corporal in the Zouaves? Where is your uniform? How is it that you speak a little Russian?'

'I speak a little of quite a few languages. Turkish, Russian, German – even a little English. I am a resourceful man.'

The lieutenant finally removed the sword point from Crossman's throat.

'And where is this resourceful deserter going?'

'Home,' replied Crossman. 'To France.'

'You are *walking* back to France?'

Crossman grinned. 'I don't have any other alternative. They wouldn't let me have a horse. I'm a foot soldier, as you can see. I was hoping to get a ship somewhere up the coast. Perhaps you can give me the name of a good cargo vessel, bound for the Mediterranean. I live in Marseille.'

'So you said.'

Crossman bit his tongue. He was overdoing it. He was not yet good at subterfuge and deceit.

The Russian spoke again. 'You must be a sailor to speak so many languages.'

'I'm no sailor. I don't speak them fluently. I have simply heard them in the waterfront cafés of Marseille. May I go now?'

The lieutenant turned to his men and repeated the last sentence in Russian. Now they roared with laughter. Soldiers came forward and prodded him with their bayonets. Then he was herded, out of the cover of the rock hang and down the hillside. Here he saw with astonishment that there was a whole army on the march. At least two divisions. He noticed by their insignia they were from Odessa – the 4th Army Corps.

The 4th Corps! Heading towards the Russian Army now camped on the Heights of Inkerman. Something was in the wind. A fresh assault by the Russians?

2

Crossman underwent a perfunctory search for weapons and was then bullied into a scramble down the slope. When he reached the bottom he tripped and rolled over in the dirt. His sheepskin flew open to expose his British Army coatee. The lieutenant who had captured him rushed forward and shouted an order to two soldiers. They tore the sheepskin from Crossman's back revealing the now purple coatee and its faded sergeant's chevrons. When he objected he received a rifle butt on the cheekbone, making him reel back and spit blood.

'A French deserter?' shouted the officer in his face. 'I think not. I think you are British.'

'British, French,' muttered Crossman, taking back his sheepskin coat and putting it on again, 'what difference does it make? I'm a deserter.'

'Perhaps not, perhaps not. There is talk of a British sergeant who has given us a great deal of trouble. A spy and saboteur. Our people are looking for such a person. You may be he.'

Crossman shook his head. 'I try to give no man trouble.'

'How is it,' continued the officer, now drawing other officers to the scene, 'that you speak good French? A sergeant in the British Army? This is unlikely, is it not? I think you are the spy.'

An infantry captain drew his sword and stepped forward. He said something in Russian to the two soldiers standing near him. They reached out and each took one of Crossman's arms. The sergeant was forced into a kneeling position with his arms bent painfully behind his back like two open wings of an angel. He realised now he was about to be executed. The captain was going to decapitate him with his sword.

'Wait!' cried Crossman in French. 'I can be of use. I – I know the disposition of our army.'

Crossman was desperately trying to buy some time. It did not matter what he told them. He could make it up. They were surely fresh from the Russian hinterland. They would know very little about the situation here in the Crimea. It seemed he was wrong about this however, for the lieutenant standing beside the captain laughed.

'You think we do not have our spies too? What is there to know? That you have your battalions stretched thinly from Balaclava to Sebastopol? And that you have the French Army on your left covering the Chersonese Uplands? Let me tell you that the French and British Headquarters both lie five miles directly south of Sebastopol and that the camps of your depleted cavalry units are to the right and rear of your so-called siege line. What more can you tell me, sergeant?'

Despair filled Crossman. He knew he was about to die and he was terribly afraid. He was a young man with a stout heart, but waiting for a sword to descend upon one's neck was enough to fill the bravest soldier with terror. At the last moment he looked up, to see the sword poised. There was fear on the face of the man who wielded the weapon too, and the guards who held Crossman looked on in horror. An execution is no easy task for any man with feelings in his breast.

Suddenly, there was a shout. A red-faced colonel rode forward on his horse, barking an order. The captain let his sword arm fall by his side. For the moment at least, Crossman was reprieved. He let out a short sob of relief. The two soldiers pulled him to his feet as the colonel rode up.

Crossman stared up into the fat red face with its huge, white, bristling moustaches. The man stared down at him, keenly searching his face. Then another order was barked and the colonel rode off to the front of the corps, which was now on its feet and preparing to march.

'You have been given a short while to live,' said the lieutenant. 'Our colonel wishes to question you.'

'I told you I had information about the disposition of our troops.'

'Bah!' scoffed the lieutenant. 'We can find out all about that from *The Times* newspaper. Our best spies are your war correspondents. What my colonel wishes to know is whether your soldiers have any heart left, after we smashed you at Balaclava . . .'

'You didn't smash us,' replied Crossman, angrily. 'We held you.'

'Yes, but at what cost? You have lost your precious Light Brigade. We took many of your guns. We captured your redoubts on the heights overlooking the Woronzoff Road. Your generals are in disarray, arguing amongst themselves, not wishing to speak with the French whom they regard as an old enemy, and not wishing to use the Turks whom they believe failed them at Balaclava. You see, we know everything.'

'What's my grandmother's name?' snapped Crossman, as his hands were bound behind him.

'What? Don't be foolish.'

'You see,' he sneered at the lieutenant, 'you don't know everything.'

The lieutenant's face went stiff and formal.

'So, this is the famous British humour we hear about — it is not funny at all.'

'It's not meant to be. It's meant to be a put down.'

12

'I do not understand this gibberish.'

Crossman was led away on the end of a leash attached to his hands. The two guards assigned to look after him were young men with peasant faces. They seemed pleasant enough, not like the guards he had had when he had been captured on a mission in Sebastopol. They had beaten him to within a shade of his life. One of them smiled shyly at him with worried crinkled eyes as he studied the man's face. Crossman had no doubt these young men were as apprehensive as any soldier in a war.

Towards evening, the march stopped and the Russian corps made camp. No tents went up and no fires were lit. They simply formed huddled rings around stacked rifles, while sentries were posted on the periphery.

His hands untied, Crossman was taken to the red-faced colonel. The young lieutenant was there, looking immaculate. He also looked pleased with himself. No doubt he would have been given credit for Crossman's capture. Something to write home about to his aristocratic family in St Petersburg or Moscow or one of the other cities in his vast country.

Crossman too came from aristocracy: a fact he preferred to put behind him. He hated his father, a major in the 93rd Sutherland Highlanders, for seducing his mother and leaving her to die unmarried and alone. It was the reason for him being in the ranks, under an assumed name.

The colonel, who like most aristocrats also spoke French, asked Crossman some pertinent questions.

'Why are you dressed in a Frenchman's jacket?'

'It's warm. I purchased it from a French soldier, who had taken it from the body of a friend who fell in battle.'

The colonel snorted. 'You rob your own dead?'

'I understood the money was to go to the dead soldier's widow.'

There was a nod of approval from the colonel.

'And the money for that Russian headgear you wear? Is that to go to the widow of the soldier who owned it?'

Crossman looked a little shamefaced.

'I admit I stole this fur hat.'

Again, another nod. 'You know what I think? I think you buy and steal clothes because the British Army does not supply its own troops with such items. I think your great Army of the East is in chaos. Admit to me. The men are dispirited, are they not? Their morale is low, they are under-provisioned, they die of sickness in the siege trenches, they freeze on cold nights, they have nothing left in them with which to fight?'

Crossman would have liked to argue all points with the colonel, but he did not, instead he confined himself to the last part of the question.

'A British soldier will always have something in him with which to fight.'

The lieutenant standing behind Crossman snorted with mirth. But the colonel merely stared into Crossman's eyes, seeking some sort of truth.

Then he said, 'I think you know your army is at a low ebb, far from home, its faith in its leaders gone. The cholera is killing you by the hundred. Your cholera belts are no protection against this deadly disease. I think you know you are finished.'

'Then I must know it, if you think so.'

'I do, I do. I am sorry for the common soldier. You should have come after us when we retreated from the Alma. You should have gone into Sebastopol immediately. Your leaders are making too many mistakes, costing many lives. Now we have our defences and a stronger army building. We will destroy you all and send the survivors home to a nation in sorrow.'

Crossman shrugged. 'If you think so.'

'I do, I do.'

After this interview, Crossman was led away by his guards and his hands were retied behind his back. His ankles were also bound this time, since there was no marching to do. He was made to sit with his back against a boulder. A kind of peace settled down over the area, though the sound of distant guns both from the city and the allied armies punched at the hollow sky.

Gradually men fell asleep all around. A Russian soldier's uniform, unlike that of a British soldier, was full and warm. They were not even issued blankets, their thick greatcoats serving that function. Finally only one of Crossman's two guards remained awake. He was staring into the middle distance, not paying very much attention to his prisoner, who he believed to be secure.

Indeed, Crossman himself felt helpless. The ropes were tight around his wrists. And while his ankles were bound he could not creep away into the night. He tried scraping his bonds against the boulder, but they remained secure and unyielding under his efforts. After looking up at the stars for a while, he too dropped into a doze.

At around two o'clock in the morning he suddenly woke to feel someone slicing through his bonds. Glancing behind him he saw the rotund shape of a man using a sharp knife. Quickly he looked at the two guards. Both were asleep now, one sitting hunched over his musket, the other with his back against the same rock against which Crossman was propped.

The bits of rope dropped away. The knife was pressed into his right hand. He swiftly cut through the cords around his ankles. When he looked up he saw his rescuer was just about to slit the throat of the soldier closest to him. Crossman gripped the man's wrist and shook his head. The man shrugged and the pair of them then sneaked away into the darkness.

The man who had saved Crossman from what would surely have been a summary execution, was Yusuf Ali, the Bashi-Bazouk with whom Crossman had shared many missions, many fox hunts. The sergeant did not pause now to ask why the Turk was there, but simply followed him as he snaked through the tall grass between two Russian sentries. Once they were safe in the hills however, Crossman asked the obvious questions.

'What are you doing here, Ali?'

'I follow you,' replied the Turk, wiping mud from the blade of his knife on to his red pantaloons. 'You go without me!'

This last sentence was uttered in an incriminating tone.

'I was ordered to go alone. You should not have come.'

'Ha – I no come, you be dead in the morning.'

That was true enough. 'You saw me leave then?'

'I walk with Mr Jarrard. We both see you go off into the hills. I follow you.'

'Rupert Jarrard saw me leave too? What kind of spy am I? The whole allied army must have watched me go.'

It was distressing, considering the nature of the fox hunt.

'No – just me and Mr Jarrard.'

Jarrard was an American war correspondent and Crossman's particular friend. The two had a lot in common – an interest in modern inventions and discoveries, a dislike of the aristocracy, a keen appreciation of beautiful women – and they spent time together discussing these things when they could. Crossman wondered whether Rupert would approve of assassinating traitors without a trial. Knowing the man, he thought not.

Yusuf Ali, ever practical, now asked, 'You lose your weapons?'

Crossman shook his head. 'My revolver is in a hidden pocket in the hem of my sheepskin coat and my knife is where any self-respecting Scotsman keeps his *sgian dubh* – in the top of my hose.'

'They not search you?' asked the Bashi-Bazouk in surprise.

'They did – but badly.'

'Where we go now?'

Crossman set his mouth in a firm line.

'I am going north, but you are going back to Major Lovelace. It's no good shaking your head like that, Ali – you must. Someone must tell our generals that Sebastopol is being reinforced with new troops. It's my belief they're about to make another assault on our lines. The information needs to get back. Tell Major Lovelace that the 4th Army Corps from Odessa is on the move towards Sebastopol and will be there tomorrow.'

'I go with you,' said Ali, stubbornly.

'Please, Ali, don't argue with me on this. Come out after me if you like once you've delivered the message, but someone must go back and I have an unpleasant job to do.'

The Bashi-Bazouk scratched his brow under his turban, and then finally nodded.

'I go.'

3

It was a blood-red dawn which rose over the eastern hills. Crossman lay in a hollow on a rise above Mackenzies Farm and watched the sunrise. It was a beautiful sight. Normally he was too cold and wet, too weary to appreciate such things, but this morning there was no rain and he was out of the wind. He could afford to let his mind wander on poetic lines.

Lavinia Durham would like such a dawn. Perhaps she was watching it at that very moment, from her little house in Kadikoi? Crossman had not spoken with her since the duel between her husband and Lieutenant Dalton-James. Crossman had managed to avert any bloodshed on that occasion. Just as a joke, Crossman had led the lieutenant to the belief that Lavinia Durham had requested a tryst with him, but the whole episode had unfortunately turned nasty. Crossman felt doubly guilty, since he had been the one having an affair with Mrs Durham, a sweetheart of his before she was ever married to the quartermaster, Captain Durham.

He was not proud of his behaviour, even though he had been under the influence of pain-killing laudanum at the time. In point of fact, Lavinia and he had effectively been laying an old ghost to rest.

Something was happening in the farm below – a lamp had

been lighted – and Crossman's mind was yanked back to the task in hand.

His 5-shot Tranter revolver was in his hand, ready to kill the man who walked or rode up to the farmhouse. It was not a chore he relished, this cold-blooded murder without any real sort of proof or any kind of trial.

What if someone quite innocent of any wrongdoing were to be there first? Perhaps an employee of the farmer, who lived in one of the outlying villages? Or the real traitor did not turn up, but decided to deliver his information elsewhere, and another man by coincidence happened to be passing the farmhouse on his way to another location?

Crossman's palms were sweating. This was ugly work. There might even be retribution later. What if Major Lovelace were killed in battle? There was no written order in Crossman's possession. Only the word of an officer. If Crossman were accused at a later date of committing what was in truth a crime, there would be no one willing to stand up for him. A few, his enemies, would wallow in his downfall.

This was of course the worst scenario, but in times of stress such outcomes did not seem unlikely.

A figure was coming up from the south on foot, heading towards the farm! It seemed the man wanted to be as inconspicuous as possible, for he kept to the shadows of the hills, skulking in the half-light, constantly looking about him as if he expected to be followed. A child could not have looked more guilty, sneaking down to the pantry at night.

Crossman checked his pocket watch. It was just coming up to six o'clock.

The sergeant saw that the man would pass an outcrop of rocks, and he slipped silently down the slope to position himself behind those boulders. When the traitor passed that spot all Crossman would have to do would be to step out and shoot him in the head at point-blank range, then drift back into the hills again before anyone from the farm could investigate. Crossman knew he should use the hunting knife, silently and swiftly, but he did not trust himself to kill instantaneously. Even a traitor deserved to be executed without a lingering death.

It was a simple action, but his heart was hammering in his chest. The Tranter felt like a ton weight in his right hand. He used the trigger under the guard to cock the weapon. In the silence of the hills the metallic *click* seemed loud and intrusive. Crossman winced. A quick glance at the oncoming man, however, told him that the sound had not been heard.

Feet crunched on gravel and shale, coming closer and closer. An elongated shadow stretched into view at Crossman's feet. Suddenly, the man was there. Crossman stepped out quickly, his arm outstretched. He pointed the muzzle of the revolver at the side of the man's head. In that second the other turned his face, startled, suddenly aware of Crossman's presence. There was an expression of puzzlement on the man's features.

Crossman began to squeeze the trigger, but at the last instant relaxed.

The face before him, albeit hidden under a layer of grime, belonged unmistakably to Lieutenant Dalton-James.

'Sergeant Crossman?' cried the lieutenant, his eyes full of surprise, 'what are you doing?'

Dalton-James was the traitor. Dressed in the clothes of a Tartar, his face purposefully dirtied under a filthy fur-lined leather hat with earflaps, he had a waterproof envelope beneath his arm which probably contained the papers he was about to sell to the enemy. The lieutenant looked every inch the spy and traitor he obviously was. It was difficult to believe that such a man, from a good family, would betray his country, his queen, and his friends, but such seemed the case.

Crossman tried to squeeze the trigger again. He found it impossible. His finger had frozen. He could not assassinate the lieutenant in cold blood. The trigger might have been welded to the pistol. His finger might have been made of granite. He let out a sob of frustration, angered by his own ineptitude.

Unable to do the deed at that moment, Crossman vowed to himself he would do it later. He had to talk to the man. Find out why he was selling his soul. Perhaps Crossman could build up enough courage to kill him later. After some sort of trial at least. Even if he had to be the judge and jury all rolled into one.

'Move!' he said, prodding the officer. 'Up the slope. Quickly. I swear if someone comes out of that farm and catches us I'll shoot you dead where you stand.'

If Dalton-James had been about to protest, there was something in Crossman's expression which prevented the words coming from his mouth. He certainly looked outraged, but held his tongue. The lieutenant allowed himself to be prodded up the slope, away from the farm. Crossman hurried his prisoner over the ridge on a goat track which was hidden from the farm's view. Whenever Dalton-James opened his mouth, Crossman warned him to save his breath and keep walking.

'How dare you! How dare you! You will suffer for this, sergeant,' snarled the lieutenant. 'I'll see you broken on the wheel. I'll have you flayed until you bleed.'

If it was acting, Dalton-James was good at it. His sense of drama was perfect. The officer seemed so incensed he kept tripping over his own feet in frustration, but Crossman merely kicked him on with his right boot, anxious to put some distance between the farm and himself. When Dalton-James turned to protest at what he considered to be disgraceful treatment, the taller and stronger Crossman grabbed him by the back of his collar and literally manhandled him up a gradient.

Finally the lieutenant could take no more of Crossman's bullying, and with a cry he reached into his pocket for his own revolver. Crossman brought the barrel of the Tranter savagely down on the man's wrist, hearing the bone crack. Dalton-James let out a sob of pain and dropped his gun. Crossman picked it up and put it in his own pocket.

Dalton-James stared into the sergeant's eyes. For the first time he seemed to realise he was in serious trouble. He held his broken wrist and stumbled on white-faced in front of Crossman, who prodded his back.

Finally, they reached a spot where Crossman felt it safe to stop, in amongst a covering spinney.

'My arm-bone is fractured,' complained Dalton-James. 'It needs attention.'

'You won't be worrying about the pain for very much longer,' replied Crossman. 'Just tell me why you did it. Why did you turn traitor? You know I have orders to kill you? I should have done it back there, but I was shocked to find it was you selling secrets to the enemy. Tell me, and then we'll get it over with quickly. It's no use pleading – there can be no other way.'

Dalton-James blanched even more at these words, the blood draining from his face.

'I'm no traitor,' he said, in an obstinate tone. 'I'm following orders too.'

Crossman reached forward and snatched the oilskin envelope from under the lieutenant's arm. He opened it, keeping a wary eye on his prisoner. Inside the envelope there were drawings of British and French positions along the siege line. Crossman held one up so that the lieutenant could see it.

'What's this, sir?' he asked. 'A plan of a child's nursery?'

Dalton-James peered at the sketch. 'Don't be facetious, sergeant. You know what it is. My orders were to deliver this package to a lieutenant-general of the Sardinian forces, who has landed secretly in the Crimea. The Sardinian Bersaglieri, don't you know, are considering joining the allies in their fight against Russian expansion. The general wishes to assess the situation before committing his own army to the cause.'

Crossman considered this explanation, seeing how flimsy it was when held up to inspection.

'Why would a Sardinian general want our troop positions at this point in time? Surely if he was considering joining us he would take a ship to Balaclava and see the position for himself? He would not land at some other port and then hide in a farm in what is effectively enemy territory.'

'These are not questions I have the authority, nor even the knowledge, to answer. I am merely a courier. I have been given my orders by a senior officer. The explanations which lie behind these devious schemes are unknown to me. You and I are part of a complex espionage network created by Major Lovelace under General Buller's orders. We do not question. We merely obey orders and leave the complicated machinations to those above us.'

Crossman became irritated with the lieutenant.

'Are you telling me, sir, that you obey orders without considering their implication?'

'It is a soldier's duty.'

Crossman said drily, 'The Light Brigade can attest to that.'

'Mistakes will happen. That is inevitable,' said Dalton-James, rubbing his now swollen wrist. 'I do not understand how you, a common soldier, can consider questioning the wisdom of our superiors, while I – a commissioned officer – am willing to die without lengthy enquiries as to the nature of the intelligence of our orders. I am proud to serve without question. I cannot live in distrust of those whose acumen I admire. We neither of us understand the other, sergeant, and that is a fact.'

Crossman realised this was quite true. He knew he was unusual in the army, for being a sceptic. It was probably down to the fact that he had grown up with a father who he considered to be infallible, and had found out quite suddenly later that his hero was a blackguard. That sort of shock tends to turn a man into a sceptic: into a man who questions authority at every turn.

'Who is the senior officer who ordered you to take this envelope to the farm?'

Dalton-James lifted his head, his expression defiant.

'That I would not tell you if you broke my other wrist and my legs too. I am under an obligation to keep the officer's name in complete confidence.'

'Was it Major Lovelace?'

'I cannot say.'

'General Buller?'

'I refuse to say.'

'You, sir,' cried Crossman, angrily, 'are a blamed fool.'

Dalton-James's head came up and some of the old fire of his prejudices and bigotry entered his voice.

'How dare you? I will not be insulted by a common sergeant from the ranks. If you are here to murder me, do so now. Shoot me and have done with it. But I will hear no more of your abuse. It offends my dignity to speak with you further.'

'Fair enough. I hope you realise it was Major Lovelace who ordered your assassination. I am merely the executioner. I think you are entitled to know that your judge and jury was he. You may go to your death cursing his name if you wish.'

Dalton-James stared in disbelief.

'Lovelace? No, you are lying, sergeant.'

'I was told to wait at Mackenzies Farm for a traitor and to execute him. No name. Just a man delivering secrets to enemy agents at the farm. You are he. Major Lovelace's orders, I'm afraid, and according to you I should obey without question.'

For the second time Crossman raised his revolver to the head of the officer he had despised long before he had discovered he was a traitor. Dalton-James's eyes widened and his lips began to move as if in silent prayer. Crossman's hand started to shake as he squeezed on the trigger. Finally, he let his arm fall to his side without firing. He cursed out loud.

'Damn you! I can't do it. I'm a bloody failure as an assassin. I'm too bloody soft.'

Dalton-James's legs gave way and he sank to his knees, the sweat shining on his brow.

He said in a choked voice, 'Forgive me for saying so, sergeant, but right at this moment I'm of the opinion that such a feeling does you credit.'

Crossman allowed the man before him some time to gather his faculties together and collect himself. Both men were considerably shaken. Dalton-James knew that he had escaped death by a whisker, and Crossman knew that he had almost murdered a man in cold blood. The threat of violence had clouded the atmosphere with red mist for a while. It took a few minutes of reflection to reintroduce a calmness to the scene.

'I must confess, sir, I don't know what to do with you now. I can't kill you – not this way – and I can't take you back with me. Major Lovelace does not want a scandal. It was to be done quietly and without any fuss, so as to save embarrassment to family, friends and regiment . . .'

'Oh, that's capital!' said Dalton-James, with bitter cynicism. 'Never mind that it's murder, so long as no one is embarrassed.'

'Well, I have to say I agree with your sentiments there. I believe in a candid and open assessment of such damage, but I have superior officers who believe otherwise. Major Lovelace also has to take his orders from those above him.'

'Major Lovelace again,' said Dalton-James, darkly. 'Major Lovelace? Has it not occurred to you that Major Lovelace might be getting rid of us both, for his own reasons? What if *my* mission were genuine and yours the one which is false? Do you know for sure that Major Lovelace was given orders to have me – all right, you didn't know it would be me – but the courier then – do you know for sure he had orders to assassinate the courier of these papers?'

'No,' replied Crossman, hollowly.

'What if Major Lovelace is steeped in some dark plot or other and needs a scapegoat? Perhaps he is the traitor and thinks that by assassinating me he will divert attention from himself? Once I am dead there will be no need to look for the traitor any longer. And you. He would have a stranglehold over you for the rest of your life. You would be the murderer of a lieutenant of Her Majesty's Rifle Brigade!

'Have you thought of that, Sergeant Crossman, or is your idle brain incapable of entertaining such ideas?'

Crossman did not know what to say to this logical argument. It seemed to boil down to a choice between believing his lieutenant, or believing his major. Neither one seemed a likely candidate for a traitorous career: neither one was so spotless he could be chosen over the other. Crossman was stuck between two unknown quantities and with no means of answering any questions.

'I don't know,' he replied at last. 'I just don't know.'

4

Crossman brooded on his problem as they walked through the hills. He knew now that he could not shoot Dalton-James. Yet if he took him back to camp there would be a terrible scandal, which was just what Lovelace did not want. It boiled down to the fact that he, Sergeant Crossman, had been sent out to do a job and had failed. He felt thoroughly miserable.

'We can't wander these hills forever,' said Dalton-James, bringing the problem to a head. 'You have to make up your mind what to do with me.'

'Perhaps Yusuf Ali will come out to us? He's good at finding me when I don't need him with me, so let's hope for once he finds me when I do. I shall send a message with him back to Major Lovelace. Then we'll see.'

'And if Lovelace is the traitor?'

Crossman did not know what to say to this.

They stopped for a rest by a narrow brook which ran down through a cleft in the rocks. Crossman used a strip of torn shirt to bind tightly the broken wrist of Dalton-James, employing a piece of slate as a splint. The lieutenant winced several times during the operation, but once it was done he looked relieved. He rubbed the wrist, then nodded.

'Thank you,' he said, though Crossman knew the words almost choked him. 'A competent job.'

There was not a great deal of surface water to be had in the region, despite the autumn rains. It seemed judicious to fill their water bottles, and Crossman asked Dalton-James to perform this task.

As the lieutenant bent down to do this, he was shot in the face.

Dalton-James flew backwards with the impact of the bullet, colliding with Crossman and knocking the sergeant off his feet.

The pair of them went tumbling down a slope. Even as they rolled, another bullet zinged from a rock, stinging Crossman's face with a shower of granite splinters. At the bottom of the slope Crossman scrambled behind a rock. Another shot rang out, the round narrowly missing the sergeant's head. Dalton-James was still exposed to the fire. Crossman was about to risk his life and dash out to drag him to cover, when the lieutenant scampered away of his own accord, hiding behind a natural rock buttress.

The two men were about ten feet apart.

Dalton-James was lucky to be still alive. The ball had entered his mouth obliquely and exited through his left cheek. He looked a little dazed, but essentially his wound was not serious. He had probably lost a couple of teeth in the bargain, but he still had a beating heart. An inch or so higher and the ball would have gone through his left eye.

'Who is it?' called Dalton-James, with a strange-sounding flurry to his tongue. 'Who's up there?'

Crossman glanced upwards, to a narrow pass between a rock face and a tor-like needle. This brought another shot in his direction, which ricocheted off some stones near his feet.

'One man, I think,' said Crossman. 'Up on the heights to our left. He's a good shot, but not brilliant. If that had been Peterson up there, one of us at least would be dead.'

'A single man?'

'A Cossack, perhaps.'

'Why should it be a Cossack? Why not an infantry soldier?'

'I don't know. Just a feeling. Those bloody Cossacks have been trying to kill me ever since the Alma. We've got a personal vendetta going. I'm sure it's a Cossack, even though they usually operate in threes.'

'What are you going to do about him?'

Dalton-James dabbed his cheek with a handkerchief as he spoke. There was blood oozing from his wound. He did not seem too perturbed by this second injury. Crossman reflected that the officer must be tougher than he appeared.

Crossman considered the situation carefully. There was a natural rock chimney on the other side of Dalton-James, hidden behind a spur. He would have to dash over to the lieutenant to get at that chimney, then ease his way up and perhaps be able to get on a level with their ambusher. That was if their attacker remained where he was for the next thirty minutes.

If he did not, all well and good, they would both escape with their lives.

Crossman reflected that if Dalton-James were to be shot during this fracas, it would solve his problem of what to do with him. It would not, however, tell him anything about the real situation, which was obviously more complicated than he had previously been led to believe. He would hate to think he was partly responsible for the death of an innocent man, even someone he heartily disliked.

'I'm coming over to you,' he whispered to Dalton-James.

'No – there isn't room.'

'I'm coming.'

At that moment a shot clipped the point of Crossman's boot, where his toe was sticking out from behind the rock.

'You'll be killed,' said Dalton-James, matter-of-factly. 'That Russian is no marksman, but you'll be a sitting target.'

'I'll wait until he's fired again, then do it while he's reloading.'

'He may have two firearms.'

Crossman considered further. Dalton-James was probably right. The man was no doubt using a rifle or carbine for better accuracy at the distance. However, there was every reason to suppose he had a pistol too. Which meant there was a good chance Crossman would be shot crossing the gap. If their attacker got him, he would get the lieutenant too, eventually.

Crossman made a decision and reached inside his tunic. He took out the lieutenant's side arm.

'Here,' he said, 'try and catch this with your good hand.'

He tossed the revolver to Dalton-James who caught it neatly one-handed, like a good cricketer in the slips.

'Can you fire it with your left hand?' enquired the sergeant.

'Of course. I practise with both hands. I'm almost as good with the left as I am with the right.'

Dalton-James checked the chambers, cocked the weapon and then looked across at Crossman. The sergeant stared at the pistol in the lieutenant's hand. Was his superior officer going to shoot him, now that he had a weapon? If Dalton-James was a traitor, that would seem the sensible thing for him to do, then perhaps shout to the man in the rocks and give himself up. If he were taken to the Russians by this ambusher, he could explain later that he was actually on their side.

However, the lieutenant did not fire. He touched the wound on his cheek once and then began climbing up to the hidden chimney. Crossman, to distract their attacker, drew his Tranter and stuck his hand out only, firing blindly up at the rocks above. Five shots went singing up into the pass without a hope of hitting the ambusher. A single shot whistled down by way of reply, but accurate enough to have the sergeant whip his arm back to the safety of the boulder.

He fitted the Tranter with another loaded cylinder, risked two more shots over the top of the boulder without looking, then waited.

It seemed forever until he heard Lieutenant Dalton-James use his weapon, the sound of the firing coming from high up to the far left. Crossman waited until he heard a reply shot from their man, then he left the cover of the boulder and began to scramble up the slope. He could see Dalton-James up on a rock shelf, aiming at the gap between the face and the needle.

Crossman fired into that gap too, hoping to hit the attacker by chance.

Two shots now hummed over his head. Crossman decided the man had indeed been using a rifle before, but now that he was being attacked on two sides he had drawn his revolver.

Desperately Crossman clawed his way up the incline, his race to get to the man similar to that of an animal charging down a hunter who is taking careful aim. The sergeant could see part of their target's body now, as the figure leaned against the edge of the rock face, to get support for a better shot.

Then Dalton-James fired again and the figure fell backwards with a shout.

'Hit him!' cried the lieutenant, triumphantly. 'Got him, by God!'

Sergeant Crossman continued his race up the incline to the track above. There was an angry growl from the lieutenant's victim, then the man appeared again. He was concentrating on Dalton-James now. Crossman only had a narrow side-view of half the man's torso. Gasping for breath, the sergeant took quick aim and fired twice. His target fell away with a groan and a firearm went clattering down the hillside.

The man drooped forward, staggering, using a carbine as a walking stick to steady himself. Then he raised this weapon one-armed, pointing at Crossman. Without hesitating, Dalton-James, who had full view of their attacker now, shot him in the chest. There was a gargled scream, then the man slumped forward and fell down the gap between the rocks, following the path his pistol had taken just a few moments earlier. He landed in a crumpled heap at the bottom of a narrow gully.

Both Crossman and Dalton-James scrambled down from the hillside after the body. The lieutenant, being closer, reached it first. He turned the figure over and let out a gasp. Crossman, coming up behind him, stared hard. Clearly Dalton-James knew who it was, though Crossman had never seen the man before.

By the time Crossman got to them, Dalton-James had opened the overcoat of his victim. There was a fatal wound over the man's heart. It was not the bloody hole in his chest which drew Crossman's attention though. It was the uniform he was wearing beneath the greatcoat.

It was that of a British infantry officer.

'Captain Charles Barker,' murmured Dalton-James, stepping back with a pale face. 'We've murdered one of our own officers.'

'He was trying to kill us, don't forget,' reminded Crossman, though he too was appalled by what they had done. 'He fired on us first.'

'He may have thought we were Russians. We're not exactly displaying regimental insignia, are we?'

That was true. The pair of them were dressed like Tartars.

Yet there had been no challenge from the captain either. Nor any call for surrender when he had them pinned down. He must have heard exchanges in English between the two when the fight was in progress. Why had he not called out at that point, asked them who they were? No, something was not quite right about this situation. Dalton-James was keeping something back too. He seemed more than shocked on seeing it was this particular captain.

'Is the captain a friend of your family? How do you know him?'

Dalton-James straightened his back and turned on Crossman with cold and angry eyes. He had his revolver in his hand and clearly no longer needed to be intimidated by the sergeant. They had equal status now. It was simply a matter of who fired and killed the other first.

Crossman was not about to be bullied. 'I asked you a question, sir, which you will please answer. You know this man we have killed. How do you know him? Is he a friend or simply an acquaintance? Remember, I have orders to kill you and I will do it, though it costs me my own life.'

'You never stop, do you, sergeant? You're like some nasty little terrier, snapping at my ankles. Insubordination means nothing to you.'

However, Dalton-James lowered his pistol and stared at the corpse.

Dalton-James continued. 'I hardly know the fellow. I've spoken to him once only before in my life. This is the officer who ordered me to take those papers to Mackenzies Farm,' he said, quietly. 'He said he was replacing Major Lovelace. I was pleased about that. I do not like Major Lovelace.'

'What?' said Crossman, taken aback. 'What do you mean, replacing Major Lovelace?'

'I don't know what I mean. All I know is this officer came to my quarters late yesterday afternoon and said he had been sent by General Buller. I was to take the papers to the farm and put them in the hands of a Sardinian general. Those were my orders from a superior officer. I had no reason to doubt them.'

'You didn't check with Major Lovelace or General Buller?'

Dalton-James looked unsure of himself for the first time since this business had started.

'There was no reason why I should. Although we hadn't spoken before, I'd seen Captain Barker in the camp. He's no Russian in disguise. Besides,' confessed the lieutenant, 'the idea of a field assignment – a fox hunt – greatly appealed to me. I'm stuck behind the lines while you and that *peloton* of yours go roaming over the countryside having all the fun.'

'And risking our lives. But was that it? You saw your chance to get in on the action at last and couldn't wait to take it? Not even just to check with General Buller?'

'After all,' confided the lieutenant, nodding ruefully, 'General Buller might have changed his mind and forbidden me to go – he might have decided in the meantime that you or Lovelace should do it, and I would have missed out again, wouldn't I?'

Crossman decided he believed the lieutenant's story.

He stretched out his hand. 'Give me your pistol, sir.'

'What?' Dalton-James stepped back. 'Not this time, sergeant.'

'Give it to me and I will take you in. We'll go to General Buller together. If your story is true, you have nothing to fear from me. I was sent to kill a traitor. If what you are saying is true, then that traitor lies dead at our feet.

'However, there is still some small element of doubt in my mind and I would be grateful if you would hand over your weapon. Otherwise we are back at a stalemate again.'

Dalton-James stared at the sergeant for a good few minutes, then passed the pistol to him. He rubbed his broken wrist thoughtfully before testing the hole in his cheek with his tongue. Finally, he sighed.

'I'm no chess player, sergeant. I hate the game. Give me a good rubber of whist any time.'

'Sir?'

'Stalemate. It's a chess term. You obviously play chess.'

'Like a one-legged man runs a race,' replied Crossman, smiling. 'Come on, sir, let's get this mess sorted out so we can revert to our former roles. I do not like having to threaten one of Her Majesty's commissioned officers, any more than you like being held prisoner by a common sergeant. Let's cover this bastard with rocks and then get back to camp.'

When they were half-way through their task, the Bashi-Bazouk, Yusuf Ali, turned up to assist them. Crossman was glad of the Turk's company on the way back to their lines. It meant that Dalton-James remained silent. Despite having shared a dangerous time together, the two British men had very little to say to one another that was not contentious.

'How you kill the officer?' asked Ali, simply out of idle curiosity. 'You cut his throat?'

'We shot him,' replied Crossman. 'Through the heart.'

The Bashi-Bazouk gave a noncommital grunt. It really did not matter to him. He asked no further questions. If the sergeant had deemed it necessary to kill a captain in the British Army, that was fine with Yusuf Ali. So far as he was concerned, the sergeant was to be trusted in all things.

5

When Crossman and Lieutenant Dalton-James got back to Kadikoi village, there was an open-air church service in progress. There were rows of men standing in silence before a makeshift altar consisting of a door on two upright barrels covered with a cloth. Out in front a priest was intoning, assisted by a drummer boy in his role as an altar lad.

Anxious to impart their news to General Buller, they looked to see if he was among the congregation. He was there, but right up at the front, standing with Mrs Durham and her quartermaster husband.

Next to Lavinia Durham was the young widow of a common soldier who had been killed at Balaclava. She was a small, pretty woman with bright eyes. Even before her husband had died she had built herself a reputation. Whether the reputation was deserved, Crossman had no idea. Molly Kennedy was known to enjoy flirting, but any more was supposition and hearsay. Mrs Durham had taken Molly Kennedy under her wing and she was now the quartermaster's wife's constant companion.

Mary Seacole, the West Indian lady who ran the refuge she called the British Hotel, was also there, sharing a hymn book with Dr James Barry, a medical officer. The eucharist was in progress. Brigadier-General Buller and others were about to take the sacraments.

Catching sight of the two men from the back row, however, was the figure of Major Lovelace. He came over to them and guided them with his hand to a place out of earshot of the congregation. They stood in the mud not far from the spot where the 93rd Sutherland Highlanders had held their line against four squadrons of Russian hussars just a few days previously.

'Lieutenant? Sergeant? You have a serious look about you both. Do you have something to tell me?'

Lieutenant Dalton-James said, 'It seems I am under close arrest. The sergeant here has taken it upon himself to relieve me of my side arm and will not release me until someone in authority assures him that I am not a Russian spy. I have recently narrowly escaped assassination by the sergeant, but some tender spot within his rough exterior is responsible for my survival.'

Lovelace, who had been staring at the wound on Dalton-James's cheek, was thoroughly taken aback. 'What?'

Crossman continued the story. 'You sent me out to assassinate a man who was to be in a certain place at a certain time. That man proved to be Lieutenant Dalton-James. He should, if I had carried out my mission to the letter, be lying dead in the dirt of Mackenzies Farm. However, I failed in my duty, and here he is, standing before you.'

'You shot the lieutenant in the face, but the wound proved not to be fatal?' murmured Lovelace, entirely bewildered.

'No, I broke his wrist. Someone else is responsible for the hole in the lieutenant's cheek.'

Lovelace shook his head as if he were being bothered by flies.

'You are the traitor?' whispered Lovelace, turning to Dalton-James. 'I don't believe it.'

'Fortunately,' said Dalton-James, his hands clasped behind his back, 'in his heart of hearts, neither did Sergeant Crossman, or I should indeed be meat for the Crimean crows. Sir, do you know of a Captain Charles Barker . . .?'

Dalton-James gave the name of the captain's regiment and its commanding officer.

'I have heard of him. I've seen him around the camp.'

'Captain Barker came to me with papers, saying General Buller had sent him. He said I was to take these papers to Mackenzies Farm, to a Sardinian general who would relieve me of them at precisely six o'clock on the following morning. Barker intimated that he was taking over from you as head of clandestine operations in the Crimea.'

'Good Lord!' cried Lovelace. 'He's our man then.'

'Correction, sir,' Crossman said, 'he *was* our man. We shot him dead out in the hills. He attacked us on our way in to camp and we were forced to kill him. We have buried the body under a pile of rocks.'

Things were beginning to click into place in Lovelace's mind now. He stood there for a good five minutes in silence, thinking things over. Finally, his eyes narrowed and he spoke again.

'Let me try this on you both. This Captain Barker somehow got wind of the fact that he would be in grave danger taking the documents to the farm himself. So he pretended to be my replacement, coupled it with a sense of urgency and secrecy, and sent the lieutenant with the papers instead. To make sure the lieutenant did not return, he followed at a safe distance, waiting to see what would happen. When he saw Sergeant Crossman capture you, he knew he had to kill you both and retrieve the papers, which of course had not been delivered to his Russian masters. I think that fits the scenario quite nicely.'

'So,' said Crossman gravely, 'I am not to be allowed to shoot Lieutenant Dalton-James on this occasion?'

'I'm afraid not, sergeant,' said Lovelace, joining in with Crossman's warped sense of humour. 'It is a great shame, but you will have to wait until the lieutenant decides to sell more secrets to the Russians, and then perhaps we'll give you another go.'

Dalton-James rubbed his broken wrist. 'I fail to see any drollery in this situation. I have been wounded twice – most painful of which is my wrist, caused by the sergeant's zeal in protecting himself.'

Crossman handed the lieutenant back his pistol.

'I do apologise for that, sir, but I'm afraid you would have shot me had I permitted you to fire your revolver.'

'You're damn right I would. Now, if you'll excuse me, Major Lovelace, I shall seek medical advice.'

He saluted and then walked off over the mud towards Kadikoi hospital: a small house which had been taken over for the purpose.

Major Lovelace watched the lieutenant go and then said, 'Say nothing of this to anyone, Sergeant Crossman.' He stared at the bruise made by the Russian rifle butt on Crossman's jaw. 'You should get that nasty thing looked at too, sergeant. Did the lieutenant do that?'

'No, sir. If he had, there would be a few similar marks on his own face.'

'I'm sure you're right. Now, about this traitor . . .'

Crossman looked at the major in such a way as to cause the other to add, 'What?'

'Nothing, sir – except that the lieutenant and I – at one time . . .' Crossman was hesitant to say what was on his mind, but then decided nothing could be gained by keeping it back. 'We thought you might be the traitor, sir. You are the one who ordered confidentiality. It would have been easy for you to have set everything in motion, to cover your own tracks.'

An expression of intense anger swept across the major's face like a dark squall over sea.

'You have my word that I am not – the word of an officer and a gentleman.'

39

'I do beg your pardon, sir, but that very same description fits a captain buried under some rocks on the other side of the Woronzoff Road,' replied Crossman, stubbornly.

The major stared, his eyes still sparkling with annoyance, then his brow cleared at last.

'I suppose you have every right to question me, sergeant. I thought we trusted one another now, but it seems I still have to win that privilege. If you wish, we can go to General Buller and speak with him on the matter. Perhaps we ought to take Lieutenant Dalton-James along with us. He probably harbours the same suspicions as yourself. I'll go over to the hospital now – you join us in an hour.'

'Yes, sir.' Crossman saluted smartly. Then he said, by way of an afterthought, 'We have chosen a very untrustworthy occupation, sir. Nothing personal.'

The major smiled grimly. 'I should have said that. You're learning fast, sergeant. In an hour then.'

Before they finally parted, Crossman asked, 'Did Yusuf Ali warn you about the Russian 4th Army Corps?'

'Yes, he did. I forgot to thank you for that, sergeant. As far as I'm concerned it was well done.'

'As far as you're concerned?'

'And General Buller, I should have added. Lord Raglan, however, seems to attach little significance to it. When he found out it was one of our own spies, and not a Russian deserter, who was responsible for the information, he dismissed it. I imagine his words were, "If I have to learn these things from skulkers, I'd rather not learn them at all." But General Buller is pleased with you. You rise every day in his estimation.'

'Thank you, sir.'

At that moment the guns began pounding along the siege line a few miles away. Picquets would be sniping at each other on both sides. Captain Goodlake of the Coldstream Guards would be leading his hand-picked marksmen through the gullies and ravines beyond the Sapouné Ridge. Russian sharpshooters were picking their targets from amongst British and French gunners. Men were being crippled. Men were dying somewhere nearby.

In contrast to the noise of the guns, bells tolled in Sebastopol. This otherwise pleasant sound was treated with suspicion by the British forces. The bells had pealed loudly on the day the Russians had launched their last offensive, in order to bolster the courage of their troops. It was unlikely, however, that the Russians were attacking so soon after their probing offensive on the heights near the Inkerman ruins.

It was common knowledge that Lord Raglan, the commander-in-chief of the British forces himself, had remarked to an officer of the Engineers, when advised to strengthen his forces near Inkerman, 'Nonsense! They will never dare come that way again.' Not that the general had visited the area in question, nor did he intend to. General Canrobert, the French commander-in-chief, probably knew better than Lord Raglan what were the strengths and weaknesses of the post-road which came out of Chernaya Valley, though his responsibility was for the Chersonese Uplands.

Crossman made his way back to the hovel just as the church service ended. Some of the 88th Foot were coming away from the open-air church and he heard one of them mutter, 'There's Fancy Jack. Dressed like a Tartar as usual . . .'

Crossman smiled to himself. At one time he had hated his nickname, but these days he did not care. An obvious aristocrat in the ranks, he was regarded with suspicion by common soldier and commissioned officer alike. The first group thought he was there to report on their misdemeanours, the second, because he had done something of which he was ashamed. Neither was true.

He hurried away from the scene, not wanting to meet Mrs Durham face-to-face. She might just confront him, even with her husband in attendance.

There was a problem with Lavinia Durham. She knew that his real name was Alexander Kirk and that his father and brother were serving with the 93rd Foot in the Crimea. This was information which Crossman wanted to remain secret. So far Mrs Durham had not used her knowledge, but there was no telling she would not in the future.

On reaching the hovel, Crossman found his small *peloton* lounging around within. There was Corporal Devlin, Lance-Corporal Peterson, Lance-Corporal Wynter and Private Clancy. Since they had earned some prize money – the silver coins which had been intercepted on their way to the traitor Barker – they had begun to get a little uppity. Crossman had sent them back to the front to remind them they were ordinary mortals – soldiers of the 88th Connaught Rangers – and they were now a little more subdued.

''Ello, sergeant,' remarked Wynter as Crossman entered the room, 'come to rejoin the happy band?'

The biggest troublemaker of the group, Wynter, was never without words. Peterson, a woman disguised as a man, whose real identity was known only to Crossman, sat in the far corner of the room cleaning her precious Minié rifle. She was the best shot Crossman had ever seen, and for that reason alone he kept her secret. Private Clancy was lying on his cot, his hands behind his head, probably dreaming of India, where he had been raised as the son of an Irish clerk and an Indian mother. Corporal Devlin, a steady and reliable married man, was scraping mud from his boots.

'Well, well, my boys,' said Crossman. 'Back from the ditches of hell, eh?'

'We're back, sergeant,' replied Wynter with a sour look. 'You're lucky we're all alive. We could've been killed. Shell and round shot fallin' like rain out there. Whistlin' Dicks scarin' the living daylights out of you. Musket balls whizzing through your breakfast tins. Ain't right.'

'You should be proud to do your bit for your regiment,' said Clancy from his cot. 'I am.'

'Listen to old dusky,' replied Wynter with a sneer. 'Anyone would think you was British.'

'He's as British as we all are,' Peterson said hotly. 'And don't you forget it, Wynter.'

Devlin however, disagreed. 'I'm not British, I'm Irish – and so's Clancy as far as I'm concerned. A man with an Irish father?'

'I'm not Irish, I'm Anglo-Indian,' remarked Clancy. 'Even the sergeant knows that.'

Crossman, who regarded himself as Scottish, even though he had an English mother, smiled to himself at these exchanges. If they all came from the same county, they would be arguing their differences, saying their village or town was superior to any other. The human race is so territorial, he thought. We would argue for our own back yard if there were no nations.

He cleaned himself up at the communal wash bowl and then joined Lieutenant Dalton-James and Major Lovelace at the hospital. The major had more information on Captain Barker. It turned out that Barker had been born in Bulgaria, his father being an English merchant there. No one knew the nationality of his mother, but there was enough evidence to suggest that his traitorous activities had more than just a mercenary motive.

'I'm afraid General Buller is not available for a few days now – I think you will have to trust me after all,' said Lovelace.

Crossman nodded. 'It seems I have little choice, sir. I will give you the benefit of the doubt. This Captain Barker – you think his mother may have been Russian?'

'It's possible.'

If Barker's mother had been Russian, or from a country sympathetic to Russia in this war, and she had been mal-treated in some way by his father, then Barker might have reason to assist the enemy. Who knew? Dalton-James was inclined to think that it was pure greed which had turned the captain's head, but this was too simplistic an answer for Crossman.

43

'The trouble with you, sergeant, is that you think men are complex creatures,' said the lieutenant, on their way back to the hovel. 'I, on the other hand, believe them to be basic creatures who would sell their own grandmothers for gold.'

'That's a very cynical view,' said Crossman. 'I would despair for mankind if I held such an opinion.'

'Nonsense. Take a man like Wynter, for instance. If the Russians promised him enough, he would fight for them against his fellow countrymen. Some men are incorrigible.'

'I hope not,' replied Crossman, with feeling. 'I sincerely hope not.'

6

Crossman once again settled for a short time into camp life. This was better for him than most company sergeants, who spent their time soaked to the skin on picquet duty, sleepless and weary, and whose only entertainment was a dreary canteen. Crossman's colleagues up in the trenches and on the picquet line were having a hard time of it. They were being bombarded relentlessly by the Russian guns, forever crawling through mud and mire, and were lucky to snatch an hour's sleep.

Every day too, there were skirmishes going on between picquets and forward patrols. Men were being killed by musket fire, the bayonet and cannon. Sharpshooters picked off those foolish enough to show their heads above the trenches. Round shot and shells fell in trench and on barricade. Cold steel entered the breasts and bellies of soldiers of several nations. Bodies were being collected during armistices by both sides.

One such typical incident was that experienced by Private McGuire of the 33rd Foot, who was taken captive by two Russian soldiers. McGuire had been on advanced sentry duty at the time when the Russians came across him and disarmed him. They marched him between them towards Sebastopol.

But McGuire was not going to be taken that easily. He waited until his captors were inattentive, then snatched back his Minié, to blast one of the Russians. He then turned on the other and struck him with the butt of the rifle, felling him to the ground. Private McGuire ran off and made it back to his own lines safely.

Crossman, although his work was dangerous, did not have to spend days and nights in freezing trenches. That deadly strip of land around Sebastopol was the responsibility of others. And at least he had a roof over his head and a straw mattress to sleep on.

The evening of the day he had returned with Lieutenant Dalton James he had a visitor from the 93rd Foot.

'Sarn-Major Jock McIntyre,' he said, as the Scotsman walked through the doorway in his splendid Highlanders' uniform, 'to what do I owe this great pleasure?'

The sergeant-major was one of the few people in the Crimea who knew Crossman's real identity. He was a solidly trustworthy man, whose loyalty was unquestionable. Crossman felt no concern at the fact that McIntyre knew his secret.

'Thought I'd come and share a dram with ye,' said Jock, looking round at the other men. 'Is there somewhere private we can talk, man?'

'Certainly. Step upstairs to my drawing room.'

The sergeant-major followed Crossman up to the room above, where he and Major Lovelace had their sleeping quarters.

'An' if I hear one whisper about ladies in skirts,' the kilted McIntyre warned Wynter and the other soldiers below, 'I'll personally tear the man's ears from his head.'

The sergeant-major of the Sutherland Highlanders was a formidable looking man, square of shoulder and of jaw, and even Wynter kept his peace this time.

Once in the privacy of the upstairs room Crossman lit a cheap tallow candle. Major Lovelace was out and about somewhere, employed with the duties of the night. By the flickering light of the poor flame Jock confided to Crossman that there was a problem with Crossman's brother.

The first thing McIntyre said was, 'Where'd ye get the bruise on yer jaw, laddie? It looks like a plum.'

'Not from fighting with the soldiers of other regiments, Jock,' Crossman said, smiling. 'A Russian rifle butt is responsible.' He ran his fingertips over the bruise, having forgotten it was there. It was still sore to the touch. 'The 4th Corps from Odessa was passing by and took a fancy to me. It's my belief there'll be another Russian assault soon, but our generals don't agree with me.'

The Highlander shrugged and nodded, then got down to the business he had come about.

'I hope ye dinna mind me coming here with tales, man, but I'm feared for your brother. He's a gude officer, a wee bit inclined to follow his fether's lead, ye ken, which is nae always the best way to go – but he has the makings of a fine soldier. Lord knows we need gude officers in our regiments during these hard times. We need reliable leadership – steady, dependable leadership.'

'You know I asked you to look out for him,' replied Crossman. 'Has he got himself into some sort of scrape?'

'Well, yes, and he's getting deeper all the time.'

'Is it a woman?' asked Crossman, knowing his own weakness. 'Has he fallen for one of the camp whores?'

'No, not that, though he does visit places where they are to be found. Nor is it the drink – which reminds me – I've a quart of gude malt whisky here. Would you like a spot?' Jock pulled a bottle from inside his tunic, took out the cork, and offered the bottle to Crossman.

Crossman took a long swig of the amber liquid, feeling it burn his oesophagus on its way down to his stomach.

'That was good. So tell me. What's my brother James been up to?'

'Gambling,' McIntyre said flatly. 'He's taken to the cards in a terrible way. His debts are as long as ma arm and

47

growing longer by the day. I've said nothing to him, of course, for it's no ma place. But I thought ye ought to know.'

'And my father, Major Kirk?'

'Major Kirk disna ken what's going on, Jack. The major, well he's likely of an evening to be frequenting those places we mentioned earlier – visiting the ladies. Lieutenant Kirk spends his time wi' the young subalterns.'

'Chasing women is a family failing. But gambling? Even my father has never been much interested in gambling. He likes to keep his money in his pocket too much to give it away to someone with a better hand of cards. Oh, he has the odd wager on who is the best shot with a sporting gun, or who can jump a high fence on a hunter, but nothing more than that.'

'I think your brother is already down some two thousand pounds,' confided McIntyre.

Crossman whistled, sitting bolt upright.

'As much as that? My father's only worth about five thousand a year. James will ruin the family.'

It was funny. It was the first time since he had left home that Crossman felt any consideration for the family as a unit. He was concerned for the woman he had always called 'Mother', and occasionally he thought about his brother James, but he believed he was over worrying about 'the family' as an entity of concern. He could not in fact care less whether his father's estate was ruined or not, except that it would affect his step-mother.

'Will yer fether pay yer brother's gambling debts?'

'I doubt it, Jock. Not to the tune of two thousand or more. I think he would sooner fling James out. My father's not one of those Scottish aristocrats who cares much about the honour of the family. I've got to stop this thing somehow. Who is the main holder of the debt?'

'I should say that would be Captain Campbell. He's the man with a flair for the cards. I should say every officer in the

48

regiment who has ever held a playing card in his hand is in debt to Captain Campbell in some form or another.'

Crossman took another swig of whisky, this time out of necessity.

'What kind of man is he? This Campbell?'

'No as flashy as ye'd expect considering his favourite pastime. No a bad sort o' man, outside the gambling. Reliable enough on the battlefield, a wee bit too cocky off it, but there's many an officer follows that description, Jack.'

'Could I appeal to him, do you think?'

'Whut? Ask him to put the debt aside? Jack, Jack, ye know better than that, lad. How many men could ye ask to do that? Yer very best friend, perhaps, someone ye grew up with, saved from drowning, and who owes ye his life. But merely a brother officer?'

Crossman sighed. 'Yes, I know. Well, thanks for coming here tonight, Jock.'

The sergeant-major smiled. 'Always a pleasure to see the man who saved ma life. If it was me who held yer brother's debts, then ye could forget them. Unfortunately, it's another. I'll see ye on the battlefield, for it's certain sure we havnae seen the last Russian coming at us. A new assault ye say?'

'I think so.'

'Then I'll keep ma powder dry.'

Just before he left, the sergeant-major spoke to Crossman one last time.

'Ah said Campbell was no a bad sort o' man, outside the gambling. But I have tae tell ye, inside it he's the very devil. I've been told he cheats. Ah don't think anybody's ever proved it mind and the last man who accused him of cheating is lying in some French cemetery outside Paris.'

'A duel?'

'Among his other skills, Captain Campbell is an excellent shot – ah ken no better.'

'If he cheats, how does he get people to play with him?'

'Laddie, laddie, ye know so little about the underside of life. It's mah guess he disna cheat with everybody. He'll pick a victim – a raw card player like yer brother – and he'll milk him. He's never been caught red-handed, mind. It's just a whisper from his batman, ye understand. A servant's loose tongue. It may not even be true.'

'But you think it is?'

'Ah've seen too many green officers destroyed by him.'

The next morning, Crossman made enquiries about Captain Campbell. It seemed the man had a reputation for gambling with high stakes and that there was some taint of cheating attached to him. There was also no reason to suppose that Campbell was a philanthropist: it seemed he always collected money owed him, one way or another. In fact, Crossman managed to catch a look at the man as he passed by his tent. Campbell was shaving with a cutthroat razor in the light of the dawn. He looked up and frowned on seeing he was being observed.

'Can I assist you, sergeant?' he said with some hauteur, his face still half-covered in shaving soap and his razor hand poised above his chin. 'Are you waiting to see blood?'

'No, sir – sorry, sir,' replied Crossman, hurrying on.

There was no point in getting into an unpleasant exchange with the officer.

That single encounter had told Crossman a great deal. The sergeant had seen the look of steel in the captain's eyes. It had been uncompromising. No quiet reasoning would work with this particular man. Captain Campbell, immaculate of dress and bearing, was obviously one of the old school: he would rather call a man out than allow him to welch on his debts.

Crossman returned to the hovel with a heavy heart. The first thing to do was to stop James from getting in any deeper. His brother had to be dissuaded from further gambling. Then they had to settle the debts in any way they could, preferably without their father getting wind of it.

Major Lovelace had returned and Crossman broached the matter straight away. Lovelace was poring over some charts. The small mean window of their sleeping quarters allowed only a dull grey light into the room, and he was having to peer closely at the charts, his attention absorbed by their faint lines. Crossman cleared his throat and spoke with great difficulty.

'Sir, is it possible to advance me my prize money? I believe I have two thousand in Maria Theresa dollars coming to me.'

Lovelace looked up sharply from the map he was studying.

'You must have good reasons for asking that question,' said the field officer at last. 'You know the answer.'

'I have very good reasons – family reasons. The money would not be for me. It is desperately needed elsewhere.'

Lovelace sighed. 'Unfortunately, the decision is not mine to make. I'm sorry, I can't help you. If you will take my advice, which of course you have no need of, you will drop the matter straight away. It can only lead to disappointment.'

'You think there's little chance?'

'I believe there's *no* chance whatsoever.'

'I just thought I would ask. I'm sorry to have embarrassed you, sir.'

'On the contrary, sergeant,' replied the major, quietly, 'it appears to be you who is embarrassed. I'm sorry about your domestic problems. Is it anything I can help you with personally?'

'No, sir, I'm afraid not. Thank you anyway.'

Major Lovelace nodded, no doubt thinking that one of Crossman's parents was desperately ill and in need of funds.

Crossman was squirming inside. He hated even having to mention the fact that he had problems. It was a family matter and had to be settled by family. He wanted no one outside the small circle who already knew to find out about his

51

brother's foolishness. James, of course, was entitled to gamble if he wished, but not with money he did not own. On doing so he had abrogated any entitlement to privacy.

'Sergeant?' said Lovelace, and Crossman realised the officer had been speaking to him about another matter while he had been reflecting on the situation.

'Sorry, sir. Yes?' Crossman's concern for his brother would have to wait: there were more important problems in hand.

'We have a fox hunt. You and your men. Any of you been in the navy at all?'

Crossman was a little taken aback. 'Not to my knowledge.'

'Pity, we need some sailors on this one. How are you with a canoe?'

Crossman frowned, wondering what this was leading up to.

'You mean like Red Indian canoes? My friend Rupert Jarrard might know a thing or two about canoeing. He was an American frontiersman, before he became a newspaper man, or so he informs me.'

'Then we might have to recruit this Jarrard. Come over here and look at this map.'

Crossman did so. It was a map of the Crimea and part of mainland Russia.

'Now,' said Lovelace, pointing with his pencil, 'here we have the Crimea three-quarters surrounded by waters of the Black Sea. You see this stretch of water on the north-east shoulder of the peninsula, almost enclosed except these straits? This is the Sea of Azov and the straits are known as the Straits of Kerch.'

'I am familiar with the local geography, sir.'

'Right, yes, of course you are. I sometimes forget you were educated at Harrow like myself. However, we did not always swallow the stuff Professor Damien threw at us,' said Lovelace, recalling one of the tutors at the school, 'so perhaps you'll forgive me if I go over a few details.'

'I think it was "Piggy" Allendale who taught geography,'

replied Crossman, quietly, knowing Lovelace was trying to catch him out. 'Professor Damien, or "Bottleneck" as we used to call him, on account of his rather reedy-looking throat, taught history.'

'Quite so, quite so, sergeant,' said Lovelace with a wry smile. 'Put me in my place, eh? Well, on to more serious matters.'

He continued to bring Crossman's attention to sections of local geography and topography and finally came to the crux of his plan.

'This is the Russian supply route. They ship men and provisions across the Sea of Azov, to Yenikale and Kerch, here on the panhandle of the Crimea. These are then taken overland to the Russian Army or Sebastopol in the west. I think we can harass their craft a little. Blow up one or two of their supply ships before they realise what we're doing and it becomes too dangerous. I have two ships in mind – the *St Petersburg* and the *Yalta*. They should, at the time you destroy them, be floating arsenals, magazines carrying explosives and ammunition.

'They'll light up the sky a little for us and give us a certain psychological advantage in this Russian attack you tell us we must expect.'

7

A boatswain by the name of Peter Brickman had designed a canoe which would serve Sergeant Crossman and his men in their efforts to sabotage Russian ships in the Sea of Azov. The canoe was fashioned to carry two men with cargo space for their bombs between them. Three of these grey-coloured canoes had been built to carry the six men: Crossman and Ali in the first, Devlin and Wynter in the second, and Peterson and Clancy in the third.

Rupert Jarrard, as the only man they could find with canoeing experience, agreed to help train the men in the use of the craft.

'There's nothing to it,' said Jarrard. 'Most Americans are born able to paddle a canoe.'

'If we were to listen to you,' grumbled Crossman to the American correspondent, 'we should believe that most Americans can do anything and everything. I recommended you, I know, but are you sure you should be assisting us?'

'Can't help it,' replied Jarrard, always itching to be in on any action. 'In my blood. You don't know how frustrating it is, sitting on the sidelines, watching this scrap go on around you, yet barred from assisting. It's like witnessing a fist-fight in a saloon and not being able to join in. Anyway, you could

54

hardly call this training exercise "combat" could you? All I'm doing is showing you how to use a canoe. Something we Americans . . .'

'Yes, yes,' interrupted the piqued Crossman, 'something you do instinctively from birth. You're all little Moseses, paddling down the river in your pitch-caulked cradles, fighting off Sioux Indians with one hand and shooting rattlers with the other.'

They were standing on the quayside of Balaclava harbour. Crossman and his men were preparing for their first try in the canoes. Wynter was staring dubiously at the flimsy craft bobbing in the water below him. Clancy, Devlin and Peterson were not looking too happy at the prospect of canoeing in the choppy water either. They were not used to the water, any of them. Three had been farm labourers. Clancy had had various occupations, but none of them involved close contact with water.

The boatswain who had designed and built the canoes had hold of the lines which were attached to the bows of the canoes. Peter Brickman looked like a proud man with his hands on the leashes of three frisky dogs, about to walk them in the local park. These were his pedigree puppies and he was sure they would be up to the work for which they had been fashioned.

'Sergeant Crossman and I will take out the first canoe to test it,' said Jarrard, with a certain satisfaction in his tone, 'so you men can relax for a few minutes.'

The soldiers of the 88th Connaught Rangers looked relieved. The Bashi-Bazouk, Yusuf Ali, merely nodded. Boats held no fears for the Turk. In fact there was little in the world which did scare the man, who looked like a cross between a renegade Santa Claus and a Corsican bandit. He had a mother-in-law of uncertain temper of whom he was wary, and he was not overfond of large snakes, but since he did not come into contact with either of these horrors in the Crimea, his heart rarely felt a flutter of panic.

The first thing Jarrard did was pick up one of the double-ended oars and snap it in half over his knee, so that there were two short one-bladed paddles. Brickman looked on in consternation, but said nothing. The sailor realised that the American would have a good reason for breaking the paddle he had spent so much time shaping with his spokeshave.

We don't use those kayak paddles where I come from,' Jarrard said. 'They're no good for manoeuvring in narrow channels. If you have to go between two ships or between a ship and the dockside, you'll be smacking something noisy with the tips of the blades. Better to use the short Canadian paddle. It's easier to control and therefore quieter to use. A single splashing sound might mean your life. You put it in the water like this.' He held the blade of the paddle in line with the side of his body. 'Propel the canoe forward, gently, so as to minimise the noise it makes, and then twist the oar sideways so that it's parallel to the canoe and automatically forms a rudder. Thus the end of the propelling motion helps to steer the craft. And while in this position, the paddle slips out quite silently from the water without so much as a drip.'

Crossman had to admit to himself that Jarrard really did look as if he knew what he was doing.

'I see,' he said, taking up the other half of the broken paddle. 'Like this?'

He copied the sequence Jarrard had demonstrated.

'Looks fine to me. Now take off that sheepskin coat and those boots. If we turn over they'll drag you down. Keep the rest of your clothes on or you'll freeze in two minutes in the water in this weather. Right, are you ready?'

The two men went down the quay steps. Jarrard held the canoe steady while Crossman climbed into the back seat. Then Crossman held on to the quay while Jarrard took his place at the front. The two men paddled out into the harbour, Crossman copying the strokes of the man in front of him. They seemed to be doing quite well. The surface of the water in the harbour was calm and Crossman was beginning to wonder what all the fuss was about.

'This is easy,' he said.

At that moment a seagoing ship cruised into the harbour, its bow wave creating a rather different surface to the water. Suddenly Crossman found himself fighting to keep the canoe stable, as it rocked violently. Jarrard seemed quite easy with the motion, using his paddle to keep the craft steady, but Crossman was rocking at the hips, unable to control his upper body movements.

'Don't panic . . .' cried Jarrard, but then the canoe was over and Crossman found himself in water that was so incredibly cold it sent a shock wave through his body. His lungs seemed to shrink to pebbles in his chest. His bones were brittle sticks of ice. He sank like a brick at first, the grey-green water passing before his eyes, but then fought his way back to the surface, the low temperature eating deeply into his flesh.

When he broke the surface he instinctively reached out for the canoe, as a drowning man will claw at thin air, but Jarrard had somehow remained inside the craft and had paddled a little out of his reach.

'Jarrard,' gasped Crossman, 'for God's sake, man.'

'Stop flailing,' ordered the American. 'Calm down. Tread water. I'll bring the canoe to you, but just use it as a balance aid. If you tip it over again, we'll both be in trouble. Grasp the stern of the craft with one hand.'

Jarrard was wet through. He paddled the canoe closer to Crossman, who gripped the stern as he had been told and thrashed with his legs to keep himself afloat. Fortunately they were only about twenty yards from the quay. When they reached the edge, Ali grabbed the sergeant by the coatee and pulled him from the water. A blanket was wrapped round him immediately.

The freezing Crossman turned to Jarrard, who had climbed out of the canoe and was now also covered in a blanket.

'How did you do that?' said Crossman, his teeth chattering. 'How did you stay in the craft? I thought it turned over?'

'I turned it back again, with my weight and the use of the paddle.' Jarrard looked round. 'Right, now who's next . . .?'

But Wynter and the other soldiers, looking as pale as death, were already half-way back to Kadikoi.

Once Crossman and Jarrard were dried and ready for another session, the terrified soldiers were dragged back to the waters of the harbour. They were forced into the canoes and made to practise within a short distance of the quay. A bonfire was lit on the quayside, to dry those who fell into the water. This scene attracted the attention of the sailors in and around the harbour, who hung over ship rails to yell encouragement or to heckle the soldiers in their efforts to become instant mariners.

'Perhaps,' said a watching Mary Seacole, to Major Lovelace, who had come down to the harbour to watch the fun, 'you should use sailors, instead of farm boys?'

Major Lovelace shook his head. There was much to admire in this army officer, who was not afraid of generals and who wanted to create an espionage network in the face of official opposition. But like many other army officers, and indeed their naval counterparts, he had the vice of pride. Proud army men do not allow navy men the opportunity to prove they are better. Proud army men would rather die first. Or let their men do so. The maxim, 'My cousin and I are against the enemy, but I am also against my cousin,' suited both services admirably.

'No, it was our idea, and we use our own. Besides, half those jeering jackals on those ships can't swim either.'

'They know the sea better,' the West Indian lady pointed out. 'It's supposed to be in their blood.'

'They know tall ships and steamships, but do they know canoes? I think not. Naval ratings are used to rushing about a big deck, tying knots in things. My men will improve more quickly, since they are more resourceful. Out in the field they have to use their intuition in order to survive. Those salty chaps simply follow a procedure time and time again.'

Mary smiled to herself and walked away shaking her head.

Gradually Crossman, Wynter, Devlin, Peterson and Clancy did improve. (Ali seemed to take to it naturally, as he did with everything else.) Soon they were able to go out of the harbour into the real ocean, where the choppiness of the water created quite a different and much more difficult task. They learned, however, to keep their canoes together like a flotilla in tight formation, so that they could steady each other.

Wynter never quite got used to being on an uncontrollable surface, and his face often went from the red caused by exertion, to an ashen colour within the space of a few seconds. He was terrified of drowning and did not mind who knew it. He considered being on the water an unnatural custom, only one stage removed from the practice of eating one's own young.

Finally, after a day and a half of intense training, Lovelace announced them ready. There followed a short course on navigation from Peter Brickman, but he ended with, 'Hopefully you'll just have to set course for one set of lights or another. The captain of the *Antigone* has promised to hang lamps from the yardarm, so that you can find his ship on your return journey. Just remember one or two principles . . .'

The next part of the training was in the use of the bombs they were to carry in their 'holds'.

The bombs consisted simply of explosive charges which would be detonated by a slow-burning underwater device known as the Beckford fuse. There were spikes on the casings of the charges which would enable the bombs to be stuck to the lower hull of a wooden ship, below the waterline. Even if the explosive did not start a chain reaction in the doomed ship, the vessel would sink where it was and thus create a future shipping hazard, with its unstable cargo forever menacing the seaway.

Each of the canoes had four of these bombs.

Finally, the expedition was ready to depart. A new fox hunt was under way. The canoes and their crew would be carried eastwards along the Crimean coastline to a point just outside the Straits of Kerch, where they would be lowered into the water at night and would have to paddle up through the straits and into the harbour of Kerch itself. There they would light and plant their bombs on the *Yalta* and the *St Petersburg*, and then paddle back to the point where HMS *Antigone* was anchored, waiting for them to board again.

'All very straightforward,' said Lovelace. 'You should have no problems.'

Crossman spent the last hour before embarkation with Rupert Jarrard in a quayside canteen.

'Thank you for giving us the benefit of your knowledge,' said Crossman, 'hard-earned no doubt on the frontiers of the New World.'

'Hard-earned? You betcha. Did I ever tell you of the time I was swept over some rapids on the river . . .'

'Once or twice,' interrupted Crossman, smiling. 'I forget how many times exactly.'

Crossman was smoking his beloved chibouque, that marvellously long-stemmed pipe purchased in Constantinople. Smoke billowed in clouds from the bowl of this instrument. Jarrard was sucking on an old cigar, his smoke too adding to the dense atmosphere within the canteen.

'You still carry that fancy 5-shot Tranter?' asked Jarrard.

Crossman patted the pocket which contained the illicit revolver.

'I certainly do. Just as you have your beloved Navy Colt.'

'Well, keep your cartridges dry. You may need that pistol before your expedition is over. Lovelace may think this fox hunt is a piece of cake. I think it's highly dangerous.'

'So does he,' replied the sergeant, 'but he's not going to say so to a bunch of men terrified of the sea, is he?'

'I suppose not. So what's the latest in the world of inventions? Have you heard of anything new?'

This was a subject dear to the hearts of both men and the thing that had bound them together as comrades from the start of their acquaintance.

'I am reliably informed by a French soldier that a countryman of his, a one Charles Gerhardt who works at the University of Montpellier, has synthesised a substance called acetylsalicylic, or *aspirin* as he calls it.'

'And?'

'Aspirin is a drug which appears to be excellent for the relief of pain when taken orally as a powder or a pill. Having used laudanum, for the same purpose, and having become addicted to its opiate qualities, I welcome any new advance in medicine of this sort. It seems that aspirin is happily *not* addictive in any way.'

'Well, that certainly is good news. Now I have something for you to ponder on while you are ploughing through the dark billows and furrows of the Black Sea. Staying with France, and also relevant to our situation here in the wartorn Crimea, the United States has been importing a new kind of ammunition – the Flobert cartridge – so-called because it was invented by a Parisian gunsmith called Nicolas Flobert. The ball or pellet is actually fitted to a case containing the powder, which goes in the breech of the rifle as one single piece. The modern cartridge they call it. This has been greatly improved by our own gunsmiths of course and has led to the development of a weapon called the .22 Long Rifle.'

'Marvellous,' said Crossman.

'Brilliant,' agreed Jarrard.

They both puffed away happily on their respective tobaccos.

8

Sergeant Crossman's *peloton* – or platoon – boarded the man o'
war, HMS *Antigone*, late in the afternoon. There was a fresh
breeze blowing and the *Antigone*, one of a dying breed of
wooden-built, sail-driven battleships in the British Navy now
that steam power was the order of the day, set off along the
coast towards the Straits of Kerch. They had roughly a
hundred and fifty miles to go, before anchoring offshore.
There they would deposit canoes and men in the sea.

'This is a job for marines,' grumbled Wynter, gloomily,
staring out at the dancing grey-green sea. 'We shouldn't be
here at all, doin' this kind of thing.'

'Better than fighting in the line, eh?' Corporal Devlin
answered him. 'Better than the trenches?'

'I like the sea air,' said Clancy, his dark skin glistening
with salt from the spray. He sniffed in the cold clean air
deeply. 'It fills your lungs well, don't it? No gunsmoke out
here. What do you say, Peterson?'

Peterson did not reply. She was busy being sick over the
rail. Peterson hated the sea. She only had to look at a rowing
boat and she felt sick. This was not the best of fox hunts, so
far as she was concerned, but since she had grit and determination she refused to let a little thing like seasickness prevent

her from going on the expedition. At least, it had seemed a little thing, before they had set sail. Now she believed she wanted to die.

Ali was sitting at the base of a mast, cleaning his many weapons, wrapping them in oil cloth and trying to keep them from the corrosive effects of the ocean. He was a walking arsenal, the Turk, while the others carried only Victoria carbines. These latter were not a favourite weapon with the soldiers. Victoria carbines were not very accurate, not very efficient, not very anything really except that they fired a ball.

Crossman was on another part of the deck, trying to write a letter despite the motion of the ship. He was under a canvas shelter, so he was able to keep the pages from becoming thoroughly wet. But it was impossible to keep out the dampness altogether and he was having trouble with the ink, which tended to blur at the edges of strokes.

He was writing to Lisette Fleury, the French woman he had fallen in love with when he had commandeered a farmhouse on the Crimean peninsula. Lisette's uncle had owned the farmhouse, which had been attacked by Cossacks. Crossman and his men had helped to defend the place. He and Lisette, who was now in Paris, had an understanding that one day they would marry.

Crossman had seen a great deal of action since he had been in the Crimea, though only in small part on the actual battle front. Only a handful of people knew what he had done off the battlefield. It was unlikely he would ever be rewarded for his services in medals or promotion. Major Lovelace had been promoted, so had some of Crossman's men, but there was really nowhere for Crossman to go. The next stage up was colour-sergeant, the senior sergeant in an infantry company, who had duties to his company which needed his presence. Likewise with a sergeant-major, the one above that. A colour-sergeant and a sergeant-major were needed in the regiment at all times.

In a general reshuffling, Crossman had recently been

transferred from a centre company to one of the flanks of his battalion. There were eight companies altogether in a battalion of a line regiment such as the 88th Connaught Rangers. Six of these were centre companies, or Battalion Companies as they were known. The other two were flank companies.

One of the latter was the Light Company, usually on the left flank and used as skirmishers. The other was the Grenadier Company, traditionally on the right flank. Crossman had been transferred to the Light Infantry Company, due to some idea that he was on skirmishing duties elsewhere, and therefore it would be more appropriate to place him there, along with his normally absent soldiers.

Crossman looked on his transfer as some sort of recognition that he was engaged in dangerous duties, even if his battalion and company commanders did not know exactly why they had done it.

Crossman told Lisette about the problems he was having with his brother. By the time his fiancée answered, of course, it would be too late. But it helped Crossman to ponder on the problem, sharing it with the absent Lisette.

The *Antigone* ploughed her way along the coastline, a brisk wind from the north-west driving her through fairly high seas. White-maned seahorses slapped at her hull. In the late afternoon, lamps began to be lit in houses and villages on the shore. A low mist was forming, but not dense enough to prevent the lights from the land being seen by the crew. Before the darkness fell completely, however, another vessel hove into view.

Suddenly, HMS *Antigone* veered sharply, changing her course swiftly and smoothly. She began to run with the wind, flying south-east like a racehorse given its head. The crew were ordered aloft and more sail was unfurled. Peterson was violently sick all over Wynter, who registered his disgust by shouting for the sergeant. It was this whine from Wynter which broke Crossman's reverie, rather than the change in course. Once it had impressed itself on Crossman's mind, he went straight to a naval officer.

'What's happening, sir?' he asked. 'Why has the captain changed course?'

The young officer was in a high state of excitement. He pointed with great drama at the ship in the distance.

'See that! It's a Russian warship! We're going to attack.'

'Good God,' muttered Crossman. 'One foot on a tub and we go straight into battle.'

'This is not a "tub",' said the officer stiffly. 'This is HMS *Antigone*, a third-rate ship of the line, pride of Captain Montagu Collidge, and it might be our last chance ever for some action. We have seventy-four guns on board this vessel and we're going to show the Russians that the old *Antigone* is not obsolete yet.'

Crossman, who knew next to nothing about naval warfare, was appalled.

'You mean there are people who think it is? In other words, we're going into battle in a boat that many think is out-of-date and will be scrapped as soon as someone gets round to it?'

'Boat?' screamed the midshipman. 'This is a *ship*, sergeant, and don't you forget it. Boats are driven by oars!'

Crossman glanced up at the bridge. He could see Captain Collidge standing there, one hand under his coat lapel in a Nelson-like pose, looking as if he had just been taken out of a long retirement for the action of his life. There was the glint of battle in his eye. Crossman could see he was about to enjoy himself in the line of duty.

His first officer had his eye glued to a telescope and was shouting instructions to somebody, Crossman was not sure who. Men were coming up from below and spilling over the deck like ants.

Gunners were manning their stations. Crossman had heard a rumour that the Navy never yelled 'Fire!' when they used their guns, they cried out, 'Shoot!' The reason being that the word 'fire' might have men rushing backwards and forwards with buckets of water and hoses. He waited with interest to see if this story were true.

'Prepare to engage the enemy,' cried an officer on the bridge, though it looked as if everyone was already feverishly preparing for the battle.

There was a crack of sails above as the main and fore royals and upper main and fore topgallants were dropped and instantly filled with wind. The *Antigone* shot forwards in the water, spray streaming from her bows. The wind and spume hissed through stays and lanyards. High above Crossman's head, men were scrambling up rigging, pulling on ratlines and buntlines, scrambling back down again. These sailors seemed to have no fear of heights, or if they had once, they had conquered them.

Lance-Corporal Wynter came excitedly to Crossman's side.

'This will be worth watching, eh, sergeant? A sea battle, by jingo. I wouldn't give much for that Russian's chances.'

'You wouldn't, would you? Well, considering she's just as big as we are and seems to be carrying the same number of guns, I think it'll be a fairly even fight. And I hate to ruin your day, Wynter, but we'll be fighting too. You get back over there and tell the others to load their carbines. If I'm not mistaken, we're in the marines now – at least for the duration of this battle.'

'Eh? What have we got to do with this? We're army.'

'We might be crab bait if we don't help. You think the Russians are going to say, "Oh, don't touch those army men there, they're nothing to do with a naval battle"? I think not, Wynter. I believe we're in it up to our necks.

'I wish the captain had remained on course for the Straits of Kerch, but out here on the high seas captains are gods and follow their own wishes and desires. Captain Collidge obviously thinks it will add more of a flourish to his career to conduct a sea battle, than to transport six soldiers and their canoes safely to Kerch and back again.'

Wynter slouched back to the group by the rail, who were watching with great interest as the *Antigone* gradually over-hauled the Russian warship. The sea was in a very choppy state, with huge waves crashing against the hull.

The *Antigone* used the relatively calm wake of the Russian ship as a sailing lane, and in the process robbed the ship in front of wind. A bow cannon opened up simultaneously as two great splashes appeared one either side of the *Antigone*, the sound of the Russian guns following up from behind like trailing long-distance runners.

Captain Collidge suddenly tacked to port, to bring more of his guns to bear on the running Russian. The British gunners below were obviously used to this manoeuvre by their captain, for they were ready to send shot crashing into what they could see of the port side of the Russian ship, whose name *Czarevna Alexandra*, was now clear to the soldiers of the 88th Foot, as they waited to do their bit.

Shattered timber and other debris flew into the air as the shot and shells impacted on the enemy ship. A sail was hit by a cannonball and went flying away like a ghost. A fireball landed amongst some sailors and the clothes of one caught alight. He ran the full length of the deck, blazing, the wind fanning his flames. Only when he fell did someone think to throw a bucket of sand over his twitching body. A Russian gun, and the men around it, disappeared completely under a hail of iron. The mizzen mast lost its spanker gaff, which fell to the deck of the enemy ship amid a welter of heavy canvas.

'Got you!' roared a sailor nearby. 'That'll sting!'

The noise of the guns was appallingly loud to the army men, who were used to having a certain distance between their ears and the cannon. Thirty guns blazed away again a minute or two later, acrid-smelling smoke filled the air. There was a hollow booming sound over the water. Some cannonballs fell short, sending geyser spouts high into the air, the spray of which was blown back to the *Antigone*. A rocket fired from the bows dipped into the sea, and skipped like a flat stone thrown by a boy.

The *Antigone* listed momentarily with the recoil of the cannon, then was back up again and swishing through the foam, her gunners working feverishly to reload.

A return volley came smacking into the side of her now, and all around the ship were white founts of water from the shot which had missed. Shells were bursting overhead with black smoke, sending sizzling hot fragments of iron like rain to clatter on the deck. A sailor struck by a piece of shrapnel folded like an empty sack. He lay in the gunwales for a few moments before some comrades dragged him back.

There were one or two fires on board the ship now, which were being efficiently attended to by sailors. The wounded were for the most part having to fend for themselves. One man had lost both his legs to a round shot, and his stumps had been stuck into twin barrels of hot tar by his comrades. The poor fellow had been left there, half-swooning, held up on the edges of the barrels resting against his crotch, while his comrades went about other tasks.

A 32-pound ball of solid iron crashed into the deck in front of the soldiers from the 88th. Slivers and chunks of lumber flew and hummed around them like crazy insects. Crossman's coatee and hair were covered in tiny pieces of wood the size of matchsticks. Wynter fell to the deck with a scream, a foot-long hunk of jagged oak sticking from his calf. He began to seep blood on the deck from this ugly wound, which he clutched with both hands.

'Get it out! Get it out!' he shrieked.

Peterson, her seasickness forgotten for a moment, dropped down beside him and wrenched the piece of wood from his leg. Instantly the blood pumped out in a stream, no doubt from an artery, much to the horror of Wynter. He clutched at the hole, trying to keep the blood back with his fingers.

Crossman quickly made a tourniquet out of his belt and fitted it over the thigh of the writhing soldier. He twisted and got the blood flow under control, while Peterson applied some lint pads she always carried to the wound. Ali wrapped them around with a tight strip of canvas torn from a sail bag. Peterson put her finger on the knot while Ali tied it, then she was sick again, luckily in the guttering which ran along the gunwales.

'You stay there,' she ordered Wynter, when she had recovered from another gut-wrenching bout. 'I've got to get some shooting in.'

'I'm not going anywhere,' said the soldier, looking at her as if she had lost her reason. 'I'm stuck here, ain't I?'

The battle still raged with the soldiers at the centre of it. They were close enough now to *Czarevna Alexandra* for the 88th to follow the lead of the marines along the deck, and to fire their carbines. Led in this by the unperturbable Turk, Yusuf Ali, they began to pick targets from amongst the Russians. Ali killed a man with his first shot and Peterson fired directly into a porthole behind which faces could be seen.

'I wish I had my Minié,' she complained, reloading her hated Victoria carbine. 'Could pick them off easily with that.'

Fire was coming back from Russian marines now and musket balls clipped the rigging and ricocheted off the rail. There was a great clamour on the Russian vessel, as the captain tried to run the *Czarevna Alexandra* off again, to the south-west. Collidge was up to this however, and the *Antigone* veered to windward, following the line of the Russian wake.

A loose sail began flapping madly above the 88th, having lost one of its sheets. This noise was even more distracting than that of the guns and muskets. It was as if some insane giant creature were trying to escape from a snare above them.

Darkness was falling rapidly all the time the battle raged, and the flashes of the guns were getting brighter.

Suddenly, the desperate *Czarevna Alexandra* tacked to the

south-east and headed for a bank of mist, which, combined with the darkness, folded around her when she reached it. The *Antigone* followed her in, but it was obvious after a short search that they had lost their quarry. There were moans of disappointment from the bridge and the quarterdeck.

After some time cruising around in the fog, the *Antigone* once more set course for the Straits of Kerch. The captain went below while the first officer gave a little speech to his weary men, telling them how bravely they had fought. One man cried it was a 'shame' that they had not engaged the Russian an hour earlier, when the darkness could not have swallowed her up.

'We gave her a bloody nose,' said the first officer, with some satisfaction in his tone. 'She'll think twice about coming up against another British naval vessel of our size.'

A ragged cheer went up from the men at the guns, and the task of clearing up the debris and putting the ship to rights began. The wounded, including Wynter, were taken below, to be looked at by the ship's surgeon. The deck cannon were secured. The flapping sail over the heads of the 88th was set again. Fires were doused and debris gathered from the corners and thrown overboard. The ship's carpenter and the surgeon would be the busiest people on board for a time.

A midshipman came to Sergeant Crossman with a message from the captain to assure him the *Antigone* was in good enough shape to complete the mission.

'We can still drop you off at the agreed point,' said the sailor. 'The damage we sustained won't hamper the ship's performance.'

Crossman went back to the 88th with this news.

'Well done, men,' said Crossman. 'You played your part.'

Peterson went back to being sick over the rail. Crossman made a mental note to leave her behind, with Wynter, now that one canoe was without a full crew. Ali and Clancy would go as one team and he and Devlin as the other. They could not carry the extra bombs between them because a rehearsal had shown they were already very low in the water. One more piece of weight and the canoes would start swamping. Crossman would have to do the job with two canoes and eight bombs.

9

The mariner who had lost his legs died within half an hour. Wynter had to witness his going in the cramped quarters below deck. It did nothing for the soldier's spirit, even though it had seemed a likely end for the poor fellow. He went out of the world crying for water: death had provided him with a thirst which was almost immediately redundant. Wynter wondered about that: why a man suddenly craved the stuff of life on the point of death. It seemed to him to be a cruel joke.

Wynter's wound was treated and dressed. The sailors were far better provisioned than the soldiers in the field in that respect. They had bandages, salves and balms. When Wynter had rested, he heaved himself up to the deck again, and Crossman told him he was not going on the mission. The soldier felt a sense of disappointment mingled with relief. He understood the latter, but had no idea where the former had come from.

Crossman explained the change of crews in the canoes.

'Ali is the best navigator amongst us,' said Crossman, 'followed closely by me. It seems pointless to put all our eggs in one basket, so I'm splitting the two of us up . . .'

They were drawing near to the shore now. It was daylight

again and they would have to cruise until nightfall. As soon as it was dark, the canoes could be launched.

The journey along the coast was quite dreary: the land itself was a charcoal-grey grimace against an unpleasant sky.

There was really nothing for the men to do but stare at the waves, which remained endlessly similar. Peterson had recovered a little from her seasickness, but was so weak she could do nothing but lie in a corner of a cabin below and shiver. She still wanted to die, but not quite as much as before.

When they reached the place where they were to launch the canoes, the captain sent for Crossman. The infantry sergeant was taken down below to a cabin which was luxurious when compared with an army officer's quarters on the front, but tiny in comparison with any other form of accommodation except a cell in one of Her Majesty's Prisons. Even then the ceiling was lower.

'Sergeant Crossman?' said the captain, who was sitting behind a desk covered in charts. 'I thought I would wish you good luck in your mission. Would you join me in a glass of port before you go?'

Crossman's eyebrows shot up at this invitation. It was quite unorthodox, perhaps even unseemly, for the captain of a British warship to offer to drink with a common sergeant. He wondered what might be behind this gesture and decided no harm could come of waiting to find out.

'Thank you, sir, I will,' said Crossman, taking the seat offered him. He had to duck and weave under the beams, but managed to avoid injury.

'Mind you don't damage my deckhead,' said the captain, incomprehensibly. 'You're a bit too tall to make a sailor.'

A pale cabin boy of about eleven years of age poured them each a glass of port with a trembling hand. It was hard not to notice how the child's hand shook. The captain nodded thoughtfully.

'It's young Simpson's first taste of battle, eh, boy?'

'Yes, sir,' answered the cabin boy, quietly.

'Well, it's not a pretty time for a youngster. I remember well the first time I heard the guns fired in earnest. I thought my head would fall off. Different when you're present at a salute, somehow. The guns seem quieter then.'

'You've seen a lot of action then?' asked Crossman, for something to say. 'Were you at some of the earlier battles of the war, in the Baltic, sir?'

'My dear boy,' replied Captain Collidge, a portly man who now leaned back in his chair, 'I was at Trafalgar with Lord Nelson. I was twelve years old. Frightened the living daylights out of me. It don't worry me now of course, but I'm getting a bit too old for it all. Probably why I lost that damn Russian warship. Losing my touch. Not the same now as it used to be. Too much slaughter these days. Too much carnage.'

'Carnage, sir?'

'Why yes. Take that fracas at Sinope. Damn slaughter. No other word for it. Once upon a time it was considered a coup to take a ship whole. Prize money and all that. Now they just sink 'em as fast as they can. Sinope's a good case in point.'

At the outset of the war between Turkey and Russia, before France and Britain had officially entered into the fighting, the Russian Black Sea Fleet had attacked a Turkish squadron under the command of Omar Pasha at a place called Sinope. Seven Turkish frigates and two corvettes were sunk outright by the Russians, superior in weight and number of ships. There were reports that five thousand Turkish sailors had perished, many of them being blasted with canister and grapeshot from Russian ships' cannons, as they struggled to survive in the water.

'Turkey and Russia were at war,' pointed out Crossman, 'but I agree if the reports were true then it was a needless massacre.'

Captain Collidge shook his head sadly.

'There you are, there you are. Few gentlemen o' war left in

these times. That's a pun on man o' war, by the way, but you don't have to laugh.' He smiled benignly.

'Take your expedition for example. Don't approve. Can't approve. Sneaking out in the night and sticking a bomb on a helpless ship at anchor. Blowing it to smithereens while sailors are sleeping and the watch is staring dreamily at the stars. Destroying the tranquillity of a peaceful evening. How can I approve? Still,' he took up his glass and motioned that Crossman should do the same, 'not my decision. Not for me to approve or disapprove really. When this is all over I shall just be glad to collect my half-pay and go into retirement.'

He lifted his glass. 'To the Queen,' he murmured.

Crossman lifted his also and automatically stood to attention. He cracked his head hard on an overhead beam. Sitting down again abruptly, he felt his mind spinning. He rubbed the sore spot.

'Told you you were too tall for a sailor,' laughed the captain. 'Said you'd damage my deckhead, didn't I? Don't you know sailors never stand for the toast? There's why, my boy. There's why. End up banging your noddle on a deckhead.'

Crossman felt a little better after he had drunk his port, but refused a second glass.

'I need to keep my wits about me, sir. I'm sure you'll understand.'

'Of course, of course. Well, good luck to you – no don't stand up so quickly, sergeant – take your time.'

Just before he left the cabin, Crossman turned, and with a puzzled frown, asked, 'This is not usual, is it, sir?'

'What, my boy?'

'Drinking with a non-commissioned officer.'

The captain's eyes twinkled.

'Oh, an old salt like me can afford to flout convention from time to time. Look at these heavy-swell side-whiskers of mine.' He plucked at the fluffed hair on the sides of his face. 'Not considered good form for a naval man. Get me into trouble all the time at the Admiralty. "Horse Guards next door," the first lord once roared at me when he saw them. Don't care any more. No more promotion coming this way, eh?'

'But is that all?'

'No, Major Lovelace mentioned you was at Harrow. There meself y' know. Should stick together us Old Harrovians. Too many of these Etonian bouncers about. Take all the best government jobs. Well, good luck again. Don't know what an Old Harrovian's doing in the ranks of the British Army, but I daresay that's your business, sergeant.'

'Yes, sir, thank you, sir.'

'Not at all.'

Crossman went back up on deck. His men were waiting there. The ship was now at anchor offshore and two canoes had been lowered into the water. It but remained for Crossman and the other three who were going with him to scramble down the nets and take their positions in their canoes.

Once they had done this and were ready, they cast off, paddling away from the tall ship into the blackness of the night. Now that they had come down from the high decks of the warship, the waves seemed much larger. There was a swell running from east to west, which created great watery canyons. The canoes slipped down into these monsters easily enough, but paddling back up the other side was hard work. Soon Crossman's arms were aching.

'Are you all right, Devlin?' he asked the man behind him.

Devlin was grunting with the exertion. 'All right as all right can be,' replied the Irishman.

Now that they were down amongst the waves, the coastline kept disappearing and reappearing too. It was not easy to navigate amongst the changing folds of the sea. Shore lights twinkled into existence, then just as quickly were lost again, having disappeared behind flowing, liquid horizons.

'We've got about ten miles to do,' Crossman said. 'At this rate it'll take us all night. Where's the other canoe?'

'Not far behind us, sergeant.'

'Signal for them to come closer.'

Devlin gave out a low whistle and then steered their craft towards Ali and Clancy.

Crossman called out to the two dark silhouettes when they were within range.

'We'll have to go in closer to the shore. This headwind may be less fierce there. Not too close though. We don't want to get caught up in any breakers. The onshore drift may well carry us on to rocks or into cliffs if we're not careful.'

Ali waved to say he understood.

There was no telling what the coast was like at this point. Whether there were beaches or rocky cliffs could not be discerned in the darkness. They could see black lumpy masses in the starlight against the dark sky, but could make out no real definition. Here and there small points of light glowed like stars upon the ground – probably the lamps of farm-houses. In one place a fishing village added some cheery light to the otherwise gloomy landscape.

On the other side of the canoeists was the vast open sea: an inky blackness that stretched out into infinity. Staring that way made Crossman feel very small and vulnerable, and the canoe just a flimsy piece of material beneath him. The waves were quite vigorous, and it took all their strength to keep the canoe upright. Should they overturn they would be lost. They might cling on to the canoe and try to swim it to the land, but they were in fact about a mile out to sea and would die in the freezing water within a few minutes. It was cold enough to kill a man outside the water, let alone in it.

'Keep paddling,' he said to Devlin.

The Irishman had not in fact stopped paddling, but Devlin seemed to understand that these superfluous words had been used for the purpose of seeking comfort. There was little enough comfort to be had out there on the water. Thoughts were as dark as the sea and the night: deep gloomy ponderings that might drag a man down with them to the depths of despair. If one let it, a black panic might overtake a soul and create its own problems.

The wind, low as it was, bit into the faces and hands of the canoeists. Spray constantly flicked up over the bows of the home-made craft, stinging Crossman's eyes, soaking him in the bargain. Although on the one hand his exertions were making him sweat, he was constantly shivering inside his clothes. Rivulets of water ran from his hair, down inside his collar, to his chest and back.

There was nothing for it but to keep paddling, for what felt like an eternity. Hour on hour seemed to drag past, though each hour might only have been a quarter of real time. Sometimes Ali and Clancy overtook them, to take the full brunt of the wind and give them some relief. It was, of course, much easier to trail in the wake of the leading canoe.

Finally they came to a headland on which a light brighter than most stood, like a beacon in the dark wilderness. Its rays shone over the waters. Crossman guessed this was some sort of warning to shipping, that there were rocks around. Beyond the light was a stretch of black lapping sea which seemed to have no end. They had come at last to the Straits of Kerch. All four men were very tired, yet they knew they now had to battle against the notorious currents which ran in the straits.

Once again they dug deep into their reserves. The paddles went in and came out automatically. Somehow the canoes moved forward, but it seemed infinitesimally slowly. The bright light seemed to grow no nearer. In fact at times it seemed as if it were moving away. Finally, as the two canoes were abreast, Clancy let out a choking sob.

'What's the matter?' asked Crossman.

'Cramp! I've got cramp in my legs. Oh, God, sergeant, this is agony. My feet were cramped a few minutes ago. I can stand that, but not my calves. It feels like my muscles are being squeezed and knotted in a washing mangle.'

'Grit your teeth. Bear it until it goes away.'

'I can't do this, sergeant. My arms are falling off. My

whole body aches to death. I've got to stop. This is killing me. I've got to get out and walk a bit. I'm no coward. I'll go at the guns any time. But this is agony. This is murder.'

Crossman knew how the man felt. His own hipbones felt as if they were cracking and crumbling within him. He too had had cramp in several places, which had been incredibly painful. But in addition to that there were constant shooting pains and aching in his joints and up and down his limbs. His shoulders hurt too, with the constant use of the paddle.

The canoes had been designed so that the paddler sat on his own calves, his legs folded under him. There was no relief from the agony of ache that attacked a man's lower back and legs in this position. One could slip down a little on to one's heels, or kneel upright for a moment to relieve the pain on the legs. But the paddler could not move too often. It was dangerous. If one kneeled upright the canoe became unsteady and threatened to topple sideways. It simply had to be a quick shift of position and then back on the calves or heels.

'Paddle towards the shore a little. See if there's a beach where we can stretch our limbs for a few minutes. Otherwise we'll all be in trouble,' said Crossman. 'Easy now, we don't want to end up on any rocks.'

Ali and Clancy led the way to the shore, listening carefully for breakers or the sound of waves on rocks. Crossman and Devlin followed on behind. No one, not even Ali, objected to the halt, though it was clearly an extremely perilous thing to do on a mission of this sort. There were unseen risks out there in the darkness, on solid ground, which were better avoided.

10

They found the waves lapping on a gently-sloping shore and gratefully took the canoes in. Crossman climbed out into the freezing shallow water and immediately his legs cramped. He staggered to the beach and fell over, groaning and massaging his limbs. Similarly, the others climbed from their floating boxes and walked like puppets. They stretched their arms and legs, trying to get some life back into them. Clancy complained about his back and Devlin said his neck would never be the same again.

Crossman looked around him. In the starlight he could see they were on the beach of a small cove, encircled by shallowly-rising cliffs. White-veined tracks ran up the slopes to the top of the cliffs, where a single light shone. Apart from that one habitation, it appeared to be a fairly deserted place. There was the sound of goats or sheep coming from above, accompanied by a faint smell of manure on the night air.

'Ten minutes,' said Crossman, 'then we've got to be on our way again. Walk up and down. Get your circulation going. Rub some life back into your limbs.'

They did as he suggested.

As they walked up and down there was a cold shaft of wind blowing along the beach. Starlight twinkled on minerals in the rocks. Along the beach was heard the rustle and sigh of the wavelets as they slipped over the pebbly shore.

'Right, time to go,' called Crossman, softly.

The men gathered by the canoes. There were only three of them. Ali was missing.

'Ali?' called Crossman, staring into the darkness of the beach. 'Are you there?'

No answer.

Crossman felt a surge of panic. The second canoe could not possibly continue without Ali. Clancy would not have the strength to paddle it on his own, it was difficult enough with the two of them. They could not leave the Bashi-Bazouk here either. Crossman knew his chances of relocating this small cove again on the return journey were negligible. And Clancy would never find his way back to the ship on his own: not without Ali to guide and encourage him.

'Ali,' called Crossman, a little louder. 'For God's sake, where are you?'

At this call there came the sound of a clattering amongst the rocks and scree.

Crossman felt relief wash through him. Perhaps Ali had gone off to perform his toilet. Muslims were very particular about privacy. He waited, but when the sounds simply continued, without any sign of Ali, his apprehension rose again.

'Ali, is that you?'

Still no answer, but the noise of heavy footsteps came closer, as if heading towards the sound of Crossman's voice.

'Russians,' said Clancy, reaching into his canoe for his carbine.

Crossman was not so sure. If it was the enemy, how were they able to approach without some sort of light? It was almost pitch black amongst the rocks. And why come any closer? Why not just open up with guns or rifles and kill the British where they stood? These thoughts raced through the sergeant's mind as he drew his revolver.

'Ali, if that's you, damn you, man, speak – or we'll have to fire upon you!'

Still no answer. The noise of the feet on the pebbles now indicated that it was more than just one man. It was too loud, certainly for Ali, who walked like a cat. There was the accompanying sound of heavy breathing too, and a strange kind of smell, a musty stink. Soon, whoever it was would be out of the deep shadow of the cliff, and into the starlight. They would at least be able to see a shape.

'It's a monster!' cried Clancy, the superstitions of his Indian childhood rushing to the fore. 'It's a ghost. I can smell it.'

'Don't be stupid, man,' said Crossman, but he had felt the hairs on the back of his neck rise at these words. 'Keep your voice down.'

At that moment a huge form loomed above them, coming out of the darkness. It had a peculiar loping walk and its large eyes shone in the starlight. A thick-lipped mouth hung open, dripping saliva and goo, which splattered on the smooth pebbles of the beach. It's long neck arched out as it gave first a short snort, then a mooning bellow, on seeing the three men.

Crossman lowered his pistol. 'A camel,' he muttered. We've been frightened by a dromedary. Clancy, here's your monster-ghost. It probably belongs to that dwelling up on the cliff and has wandered away from its tether.'

Clancy gave out a little sob. 'I – I thought it was *Muru*, the Demon-with-seven-thousand-sons, come to slaughter us.'

'Well, it's not,' said Devlin, who had been thinking of the Banshee himself, 'it's only a ragged old camel, you idiot.'

The camel's breath stank of whatever herb or weed it had been chewing on when the group had disturbed it. Crossman tried to shoo the beast away, but it remained shuffling its feet before them. It had found company in the long cold night and it was obviously a gregarious beast, happiest in society.

Now that the emergency was over, Crossman began again

to fret about the disappearance of Ali, but no sooner was he considering organising a small search party to scour the beach area, than the Bashi-Bazouk appeared beside him.

'Where the hell have you been?' asked Crossman, angrily. 'We thought you'd been taken.'

A delicious smell wafted up from a battered metal pot in the Turk's hands.

'Stew, sergeant,' Ali said, simply. 'Warm our insides.'

'Stew?' murmured Clancy, stumbling forwards. 'You mean, real *food*?'

'Good Lord, deliver us,' said Devlin. 'I could use some o' that.'

The pot was placed on the ground and the men simply dipped their hands into it and began eating the contents. It appeared to consist of potatoes, carrots, cabbage and some kind of meat.

'Mutton,' said Devlin, in ecstasy, 'or goat. I don't much care which of them. It's a miracle.'

'Where did you get it?' asked Crossman, as grateful as the others for something to warm him through. 'At that place on the hill?'

'Tartar farm,' Ali replied. 'Always they have some stew on the embers, ready to eat in the morning.'

'Lord bless 'em,' Devlin said. 'I love those Tartars.'

Once they had eaten, Ali placed the empty stew pot carefully above the high tidemark on the beach. The food had been a godsend, but Ali had no wish to steal the pot from the family who had provided it. Such a pot was a valuable item to poor farmers scratching a living from the soil. There had been local goatherds who thought themselves suddenly wealthy after having found a British soldier's camp kettle on the trail.

The dromedary lumbered off and began to lick the metal pot, which made a clanking noise on the scree.

The men boarded their canoes and once more set off towards the harbour which was their destination.

The stew had put new life into their paddling, but the wind, the cold and the twisting currents made their journey a bitter one.

Eventually they came in sight of a town which, by its size, they realised must be Kerch. Crossman signalled silently to the canoe behind to follow his lead.

They slid into a harbour full of ships as silently as two deadly crocodiles. There were one or two lamps lit on board some of the vessels. Others lay in darkness. Perhaps on most ships there would not even be a watch, for the Russians believed they were in a safe harbour, protected from any mainland attack by their army. Of course the British Navy might sail round and try to capture the port, but that would have been seen from miles away and reported all the way up the coast.

The canoes then slipped in amongst some very sleepy vessels. All that could be heard was the creaking and groaning of timbers disturbed by the currents. Crossman now began a patient search amongst the ships with their forest of masts and booms. Each likely craft, one that matched the silhouette imbedded on Crossman's mind, had to be approached and studied in the poor light coming from the ships themselves, and from the port, to discover their names.

It was a long and painstaking task, fraught with the possibility of discovery at any moment. All it took was one sailor with insomnia to lean over the rail and look down into the water at the right time.

Finally their seeking was successful and they found their quarry: two large ships anchored together, one either side of a wharf.

Crossman motioned for Ali and Clancy to take the *St Petersburg*, which was furthest away, while he and Devlin took the *Yalta*.

The *Yalta* looked alarmingly high in the water. Crossman suspected that at least some of the ship's cargo had already been unloaded and was stored somewhere nearby. It was a hopeless task to go searching the warehouses, for the explosives could be anywhere, not necessarily on the quayside. He had to hope that there was enough ammunition and gunpowder left on board to make a bang worthwhile.

Devlin made ready a small charge first, to be fitted to the hull just under the waterline of the bows. This was what Devlin called the 'mercy bomb' which would explode first and allow any sailors on board to evacuate the ship. Crossman had ordered this little device himself at the instigation of his men: Lovelace had no knowledge of it. The men – and Crossman had to admit, he himself – had a horror of blowing up mariners still asleep in their hammocks and bunks, who would otherwise have no chance whatsoever of surviving a night blast.

The 'mercy bomb' would merely blow a hole in the bows and start the ship sinking. If they had any sense at all the Russians would disembark from a ship full of explosives on which bombs were being detonated. Ten minutes afterwards the main charges would detonate and the vessel would be matchwood floating through the skies.

Of course, Devlin had argued, they might be foolish enough to stay around and look for further bombs, but that was their business, and at least they would be wide-eyed and awake when they were sent to kingdom come. It was highly unlikely they would look *outside* the ship for the cause of the explosion. It was more likely they would believe it to be accidental and would simply evacuate until there were no signs of further blasts.

They lit the Beckford fuse of the first bomb and tried to screw it into the ship's hull. Despite the sharp threaded point on the bomb's spike, it was not as easy as they had imagined. The wood was hard and the spike would not penetrate at first. Eventually, with the help of some silent swearing, the first bomb was in position.

Now they went a quarter of the way along the ship and placed the second, and a little further along, the third charge. Then they went around to the other side, away from the jetty, with no protective screen above their heads. Finally, all four charges were lit and in position. Just as they were about to paddle out into the harbour, to meet up with Ali and Clancy, they heard voices above. A lit cheroot end came floating down to hit the water near them and sizzle to extinction.

Crossman immediately eased the canoe under the belly of the tall ship, out of sight of anyone above.

There were low voices. Clearly two or more men were leaning on the rail, talking about something: their sweethearts, their wives, or perhaps even the war? It appeared to be one of those earnest discussions that men have in the early hours of the morning when they believe their minds are functioning best. In fact most ideas formed at these times are likely to be less than reasonable, but such chats are cosy and enjoyable for men who have nothing to do except wait for the world to wake.

Crossman looked at Devlin and the Irish corporal's eyes told him that the other soldier was wondering the same thing: the fuses had been set for fifteen minutes. Both men had had talks like this on sentry duty and knew that such a discussion as the one above was likely to go on for an hour or more. The sailors on the deck had all the time in the world.

They had spent nearly ten minutes putting the other four charges around the ship, after planting the 'mercy bomb'. In just a few minutes that first bomb would explode, smashing a hole in the bows of the *Yalta*. If the garrulous mariners above had not moved away from the rail by that time, Crossman and Devlin would have to make a dash for it across the harbour, hoping there would be too much confusion and chaos on board to spot them canoeing away.

They waited in apprehension, the sweat visible on Devlin's brow in the lamplight from the ship.

Crossman could see Ali and Clancy in their canoe, crossing the harbour. Suddenly, one of the men above let out a yell. He had seen them too.

'Let's go!' said Crossman. 'Paddle for all you're worth, corporal.'

They shot out from under the ship, just as a Russian sailor came to the rail with a musket. Something was shouted, the musket was fired. A 'plop' sounded in the water near the front of the canoe. Then came a second shot, presumably from another musket, which sang past Crossman's ear. Devlin reached for his carbine, already loaded, and before Crossman could stop him, aimed and squeezed the trigger.

The powder was damp from seawater and the carbine failed to go off.

'Thank God it didn't fire – you'd have had us over with the recoil, corporal,' said Crossman. 'We were side on. We'd have rolled and capsized.'

'Forgot about that,' Devlin acknowledged. 'Sorry, sergeant.'

'Let's just get out of here. Follow the two in front. As fast as you can.'

A bell was going ten to the dozen on the deck of the *Yalta* now and some sailors were launching a longboat. When the boat was half-way down to the water, the first of the charges exploded. The *Yalta* shuddered from stem to stern and rocked violently in the water. The bowline of the longboat was released and the small craft tipped over, spilling men into the sea.

Fortunately for the Russian mariners, the water was so cold they wanted to get out of it as soon as possible and began swimming for the quayside, some helping others.

A half-a-minute after the first mercy bomb had exploded, the one attached to the bows of the *St Petersburg* went up.

More shots were fired from the deck of the *Yalta*, but these fell short of the canoe. The harbour currents had helped to take the British soldiers beyond the range of shipboard muskets. On board the *Yalta* someone was screaming orders in an incomprehensible voice. Crossman and Devlin paddled like mad, hoping to put a good distance between themselves and the two craft which were soon to go sky-high.

The *Yalta* was now listing badly and going down at the bows.

11

When the bombs around the *Yalta* finally exploded, the effect was relatively disappointing. The ship was destroyed, but no secondary explosions took place. Clearly the Russian explosives which had been on board had been unloaded. The 88th had blown up an empty ship.

Still, the blasts were impressive, and sent timber and other debris flying through the air. A series of large waves was created which came rushing towards the two canoes. Crossman saw with alarm that if they did not point the front of the canoe at the oncoming wash they would be overturned. Clancy and Ali had already assumed that position.

'Get the canoe round, Devlin,' he yelled. 'Copy Ali's manoeuvre!'

They managed to get the craft in line just as the first wave hit. Riding it with difficulty, they took some water in the bomb hatch which had a chilling effect on their thighs. The next wave was slightly smaller, and so on, and finally they were able to relax a little. They were near to a stone quay now. Ali and Clancy had climbed out of their canoe and were standing on some steps. Crossman and Devlin joined them.

Crossman was anxious. Where was the second series of explosions? Surely they should have been detonated by now?

He did not have to wait long. He had just managed to disembark and take their canoe out of the water, when the whole harbour area was ripped apart by a deafening set of blasts which were so close together they were almost one. This time the distant wharf, jetty, the *Yalta*, the *St Petersburg* and several other ships, vanished amid a storm of wood, water and flying metal.

Crossman instantly dropped down alongside Clancy and Ali. Devlin, a little slower in his thinking, was blown off the quayside by the blast, and into the harbour. He managed to grab a mooring post and cling on, waiting for the aftershock.

A hot wave of choking air buffeted the soldiers, sweeping over them. This was followed by a downpour of pieces of lumber, bits of iron and a deluge of water. Despite being fashioned mostly of stone, the quay on which they lay rocked violently. Monstrous waves swept through the harbour, carrying timber on their crests. Devlin had to shelter behind the thick mooring post, clinging on to the iron mooring ring to avoid being struck by wayward beams and other ships' trappings.

A pretty display of pyrotechnics was now cascading over the harbour area. Rockets flared away into the night like mad fireflies. Shells burst and whizz-bangs were shooting here, there and everywhere. Secondary fires were being started by these wayward explosives. Shed roofs were catching alight. Stores of hay and straw were going up in flames. Frightened livestock was charging around, colliding with people and objects, scattering bales and boxes over the waterfront.

For at least two minutes afterwards timber was still raining from the skies, falling into a choppy harbour. Buildings around the harbour were being pelted too. During this time, immediately following the firework display, there was relative silence. Stunned and bewildered Russians tried to gather their shattered wits.

Then there was pandemonium again. Bells began ringing, people began shouting, and there were the cries of the wounded and dying. Loose horses and oxen were rounded up. Carts were pulled out of the way of raging fires, and goods were being dragged free of the flames. At first there were only a few night owls to deal with the situation. Then the rest of the population began to emerge, somewhat confused at first.

To give credit to the garrison, these people were soon organised by the soldiers and sailors on night watch. Many of those who came out of their houses and billets were still in their nightshirts. They looked like ghosts as they ran back and forth with buckets of water, their night clothes billowing, their faces pale with the shock of a disturbed night.

No one took very much notice of three men on a jetty, who were trying to rescue a fourth from the water.

Devlin swam through the rubbish to the quay and was hauled up by the other three soldiers. They quickly relaunched their canoes. Still no one paid the slightest bit of attention to them. The populace was still in a state of shock and was too busy with the tasks in hand. Many were intent on kicking or sorting through debris with their hands, as if they expected to find lost comrades there.

'That was pure murder,' murmured Devlin, just as shocked as any of his Russian victims. 'I hope I'll never be doing the likes of that again.'

Crossman said nothing, but in his own mind he agreed with the corporal. The hold of the *St Petersburg* must have been full of explosives and ammunition. It had devastated the harbour and its surrounds. God only knew how many dead and injured there were. The damage they had caused was astonishing, considering they were but four men in two canoes. The Royal Navy could not have done worse with a dozen men o' war. Crossman's instinct was to pitch in and help try to save the casualties from further injury, but of course that would have been pure stupidity.

'Let's get away from here. If they catch us they'll hang us from the nearest post, and I can't say I would blame them.'

The two canoes paddled along the coastline toward and

out of the straits. Their journey was made all that much more difficult at first due to the amount of debris in the water. The canoes kept striking logs and platters of wood. Once they were round the first headland, they found themselves clear of this rubbish and were able to make better progress. The currents that had hampered them so much going into the straits, were now assisting them in their escape, and very glad they were to have them.

Soon they were well on their way. They ached in every part of their bodies, but they were heading back now. Return journeys are never as bad as outward ones. There is the promise of a warm bed and a sleep at the end.

Devlin was soaked through to the skin and shivered constantly, but the others were not much better. They had a good few inches of water in the bottoms of their canoes, and the constant spray over the bows made sure their upper halves remained wet too. Even after the light of dawn was in the sky it was still bitterly cold. They crept along the coast, their arms paddling mechanically, desperate for sight of the ship.

Two hours after the explosion in the Russian harbour, they sighted the *Antigone*. They were two miles away from the craft when a strong wind began sweeping across the water. The deep darkened and white horses appeared on the waves. Ali pointed and shouted with alarm, his finger indicating that something was coming from the south, a weather front moving up swiftly. It was clear the two canoes were going to be caught in a squall.

To make matters worse, the *Antigone* had obviously seen the squall coming too and had upped anchor and was moving closer to the shore, to take refuge in a wide bay with curving headlands shaped like two cow horns at either end.

'They're leaving us,' cried Clancy, paddling furiously. 'They're leaving us to die.'

'Head for the shore,' Crossman ordered.

They raced for the coast, which was at least half a mile away. Before they could get very far the squall hit them with great force. At first Crossman and Devlin were carried on the crest of a wave, on its surf, like a piece of flotsam.

Then Crossman felt himself being lifted up and thrown down hard. It went black and cold, freezing cold, as he found himself surrounded by water. The night air had suddenly turned liquid. He tried to breathe and took in seawater. He gagged and choked, his eyes starting from his head in pain and fear. Which way was up and which was down? The stars had gone, the wind had gone, there was no spray on his face. He dared not breathe again even though his lungs burned with a horrible yearning pain.

The pain became a blinding white agony in his breast, searing all from his brain but sheer demented terror. There was no thinking straight, no sensible survival thoughts. The pain took all his concentration for a few moments. Then, fortuitously perhaps, secondary pain came from his legs, as his muscles constricted with cramp. It was this secondary pain which shook him out of his funk. It jolted his attention into focus again. A conscious thought penetrated the unreasoning fear. He realised if he did not get oxygen soon he would be dead.

Panic continued to rush through him as he thrashed and fought to get out of the canoe. He had lost all orientation, seeing nothing, feeling only freezing water and that terrible increasing pain in his chest. Finally he managed to struggle out of his cockpit. Once free he battled his way to the surface of the sea. Fortunately he went the right way, by pure instinct or luck, for there was nothing to guide him.

He was surprised to find the sea was still in turmoil.

He clung to the side of the canoe, coughing and spluttering, warm salty water coming up from deep in his lungs.

Only after a minute or two did he start wondering whether Devlin was still underneath the canoe.

Then he saw the Irish corporal, a few yards away, his right hand gripping the line which ran out from the stern. The canoe had been literally upended, the stern going up and over, and the canoe coming down the wrong way up in the raging sea.

'Pull yourself in,' croaked Crossman with great effort. 'Get to the canoe.'

Devlin's eyes were wide with terror. It was obvious he thought he was going to drown. But with supreme labour he began hauling on the line, either pulling the upturned canoe towards himself, or himself towards it, Crossman was not sure.

The waves were reaching mountainous proportions now. One minute the pair would be at the bottom of a deep trough of water, the next they would be lifted up high into the air and carried towards the land. Crossman was concerned that they would be sucked into the maw of a wave, once the great rollers began hitting the shoreline and curling into booming surf. Rocks were the greatest fear. They would be smashed and ripped apart by the teeth of any jagged rocks they might encounter.

Finally, the exhausted Devlin managed to reach the canoe and Crossman gripped the corporal's sleeve. There was no sign of the other two men. The air and the sea were one frothing mass of white water and spume. Wind screamed around them, whipping the waves to a fury, creating forces that not only carried them up and down, but spun and twisted them round like a twig in a whirlpool.

'Sergeant,' screamed Devlin. 'I touched bottom – I did – I did.'

But Crossman's flailing feet found no purchase below.

The trouble was, they might be a hundred yards nearer shore one moment, then be back where they started the next. The shifting waters of the ocean moved alarmingly swiftly. There were storm-formed eddies and currents now, erratic and unpredictable, not like the strong but gentle currents created by a stormless ocean. They took men and canoe and played with them like toys, throwing them this way and that, sweeping them down rushing channels in the flood, tossing them in the air, then rushing off again perhaps in a different direction.

The canoe began breaking up. It had never been anything but a home-made and necessarily very light craft. The nails that held it were wrenched from their beds, squealing and squeaking. Joints were torn apart. The deck went first, was ripped away and shredded by the savage waves. Then the whole length began to break in half.

'I can't hold on, sergeant,' sobbed Devlin. 'I'm going to let go. My arms won't hold me. Speak to my wife. Tell her I died in battle. Don't let her know I drowned like a rat in a bloody bog.'

Crossman, barely able to keep his purchase on the canoe himself, tried to yell encouragement to the corporal, but lack of breath would not let him get the words out. Then he found his own fingers torn from the canoe, and was taken on a high wave, and thrown bodily on to shingle which shifted like quicksand beneath him. The next wave landed Devlin on top of him, the pair crashing together, painfully bruising one another. Bits of broken canoe struck Crossman's head and chest.

Another breaker lifted Crossman off his feet again and carried him yet further up the shore, where he managed to scramble and claw his way out of the reach of the waves.

He lay there dazed for a few minutes, his head spinning. Then he sat up to choke more water from his lungs. When he found his voice again, he yelled out.

'Devlin – are you there?'

There was no answer at first, but then a faint, laboured reply reached his ears.

'I'm out of the water, sergeant.'

The two men lay where they were for quite a long time, trying to get some strength back into their exhausted bodies. Crossman could see the sky getting lighter with every minute and after a while the squall passed over, leaving the sea still raving, but getting calmer all the time. He finally managed

to get to his feet and stagger down the shore to where Devlin
lay amongst seaweed, tossed there like a seashell by the squall.

'Are you well, corporal?'

Devlin let out a slightly hysterical laugh.

'Am I well? I'm a bloody ruined man, sergeant, that's what
I am. I've been tortured with paddling for hours on end, I've
been blown up and thrown this way and that, and I've been
near drowned in a bloody storm. Am I well? I'm alive, is all
I'm saying, but as to being well, only the Lord knows.'

'A fine speech,' Crossman said, wryly. 'You must be as fit
as a fiddle. I haven't the strength to make such a speech.'

Devlin sat up and looked down at his soaked clothes.

'We're in a pretty pickle now, sergeant. We've lost our
canoe and it's a long walk home, through enemy territory. Do
you think the others made it?'

'I don't know. Let's go and look.'

They got to their feet somehow and began a search of the
immediate area. There was no sign of either Ali or Clancy. It
appeared they had not made it to the shore. The two men
climbed up to a higher point from where they could look
down on several small bays. In one there was something which
looked bulky, like a body lying on the sand. The two men,
cold and shivering, scrambled down the slopes which led to
this bay.

It was Ali, and he was unconscious. Clancy was nowhere
to be seen. They carried the inert Ali, a heavy load, up the
track to the top. There Crossman scoured the landscape for
signs of habitation. Finally he saw smoke rising from the
west. He and Devlin managed to half-carry, half-drag the
bulky Turk in this direction, until they came upon a large
farmhouse. Smoke was curling skywards from the chimney.
All the windows had shutters, which were still closed. A
thick, roughly-hewn door barred their entrance to the
dwelling.

Crossman hammered on the door with a rock.

12

The door opened and an elderly woman stood there. Her hair was completely grey and hung in a single plait down her back to her waist. Her face was tanned and weathered, with more creases than a well-used war map. She stepped back, her mouth dropping open, as she beheld the three drenched soldiers. A single word which sounded like an exclamation escaped her throat, but Crossman did not understand it.

Crossman waited no longer to be offered entrance. Still holding Ali's legs, he pushed past the old woman with a murmured word of apology, which he guessed she would not understand. Devlin came up behind. Between them they carried the body of Yusuf Ali, whose eyes were now open. The Turk seemed to be having trouble focusing, but he was breathing regularly. He said something to the woman, who made a gesture which was incomprehensible to the other two soldiers.

The woman stared at the Turk for a short while, then left the room. Crossman was wondering whether he ought to follow her. Perhaps there were men in the house? In their present state the three soldiers could be overwhelmed very easily. But in fact he felt too cold and weak to do much more than wait for the outcome. Devlin had already collapsed on to a chair and lolled there like a rag doll. Ali remained on the floor.

The woman returned, not with assistance, but with a warm blanket and some hot soup.

She wrapped the Turk in the blanket and then began to spoon-feed him some of the soup. When it seemed he had had enough, she handed the remains in the bowl to the other two men. There were the embers of a fire in the grate. Crossman took the liberty of placing some logs on the hot ashes. When he looked at the woman, her eyes revealed her approval.

Once the logs were blazing, all three men sat in front of the flames and warmed themselves through. They let their clothes dry on their bodies. Soon Crossman was feeling a great deal better and more able to cope with the situation, both mentally and physically. He was desperately tired, but he had been in that position so many times before. It was enough that he was warm and dry now, with some food inside him.

'Don't fall asleep, Devlin,' he warned his corporal, whose eyes he had seen closing. 'We have to get out of here. They'll be looking for us. And if we don't get to the ship soon, it'll leave us here, thinking we are all dead.'

'The sergeant is right,' Ali said. 'We must find the ship. It is too many miles to walk. Too much danger.'

He then spoke at length to the elderly woman, who stood with her arms crossed in front of her chest. It seemed to Crossman that the pair were arguing, but he had often made this assumption in the past with regard to foreigners, and often found to his amazement that the stiff words and raised voices meant nothing more than a mutual agreement over some third action or party. Such seemed to be the case here, for the woman left the room and returned a little later with two ancient muskets. There was also a tin box which contained powder and balls.

'The carbines went down with the canoes,' explained Ali. 'I ask her to sell us some guns and dry powder.'

He gave the woman three coins which instantly disappeared in the folds of her dress.

'With that her husband can buy a new rifle. He is away at market in Yalta,' explained Ali. 'They are Tartars. They not care too much for the Russians, who eat their food and pay nothing. They not like the Cossacks who is their old enemy, from old, old times.'

'Tell her we appreciate her generosity very much. What did you give her?'

'I give her Maria Theresa dollars we steal from the Russians.'

Devlin said rather indignantly, 'You're not supposed to have that. It's to be shared out amongst us after the war is over.'

The Bashi-Bazouk never let criticism go unanswered.

'I only take a little. I take some for good use. Maybe I not live until after the war. Maybe the Russians shoot Yusuf Ali and then I not able to spend the money,' replied the unrepentant Turk, who always seemed to manage to get hold of things he was not supposed to have. 'If I not take money, maybe Russian blow your head off with his gun, and you not able to stop him, eh?'

There seemed to be no answer to this, since Devlin certainly carried no international coin on his person.

Crossman now asked the question which had been worrying him since picking up the Turk.

'Ali, is there any chance that Clancy survived the wreck of your canoe?'

Ali sighed. 'I think not, sergeant. I saw him go under the wave. He not come up again. Yusuf Ali try to swim to him but another big wave come. I think he drown. Sorry.'

'Not your fault, Ali. Not your fault at all. Devlin and I could not have saved one another either. We had not the strength nor the fortitude. I'm sorry the boy's dead though. I liked him in a lot of ways.'

'Me too, sergeant,' said Ali. 'Private Clancy was like me – not afraid to kill a man with his hands.'

'Well, that's not a thing I'll miss in him,' Devlin said, 'but it's a crying shame, just the same.'

'Time we were on the move,' said Crossman, standing now. He picked up one of the muskets. Devlin quickly took the other. Ali shrugged and smiled. He and Crossman had dried their pistols by the fire: had reloaded them with fresh powder. So long as Ali had his various weapons about him, he did not worry.

They said goodbye to the elderly woman, whose thin worn face broke into a creased smile.

When they opened the door, however, figures were coming up the track to the farm. Figures in indigo. They were on horseback and they carried lances.

'Cossacks!' cried Crossman, slamming the door. 'Bloody Cossacks.'

'Did they see you, sergeant?' asked Devlin.

'I don't know. There's five or six of them. They're probably part of a wider search for us. If we start shooting, we may bring the whole damn Russian Army down on us. How far are we from the sea? Did you notice when we came up here?'

'About two hundred yards, I'd guess at, sergeant,' Devlin replied. 'We're up on some cliffs. What are you thinking? That we swim out to the *Antigone*? If you try that, sergeant, I'm not coming with you. I'll take my chances here. I've had enough of the water to last me a lifetime.'

The Irish corporal's mouth was set in a firm line. He was usually the first to obey an order, but clearly the thought of another dip in the freezing water did not appeal to him. Even the threat of a court martial would not change his mind, that much was obvious from his eyes.

'No, not swim. We wouldn't stand a chance in that cold sea. I was thinking we could make our way along the beaches until we come to some sort of fishing village. There are dozens up and down this coast. We could steal a boat and row out to the ship. What do you think, Ali?'

'I think this is the best plan. Yusuf Ali not want to go into the sea again today. Not without boat.'

The old woman showed them a window at the back of the farmhouse. They climbed through it and ran towards a ramshackle barn about fifty yards from the main house. Crossman and Devlin made it without being seen by the Cossacks, but the Turk was less lucky. He was just diving through the wide doorway into some hay beyond when a shot crashed into a wooden upright beam.

'They're on to us,' cried Devlin.

The Irishman lay down behind a bale of hay in the open doorway as the Cossacks came riding round the corner of the house. He fired the old musket and spun one of the riders sideways on his steed. The other Cossacks reined in their mounts and looked for cover. Crossman had joined Devlin behind the bale and he too fired, but missed his target.

Four of the Cossacks turned and rode back behind the house. One, however, looked keenly at the two men behind the bale and saw that they were reloading their muskets. He charged forward, pointing his lance and yelling at the top of his voice. He was half-way across the yard, scattering chickens and pigs with his mount, when Ali appeared from behind a water trough at the entrance to the barn.

The Bashi-Bazouk had two pistols in his hands. He blazed away at the charging rider, until the hapless Russian fell from his saddle. The Cossack's right foot remained caught in his stirrups and he was dragged along with the runaway horse. The creature went back to where the other horses were hidden, and on swinging round the corner of the house smashed the body like a toy on the end of a ribbon against the woodwork.

'Two down,' muttered Devlin.

At that moment carbines opened up from the right corner of the house. Heavy rounds began smashing into woodwork around the three soldiers. Cows inside the barn began to panic, making a din. Devlin suggested setting fire to the team and getting away out through the back while there was confusion amongst the Cossacks.

Crossman rejected this idea. It would have been devastatingly unfair to the old woman and her husband.

'Well, what are we going to do, sergeant? There's a hundred yards or more between us and the path down the cliffs. If we don't move soon, we'll be overrun.'

'Right, Ali, you make a dash for the cliff edge after the next volley from the Russians. Devlin and I will remain here and cover your run. Then Devlin can go, while we cover him from two different positions. I'll come up last.'

After the next fusillade of carbine shots struck the hay bales and the barn, Ali swiftly ran out and made for the cliff path. One of the Cossacks had a loaded weapon and showed himself to fire. Both Crossman and Devlin blasted away at this figure, which dropped back behind the right corner again.

'Did we get him?' asked Devlin, ramming another ball down the barrel.

Crossman shrugged. 'I don't know. You'd better make a run for it now. We can't wait for them to fire. They're on to that trick now. Off you go.'

Devlin leapt out and ran to join Ali. This time no one appeared from behind the corner. Crossman waited, wondering whether he himself should try for the cliff, where Ali and Devlin both lay. He was just about to go, when three Cossacks appeared from behind the left-hand corner of the farmhouse. They had gone round the house at the back to the opposite corner.

Surprised, Crossman turned and squeezed the trigger of the ancient weapon. Nothing happened. It was a misfire. The Cossacks, seeing this, and hidden by the barn from the fire of the other two soldiers, stormed towards him. Reaching under his sheepskin coat he found his revolver. Whipping out the 5-shot Tranter he put one Russian down at twelve yards. It took three shots. The last pair came on, both whirling sabres.

Crossman shot one in the face. On falling, this Cossack's sabre struck him on the breast, but without weight behind it the weapon bounced off. His final shot missed the last Cossack. Crossman fell sideways under a blow from the man's sword, which cut deeply into his shoulder. While down in the mud Crossman swiftly reached under his coat again and found his German hunting knife. He sliced at the Cossack's ankle, the nearest part of the man's body to him, in a kind of panic.

The blade cut through the man's boot and the back of his ankle and severed a tendon. The Russian fell with a grunt of pain beside the sergeant. Crossman leapt on top of him, pinning his sword arm to the dirt. Then the sergeant plunged his hunting knife deep into the man's chest, several times, until the Cossack no longer struggled.

Without waiting to check if the man was dead, Crossman got to his feet and ran for the cliff edge. A mortally wounded Cossack, dying by the corner of the house, fired wildly after him. The shot cut through the dirt of the yard, creating a small channel about twenty yards long. Crossman, however, was half-way to the cliff path, where Devlin and Ali were waiting anxiously for him.

'I think we've got them all,' gasped Crossman, falling down beside the other two men. 'I killed three.'

'Listen!' Ali murmured.

There were seagulls and other wild birds screeching around the cliffs, but a low note could be heard coming from beyond the farmhouse, slipping under these sharp sounds.

'More of them,' Ali said. 'We must go quickly.'

The Turk then noticed the blood on Crossman's coat.

'You wounded, sergeant?'

'Good God!' cried Devlin. 'You're soaked in blood.'

'I feel fine,' lied Crossman. 'Come on – down the path to the beach. We have to put some distance between us and those Cossacks.'

The three men scrambled down the path. They reached

the beach at the bottom and waded through shallow water around a small headland to the next bay, which proved to be a long curving one about two miles in width. They half-ran, half-walked around this crescent, constantly looking behind them for pursuing Cossacks. Soon they saw them, blue figures without their horses, running on behind, too far away to exchange any fire.

Crossman was by now beginning to feel a little weak and dizzy from loss of blood. Ali saw the sergeant falter once or twice and then ordered a halt himself.

'We must stop the blood, sergeant. Devlin, give me the shirt on your back.'

Crossman was too weak to argue. He saw Devlin rip off his own coat, followed by his shirt. Ali used the dirty shirt to pad the wound in Crossman's shoulder, tying it on with a strip of rag. All the while the Cossacks were getting closer, but Ali did not seem interested in these advancing figures. He worked calmly and efficiently, until he heard the report from Devlin's musket, as the Irishman fired on the Cossacks.

'They're still too far away,' said Devlin, reloading, 'but it'll give them something to think about. Is the sergeant ready, Ali?'

'Ready,' grunted the Turk, wrapping Crossman's good arm around his thick neck, in order to assist the sergeant. He took a quick look at the Cossacks. 'We must go now.'

13

The three men continued along the beach, but since there was nothing in sight – no farmhouse, nor any kind of building – they struck out inland again. They searched the landscape vainly for some hiding place. There were four Cossacks behind them. These men in indigo doggedly followed the three British soldiers, keeping them in sight. Devlin was in despair.

'We're caught this time, for sure. Even if we find a boat up here, we'll never get it down to the beach. What shall we do, sergeant?'

Crossman's dizziness had subsided for the time being. He tried to think clearly. Looking around him for a suitable place to make a stand, he saw a copse ahead. The trees were thick-trunked and close together. They would offer reasonable cover. They could wait there for the Cossacks to attack them and hope to beat them off. There were only four of them, after all, though probably more were coming on horseback.

He had to admit to himself that the more likely end scenario would be that the Cossacks would send for reinforcements and storm the position in the copse, giving the 88th no chance. But there was little choice for the three men. They would have to be thankful for the cover and take what came on after.

'Those trees,' Crossman said.

'Good, sergeant,' said Ali. 'We fight from there.'

They reached the trees and hid themselves, waiting for the four Cossacks to emerge over the rise from the beach.

Before they appeared, Crossman heard the sound of hoof-beats. As he had thought, more Cossacks were coming on horseback. Without waiting to be told, Ali covered the track down which the horsemen were coming. He sat there, behind a pine trunk, a pistol in each hand. A moment later however, the Turk whispered in excitement.

'Only one, sergeant – leading four horses.'

Crossman took his eyes from the beach and stared in the direction of the oncoming horses. Ali was right. One horse-man, leading four mounts, no doubt those of the Cossacks chasing them along the strand.

'Forget the boat, corporal,' he said to Devlin, pointing. 'We ride out of here instead. You take him. My shoulder's too sore.'

'I'm no sharpshooter, sergeant. I might miss.'

Ali said, 'I shoot him. Give me musket, Corporal Devlin.'

Devlin passed the old musket over to the Turk, who wet the sights and took careful aim.

'Get ready to take horses,' Ali whispered. 'Or they bolt into the hills.'

He waited for the Cossack to get closer.

The indigo rider looked for all the world as if he were out for a jaunt. He was casually trotting his mount, holding the reins of four others: two in each hand. He was a big man with a large crooked nose. The only small thing about him was his eyes, which glinted like gems in the daylight. They peered this way and that as he came on, though not with any urgency evident. It was as if he expected his brother Cossacks to come up from the beach laughing and joking, dragging either dead bodies, or herding prisoners before them.

Ali shot him just above his big bent nose, between the jewel-like eyes. For an instant his expression was one of puzzlement. He swatted at the hole in his forehead, as if it were a bee sting. Then the big man's muscles collapsed and he slid from the saddle, dead as driftwood.

The shot had momentarily startled the horses, but had not alarmed them unduly. They were used to the sound of gunfire. Two of them shied and backed away from the three men who came running out of the copse. But when the other three horses merely stood, shuffling around the body of the Cossack, they stopped a little further up the trail.

Crossman heaved himself up into the saddle of his chosen mount. Ali and Devlin were already on their horses. A shot whistled by from the beach. Excited men in blue were running towards them, firing carbines. Crossman knew there would be great emotion raging in the breasts of the Cossacks, not because the three infantry soldiers had killed their comrade, but because they were stealing their precious horses. A Cossack's charger was more dear to him than his own son.

Ali fired two shots in the direction of the running Cossacks and then rode forward, yelling at the two spare horses. He drove them into a panic and they bolted down the track, away from the men on the beach.

'Let's get out of here,' cried Crossman. 'Up into the hills.'

The three men rode north, while the furious and frustrated Cossacks were reloading their carbines. Looking back, Crossman could see tears of helpless anger streaming down the face of one man. To have his mount stolen from under him was nothing less than a complete disaster, a terrible and shameful thing: it was no wonder he wept in misery and rage.

He and his fellow Cossacks would take out their anger on the dead Cossack, kicking the body of the man who had lost their horses for them, before the ignominious walk back to their camp to face the wrath of their commander and the ridicule of their comrades. They must at that moment have considered themselves among the world's unfortunates. They were probably praying to God to give them a second chance at the thieves.

106

'We'd better put a good distance between us and those four back there,' said Crossman, as they rode on. 'If they catch us they'll spit roast us slowly over a low fire.'

'Did you see their faces?' grinned Devlin. 'I swear if looks could kill there'd be nothing left of us but skin and bones, sergeant.'

Crossman did not answer his elated corporal. His shoulder felt as if it were on fire. It seemed as though the bleeding had stopped, but the wound was raw. Pain seared through him with every step the horse took. Ali saw his discomfort in his eyes and said, 'We stop in a minute, sergeant. I make good the wound with some herbs.'

Ali had done this sort of thing before, when the men had received wounds and injuries. The Turk had a wealth of natural medicines at his fingertips. It was the sort of knowledge a young man's grandmother might have, back in Britain, but an art which was not passed on to the young men themselves, simply because they were not interested in learning it.

The Bashi-Bazouk, however, had obviously listened to the older generation in his family, and he had inherited the techniques of poultices made from moss and the leaves or roots of wild plants.

'Thank you, Ali,' said Crossman. 'You're invaluable.'

Those on board the *Antigone* had almost given up on those members of the Connaught Rangers who had gone on the expedition. The first officer scoured the coastline and the seas with his telescope, but could find no sign of the missing 88th. He reported to Captain Collidge late in the morning.

The captain, hands behind his back, stared at a chart on the wall of his cabin.

'What's your impression, Mr Sanders?' the captain asked the first officer. 'Should we wait any longer?'

'Sir, I have the feeling they've been caught. We believe

their mission to be successful, because we heard the explosions, but that was in the early hours of the morning. If they escaped, they would be here by now.'

'What if they're hiding out in some cove, avoiding detection, and plan to continue once their pursuers are gone?'

The first officer nodded. 'That's a possibility, sir.'

'At the same time,' the captain turned to face Lieutenant Sanders, 'we could be needed elsewhere. We missed the 17th of October, lieutenant. I should hate to miss another such action.'

Lieutenant Sanders replied, 'Yet there was no real glory in that day, captain. Not for our side.'

'Oh, I don't know. I should like to have been on board the *Vengeance* or the *Sanspareil*, wouldn't you?'

'Or even the *Agamemnon*, but forgive me, captain, not the dear old *Antigone*.'

Captain Collidge sighed. 'I suppose you're right.'

The two naval officers were speaking of the cannonade of Sebastopol, when eleven British warships and fourteen French warships took up positions near the entrance to the harbour and bombarded the city. The British ships were all towed into battle by steamers lashed to the port side. Over a thousand guns boomed and bellowed at the Russian forts that day, but the end result was poor. Hardly any damage was inflicted on the Russian defences, while seven British warships were seriously damaged.

'Go back to the bridge, Mr Sanders. Please send me one of those soldiers the sergeant left behind.'

'Yes, sir.'

The lieutenant left the cabin.

The captain sat in his chair and tapped on the desk top with a pen. He was troubled. That sergeant had made a favourable impression on him. Dependable. Reliable. Good head on his shoulders. Harrow too. It would be a shame to leave him to the enemy. The captain's orders had been to wait until midday. It was already two hours past noon. When he spoke to the admiral he could blame his tardiness on the previous day's battle with the Russian warship. There had been some repairs to carry out, to make the ship totally seaworthy, but it would not do to wait very much longer. The admiral was not a patient man.

There was a tap on the cabin door.

'Come!' the captain ordered.

A slim, wiry soldier stood before him. The soldier was ashen-faced and looked very ill. Of course, the sergeant had left him behind because of seasickness.

'Ah, yes, who is it?'

'Lance-Corporal Peterson, sir, of the 88th Foot.'

'Yes, of course, lance-corporal. I take it being a foot soldier, you *don't* carry a lance.' Peterson stared at him blankly, and he saw that his joke had gone well wide of the mark. He got down to the unpleasant business in hand. 'Well, I'm sorry to have to say we can't wait for your comrades any longer. I've stretched my time to the limit. What's your best guess as to their whereabouts? You know the sergeant quite well, I take it? Do you think he's in the hands of the enemy?'

'Not Sergeant Crossman. Nor the others either. They'd die before that. The Russians would hang them anyway. We've killed a lot of Cossacks, you see, sir. They've been after us for a long time.'

'So, you think they've either been shot or blown to pieces by their own handiwork?'

'Or maybe drowned away in the sea. We're not good sailors, sir. It's not in our work. There was that storm in the morning.'

'The squall, yes.'

The captain acknowledged this with a curt nod of his head.

He said to the soldier, 'So, you think they're not coming back?'

'I would hate to think it, sir, but I suppose I have to say no.'

'I'm afraid I do too. All right, thank you, lance-corporal. Go back on deck. Fresh air is the best cure for what you've got. Stay away from the smells of the galley.'

'Thank you, sir.'

Lance-Corporal Peterson left the cabin.

The captain stood up and put on his hat. It was a dreadful shame, he thought, to leave such men behind. But one had to assume they were dead. The wind was rising again too. It could be felt in the motion of the ship. It was best to sail now. Even if Crossman and his men were still out on the waves, those waves would soon be too high to conquer in a little canoe.

The captain made his way towards the bridge.

Lieutenant Sanders was still searching the horizon with his brass telescope.

'Make ready to sail, Mr Sanders.'

The lieutenant snapped the telescope shut.

'Yes, sir. Now, sir?'

'Now, Mr Sanders.'

Peterson had gone back to where Wynter lay on some ropes on the deck. Wynter observed the preparations for the ship's departure.

'What's goin' on?' he asked Peterson.

'We're leaving. There's no point in staying any longer. You know that. They're all dead. I can feel it, here.'

Peterson tapped her stomach.

'Oh, what?' cried Wynter. 'Can't we wait for a bit more? If we go back without the sergeant, we'll be sent up to the trenches straight away. Bloody chapped skin and sleepin' in water-filled holes. Your skin rots from your bones in the stinkin' trenches. You can smell the gangrene on the wounded enough to make you sick. Last week the surgeons made me fill a sack full of arms and legs and bury it. And I'm fed up with ducking "Whistling Dicks" and bloody Russian shells. Can't you tell the captain we need to stay a bit longer?'

'You selfish sod, Wynter. Is that all you can think about? What's going to happen to *you?*'

'I got to look after meself. Nobody else will, will they, eh? You know we got it good at the house. Keeps us away from the others. Almost everybody who came out with us from England on the boat is dead of disease. That, or they've had their bloody heads took off at the neck by some round shot. They're buryin' them by the cartload. Look at old Davidson. No bloody legs now. How's he going to walk to work when he gets home? And Childers. One arm and no eyes! Where's the future? We got it good at the house an' I want to stay there. Maybe they'll give us another sergeant, someone a bit softer than . . .'

Peterson shook her head and stared out over the sea, in the direction Crossman and the men had taken. If the sergeant and the others were still alive, they were on land somewhere. If not, they had been shot, or the sea had taken them. They would never allow themselves to end up in the hands of the enemy. God help them if that were ever to happen. There were Cossacks out there who would have sold their grand-mothers to get hold of the sergeant spy and his nest of saboteurs.

14

After Ali had put a poultice on Crossman's wound, the three soldiers were able to make better progress. They knew they had to cover some fifty-odd miles to reach Balaclava, through rough country. One of the least worrying of their problems was feeding themselves, something they were used to doing.

Ali shot two game birds on the first evening. These were roasted over a low fire deep in a cave. It was essential that the flames were not visible from the outside. Smoke could not be seen during the hours of darkness and scents were lost on the ground when cold, heavier air came down. They spent a comfortable night in the cave, knowing that any pursuers would be camped down too. Crossman recovered some of his strength with the hot food and a good few hours' rest.

In cases where a manhunt is over rough country, and in the face of ensuing winter, it is always better to be the hunted than the hunters, though this may seem a contradiction.

The hunters always want to be somewhere else, somewhere they are not. They want to be where the quarry lies and they want to be there *now*. There is a certain frenetic impatience which pervades in the hunters' camp. Night hours are spent in sleepless tossing and turning, wondering whether the prey is still on the move, or stopped somewhere, or even just a few yards away, hidden in some small hard-to-find hole.

The hunters need, by nature of their task, to be on the move the whole time, fording rivers, climbing hills, crossing wastelands. They go up high every so often to look out helplessly and hopelessly, over the vast wilderness and think, 'They could be anywhere. They could be near or far. They could be back on the trail, or forward on the trail, or have even left it altogether.'

The depressed hunter usually resigns himself to fate, thinking that if he comes across the victim it will be serendipity.

The hunted, on the other hand, merely have to stay lost. There is a certain amount of anxiety in their step, a concern in their breast, but it is not the sickness of not knowing which way to turn. So long as their hide-out is a good one, they can rest the night in comfort, perhaps even stay there the whole of the next day, and they need only move when they feel the need. If the country is broad and deep enough, they have everything in their favour.

So, it was with good heart that the three riders set out the next day, locked in the iron fastnesses of the Crimean hills. Tight shoulders of rock protected their progress through valleys from the sight of others. Even on the open stretches of the landscape there were dark clumps of pines, through which they could weave their journey. In the more rocky areas, tall stone columns, weathered to the leanness of church spires, cast their camouflaging shadows over the bare ground.

The three men had risen early and were heading west before the sun was up. They avoided using the roads and tracks, but followed their direction, using them as navigational aids. Ali led the way, his sharp ears listening for the enemy; his keen nose ready to detect foreign scents. They saw one or two eagles above them, circling and swooping. Ali was Crossman's eagle on the ground. Without such a man – his guide and watch-person – Crossman would have been lost.

Ali was a man of the earth, close to the natural world. It was not unusual for a wild animal like a fox to drift past the Bashi-Bazouk, without appearing to recognise him as a human being, and therefore dangerous. Wynter often complained that Ali smelt 'ripe', but the Turk's odours were not just due to uncleanliness. Wynter himself only washed when he was ordered to. No, it was simply due to the fact that he took on the scents of the ground, the trees, the grasses, the skins of animals. He smelt of tree bark, hides, moss, clay and mountain herbs. If there ever was such a thing as a Green Man, then Ali was he.

Twice he signalled silently that they should stop and rest the horses. On both occasions Crossman later heard the sound of bridle bits and stirrups clinking in the distance and knew that Ali had already detected the presence of the enemy.

On one rest stop, Ali mentioned to Crossman that there was an unusually high amount of troop movement along the roads.

'I've been thinking that myself,' said Crossman. 'What's your opinion of the situation?'

'I think there is big build-up of forces. You remember the 4th Corp go to Sebastopol? We see this. I think these others go there too. I have heard guns and limbers. Many horses. Cavalry escorting infantry. This is not just normal traffic on the road. This is something much more big, sergeant.'

'What's he saying?' asked Devlin. 'Does he think there's going to be an assault?'

'That's what I say,' replied the Turk, who did not like to be talked about in the third person while he was actually present. 'An attack is coming.'

'We should warn the army, then,' cried the Irish corporal. 'We should tell them the Russians are coming.'

Crossman sighed. 'We already have. No one seems to be taking it very seriously. Especially not the general staff. The only field officer to take any notice of us has been Major Lovelace.'

'What about General Buller?'

'General Buller is concerned, but he has little influence over Lord Raglan and the general staff. They think he's a pessimist. Buller can't say his spies have brought back the information, because Lord Raglan would blow his top. All General Buller can do is put his own people on the alert, especially since we don't know from which direction the assault will come.'

'So we're doing our job for nothing?' grumbled Devlin. 'We risk our lives to get this information which nobody takes any notice of, nobody wants to know.'

'For the moment perhaps, but it won't always be like this. Lovelace thinks that one day intelligence of this sort will be considered the most valuable weapon an army can possess.'

They spent one more night hidden away from tracks and roads, and set out again on yet another misty morning. By midday they were approaching their own lines. Crossman, though a little woozy-headed, recalled that there was a password, or rather an historical passname, for the day. Devlin however, already had that matter in hand, as they stumbled on the forward position of two picquets of the 93rd, and were challenged.

'Who goes there?'

'88th Foot!' called Devlin.

'Give us a name, by which we will know you.'

'Robert the Bruce.'

'Advance friend and be recognised.'

As they were going through the 93rd's lines, an officer approached them. He gripped the bridle of Ali's horse and stared up into the face of the Bashi-Bazouk. Crossman recognised the man as Captain Campbell.

'Who the devil are you?' asked Campbell of Ali. 'You look like Beelzebub himself! What are you, Tartar, Turk or Zouave? You ragamuffin types can't just come and go through our lines as you please. Explain yourself.'

'We are a special contingent of the 88th Foot, Connaught

Rangers,' replied Crossman, from behind the captain. 'That man, the bridle of whose mount you are gripping, is a member of the Turkish Army.'

Crossman did not add the customary 'sir' to the end of his sentence since he did not want this particular officer to know him as a sergeant.

Captain Campbell stared rudely into the eyes of Yusuf Ali.

'One of those that *ran* the other day, shouting, "Ship, Johnny, ship!"' said Captain Campbell contemptuously. 'You abandoned the redoubts in the face of the enemy . . .'

The captain was speaking of the battle of Balaclava, when the Turkish gunners were overcome by a hugely superior force of Russians and had retreated through the 'thin red line' of Sutherland Highlanders.

Crossman, rather unwisely, could not contain himself.

'Those Turks you speak of so scornfully fought for several hours, long and hard, and only gave up the position when it was hopeless. This man was not one of those brave souls in any case. This man has never run from a fight in his life, nor in my experience is he ever likely to. He has killed more Russians with his bare hands than you have with a pistol or sword, and I should be careful not to ridicule him if I were you, captain. He does not take kindly to such talk.'

'And just who the hell are you, sir?' the captain swore softly, turning on Crossman.

Crossman bristled with anger, the inherent pride and arrogance of a man of breeding coming to the fore. The sergeant's head went up and a cold sneer formed on his lips. He stared down at the captain as if peering at a repulsive insect through a quizzing glass. In the more clear reasoning areas of his mind he knew he was overstepping the mark, but decided to play on the rumours of Lovelace as a heroic phantom.

'I should be careful to discover a man's rank, before cursing him,' replied Crossman recklessly. 'You may have heard of a certain major, a man who works in the hills, undermining the efforts of the enemy to reinforce themselves, cutting their supply lines and blowing up their magazines?'

The captain looked unsure of himself now. Crossman's educated accent, his aristocratic bearing, despite his ragged appearance, was obviously authentic. Beneath the grime and dirt, the Tartar clothes, there was a British gentleman.

However, he too had the pride of his class, and was not going to retreat without a Parthian shot.

'Spies and saboteurs!'

'Call us what you will, captain, you have no authority over us. If you have any complaints about our comings and goings, take them to General Buller. In the meantime, sir, I should be obliged if you would step aside. I have a wound that needs attention and if I bleed to death while you bar our way with oaths and curses, you will answer to a higher authority for it. We are carrying urgent information. Delay us any more and that information may prove to be worthless. Time, sir – time is of crucial importance in these matters.'

Crossman used the word 'sir' in the way that gentlemen of equal status use it with one another, not as a ranker speaking with a superior officer.

The captain eventually let go of Ali's bridle and stepped aside. The three men rode through the silent ranks of the 93rd. Out of the corner of his eye, Crossman could see Sergeant-Major Jock McIntyre, a twinkle in his eye, watching their progress. Crossman did not dare look at the sergeant-major, for fear one of them should burst out laughing.

When they reached the Kadikoi hovel, they found Major Lovelace waiting for them. Peterson was there too, and the injured Wynter. The *Antigone* had been back in Balaclava harbour for hours. Crossman made his report to the major, explaining that one ship had been empty, while the other had gone up with such an explosion that part of the harbour was wrecked.

'I have heard of your success, from other sources,' said Lovelace. 'I'm very pleased with you, sergeant. General Buller shall hear of it too. I only wish we could reward you in some way, with a promotion in the ranks, but as we've already discussed, it's not possible at the moment.'

'We killed a lot of innocent people in those explosions,' said Crossman. 'I don't mind killing Cossacks, but the fox hunt this time was not to my taste.'

'There are no innocents in war, sergeant. Those men were in uniform. You have to learn that in modern warfare all targets are legitimate. We no longer live in an age where war is regarded as a game presided over by gentlemen. The age of the Brudenells has gone,' he said, referring to Lord Cardigan's family name, 'Napoleon's ruthlessness rules the field now.'

'If you say so, sir. You didn't hear the screaming of dying men. I find such things hard to get out of my head.'

'If you had been up in the trenches around Sebastopol lately, sergeant, you would hear the same screams.'

Suddenly, Lovelace became concerned:

'You're wounded, sergeant! Why didn't you say something? Let's get you to a surgeon, man.'

'No, sir. I prefer to let Ali look after it. If it weren't for him the thing would be festering and raw. Whatever it is he's put on it seems to be doing the trick. It's healing nicely, thank you very much. It's only a sword cut. Those Cossacks keep their blades nice and shiny and clean, so if the poultice does its work, I should escape infection.'

The major shrugged. 'You know your own body best. Now, what of Private Clancy. I see he's not with you.'

'I'm afraid he drowned, sir.'

Crossman went on to explain the flight through the Straits of Kerch and the subsequent squall which had taken the life of Private Clancy. He told Lovelace about the farm and the Cossacks, taking time to emphasise the bravery of both Devlin and Ali. Finally, he came to the part where they had come through the lines of the 93rd Foot, the Sutherland Highlanders, north of Kadikoi village.

'We were stopped and questioned by a rather arrogant

118

captain. I lost my head a little, when he came on rather too strong. I'm afraid I gave the impression I was you, sir. I didn't say as much, but I implied it.'

'You impersonated me?'

'In a way.'

This was a very serious offence, for an NCO to impersonate a field officer, and Crossman waited for the worst.

Lovelace, however, seemed more amused than upset.

'So if I get called out by some puffed up infantry captain and shot to death I have you to thank for it, do I?'

'I'm afraid so, sir, though I rather think it would be the captain who would be lying on the ground after such a duel.'

'Or both of us. Well, we'll let it pass. Don't make a habit of it though, sergeant.'

'No, sir – thank you.'

The major stared into the middle distance.

'Sad about Clancy. He was a good man to have on your team. Good at assassination. We'll have to find another silent artist for you. Someone good with their hands.'

The major might have been speaking about a craftsman good at turning wood, or stitching leather, rather than the cold-blooded killer Clancy had been.

Clancy, an ex-Thug, had been an expert with the garotte, despatching Russian soldiers in the night with his greasy piece of knotted cord.

'Whatever you say, sir,' replied Crossman.

15

Peterson wept when she heard that Clancy had drowned. Although she had been around men a long time, had seen the horrors of war at close hand, she was still a woman and had been very fond of Clancy. It was not that men did not weep on hearing of the death of comrades, but her tears were more copious than a man's, and they fell not in secret as men's tears often do, but in the full and open company of her fellow soldiers.

'Crikey!' said Wynter, surprised by the waterworks. 'He weren't that good a chap. Anyone would think he was your brother, the way you're goin' on.'

'He *was* my brother,' cried Peterson, fiercely. 'Not in flesh and blood, but he was my brother-in-arms.'

'Brother-in-arms?' Wynter repeated. Wynter did not understand what all the fuss was about. Men died every day in the Crimea. Clancy had been all right, sometimes, but no one to shed tears over. 'Life'll go on without Clancy.'

When the weeping had stopped, Wynter said, 'He weren't a Russian and that's the best I'll say about him.'

'That's because you're a pig without any feelings,' retorted Peterson.

'What makes you think pigs ain't got feelings?' Wynter

retaliated, missing the point of the insult. 'Pigs has got feelings, same as people. I've worked with pigs all me life. Pigs is quite feeling animals, I can tell you.'

Wynter was right about one thing: Clancy's death made little difference to life in the Crimea. It was said that back home in Britain, a long raggedy beard was now referred to as a 'crimea' after drawings of the hirsuit troops had appeared in newspapers. Most of the men looked wild, in odd clothes and with their unkempt hair and beards. Some still shaved, especially amongst the officers, but there are always those British who like to keep up appearances. Some of the officers still dressed for dinner occasionally, but these were few.

In general, the Commissariat was still failing in its duty to get warm clothing to the men. Ships in Balaclava harbour still remained loaded with badly needed goods and medical supplies. These were watched over by jealous purveyors, who demanded certificates signed by officials in London before they would distribute supplies to the troops.

Soldiers on the siege line spent days in damp uniforms, were worked so hard they never had the chance to get thoroughly dry or even take off what they were wearing. Even if they had, they would have nothing to change into. Their boots were often worn right through and let in water. Some had abandoned proper footwear and wrapped their feet in rags. There were no beds, no adequate toilets or washing facilities, no proper food. The result was skin diseases, scurvy, cholera, dysentery and a host of other illnesses which took men away by the hundred.

Those who were left had to fill in for those who had gone. These men should have been given rest, but they were given more duties. They were ragged with lack of sleep, weak from malnutrition. They froze at night. They staggered from one day to the next, sometimes not making it because a bullet, or shell, or bayonet, had prevented their progress. Small wounds festered into large wounds. Even a scratch was a potential killer in such conditions. It was little wonder that Wynter did not want to go back to his regiment in the line.

Apart from their clothes, their gunpowder too was often damp. Their weapons would not fire half the time, after they had been on duty in moist conditions for a few hours. The soldiers skirmished with bayonets in clammy dawns, after spending the whole night on picquet duty, unable to use their rifles. They went back to worn tents that let in the rain, and went to sleep in sodden blankets. Their workplace was damp, their beds were damp, their souls were damp.

Only a few officers, rich and able to transport their goods to the Crimea privately, were shaved, well-dressed and lived anything like a comfortable life. Many of these gentlemen were shod with Runicman shooting boots. They wore new uniforms, the colours still bright and the gold braid still gleaming. Those off-duty often appeared in brown shooting suits.

Affectations abounded out of sight of senior ranks. One young officer, fresh from North Africa, wore a fez and carried an ebony walking stick. Another dressed in a scarlet pelisse, and yet another carried tools for chipping fossils from rocks in a cowhide Russian knapsack. These eccentrics were envied by rankers and other officers alike. Being in a regiment was a fine thing, but it stunted individualism. Once in a while a man wants to be different from his neighbour.

As for civilians, 'gentlemen adventurers' were beginning to arrive, to view the fighting at first hand. They came to observe, to write, to sketch, and some to extract excitement from the war. They wandered about at will.

Mary Seacole's 'British Hotel' was dealing successfully with many cases of cholera. Mary, or 'Mother Seacole' as she was known affectionately to the soldiers, was popular with all ranks. She had gained great experience in the disease in Cruces, a frontier town in Panama, and on the gold rush trail to California, when it was hit by a cholera epidemic. After performing a secret and illegal autopsy on a young cholera victim, she devised a new method of treating the illness. This experience had later been fortified by a similar epidemic which struck her home island of Jamaica, where she was placed at the head of medical services at a British military base near Kingston.

Another woman, disguised as a man, was also much in evidence. Dr James Barry was a medical officer who went amongst the soldiers, doing what she could for their suffering. Some of the wives of the soldiers – there had been six per hundred men allowed to follow their husbands to the Crimea – also did what they could to help with dysentery and other problems.

In the meantime, surgeons such as George Lawson cut away limbs from men with appalling injuries caused by shells, round shot and other such missiles. Lawson's duties in the Crimea should by now have hardened him to the screams of men, to the weeping of men, to the dying groans of men, but it was still with a sickened heart that he added to the pile of severed limbs, knowing as all surgeons did, that a more horrible death, a rotting, wasting death, awaited those who avoided amputation.

On the Russian side of the Crimea, Prince Menshikoff was building the strength of his troops in the Chernaya Valley, immediately north of Sebastopol. He now had a hundred and twenty thousand men at his disposal: three times the number he had fought with at the Battle of the Alma. Facing these many battalions, ignorant of the size of the Russian Army, were a mere twenty-five thousand British soldiers, ill-equipped and in poor health. The French had forty thousand, also ravaged by injury and disease.

Even after the relatively small-scale battle on the Inkerman ruins, the day after the Battle of Balaclava, Lord Raglan had not reinforced the British front in that weak area. The 2nd Division were camped on Home Ridge, the Guards Brigade was close to the post road, near an old windmill, and the Highland Brigade still blocked the pass at Balaclava. The 3rd and 4th Divisions were stretched in a line west of the Guards camp, the former north of the Woronzoff Road, the latter south of it. The Light Brigade, or what was left of it, were encamped near the Guards, and the Heavy Brigade protected Lord Raglan's headquarters on the col at the eastern end of Wellway Gully.

Studying these positions together, Major Lovelace and Sergeant Crossman spoke about the difficulty of convincing the high command that an attack was imminent.

'You say Ali heard substantial troop movements out on the road?' asked Lovelace.

'We all did. Ali's ear is more finely tuned than mine, and no doubt he can give you an approximation of numbers. They sounded quite large to me.'

Lovelace sighed, looking away from the charts and out of the window, towards the headquarters of Lord Raglan

'Well, I'll have another try at convincing our masters of the dangers. I can't take you with me, you understand. You have eloquence, sergeant, but no credibility. No one takes seriously a gentleman who prefers the ranks to a commission.'

Crossman gave nothing away by his expression.

'No, sir. I understand.'

Lovelace spun on his heel and stared directly into Crossman's eyes.

'Why are you in the ranks, sergeant? Do you dislike your peers so much?'

Crossman took time in considering his reply.

'No, sir – at least, not all of them. I'm not overfond of the purchase system. I think we lose good officers to bad. I know captains in their fifties who should have been majors in their twenties, but because they have not the price of the next rank, they remain forever stuck in the mud.

'I have also known quite incompetent officers who have risen rapidly to the highest ranks and are colonels in their late twenties or early thirties.'

While the two men were speaking, Rupert Jarrard had

entered the room. His eyes lit up on hearing the conversation between the two Britons. Jarrard was forever picking at the intricacies of the British Army, wondering about its strange rules, its codes, its foibles. The British Army to him, and to most Americans, was an aristocratic anachronism.

Ignoring the presence of a third party, Lovelace gave Crossman a wry smile. 'You're speaking of men like Lord Cardigan and Lord Lucan?'

'I would not point the finger at any individual, sir, but those two are cases in question. Lord Cardigan is loathed by the general public at home, and many men in the army, for his empty-headed vindictiveness towards officers who served in India, for his obsession with drilling and smart uniforms, for his failure to control a violent temper. His first action in war, for which he has supposedly been preparing himself since being a subaltern, is one of the worst bungles in the history of the British Army.'

Crossman turned to Jarrard. 'Rupert, this is a private conversation. If it appears in print I shall be flogged and Major Lovelace cashiered.'

'Point taken,' said Jarrard, rubbing his hands. 'I shall use pseudonyms. Captain Smith and Sergeant-Major Jones.'

The two Britons continued their argument.

'Cardigan's courage was not at fault,' pointed out Lovelace. 'Valour is a necessary thing in a leader.'

'His bravery comes from the same source as his blind and misplaced idea that he is a good officer – his empty-headedness. He has not the intelligence to see the dangers to himself and others. Lord Cardigan, begging your pardon, sir, is like a mad bull charging around a Spanish bullring.'

'Oh, come, sergeant. *All* valour requires a little empty-headedness, even temporary. No man is going to rush at the barrel of a loaded cannon if he stops to think about it.'

'I still blame the purchase system, as it stands, for the unfairness to the individual. Sir, you know as well as I do that there are set rates for purchasing the various commissioned

125

ranks, yet these are rarely adhered to. I believe it costs five thousand pounds to become the lieutenant-colonel of a cavalry regiment, yet many will pay five times that amount for the privilege of such a command, thus sweeping aside all those officers who are constrained from further advancement because of a lack of wealth.'

Rupert Jarrard could contain himself no longer.

'I agree with Jack, Major Lovelace. The British system of purchasing commissions is ridiculed throughout the world. It is a system of privilege for no particular purpose. It's sad – and it's laughable.'

To the American's astonishment, both men stared at him as if he had made the most stupid statement of all time. It was Crossman who saw fit to put him right.

'Rupert, you have misunderstood me if you believe that I said the purchase system was for no purpose. It has a very good purpose, a high and laudable one, which works well. It has helped in preventing military revolution in Britain for hundreds of years, and with no apparent harm to our skill as a fighting force. We have won many battles, many wars, many famous victories, with the purchase system in place.'

Jarrard looked smug. 'You didn't beat *us* when we fought for independence.'

'No, but then we were heavily outnumbered, you had the French Army to help you, and we had more important commitments for our forces elsewhere in the empire. There is a myth about there being a few rugged frontiersmen protecting their rights against the whole British Army. Of redcoats marching in straight lines to be cut down by grizzled sharpshooters from the backwoods of the American continent. Balderdash, Rupert.'

Rupert grinned. 'It's a myth we like to perpetuate, none the less. Anyway, it *was* a victory. You lost, despite your assertion that you were outnumbered. You've been outnumbered in other wars, but you've won them. This was not a British victory, Jack – you lost.'

Major Lovelace came in here. 'On the contrary, it was a famous British victory.'

'How do you make that out, Major Lovelace?'

'British settlers asserting their rights over George III, a German king.'

Rupert grinned again. 'I seem to have heard that one before – you lost – sorry. End of tale. Anyway, what's all this poppycock about the purchase system being good for Britain? Even if it doesn't damage your ability as a fighting force, that's a load of hogwash, isn't it?'

'Not at all,' replied Lovelace. 'Not even a trace of pigdip in it. The purchase system is seen as necessary to the safety of the nation as a whole. It ensures that those in the highest ranks of the army will have a large stake in the country and will have nothing to gain through revolt against a civilian government by trying to form a military regime.

'Aristocrats and landed gentry, the most wealthy of Britons, have the most to lose by reverting to a military dictatorship. Under such lawless conditions their lands might be forfeit to the greater cause, that of a military regime which needs money to fight its wars. You only have to look at other European countries which do not have the purchase system, and you will find they have had military regimes at one time or another. France and Austria are two examples.

'Military adventurers like Napoleon will milk a country dry without a care. There is never enough power for them, so they build huge armies and seek more, and even more. There is never enough money in a country to sustain such constant conflict. Napoleon was a poor man, who had nothing to lose. In Britain your earls, lords and barons are already rich, and their estates would suffer if the country were plunged into economic disaster. No, the system has worked well for the country as a whole, Mr Jarrard. It ensures economic stability. Individuals may suffer, but the nation is protected against military opportunists.'

Jarrard acknowledged he had no answer to that one.

Lovelace, however, was a little piqued that the American had come in when he did, for the reason that he, Lovelace, was no nearer to discovering Sergeant Crossman's secrets than before.

16

Crossman had now to try to help with his brother's gambling problems. It was difficult since he did not want his brother to know he was there, serving as a sergeant in an infantry regiment under an assumed name. Knowing James, the older man would not be able to keep Crossman's presence a secret from their father, Major Kirk, also serving in the 93rd Sutherland Highlanders. So Crossman had to tread warily, work from the wings.

Sitting up late at night in the hovel, the candlelight flickering on the rough white walls, he devised a two-point plan. The first thing to do, he decided, was to break James's gambling habit somehow, then deal with the debt to Captain Campbell later. James had an obsessive personality. Once he was consumed with some interest, he thought of nothing else.

Crossman remembered when they had been children. James had been a collector. At one time, he collected birds' eggs, at another time, minerals and rocks, then seashells, then fossils, and when he was older it was grown-up things like snuff boxes or porcelain figurines.

However, he was never interested in two things at one time. When it was birds' eggs you could have showered him with seashells or minerals or fossils and he would have scorned you and gone back to his preoccupation of the time. James's mind ran on a single track, and the habit had to be broken naturally, through time and a waning interest, or some dramatic change.

Crossman sat for a long time, with his soldiers snoring and grunting in their sleep, each one tucked in a separate corner of the room. Finally, as the dawn rays came through the window, he had the kernel of an idea in his mind. It was a very loose idea and he was not at all sure it would work, simply because it involved the chemistry of human beings and their emotions.

He deduced that here, in the Crimea, men were generally starved of affection and the company of ladies. In such circumstances many men would go out of their way just to speak to a woman. They went to the French canteens to gaze passionately at some *cantinière*, who was not particularly good-looking in any way, but who represented the softer side of humanity of which the men were deprived and desperately missed. The officers were no different from the ranking soldiers.

Crossman decided that if he could get his brother interested in a woman, James would forget about gambling. There was a woman available, who might be interested in a flirtation with a young and handsome lieutenant. Crossman decided to go now, while the day was young, and intercept the one woman who could help him. He knew she rode out in the early morning on Bob, her favourite horse, and always passed a certain dead tree. The sergeant left the hovel to meet her there.

Sure enough, at a certain time, Lavinia Durham came cantering past the spot where Crossman waited.

'Hello,' he called, his heart in his mouth. 'Mrs Durham – Lavinia – how pleasant to see you!'

A surprised Mrs Durham reined in Bob and stared. A slow smile crept across her face. Then with a haughty but amused air about her, she trotted Bob to where Crossman stood. He shifted his feet awkwardly, knowing this meeting was going to be a difficult one for him. Lavinia always seemed to take odd situations in her stride. She might be at a loss for two seconds, but soon had herself and others under control.

'Why, Sergeant Crossman, my former lover!'

He coughed and looked about him nervously.

'I don't think you should be quite so free with that information, Lavinia.'

'There's no one here,' she replied, laughing gaily. 'Who do you think will hear? The birds? The animals in the grasses? I make no secret of my past to *them*, I can assure you. I commune with nature every day on my ride. I tell all those hidden listening ears my secrets.'

'All – all that is in the past, Lavinia. We must forget about it.'

'You can't have forgotten about it so soon, Alexander,' she said, using his real name. 'Why it was only two weeks ago . . .'

'Yes, but we agreed to – to put all that behind us, Lavinia,' he said, getting angry despite himself. 'You must keep your promises to me.'

'Just as you kept your promise to me, when I was a young girl in love?' Two angry red spots were appearing, one on each of her cheeks. Her nose was becoming white and pinched looking. 'I suppose that doesn't count, does it? To jilt a naive girl whose heart has been stolen?'

'We've been through all this before, Lavinia. I did not exactly jilt you. You know I had good reasons for going away. I would have married you, if you had waited. Instead you threw yourself into the arms of another.'

'Bertie was my solace in my hour of need.'

'Good for bloody Bertie – now get down off that beast and speak with me properly. I have a great favour to ask and arguing over our history is not going to help things.'

'What makes you think I want to help you? Perhaps I

want to see you squirm, Alexander Kirk. Perhaps I would like to see you writhe. I'm not a very kind person underneath, you know. I can be very cruel despite the fact that I'm a woman.'

'Lavinia,' he said fiercely, his tone no longer pleading. 'I order you to get down from that mount.'

'That's better,' she said, smiling demurely. 'I like you masterly, not cringing. Bertie cringes. I dislike men who cringe, even though I want them to do it, force them to do it sometimes. It makes me shudder.'

He shook his head, failing to comprehend this woman with whom he was once deeply in love.

'Well?' she said, her large round eyes on his face. 'What is this great favour? Does it involve us? If it does I will have to remind you that only a few days ago we agreed that "us" was no longer to be. We were to become "him" and "her", quite separate individuals, with different lives to lead.'

'It's my brother, James,' he said, turning away from her, hating to bring his family problems to another person, even Lavinia. 'He's in deep trouble. He has run up gambling debts to the tune of two thousand pounds. If my father finds out, he will be furious, and James could never withstand the fury of my father. No more than I could. I need to find a distraction for James, perhaps a female diversion, which will occupy his mind, take it away from his current obsession with the cards.'

Mrs Durham's eyes opened wide with astonishment.

'I hope you don't think . . .' she began, but he interrupted her quickly.

'I was not thinking of you. Despite what you believe, I am still very fond of you, Lavinia, and have the greatest admiration and respect for you. I would not dream of asking you to do such a thing. To use you like that? I would rather die.'

Her eyes, which had begun to harden, softened again.

'Oh, Alex, when you say things like that I do not wonder I ever loved you so much.'

'Well – that is beside the point. No, I was thinking of your companion, Mrs Kennedy, the wife of Corporal Kennedy, who fell at Balaclava. Forgive me if I'm overstepping the mark here, but she seems to enjoy a flirtation.'

Lavinia had a wry grin forming at the corner of her mouth.

'What you are suggesting is monstrous, Alexander.'

He took a step back, flustered and unhappy, knowing that though his motives were sound, the idea was caddish in the extreme. He was not a follower of Machiavelli himself. Ends did not justify means. The wife of Corporal Kennedy might have been misjudged by all and sundry. In any case, the fact that she might enjoy a flirtation, or even a liaison or two, did not mean that she would be willing to lend herself to an underhand scheme like playing with a man's emotions. She might even loathe his brother on sight and shudder at the thought of any kind of relationship, no matter what the reasons for the game.

'I'm sorry, Lavinia. I must think of something else.'

'I shall tell you what I shall do. I shall put the proposal to Molly herself and see what she thinks of it. Molly, like some women, does enjoy a little game-playing occasionally. If I were you, I should concern myself with your brother. How do you know he will play? He might detest her on sight.'

'That's true, but unlikely. She is very pretty, after all. One might even say beautiful.'

'Is she? Really? You think so, Alexander?' said Mrs Durham, raising her eyebrows just a little.

'Oh, not compared to you, Lavinia,' he said hastily. 'You are a nonpareil.'

Mrs Durham laughed. 'And what about her background. You don't think he will find it too – common? She is, after all, only the daughter of a blacksmith. Your brother is heir to a baronetcy. Would he even look at a blacksmith's daughter?'

'Kings have consorted with chambermaids. We're not suggesting marriage here, Lavinia. I hope we're not even suggesting anything deeper than holding hands while the moon goes down behind the masts of the ships in the harbour.'

He studied his feet for a moment, then added, 'Besides, I do not see why class should be a barrier to anything. I myself am a common soldier.'

Lavinia Durham strolled back to her horse, her riding skirts swishing as she walked. At the last moment before remounting, with Crossman there ready to help, his cupped hands under the arch of her boot, she turned and looked him in the eyes. She spoke softly in the back of her throat.

'Oh, you're anything but common, Alexander. Believe me.'

She rode off into the Crimean dawn, leaving Crossman wondering just what he had started.

Later in the day he received a message from Mrs Durham to meet her down by the quay. When he reached Balaclava harbour, he saw her standing by a capstan. There was a small dark woman with her. He recognised this person as being Molly Kennedy. Molly had one of Lavinia's parasols, which she was twirling idly over her shoulder. The pair of them watched as he approached.

'Is this the sergeant?' asked Molly.

'This is Sergeant Crossman,' said Lavinia Durham, smiling. 'Isn't he handsome, Molly?'

'He's very special, he is,' replied Molly. 'But he's not the one, is he?'

'No, the man we spoke of is the sergeant's friend, Lieutenant James Kirk, in the 93rd Foot. But you must never mention Sergeant Crossman to the lieutenant, if you are fortunate enough to meet him. I've explained to you why.'

Crossman could see that Lavinia had been instructing Molly on the correct way for a lady to dress. Lavinia would also be teaching her companion good manners, etiquette, and all those points of refinement which separated the ladies from rankers' wives. Of course, Molly would never learn to employ all these rules and codes naturally – they were too many and subtle to absorb after childhood and the peak learning years were over – but she might get by without disgracing herself in genteel company if she put her mind to it.

'Sergeant Crossman,' said Mrs Durham, 'this is Mrs Kennedy.'

'I'm Molly,' said the young woman, with a small curtsey.

'Mrs Kennedy,' he acknowledged, stiffly. 'I take it Mrs Durham has explained the circumstances?'

'Yes, she has, poor man. Your friend, I mean. I expect he's very sorry for losing all that money. I would be. Anyway, I should like to meet him. We've had a little look at him, you know, just to make sure he wasn't really horrible, but he looks nice. I don't mind meeting him, I'm sure.'

'You mustn't mention the gambling debt to him,' said Crossman, alarmed. 'I mean, he wouldn't like it.'

'Oh, no,' Molly gave an amused wave of her hand, 'course not. I wouldn't do that. A man's gambling debts is private. I wouldn't presume. I shall just pretend I'm interested in him because he's nice-looking. You mustn't think I usually do this, but I want to help my friend Mrs Durham, who said you were both in terrible straits over Lieutenant Kirk.'

Crossman found he was sweating. Was he really doing the right thing? This was not only bizarre, it was degrading, to everyone concerned, including himself. But he could think of no better plan. Of course, he was crossing bridges before he came to them. His brother might be horrified at the thought of speaking with this woman. She was as transparent as glass. Even now she was flirting a little with Crossman, though he was not supposed to be the object of her interest. It seemed to come very naturally to her, this kind of trifling.

'Thank you, Mrs Kennedy. Mrs Durham. I think I'd better be on my way now. I'm sure that you, Mrs Durham, will keep me informed of progress. Remember, Mrs Kennedy – not a word to the lieutenant about me or this scheme, if you please.'

'Course not.'

He left the two ladies standing on the quayside and quickly beat a retreat back to his hovel. When he arrived, his soldiers were just coming back from the canteen. They were all, even Peterson, a little tipsy. Crossman let this pass. They had seen too many horrors of war for him to lecture them on sobriety.

A little later he sent for Wynter to join him upstairs where he had his sleeping quarters.

'You wanted to see me, sergeant,' said Wynter, swaying on his feet a little. 'What can I do for you?'

'Wynter, do you cheat at cards?'

Wynter first looked puzzled, then indignant, and finally he managed anger.

'What are you sayin', sergeant? I never heard such rot in all my days. Me? Cheat?'

'Devlin says you do. He says he's seen you. Moreover he says you're very good at it, that if he wasn't one of your closest companions, aware of your habits, he probably would have missed your little machinations too.'

Wynter swung his whole body round to stare down the stone steps to the ground quarters.

'Why, that lyin' . . .'

'Wynter,' interrupted Crossman, not wanting all the protestations to start, 'I want you to teach me.'

The soldier swung back again, this time his face wore an expression of bewilderment.

'Teach you what, sergeant?'

'I want you to teach me to cheat at cards. If you're as good as Devlin says you are, I want you to pass on your skills to me. I have to win two thousand pounds from an officer in the 93rd. I'd like to let you do it, but I'm sure he wouldn't stoop to playing cards with a lance-corporal, so you'll have to show *me* how.'

Wynter looked positively stunned.

17

'You're going to cheat at cards?' Wynter said in disbelief. 'But you're supposed to be a gentleman of honour.'

'Let's leave my honour out of this,' replied Crossman, patiently. 'The man I'm going to play is said to be a cheat. And I intend paying the two thousand back as soon as I am able. I have – a friend – in the 93rd who has lost his life's savings to a cardsharp. I intend winning them back again. Of course, if I have to do it dishonestly, then I will eventually return the money to the cardsharp, but the important thing at the moment is to obtain my friend some relief. Buy him some time.'

'He must be a very good friend, sergeant.'

'He is – I grew up with him. Of course he must know nothing about this – nor anyone else – so I expect you to keep it to yourself. I might add that I hate doing it this way, Wynter, but my avenues are few. Since Campbell himself cheats, especially with newcomers, all the honest ways are closed to me. If I went up against this cardsharp without any secret weapons I should be blasted out of existence.'

Wynter shook his head in amazement.

'I'm not saying I cheat at cards, sergeant, but I know how

to, so I'll show you. But you need a certain skill with the deck. Nimble fingers.'

'Dexterity? Legerdemain?'

'Exactly, sergeant, if them words mean what I think 'em to mean. How much cards have you played? Good at whist, are you? I hear the gentry play a lot of whist.'

'I'm sorry, Wynter, I'm not usually a card player. I used to enjoy it as a child, but I've had little opportunity to play since then. Perhaps you'd better start with the basics.'

Wynter rolled his eyes to heaven. He then produced out of his pocket a greasy pack of playing cards. With a sigh, he fanned the pack, face up.

'I s'pose you know what the cards are. You're not going to start calling these "blackberries" are you?' He showed Crossman the ten of clubs. 'What's the name of the game you're supposed to play, with this officer of the jocks.'

'Chemin de fer, which I believe is also known as baccarat.'

'Posh French game, for officers and toffs. I take it you don't know the rules of baccarat? No? Thought not. Well, here's how it goes. You'll probably be playing with just one deck in a place like this, but it could be two. You get dealt two cards, first off, but you can ask for another one, which is dealt face up. What you've got to do is get as close to nine or nineteen as you can. The face cards count as nothin', so if you get given a six and a king, then you ask for a third card face up, and it's a two, that's eight you've got in your hand, see? If you tie with someone, all bets are off. The banker deals again.'

'There's a banker?'

'Yes, didn't I say that? One of you is banker. The other players can only bet as much as the banker bets. That's in the rules.'

Wynter was looking at Crossman's face intently. It was clear that Wynter was unused to teaching anyone anything – he had not been called upon to do so before – and it was a

138

new experience to him. He was not sure whether Crossman was taking in the intricacies of the game.

'Thank you, Wynter – I think I get the idea.'

'Oh, an' another thing, sergeant. If I'm doing this with you, teaching you things, you have to call me Harry.'

Crossman bristled. 'Harry?'

'Yep. It's short for Harrold.'

'I know what it's short for, Wynter, but I am not going to call you by your given name.'

'While we do this, you are. Otherwise, I chuck it in now and you're on your own. I get to call you Jack, you have to call me Harry – it's in the rules.'

'What rules?'

'My rules for teachin' people how to cheat at cards.'

Crossman was squirming inside, but Wynter had him dead to rights. If he did not do as the lance-corporal requested, there would be no tuition. It was as plain as that. Crossman did not know where else to go to get such tuition. There were probably several card cheats in an army of thirty thousand men, but how did one find them? You could not go and ask someone who was playing cards, 'Excuse me, are you good at cheating?' He was stuck with Wynter and there was nothing else for it.

'Right,' he said through clenched teeth, 'let's play a few games – Harry – and you can show me some sleight-of-hand tricks while we re playing.'

'Some what, Jack?'

'How to cheat, dammit!'

Wynter smiled and dealt the cards. He was thoroughly enjoying himself. Such an opportunity would not come his way again and he meant to make the most of it. It was a pity Crossman was not an officer, eating dirt, but there it was. If you had to make someone grovel, it might as well be a sergeant as anyone. It gave Wynter a warm feeling in his belly. He could not wait to tell Devlin and Peterson.

Wynter and Crossman sat there for eight hours, breaking off only to eat and drink, or go to the ablutions. Crossman's wound was still giving him trouble and occasionally he had to stop to relieve the pain in some way. A cold compress was usually the answer. At the end of the eight hours both men were exhausted.

Crossman had certainly got the hang of the game proper, but whether he was good enough to cheat at it was a big question. Wynter had taught him some basic things, like dealing a card off the bottom of the pack, thinking that anything which required a greater skill would be more likely to get the sergeant into trouble.

'Am I ready, Wynter?'

'As ready as you'll ever be, Jack – but don't forget to call me Harry.'

'Lessons are over now, Wynter. There's to be no more Harry and Jack, if you please. If you call me by my first name once more, I shall have you flogged.'

Wynter's face screwed into an expression of disgust.

'There's bloody gratitude for you.'

'I am grateful, Wynter, but you had the advantage of me, while I was in a vulnerable position. I'm out of it. Now you have to behave yourself. We're back on normal status now. One day I shall repay you for your time and effort. I'm not sure how, but we'll find some way. Perhaps when this war is over I can find you a job in civilian life.'

'A *job*? What sort of a job?'

'Gamekeeper's assistant, or footman, something like that.'

'I'd rather you gave me a kick in the pants, sergeant. I don't like working for toffs. Not in a servant capacity, if you understand me. I've got me prize money to get me started.'

'Well, perhaps I can assist you with starting up a business then? A greengrocery perhaps.'

Wynter shook his head, sadly. 'You don't understand me at all, do you, sergeant?'

Crossman grinned. 'I suppose not. Some other way, then. All right? Shake my hand, man. Thank you.'

Wynter's calloused grip closed around Crossman's proffered palm and he pumped his arm.

'You're welcome, sergeant,' said Wynter, all malice forgotten now that a reward had been mentioned. 'Any time you wants to become a better cheat than what you are now, I'll be willin' to help.'

'And if you speak of this to anyone else, I'll cut your throat, you understand?'

'Not even Peterson or Devlin?' exclaimed Wynter, upset at the thought that he could not tell them how 'Harry' and 'Jack' were such good pals. 'How am I goin' to keep it from them? They know I've been playin' cards with you all day.'

Crossman sighed. 'All right, just those two – but no one else mind. Not another soul.'

That evening, Jock McIntyre came to see Crossman after the sergeant had sent him a message.

'There's a game in the small cabin to the north of Kadikoi,' the sergeant-major told Crossman. 'It's tonight at twelve. Yer brother willna be there, since he's on duty. What are ye goin' to do, man? Yer not thinking of playing cards with Captain Campbell?'

'I'm afraid I am, Jock. Wynter has taught me the game. I shall be there at midnight. Would you speak with Captain Campbell and ask him if he would entertain another officer at the game? Tell him the officer is thought to be reasonably wealthy.'

'And who is this officer?'

'Lieutenant Tremaine, of the 2nd Rifles.'

McIntyre raised his eyebrows.

'How are ye going to get this officer of the Rifles to play for ye?'

'I shall be he. I intend borrowing one of Lieutenant Dalton-James's uniforms. We're about the same height and build. I think I shall look quite smart in Rifle Greens, don't you think, Jock?'

'With or without the lieutenant's knowledge, Jack?'

'Without.'

The Scottish sergeant-major shook his head. 'Yer taking an awful risk, man. Impersonating an officer? They'll flog ye and throw what's left out of the army. Are ye sure ye want to do it this way? Surely there's some other?'

'None that I can think of.'

'And what if ye lose?'

'Then my problem will merely be doubled. It's double or nothing, Jock. I've got to take the risk. I've sent Wynter off to steal the uniform, so there's no turning back. Wynter is our best thief, by the way. We rely on him in such matters.'

'Gude God, man. I hope ye know what yer doing.'

After McIntyre had left, Crossman set about smartening himself up. He shaved with a bowl of hot puddle water. Devlin cut his hair for him. By the time Wynter returned triumphantly bearing one of Dalton-James's best uniforms, Crossman was clean and spruce, and ready to try it on.

The fit was snug, but once in the Rifle Greens, which appeared black under most lights, Crossman looked every inch an officer in the Rifles. Peterson was enthralled by the image. She kept plucking his sleeve. There were no boots, so Crossman wore his own, but since his were Russian, taken from a dead body, they would not appear out of place. A lot of officers and rankers had taken boots from the enemy corpses after a battle. The Russian footwear was superior to anything of service issue.

A small neat undress cap was the last addition.

'How do I look, lads?'

Wynter said, wonderingly, 'It don't take much to make an officer, does it? Just a wash and shave, a comb of the hair, an' there you are, nothing to it. You look an officer right and

142

proper, sergeant. And you talk like one, so there's no finding you out that way.'

'It takes more than you think to make an officer, Wynter. It takes a lifetime of imbibing mannerisms of speech and behaviour unknown to farm labourers such as you. It's knowing when to light a cigar, how to light it, when and how to throw away the stub. It's knowing whether to stand or sit, bend or bow. It's using all the right gestures at the right times. Social graces can only be absorbed in one's formative years, to any real degree, and those who try to imitate are invariably discovered. Those who ape and parrot men of breeding appear ridiculous, even to *hoi polloi* themselves, and are rarely good enough actors to get away with it.

'I'm not saying that's a good thing, you understand, I'm just saying that's how things are. It's important to know how to *act* like a gentleman, without forcing it, by letting it come naturally. It's the small nuances of demeanour which give men away, when they're attempting to impersonate a gentleman. I was raised to those subtleties. I cannot be caught out because I am, a gentleman.'

'Well, there's a fancy speech for you,' said the delighted Wynter. 'He'll get away with it, I swear.'

Crossman heard back from Jock McIntyre that Captain Campbell would be delighted to have another victim at the card table. Consequently, at the midnight hour, he made his way over the muddy ground to the cabin. His path took him close to the house which had been commandeered by Mrs Durham's husband for the use of his wife and her lady friends. Glancing at this building, Crossman saw that a lamp was still burning.

Up at the front, the guns had ceased barking. Only the occasional crack from a sharpshooter or picquet broke the stillness of the night. Candles were burning in tents and hovels, where men were busy at some military task or other, or perhaps just reading a letter from home. Smells of wood-smoke and cooking wafted through the chill air, and in the distance the false laughter of drunks still draining their cups. A drummer boy began tapping out a rhythm on his drum until a soldier yelled at him to be quiet. Stillness, again.

Crossman reached the cabin. It had a hanging blanket instead of a door. He lifted this and stepped inside. The room was full of blue smoke from chibouques and cigars. There was a bottle of rum on the table and filled glasses. A warm, comfortable atmosphere pervaded. Crossman had let in a draught on entering and five faces turned from the table and looked at him. The only one he recognised was that of Captain Campbell.

'Lieutenant Tremaine, at your service, gentlemen,' said Crossman, removing his headgear. 'I believe I have the honour to be invited to a place at this table? Which of you is Captain Campbell, of the 93rd Foot?'

'I am. Sit down, lieutenant,' said the dealer, who was Campbell himself, 'I hope you're as green at cards as that uniform you're wearing.'

There was laughter from the other men.

Campbell continued to lay out the cards, adding one hand more by an empty chair. Crossman sat in the chair and picked up the two cards. They were a two of diamonds and a five of spades.

'The game is chemin de fer, and I am the current banker,' said Campbell. Then he suddenly stared at Crossman hard. 'Wait, I know you, fellah! You're the johnny who faced me out on coming back from one of Buller's damned furtive operations. I recognise you, even without your stinking goat-skin and your beard. What do you say now, lieutenant? This time I do know your rank, sir, and I'm glad to see I have the better of you, in that respect. I think a captain trumps a lieutenant, does it not?'

There were one or two soft laughs from the other officers.

Crossman smiled grimly. 'It does indeed, sir, and I never thought to get trumped in such a manner.' There were some more laughs from the other players. Crossman saw that he

144

had not yet said enough to placate the captain. 'You have me at a loss, Captain Campbell. I can but ask you to accept my humble apology for my rudeness. I realise I insulted you and am at your disposal if you should wish to take the matter further.'

Campbell stared at him for a few moments longer, looked back at his cards, and then waved Crossman down.

The captain obviously had a good hand.

'Play your cards, if you please, lieutenant.'

18

Even after only a few hands it was obvious to Crossman that he was hopelessly out of his depth. The game itself was not complicated, but like all simple yet absorbing games, the skill was in the playing. Crossman did not even try to cheat. He had thought he could, but now he was here, sitting at the table, he could not do it. Such a thing was not in his nature.

In any case it was patently obvious that if he used the tricks Wynter had taught him he would be discovered almost immediately. The men around the table were all hardened gamblers. They had eyes like hawks. Crossman realised he had been very naively optimistic, perhaps foolish was a better word, in thinking he could simply walk into a card game he had only just learned and beat one of its greatest disciples.

He began to lose, at first lightly, then heavily.

Soon his money was all gone. Most of it had been won by Campbell. His losses represented everything he had saved since leaving England a year ago. He was now destitute. He stared through the smoke haze at the table top in confusion.

Campbell said, 'You should have stuck to backgammon, lieutenant.'

Crossman carefully tapped the bowl of his chibouque on

146

the heel of his boot, to give himself some time to gather his wits and calm himself. Fool he might be, but he did not want to appear one. A gentleman hides his true feelings behind a cold mask of indifference.

Turning to Campbell, he said quietly, 'Backgammon is no more my game than is chemin de fer. I much prefer wagering on the horses.'

'What, owning 'em? Or racing them?'

'Both. You will find me either at Tattersalls or at any half-decent racecourse when I am at home.'

In fact Crossman had never been near Tattersalls, the famous racehorse auctioneers, and was an infrequent visitor at the races. He was desperately trying to save face and everyone in the room knew it. The best thing he could do now was leave, before he made a spectacle of himself.

Campbell puffed on a cigar. 'We will accept your markers, if you care to stay in the game.'

'I – I can't gamble with money I do not have.'

'But you *will* have more, at some time,' said a subaltern, 'surely? Why not stay?'

Crossman rose. His stomach felt like a lead weight. Failure was not a thing he enjoyed. He came stiffly to attention and bowed to the other gamblers.

'Gentlemen,' he said, 'I must take my leave.'

'Come back any time, lieutenant,' Campbell said, smiling irritatingly 'Always glad to take your money.'

Crossman bowed stiffly again and went out of the cabin.

Once outside, the cold early-morning air struck him forcibly in the face. What a fool! What an utter idiot he was. A ripple of laughter followed a remark by Campbell from inside the cabin. Crossman knew who was the brunt of the joke and he withered inside. The amazing thing was, why on earth had he thought he could do it? How many men in history had thought they could win at cards, or horseracing, or anything, simply because they felt special? There must have been hundreds of thousands. Yet here he was, a man who prided himself on his clarity of reasoning, following dumbly behind those thousands like a lemming.

He somehow managed to stumble back to his quarters and change into his sergeant's uniform. Wynter was fast asleep but Crossman woke him and asked the bleary-eyed lance-corporal to return Lieutenant Dalton-James's uniform to its correct place, before it was missed. Grumbling, Wynter did as he was asked.

When Wynter returned he asked the sergeant the inevitable question.

'No, Wynter, I did not win – I lost everything I have.'

'I knew you would,' said Wynter, smugly. Then more generously, he added, 'You're good at what you do with us lot, sergeant – you save our necks time and again – but I could have told you you was no gambler.'

'I seem to recall that you did tell me,' Crossman replied, 'quite forcibly.'

'You didn't take much notice.'

'I'm an arrogant man, Wynter.'

Wynter sighed. 'I've always wanted to be a gentleman,' he said, 'with lots of money. Not to spend it, as such, but to go and gamble at some of them posh clubs you nobs have, like White's in St James's Street in London – or Boodles, Limmer's, Watiers, the Royal Cockpit, Fives Courts or the Daffy Club. Some of the wagers that go on at those places!'

'You seem to know an awful lot of gentlemen's clubs.'

Wynter nodded enthusiastically. 'My uncle was a doorman at White's and I've read about 'em in the Dreadfuls. Did you know a Lord Alvanley once bet three thousand pounds on a race between two raindrops running down a window at White's? And my uncle told me that when a man collapsed on the steps of the club, gentlemen coming in and out straight away placed bets on whether he was dead or not.'

'I've heard the same stories.'

'Yes, but did you know that when a doctor came to give

148

medical attention, those who'd bet the man was dead wouldn't let him through the crowd, in case he was revived?'

Crossman shook his head. 'No, I hadn't heard that, but I think I could have lived a reasonably happy life without ever knowing it. What makes you so enthusiastic about the London clubs, Wynter?'

'Why, sergeant, I could have cleaned them out. With my skills as a man of cards, I would be Lord of all England.'

'Wynter, if you had been born a gentleman with those same desires, you would have been a corpse at eighteen. Someone would have called you out and shot you dead. Or run you through with a sword. They do not like cheats in White's or Boodles, any more than they do at the Hogshead Inn. Someone would have found you out and turned you into raw meat in St James's Park at six o'clock on a cold and misty morning.'

Wynter grinned. 'I can dream, can't I? I ain't saying any more. Just think on it. You got a big worry with this Campbell, but you're goin' about fixing it the wrong way. You're too soft, sergeant. Oh, I know you can be hard when it comes to duty and the enemy, but with everythin' else you're too much the gentleman. Why don't you let me, Devlin and Peterson deal with this? We'll sort it out.'

Alarm bells began ringing in Crossman's head.

'You leave me with my own problems, Wynter.'

He had visions of his three soldiers murdering Campbell in his bed and calling it common justice.

Wynter shrugged. 'Well, it's an offer.'

'Thank you, Wynter, but no.'

'Think on it.'

Crossman did 'think on it' further, but simply became more depressed as he took to his bed in the morning.

Wynter knew that the sergeant the rankers called Fancy Jack would not agree to allowing him and the other two remaining members of the *peloton* to deal with the situation for him. In which case, he decided they would do something without the sergeant's permission. He could not allow this Captain Campbell to make his sergeant miserable.

It was not that Wynter *liked* the sergeant so much: Crossman was outside that kind of reference. Wynter neither liked nor disliked the man. Fancy Jack was an upper-class toff in a sergeant's uniform. Whatever Crossman was wearing, the likes of men like Wynter did not make friends with a separate species. They were as different from one another as gorillas were from baboons: they lived differently, ate differently, thought differently. A baboon did not make friends with a gorilla.

The reason Wynter was upset was because the activities of this Captain Campbell were intruding into the cosy little world of the *peloton*. No matter how dangerous it was out on fox hunts with the sergeant, Wynter's life was preferable to that of the soldier laying siege to Sebastopol. At least Wynter was dry and warm some of the time, was master of himself occasionally, and was not treated like a moron.

So, he made up his mind to get rid of Captain Campbell for good and all, and in this frame of mind roused his two companions and told them the story. He already had a scheme in mind, which he imparted to them enthusiastically. Peterson, after hearing it, was dubious as to whether they would be able to make it work.

'Well, what do you suggest then?' asked Wynter, willing for once to listen to the views of others. 'We ain't got much time you know.'

'I think your plan is good enough,' acquiesced Peterson, 'but we need someone with a bit more rank than a corporal to make it work.'

'I agree with Peterson,' said Devlin. 'We have to find some officer to help us.'

They sat and discussed who that officer might be and came to the conclusion that anyone with a commissioned rank would not touch the scheme with a bargepole, no matter how much they sympathised with Fancy Jack. Then suddenly Devlin came up with the perfect man.

'What about Mr Rupert Jarrard – he's the sergeant's friend – let's tell him the whole story and see what he thinks?'

'Brilliant,' said Wynter, grinding some beans in the bottom of a shell case to make some coffee. 'That's the stuff. We'll get rid of Campbell all right and then things can go back to normal around here. I'm fed up with seeing Fancy Jack walking around looking like Death on a rainy day.'

The guns booming along the siege line woke Crossman up around noon. He rose from his horsehair mattress and staggered downstairs to wash his face. There was no one else about. He seemed to be alone in the hovel. Once he had washed and was feeling a little less like a warthog, he went out to seek Lavinia Durham, to get the latest news on his brother.

Mrs Durham was standing outside the British Hotel, talking with Mrs Nell Butler, a Winchester woman and the wife of a private in the 95th Foot. Mrs Butler was one of those who regularly assisted the surgeons with the sick and wounded.

Crossman managed to attract Lavinia Durham's attention, and indicated he would like to speak with her.

He went behind a row of shacks and soon Mrs Durham came tripping round the corner, holding up her long skirts with their flounces and lace with her right hand.

'Alexander,' she said, 'how nice to see you. Is this another one of our clandestine meetings? I must say I do enjoy this conspiracy. It is fun!'

As usual he became a little agitated with her flippancy.

'Lavinia, please. How is the affair between my brother and the widow, Mrs Kennedy progressing?'

'Flourishing, my dear man. He took to her instantly. I

151

must say the males in your family must be all alike. Show them a pretty face and they're lost forever. You are the same, I seem to recall, and I've heard stories about your father.'

'Lavinia,' he said, sharply, 'that is most indelicate. You can say what you like about me, but leave my father out of it.'

'Sorry. Anyway,' she linked her arm in his and walked him through the mud, 'James is smitten. It did not take long after Molly Kennedy fluttered her eyelids for your brother to start walking with her. Now they are inseparable. I think he has forgotten all about his card games.'

'He can't have forgotten *all* about them – he has a huge debt to repay.'

'Well, I can only say that his mind is preoccupied with thoughts of love at the moment.'

'Here,' said Crossman, withdrawing his arm, 'this must not become *too* serious.'

Lavinia Durham arched an eyebrow. 'My dear Alexander, you can't unleash the forces of nature and then hope to control them. You must take what comes. Your brother is a grown man.'

'Yes, I know, but Molly Kennedy – why – she's . . .'

'You shock me, sir! You're about to say "she's only the widow of a *corporal*" aren't you? Such women are all right to philander with, I suppose, but heaven forbid if it becomes any more serious than that. I thought you were this liberal-minded man, who wishes for a breakdown between the classes? You're a fake, sir – and what's more, you're a hypocrite.'

He was pained. 'No, no, Lavinia. But Mrs Kennedy! I mean, there are some of the widows who are perfectly respectable. I'm not saying I would be overjoyed if my brother married a woman from the Lancashire cotton mills, or a coach driver's daughter, but so long as she was *respectable*. You know Molly Kennedy is an outrageous flirt. She wouldn't do at all.'

'No one has mentioned marriage, so far as I know, but if they do you only have yourself to blame. You started this,

Alexander. Molly Kennedy is no different from any other woman, even if she is a flirt. A handsome lieutenant is paying court to her. A lieutenant from an upper-class family with wealth. She is both flattered and eager, and it would be unnatural if she did not want it to last forever.'

'You mean they're in love?' cried Crossman.

'Molly is most certainly infatuated and your brother is showing signs of it too. Whether these feelings will continue after a longer association I do not know, but you wanted your brother to be diverted, and diverted he is. Molly has done an excellent job of that. You may stand there with your mouth agape and your eyes rolling, but you have pushed your brother down a steep slope and can do nothing to stop him now.'

'Oh my God,' groaned Crossman.

19

Like many men who believe they have cast off the worst of their inherited prejudices, Crossman found that when it came to the heart of the matter he was no better than his father. He himself might have found a young woman below his class, fallen in love, and married her without too much discomfort of the soul. It would be all right for him, as the younger son. However, his brother James was a different matter. James was the elder and therefore would inherit the Scottish estates. For James to have an Annie Bloggs for his wife, instead of a Beatrice Hughes-Fitzwilliam or a Caroline Esterhazy, was unthinkable.

'I've started something I can't stop,' Crossman told Rupert Jarrard. 'How can I live with this?'

'You, sir, are a rotten snob,' replied Jarrard, without much sympathy. 'In the United States we allow our kin to marry whom they please, whether she is the daughter of a fishmonger, or a rich merchant.'

'Ha!' exclaimed Crossman, hollowly. 'So if your daughter, supposing you had one, came home and said she was going to marry a Cherokee Indian, you would give her your blessing? I don't think so. You *might*, but I seriously doubt it. You certainly wouldn't allow her to marry a Negro slave.'

154

Jarrard said, 'Those are different matters.'

'They are the *same* matters in different clothing, Rupert. And even closer to home than that, what if she wanted to marry a store clerk, someone with no prospects whatsoever, a man who was happy to sweep the floor of the store for the rest of his life? Or a riverboat gambler? Or a wild west gunfighter? Or even an honest cowboy, on two dollars a week and found. You would not approve. You would not, Rupert. We are all fakes when it comes to the point. Believe me.'

Jarrard shrugged. 'I think I have less snobbery in me than you do, Jack, just as I have fewer scruples.'

Crossman looked at his friend quizzically. 'What do you mean by that? Fewer scruples? Where did scruples come into the conversation?'

Jarrard looked slightly abashed, but he shrugged away Crossman's question.

'If you come down to Balaclava harbour tonight at six o'clock, I shall show you what I mean.'

Captain Campbell of the 93rd Foot was taken on board HMS *Antigone* at five o'clock in the evening, just as the sun was going down behind the curved horizon of the Black Sea. The sky was a deep red colour, a magnificent sunset, but since Campbell did not care for such things he hardly noticed it. He was thinking about the coming game of cards with two naval lieutenants, one of whom was at his elbow now, guiding him down a set of steps to a cabin below.

Campbell descended into the belly of the ship cautiously. He had never liked boats. His journeys through the Bay of Biscay, into the Mediterranean Sea and subsequently across the Black Sea, had done nothing to improve his liking of them. This gentle rocking on the wavelets created by the wind on the harbour waters was bad enough, but the great chops and swells of the high seas always made him feel very ill.

He had only agreed to a game here, on board this ship, because the two lieutenants were remarkably inexperienced card players. He had been introduced to them by the American correspondent, Mr Rupert Jarrard, a rough sort of fellow, but what passed for a gentleman in the New World.

Campbell had already taken a good deal of money from the two 'sea-green matelots' as he called them behind their backs, when they had played in the cabin behind Kadikoi. It had seemed churlish to refuse their offer to continue the game on board their ship, where they promised one or two more naval officers would be sure to join the game.

'Down here?' he said, entering a gloomy area festooned with coiled ropes and smelling strongly of tar.

One of the fresh-faced young lieutenants answered him – the one called Holliday.

'That door there, sir. We're out of the captain's way down here. He does not approve of gambling and it will serve our purpose for the better. I hope you will find us good hosts, captain, since we are going to be thrown into each other's company more than we imagined.'

Campbell did not know what Holliday meant by this veiled remark, but he took it that they meant to keep him playing until they had cleaned him out. Perhaps they believed that now they had him on foreign ground he would play in a nervous, less skilful fashion? Well, these callow youths were mistaken if they thought that getting Captain Campbell off his home ground was going to unnerve him enough to lose at cards.

He entered a cabin with a low ceiling. There was a table in the middle, fixed to the floor with strong bolts, with chairs arranged around it. In the centre of the table were two packs of sealed playing cards. An oil lamp swung in the corner of the cabin, casting a weak amber light over the room. Down here the motion of the boat was much more pronounced, but Campbell was too intent on the coming game to worry too much about any queasiness he might feel in the pit of his stomach.

'Any place which pleases you,' said Holliday. 'The choice of seating is yours, captain.'

'Thank you,' Campbell replied, taking the nearest chair, 'this will do admirably.'

'Do you drink rum, sir?' asked Blightwell, the other lieutenant. 'It is the navy's preference. We shall of course send for some claret or other drink of your choice if you wish?'

'No, rum will do fine. Let's get started shall we? Are we to be joined by any others?'

'In about an hour or so,' Holliday informed him. 'They have duties at the moment.' To Campbell's astonishment the lieutenant winked at him. 'But once they are relieved from watch they will join us. Now, if you would open one or even both packs, sir, let us play some chemin de fer . . .'

Campbell thought the wink very odd, but he had ceased to wonder at the differences between infantry officers and their naval counterparts. They were like two different races so far as he was concerned. The culture and rituals of each were as far apart as those of an Englishman and a Hottentot.

For the next hour Captain Campbell played cards.

At first his luck was in and he found he did not have to 'bend' the cards too much to make the lieutenants part with their money. He took it away from them slowly and gradually, though he could have made a quick killing. From experience he had found that men do not notice their money disappearing so much when it dribbles away. It is only at the point when they come to a reckoning of what they have left, that they suddenly gasp and go pale, realising that three months' pay has melted before their eyes like the snow when it thaws.

Annoyingly, one of the lieutenants then began winning. Campbell did his best to plug this hole, but the young man's luck was astonishing and even with some assistance from his deft fingers Campbell could not stem the flood. The strength of the rum was getting to Campbell's head, so he was having a little difficulty in maintaining his concentration. He watered down his drink from a bottle on the table, hoping to begin sobering up.

This bad patch was, he knew, merely an irritating interlude. The lieutenant's luck would eventually change — nothing is forever — and in the meantime all Campbell had to do was watch and wait, and try to clear his head. If only the damn boat would stay still for a few moments! It was probably the rum, but the rocking appeared to have increased in strength. The lamp in the corner was swinging back and forth like a pendulum in a grandfather clock. Campbell stared at it in a bemused fashion, hypnotised by its drifting light.

'Your play, I believe, captain?' said Holliday.

'What?' cried Campbell, jerking out of his reverie. 'Oh, yes — no more cards, thank you, sir. I shall remain with these two. When did you say we would be joined by others? I believe we have been playing for more than two hours.'

'Soon, captain. They are probably changing their uniforms. It gets wet on deck when one is out to sea. There is a constant fine spray from the bows, even on the calmest seas, and I believe we are heading for dirty weather at the moment.'

A shocked Campbell stood up abruptly and crashed his head on a beam, breaking the skin. He felt the blood trickling down his cheek. The two lieutenants stared at him in some concern.

'Are you all right, captain?' asked Blightwell. 'Are you hurt?'

'Damn!' Campbell cried. He took a kerchief from his tunic and held it against the wound. At this moment he was more concerned about his situation than he was about his injury. 'Look here, did you say "out to sea"?'

'Why, yes,' replied Holliday, with an innocent expression. 'You knew we were setting sail at six o'clock, did you not, captain? I understood that you wanted an excuse to leave the Crimea. You may blame it on us, sir. We do not mind in the least. Our captain is a lenient man. We intend saying we were deep in conversation and before we realised it the ship was on its way to India . . .'

Campbell felt the colour drain from his face. 'To India?'

Blightwell, his expression one of total guiltlessness, nodded his head.

'Why yes. That is our next area of duty. Part of your regiment is in India, is it not? We understood you wished to transfer to them, to join your brother in India, but your application was refused by a senior officer hostile to your family? This way it is a mere accident of fate. You were on board the *Antigone* when it set sail and were unfortunately unable to disembark, due to unforeseen circumstances. Once in India, you will be able to join your preferred battalion. These are your wishes, are they not?'

'What in the blazes made you think that, you idiot?' raged the captain, losing his temper completely. 'Are you mad? Are you both refugees from Bedlam? I shall be shot for desertion. Who put you up to this? Who told you I wished to go to India?'

The smile which was a semi-permanent feature of Lieutenant Blightwell's face was instantly removed.

'Why, Mr Jarrard, the war correspondent. He saw to it that your belongings were brought on board, after we started our game. The captain need not know it, but your wardrobe and personal effects are hidden in the hold. We can soon smuggle them on to shore once we reach Calcutta.'

Campbell's temper subsided, to be replaced by a calmer but more unpleasant feeling of panic.

'By God,' he said, slowly and carefully, a horrible feeling of sickness, quite unconnected with the sea, stealing over him, 'I sense some sort of plot here, but the reasons escape me. I need to speak to your captain. He must set me ashore . . .'

159

'I'm afraid that's impossible,' replied Holliday, with maddening logic. 'We are now too far out at sea.'

Crossman stood on the quay at six o'clock, and five minutes later he was joined by Rupert Jarrard.

'Why am I here?' asked Crossman. 'You said something about proving your scruples worse than my own. I'm perfectly willing to believe they are, Rupert, without needing any proof.'

The American was looking smug. 'See that ship out there, just dipping down over the horizon?'

'I can see a set of masts, yes – the hull appears to be already out of sight.'

'That's the *Antigone*.'

'Is it?' Crossman said. 'Captain Collidge's ship? On its way home?'

'No, it's been sent to India,' Jarrard said, gleefully.

Crossman was beginning to lose patience with his friend.

'Look, you seem to be exceptionally pleased with yourself for some reason, Rupert, but I haven't the damnedest notion why. If you've got something to tell me, say it now. It is most frustrating standing here watching you wallow in self-satisfied pleasure.'

'You know who's on board that ship?'

'I have no idea, unless you're going to tell me Wynter has stowed away and is out of my hair forever.'

'Someone – not Wynter – someone you would rather get rid of than Wynter.'

Crossman shook his head. 'There is no one in this world I would rather shed than Lance-Corporal Wynter, bless his dirty socks and foul breath.'

'Not even Captain Campbell, late of the Sutherland Highlanders?'

Crossman took some seconds to absorb this remark. He stared hard at the departing vessel, just the tip of the main topgallant mast showing now. Then he looked back again into the grey eyes of the American.

'Captain Campbell is on board that ship?'

Jarrard nodded slowly.

'And it's bound for India?'

Another slow nod.

Crossman stared at the wake of the vessel, which formed a flat wavering line snaking out to sea.

'Then we have got rid of him, at least for a while.'

'For quite a long while. Perhaps he won't ever be back. I think I'll have to get in some target practice with my Navy Colt if he does return. He probably knows by now that it was me who tricked him on board.'

Crossman shook his head wonderingly.

'Who put you up to this?'

'Why, that lovable rogue Wynter, for whom you have so much admiration and respect. He and his pals Peterson and Devlin thought it a good idea to get rid of Campbell. Your boys wanted to help you. They saw their sergeant in trouble and they rallied. They roped me in because I am a gentleman and would be taken more seriously than they.'

A strange feeling of comradeship for his men swept through a flaw in Crossman like lava through a fault line.

'You are perfectly correct, Rupert, in your assumption that you have fewer scruples than I do. In fact I believe you to have no morals whatsoever.'

'Not when it comes to dealing with cardsharps, I don't.'

Crossman, unstiffening his British reserve for once, put an arm around the American's shoulders.

'Rupert, I owe you a drink. Will you join me at the canteen bar? We shall get "my boys" and all drink to each other's lack of principles. And you, my fellow conspirator, shall be carried home tonight on a litter, or my name is not Jack Crossman.'

Jarrard smiled and started to walk forward, then he turned and frowned.

'But your name *isn't* Jack Crossman.'

'In that case it won't be whatever it really is, my Yankee friend, if you can work that out. Come on, I shall match you glass for glass, and the loser shall be carried home by the winner, like a trophy from the Greek games . . .'

20

The removal of Captain Campbell was a blessing to Crossman.

He still had to deal with his brother's infatuation for the redoubtable Molly Kennedy, but the Crimea was a strange place where events caused changes to take place every day. Crossman was convinced that a major attack was imminent, though the generals refused to believe it. Such an event would wrench his brother from the arms of Molly and thrust him into a more sobering position.

The now reduced *peloton* was gathered in the hovel. Out along the front the ordnance seemed louder and more vigorous than usual on the 4th of November, even though it had been raining heavily the whole day. Wynter said it was in preparation for Guy Fawkes night, the next day.

'We got our own fireworks,' he said, 'what with shells and all. We just need to make a Prince Menshikoff guy an' burn him on a bonfire. What do you say, sergeant? Shall we make a Guy Fawkes?'

'I quite appreciate the fact that you wish to promote our cultural ceremonies, Wynter, but I think Major Lovelace would not like it if he found us idle enough to play at bonfires.'

Rupert Jarrard, who was there with them, developed a puzzled expression.

'Who is this "Guy Fawkes"?'

'Why,' replied Wynter, 'he's the cove who tried to blast our parliament to bits.'

'I should have thought by the way the politicians have conducted this war, that you would be drinking his health, not burning him on a fire.'

Peterson laughed. 'He's not that recent. It was – when was it, sergeant . . .?'

'November the 5th, 1605. Guy Fawkes and some other Catholic conspirators tried to assassinate King James, and would have taken parliament with him if the plot had succeeded. We call it the gunpowder plot, Rupert. A quantity of explosives was found under the Houses of Parliament, I believe. Guy Fawkes and his fellow conspirators were put to death. I'm not sure they were burned at the stake, but they might well have been.'

Wynter screwed up his face. 'You make it sound as dry as dust, sergeant. You never could tell a story, could you?'

Jarrard shook his head in bemusement. 'And you celebrate this man's horrific death by burning his effigy every year since then? Am I the only person in this room who thinks that smacks a little of barbarity?'

Crossman said, 'Just harmless fun, Rupert. A few pyrotechnics, a bonfire for the children . . .'

'For the *children*?'

'It's mainly a treat for the children,' said Peterson.

Rupert Jarrard shook his head in disbelief.

'No wonder my ancestors decided to leave the shores of Britain for the New World. You are riddled with ugly rituals which corrupt the children at an early age, so that when they reach manhood they think that burning images of people is just a little harmless fun. Well, well. I'm glad I live in a civilised country.'

'Where men shoot each other in the street for some

imagined slight,' murmured Crossman. 'Come on, Rupert, we all have our little foibles.'

At that moment, two soaked and dripping soldiers appeared in the doorway. They had grim faces, as if they were on an unpleasant mission. Behind the soldiers was a young and very wet subaltern. This man stepped into the doorway, blocking out the light.

'Sergeant Crossman?' he enquired.

Crossman stood up. 'Yes, sir?'

'You are Sergeant John Crossman, of the 88th Foot?'

Crossman was beginning to think something was very wrong. This looked like an arresting party.

'I am he.'

'Sergeant Crossman,' said the subaltern ponderously, 'you are under arrest for the murder of Captain Charles Barker, formerly of the 47th Foot. You will step outside, sergeant, and be relieved of your arms.'

There was shocked silence from within the room. Then Wynter, probably without thinking, stepped in between the lieutenant and Crossman with a drawn bayonet. Whether he saw himself as a biblical Peter and would have sliced off the lieutenant's ear was a matter for speculation, for Corporal Devlin grabbed Wynter's wrist and pulled him out of the way.

'That won't do no good, Wynter,' hissed Devlin. 'Let the sergeant go with them.'

Crossman stepped forward and followed the lieutenant through the doorway. Once outside he divested himself of his Tranter revolver and his hunting knife, the only two weapons on his person. The lieutenant took these quietly, not mentioning that they were not of army issue. He then motioned for his two soldiers to march Crossman away, before turning and confronting Lance-Corporal Wynter.

'You threaten an officer of Her Majesty?' cried the lieutenant. 'You realise the punishment for such a crime? Are you all rogues here? What do you say, corporal?'

165

Peterson looked about to intervene, but Devlin stepped forward and answered in a placating manner. 'Begging your pardon, sir, we are certainly not all rogues. We are a special unit of skirmishers, for General Buller, and are often out behind enemy lines. We have to be quick with our hands, if not our wits, sir. Lance-Corporal Wynter here acted out of what you might call instinct, sir. It was not meant. It was a sort of self-protection act, if you know what I mean.'

'If I might have a word, lieutenant,' Jarrard said, stepping out of the shadows. 'I am an impartial observer – Rupert Jarrard, of the *Banner* newspaper, from the United States of America. These men have been under great stress and hardly know the time of day.'

'There are men in the trenches,' pointed out the lieutenant, 'who are under similar stress.'

'I venture to suggest they are not the same circumstances. With these men a swiftly-drawn bayonet means the difference between life and death. They live in the pockets of the Russians, lieutenant.'

The officer stared flinty-eyed at Wynter, who was now trying to look contrite.

'Sorry, sir,' said Wynter, 'I wasn't thinkin' straight. I thought you was the enemy, so to speak.'

The lieutenant remained for a few moments, his hands locked behind his back, gazing at Peterson, Devlin and Wynter. Finally, he spoke again, 'I shall overlook this incident, Lance-Corporal. Consider yourself very fortunate. You three soldiers, however, must rejoin your regiment at the front, until you know the fate of your sergeant.'

The lieutenant then left them.

Wynter grimaced at the lieutenant's back, whispering to Devlin, 'I thought he was the enemy and he bloody well is. I ain't going to no front. I'm still on the sick list with this here leg. I'm going to the hospital, I am, and they'll have to drag me out of it with a company of soldiers if they want Wynter back in the trenches.'

The trio began to gather up their belongings in silence.

The lieutenant caught up with the two soldiers marching Crossman through the driving rain towards a farmhouse. He took Crossman into the house alone, leaving the two guards outside. There, at a rickety table, sat a major. The field officer looked up as Crossman entered. He looked quizzically at the lieutenant, who must have made some sign or other out of Crossman's sight. The major's face assumed a stern expression.

'So you're the man who murdered Captain Barker?'

'I think you ought to speak with Major Lovelace, sir,' said Crossman, aware that water was running down his face from his hair as he met the major's glare. 'Or failing that, with Brigadier-General Buller.'

The corpulent major's red face looked as if it were about to explode.

'Did you, or did you not, kill Captain Charles Barker?'

Crossman realised he was not going to get anywhere by remaining silent on the issue. If there were to be a court martial, then Lovelace would be called. This major obviously knew quite a bit in any case.

'Myself and another man were defending ourselves against an ambush by Captain Barker. Unfortunately in the exchange of fire Captain Barker was fatally wounded. It was not an unlawful killing, sir, as you will discover when you speak with General Buller.'

The steam seemed to go out of the field officer now as he turned to the lieutenant.

'He admits it! What is the army coming to, when villains like this can kill a fellow soldier, an officer in his own army, and boldly state it? Young man,' he turned on Crossman fiercely, like a white-haired father on his son, 'you will be punished, very severely, for this crime. I intend seeing you hang by the neck until you are dead. Who is your accomplice? Come, give me his rank and name. It will do you no service to keep this man's identity a secret.'

'Sir,' said Crossman, with all the patience he could muster, 'you are not listening to me. Stop for a moment, I beg you, and listen to what I have to say. The death of Captain Barker was sanctioned by a much higher authority than either of us. You will save yourself and your lieutenant here a lot of trouble if you simply go to General Buller and hear what he has to say on the matter.'

The major blinked rapidly, as if he had just been slapped in the face.

'General Buller? What has he to do with anything?'

'I am not at liberty to say. I cannot tell you the name of the man who was with me and witnessed Captain Barker's death. I am not permitted to say anything, even in my own defence, beyond giving you the names of Major Lovelace and General Buller. This situation will remain beyond your comprehension, until you speak with one or both of these two officers, sir.'

The major was not a very bright individual. He was the kind of bumbling old fool who, in his middle-sixties, finds himself in a senior post simply because of the purchase system. He had bought his way through the ranks, had been kept away from any area of the army where his lack of intelligence might do some harm, and was tolerated by his peers because he came from the right sort of family. They knew him, they obliged him, but along with everyone else, they still considered him an old fool.

A more experienced lieutenant might have intervened before now, but at last the younger officer spoke up.

'Sir, the sergeant seems adamant that we ought to speak with General Buller. Shall I arrange an appointment?'

White bushy eyebrows rose up a plum-coloured brow.

'Certainly not! You think I want to bother the general with the doings of a sergeant?'

'It is murder, sir,' protested the lieutenant. 'It's not simply a case of petty theft.'

The major looked sharply at Crossman, while the lieutenant was speaking.

'Where are you from, sergeant? You speak like a man of breeding. Are you one of these clerk fellows who've got a bit of education and ape their betters? I know men like you, sir, and I don't like 'em. If you're trying to be a gentleman, you're doing it very badly. Men of breeding don't join the army as anything but officers.'

He turned to the lieutenant again.

'And before you go harping at me again, I happen to know,' said the major with some aplomb, 'that Brigadier-General Buller and this man Major Lovelock or whatever, whose names this rogue keeps bleating at me, have both gone on an expedition to the north.'

Crossman was alarmed to hear this. He was in little danger of being hung before these two key witnesses returned, but he did think that the major might do an awful lot of damage to General Buller's espionage group in the meantime. If this major went to Lord Raglan instead of waiting for Buller to return, the commander-in-chief might begin his own investigations and find that a spy network was operating. Lord Raglan, as everyone knew, detested spying in any form.

'Lieutenant, lock this man up now. I will arrange for his court martial. Keep him under close guard.'

'But sir . . .'

'Lieutenant, I do not want to have to repeat myself. That is an order.'

'Yes, sir.'

Crossman was led out of the farmhouse in the pouring rain. He was taken by araba to a thick-walled, windowless croft near to the 2nd Division Camp on the Inkerman Heights. Prisoners were held here so that they could be used as labour in digging and sandbagging defences. In the croft were several men who had broken rules, regulations or laws seriously enough to warrant temporary imprisonment. A very damp and miserable Crossman found himself a corner in the stinking room, away from the eyes of the other occupants.

Most of the prisoners were sullen men with sunken eyes

and pinched looks. They seemed bitter. Whatever they had done was probably not weighing heavily on their consciences. They were more concerned with their own plight, than admitting to any guilt. Most no doubt believed they were being wronged, whether that was the case or not. One, however, was a talkative soldier whose sleeve bore a bright chevron shape which corporal stripes had obviously once covered, the rest of the sleeve's colour having faded.

'I wouldn't sit there, sergeant – that's where we all piss when we need to.'

Crossman moved out of the corner and said he was obliged to the man for his warning. He moved to another spot, closer to the men. The talkative ex-corporal was a big, raw-boned fellow with huge hands and arms as thick as Crossman's thighs. He got up and sat down beside the sergeant, who shifted uncomfortably, not wanting company in this black hole of the Crimea.

'Daniel Johnson,' said the man, extending a hand, which Crossman found himself obliged to shake. 'I punched an officer. Take no heed of these miserable wretches,' he nodded at the other three men, 'they're all thieves and vagabonds, they are. Don't turn your back on 'em though, or they'll steal the back buttons from your trousers.'

One of the men glared at Johnson, but the large man balled his fist and good-humouredly shook it under the man's nose.

'Don't you be gettin' too big for your boots, you young spud, or you'll be earnin' a busted snoot.' He then turned to Crossman again. 'What are you in here for, Fancy Jack? Oh, yes, I know you. We're from the same regiment, see . . .' Crossman had not noticed the yellow facings in the poor light, but he saw the eighty-eight on the forage cap now. 'You and me are comrades-in-arms, me old sergeant spud. What did you do, murder an officer?'

'That's what I'm accused of doing.'

Crossman hoped that this admission would end the conversation and that Johnson would leave him alone. The three smaller men moved away a little, as if they might become contaminated. Johnson remained sitting where he was however, staring deeply into Crossman's eyes.

'By God,' said the big man, 'I believe you.'

21

Prince Menshikoff's foray on the Inkerman Heights on the 26th October, the day after the Battle of Balaclava, had convinced him that the weakest point in the siege line was on the British right flank. There, Lord Raglan's troops were stretched thinly. Colonel Federoff, with a mere five thousand men, had broken through the outlying British positions on that day, only to be repulsed by artillery fire. Now Prince Menshikoff planned a major offensive with a hundred and twenty thousand men over the same ground.

The Inkerman Heights was a piece of land east of Sebastopol, riddled with deep ravines and gullies, the largest of which was Careenage Ravine. Some of the ridges were over six hundred feet above sea level and thickly wooded. It was contained on the right by Chernaya River and to the south by the Woronzoff Road. Within the Heights was the British 2nd Division Camp, with the Light Division Camp and the Guards Camp to the rear. Despite Colonel Federoff's attack, there was no evidence that Lord Raglan had visited the Heights or strengthened his position there.

There were three main gullies to the north-east of the area: Volovia, Quarry and St Clements Ravines. In the centre was a rise known as Shell Hill. Menshikoff's plan involved getting his artillery to Shell Hill in the quickest time possible. The British and the French would be in range of these guns and could be pinned down. At Shell Hill General Dannenberg would take overall command of Soimonoffs and Pauloff's troops and drive on over Home Ridge, through the British defences, while General Gorchakoff harried the French.

Prince Menshikoff was confident that a major attack would see his Russian soldiers overrunning the British positions. Once they had broken through, they could come up round behind the French on the British left.

A mere twenty-five thousand British soldiers stood in his way, with forty thousand French unable to intervene in time.

With his staff officers and messengers gathered round him, Prince Menshikoff issued his orders.

'General Soimonoff is to advance from Sebastopol, cross Careenage Ravine, and using the road we know to exist on the east of this gully, to march with an army of nineteen thousand of our brave soldiers to take possession of Shell Hill with thirty-eight guns.'

The lieutenant who was to ride with this message to General Soimonoff came to attention and clicked his heels. He knew the plan would please the general, who was proud of his 10th Division, consisting of twelve battalions of Katherineburg, Tomsk and Kolivansk Regiments. Alongside this division would be the Vladimir, Susdal and Uglitz Regiments, of the 16th Division, who had fought at the Battle of the Alma. There would also be the Bourtirsk Regiment, the 6th Rifles, a force of sappers and a small number of Cossacks.

Menshikoff now turned to General Pauloff's part in the assault.

'General Pauloff will have the 11th Division, also the Borodino and Tarutin Regiments, half the 4th Rifle Battalion and ninety-six guns. In all, some sixteen thousand of our best troops. He will march across the Inkerman Bridge over the Chernaya River and advance along what the British call Quarry Ravine, to take up a position east of Shell Hill.'

Prince Menshikoff now paced the floor of the old hall with its vast recesses, which he was using as his headquarters. He stared up at the high dirty windows as if deep in thought. Actually, he knew exactly what he was going to say next, but he had something of the showman in him. A little drama added to the occasion. He felt sure this was going to be the culmination of the war and victory for Russia over the invaders.

Suddenly he turned on his heel.

'General Gorchakoff will have under his command twenty-two thousand men. The 12th Division, General Liprandi's cavalry and eighty-eight guns. He will draw the French under that General Bosquet from the Sapouné Ridge – also those British who are there, the Guards I believe. It is important to open a route for our cavalry. General Gorchakoff will force the French and British to attack him and so gain access to one of those routes. Am I understood?'

There was a solemn nod from one of the staff officers responsible for the message to the general.

Prince Menshikoff continued.

'Generals Soimonoff and Pauloff will link up at Shell Hill and General Dannenberg will assume overall command. The attack will take place at six o'clock this morning. We must take heart in the knowledge that the British have not seen fit to reinforce the Inkerman Heights in any way since our attack several days ago. God is with us, gentlemen. It is our day.'

The messengers went their various ways to deliver the orders.

General Soimonoff received his message direct from Prince Menshikoff's headquarters at around five o'clock. He read the order and then went to the doorway of the house he was using as his own quarters. It was still dark outside. The terrain over which his men would have to march was quite unknown to him. It was not going to be easy for his troops to wend their way across unfamiliar country. Prince Menshikoff's staff officer had explained to him that he was to advance along the eastern edge of Careenage Ravine at six a.m. So be it. It would be done.

However, shortly after the first messenger had departed, a second messenger arrived from General Dannenberg.

'Sir, General Dannenberg's compliments.'

He was handed the written order from his immediate superior, which told him to advance, not on the eastern, but on the western bank of Careenage Ravine, and at five a.m.

Soimonoff frowned and shook his head in bewilderment.

'Which of these orders am I to follow?' he asked the captain who had delivered the second message. 'One tells me the east bank, the other the west bank! One says six a.m., the other five! Surely General Dannenberg has spoken with Prince Menshikoff?'

The captain looked uncomfortable. It was not for a lowly staff officer to give opinions on the orders of high command. Soimonoff realised he was being unfair on the man and he shrugged his shoulders and dismissed him.

But what was he to do? He was not yet under Dannenberg's command, but still under the command of Prince Menshikoff. Dannenberg would have command *later*, but that was not now. Soimonoff dreaded to think what would happen if Prince Menshikoff did not know about this sudden change in his plans. It was his inclination that he should stick to the first order and ignore the second one. He would advance along the eastern side of the ravine at six o'clock.

He sighed in frustration. Having made a decision did not make him feel as good as it should do. Somehow he had the idea that he was in a bad situation. If the attack failed, whatever he did he would be accused of doing the wrong thing.

The attack would just have to succeed, that was all.

The bells of the Sebastopol churches began ringing out. It was Sunday. The citizens of the town would be preparing to go to church. The sound of the bells would help also to give heart to his troops. Perhaps they would see victory today?

175

After all, the British and French were heavily outnumbered, and the element of surprise would assist in their endeavours.

Lieutenant Kirinski served in the Tomsk Regiment, which was now marching down a narrow ravine. Mud splashed up his fine leather boots and clung to the hem of his greatcoat. Damp fog wet those pieces of hair sticking outside his headgear, plastering them to his sweaty forehead. The blade of the sword in his hand was covered in fine droplets of water, glistening like crushed diamonds in the dawn's light.

Fortified by a priest's blessing and a little alcohol, Kirinski was ready for the coming day's battle. The steep ravine walls were pressing the columns of men in on themselves, making progress difficult. Kirinski had imagined the gullies would be wider than this and not so deep or sheer. Those men who were squeezed on to the edges were tripping over themselves and there was some confusion amongst them.

'Keep in step there,' Kirinski ordered, as he came under the stare of Captain Gorbatloff. 'Keep those feet in time.'

He struck one of the men closest to him with the flat of his sword blade as a warning. Normally Lieutenant Kirinski carried a thick baton with which to beat the men into line, but today he felt happier with his sword in his hand. Other officers still had their sticks, or used their fists, without which they would have felt inadequate and unable to keep order.

The soldiers did their best. There was a need to keep silent so that their advance would be a surprise to the British. Somehow though, the fear of making a noise made them even more clumsy. Some little way behind them the wheels of the gun carriages were squeaking and groaning, cracking stones and gravel under their rims, as they had to traverse rough ground. They had been well greased of course, but heavy guns will always make a certain amount of noise.

Kirinski listened to the bells ringing out from Sebastopol and wondered whether he and his men would at last get the better of the British and French. If the Russians were the conquerors today, he felt sure he would have the opportunity to punish the Turks who had caused this war to be fought on Russian soil.

Dawn began to creep very gradually up the eastern sky, though it was still dark in the depths of the gully. Mist swirled around the swinging arms and marching legs of the men. Kirinski's eyes had become used to the poor light however, and he could see those men closest to him. He studied the peasant looks of the soldiers, with their bland faces, their wiry hair.

These men were all conscripts, serving a forced twenty-five years: coarse, ignorant fellows, who were used to beatings in civilian life. They had courage, but it was the bravery of men whose very souls were owned by their masters. It was a quiet kind of desperate courage, not the aggressive boldness of a proud man. They fought in solid blocks of thousands, mindlessly and rigidly following each order to the letter, their columns like multi-limbed automatons.

It was the opinion of Russian officers that if a man's life was not really worth living, he would sacrifice it in battle that much more willingly. Kirinski believed this might be true, but he was not sure of its effectiveness. He was an intelligent young man and saw about him much he would change, if he were commander-in-chief of the Russian Army.

The constant drilling for instance. A certain amount of drill was necessary for the discipline and order of the troops, but in the Russian Army drilling had been taken to extremes. It had reached the point where parades and ceremonies were more important than winning battles. Many of the muskets the men carried were useless as weapons of war because their parts had been polished with brick dust, so that they shone and their fittings were loose enough to rattle impressively on parade.

These muskets only had a range of one hundred and fifty to two hundred yards at the best of times, but after being rubbed down and cleaned for the thousandth time they became utterly useless except as staves on which to fit a bayonet.

We fight like African warriors, thought Kirinski, with spears.

At that moment the lieutenant's thoughts were interrupted when he noticed some figures ahead of him in the mist. He motioned for his men to stop marching. The figures came on, seemingly carelessly, calling out softly in a language that Kirinski knew to be English. These British soldiers had obviously not realised they were being confronted by Russians and probably thought this was a company from their own army.

Suddenly the British soldiers in front stopped, not a few yards from Lieutenant Kirinski. He could see their pale white faces. Their eyes gleamed through the thick swirling mists as a cold realisation entered them. Kirinski estimated that there were about fifteen of them. Not a very large coup, but hopefully the first strike in a series of successes today.

'Take them, quickly,' ordered a captain to Kirinski's left, 'before they make a sound.'

The British soldiers, bemused and shaken, were quickly gathered in, disarmed, and spirited to the back of the column.

General Soimonoffs army moved on, like a great grey centipede winding its way along a channel. Kirinski was unusually cheered by the capture of those few soldiers. It seemed to bode well for the day ahead. Victory would be sweet, after the humiliation at the River Alma. Victory today would restore Russian pride and crush the hopes of the invading army for good and all.

Then, just as suddenly as before, another set of figures came out of the mist. This time there were more of them. However, these were not weary picquets, but men whose brains were sharp and whose eyes were keen. Immediately shots rang out and the captain to the left of Kirinski fell with a bullet through his temple. His falling body hit the lieutenant with a thump, knocking the young officer sideways.

Three other Russian soldiers in the front row of the column also crumpled, one letting out a penetrating scream.

Now it has started, thought Kirinski, regaining his feet, and may God be with us this time.

21

Peterson had gone with Devlin to rejoin the 88th on the front, but she was not with the Connaught Rangers for long. Captain Goodlake, who had formed a company of sharpshooters from the Guards, heard that she had returned to the front and requested her presence in his roving band of marksmen. Peterson was known to the officer as a brilliant shot with the Minié rifle. She had been in Goodlake's sharpshooters when the Russians had attacked the Inkerman Heights less than a fortnight previously. Goodlake was pleased to get the Ranger, who was now with him and thirty of his men now patrolling the Heights.

Peterson had befriended a Coldstream Guardsman by the name of Wilkins, who admired her accuracy with the rifle. Wilkins did not know, of course, that Peterson was a woman, but he was the kind of man to whom this would have made little difference. His admiration was for the skill, not for the person behind it.

The previous day it had rained hard, and through most of the night. Dawn had seen a cessation of the downpour, but warmer air had produced thick fog and mist all over the Heights. Peterson and Wilkins were moving together, with the other sharpshooters, north-west along Careenage Ravine when they heard clinking and rattling which seemed to come from the gully ahead. Sounds were deceptive in and around the Heights however, and such noises could have come from the road to the north.

Captain Goodlake made a silent signal for the company to halt. They were used to his methods and each soldier in the company already had his rifle at the ready.

'Gun carriages?' whispered Wilkins. 'Or just ox-carts on their way into Sebastopol?'

Peterson listened carefully. 'Guns,' she said, her experience with Crossman's *peloton* serving her, 'and troops.'

At that moment a mass of grey figures emerged from the mist not fifteen yards away. At first they were phantoms moving in a formation: merely a block of human shapes with mist swirling round their dark forms. Then they began to take on features, with round pale faces and muffin-shaped hats.

It was a Russian column, filling the width of the ravine. Goodlake immediately sent a messenger off to raise the alarm in the British camps. Goodlake then realised it was time for action. He raised his hand.

When it was lowered but a moment later an enfilade of fire came from his sharpshooters. The front ranks of the Russians staggered back as men were killed and wounded.

'Lay into them, lads!' cried Goodlake, silence now unnecessary. 'Give 'em your best.'

Peterson reloaded and fired again, the ball striking an officer in the head, flinging him backwards dramatically. The sharpshooters were retreating slowly back along the ravine, with the thick mass of bristling Russians moving ponderously forward, impossible to stop due to their sheer weight of numbers.

The Russians were returning fire now, but ineffectively, hampered by their closely-packed numbers, arms and elbows getting in the way, musket stocks clattering against each other and bayonets clashing. They could not but help getting entangled and their accuracy suffered for it.

'Look for ways up the western bank, boys,' came the order from Goodlake, when they came to a slope which could be climbed. 'Find a place to scramble up.'

The sharpshooters did as they were ordered, knowing the area well. There were goat tracks they could ascend in a trice.

Suddenly, fire began to come down from the opposite bank of the ravine. Peterson peered through the mists and saw that there were many more grey columns moving on the other side of Careenage. Infantry, artillery, cavalry.

Thousands of bayonets and swords gleamed dully in the poor light. Through gaps in the mist the snouts of many brass and bronze cannons were visible. Several hundred hooves of battle steeds clattered amongst the stones. It was a chilling, sobering sight which was revealed and then disappeared as the mist drifted over the Heights, covering and uncovering the ground.

Those Russian soldiers in the gully were a small number in comparison to those great blocks of infantry on the east side of the ravine. This was no probing force. This was a major attack, with many thousands of troops and dozens of guns.

'Wilkins,' she said, after she had picked off a gunner riding on a limber, 'this is another Alma. This time it a us who are under attack.'

'I think you're right there,' said the tall, stoical guardsman. 'This is a big one.'

At that moment the Russians charged, the space in front of Peterson appearing to be a mass of shining bayonets. They came on as a solid body, not having the room to do much else in the narrow gully. There were yells and shouts from both sides as they clashed together, rifles locking with rifles.

Peterson, light-framed and not really built for close combat, was thrown backwards by the initial force of the charge. She fought to stay on her feet and somehow managed it. The impetus was with the Russians though, who crowded on, cramming their way forward in a welter of arms and legs.

182

Wilkins dragged her backwards by the collar, away from the sheaves of bayonets that prodded the air. Goodlake's soldiers were quicker on their feet, more nippy than the stolid blocks of the enemy, and they were able to dance back out of the way of the forest of points. Once again those who had reloaded amongst the sharpshooters poured a fusillade into the struggling crush of Russian grey greatcoats, forcing them to reel back and shed an outer layer of dead men like a snake sloughing its skin.

Peterson choked on the gunpowder fumes which gathered in the ravine in blue clouds. She thanked God there was no room in this part of the ravine for the Russians to bring forth one of their big guns. A blast of canister or grapeshot enfiladed down the rocky gutter of the gully would have wiped out Goodlake's sharpshooters to the last soldier.

Captain Goodlake, realising that he could do little to hold the Russians any longer, yelled for his men to retreat swiftly. He could hear picquets of other British regiments, scattered about the Heights, being fired on now, but no general alarm had gone out. The rest of the British Army had to be warned of this attack.

'Fall back in good order,' cried Goodlake. 'Fire at will as you go. Pick out the officers. Without them the Russian soldier is thrown into confusion.'

Goodlake's sharpshooters had not lost a man to the Russians. They faded back from Russian eyes like phantoms of the Inkerman ruins. The Russians must have thought they were indeed ghosts, for they were there and then gone, leaving nothing but wisps of disturbed mist in their wake. Peterson and Wilkins scrambled up a goat track and on to the ridge above.

As Peterson reached the safety of the rise, along with Goodlake's other soldiers, a man on a horse rode up.

'Who's there?' cried the rider, coming from the direction of the Lancaster battery. 'This is General Codrington!'

Captain Goodlake answered the general.

Codrington then asked, 'I heard muffled noises of movement while I was riding along Victoria Ridge. Then the sound of rifle fire. What's happening, captain? D'you know?'

'The Russians, sir, attacking in great force.'

'Damn me!' cried the general. 'I'll rouse the Light Division, captain. You try to hold 'em from up here. Don't let 'em follow you up. Anyone else aware of the attack?'

'They must be, general – the picquets are fighting hard out there in the mist – lots of isolated but desperate battles in progress over on the Heights.'

The general rode off, towards the Light Division's camp, which lay south at the crossroads along Victoria Ridge, below the Lancaster battery. From all around now came the crack and whine of rifle and musket fire. It seemed to Peterson that the whole of the Inkerman Heights were covered with Russian troops. Certainly there was great activity in the north-east, where the post road followed Quarry Ravine.

Bugles were sounding now and the crash of nearby guns punched holes in the mist. Shells and round shot began falling around the sharpshooters, as they moved back and forth, trying to find their prey in the poor visibility. Peterson recognised the bugle call of the Light Division and knew that Devlin would have been roused from his bed. The 88th Connaught Rangers were at last going to prove their worth, after being denied a chance for glory at the Battles of the Alma and Balaclava.

'They're coming up the tracks!' cried a warning voice. 'Help ho, lads. Come on! Come on!'

The small company of hand-picked men rallied quickly, the advantage with them as they fired down into the grey stocky figures climbing upwards. Peterson saw her latest quarry fling his arms wide, crumple and roll over his own fallen musket, cracking it into two pieces like a rotten stave. She reloaded and hit another full in the face from a yard's distance.

This unfortunate man's features disappeared in a swathe of

black gunpowder, like a dark rash over his pale skin. There was a sound like a trodden toad bursting under a soldier's boot, then he slid down the slope sideways.

Some of the guardsmen from the sharpshooters were using their bayonets now, employing them as spearmen might do on the ramparts of some castle, repelling an assault on their battlements. The guardsmen thrust downwards at the oncoming enemy, piercing necks, heads and shoulders. Bayonets were bending as they struck thick skulls or were caught in eye sockets. It was a grisly, horrible business, which had the bile rising to Peterson's throat. She struck out hard with the others, the long length of her Minié keeping the foe at bay.

There seemed too many of them: they were like a multitude of rats scrambling up out of drains. Brave men, to come at almost certain death in the way that they did, with brave officers leading them. One of these officers, a tall lieutenant, managed to get over the crest. He ran at Wilkins firing a pistol and waving his sword, jubilant to have a target at last.

'Look to yourself, Wilkins!' shouted Peterson in a panic.

But Captain Goodlake was there, swifter than the Russian, who had lost much energy and breath on the climb. The British officer sidestepped and struck the grey-coated lieutenant across the left shoulder with his sword. A wound gaped beneath the slit coat, forcing the Russian to drop his pistol. Then a quick thrust up into the lieutenant's underarm caused the wounded man to scream in agony as the point of Goodlake's sword found the ganglions of nerves which nestle in that region.

A startled Wilkins finished the man off with the butt of his rifle, crashing it down on the side of the officer's head. It seemed to Peterson's ears to be a merciful end to the man's agony, for he was still screaming from being stuck on three inches of Goodlake's blade.

All the while the sharpshooters were retreating, some of them stumbling backwards, hoping for relief from behind. Guns were booming all over the Heights, most of them coming from the side occupied by the Russians. A major battle was in progress now, but scattered and fought with independent units, small pockets of British soldiers were holding the swarming soldiery of the Russian columns, trying to keep them contained until the British ranks were swollen by greater numbers. All around the air hummed and sang with flying pieces of hot metal.

'Well done, my boys, well done!' cried the encouraging Goodlake. 'We pushed 'em back before and we'll do it again. Their numbers are jamming them together, working against them, so don't despair. Keep your footing. Don't fall. We'll do it yet, I guarantee.'

His bold words gave new heart to the men, who now fell back in good order, to reload their rifles and fire again at the dark shapes in the mist. Ammunition was beginning to run short. Men were borrowing from their comrades, having lost bullets from their pouches in the scramble up the cliff.

Peterson's hand was raw from ramming bullets down the barrel. Her mouth was stinging and dry, tasting of gunpowder from biting paper cartridges. Her shoulders ached and her back felt as if it would crack at any moment. There was no relief at hand though, not for the moment. They had to stand and fire, fall back, rush forward, fight and fight on. Sweat was crusted on her brow, as the dust and moisture mixed there into a cake of clay. This was the hardest fighting she had had to do yet in the whole war, and her fitness was put to the supreme test.

'I can't keep this up much longer, captain,' she called to Goodlake in despair. 'My arms are falling out of their sockets, sir.'

'I'll watch to you,' said the indomitable Wilkins, his broad face pocked with rings of dust and sweat. 'You stick by me, half-pint, and I'll carry you home if needs be.'

He almost made Peterson laugh, this big serious guardsman who seemed to toil and toil without fatigue.

'You'll watch to me all right, I'll wager on that,' she said, gathering all her reserves of strength. 'You carry me on your shoulders and I'll pick 'em off like I was on the back of a mail coach being robbed by highwaymen. You're a card, you are, Wilkins. I'll see to myself, don't you worry.'

The pair of them stood together, amongst the valiant sharpshooters, firing, loading, firing, scurrying back when the pressure became too great, rushing forward when they saw a weakness or a breach. To the oncoming Russians who came over the top of the gully they were frustrating: like snapping, snarling terriers impeding a herd of determined cattle.

23

Corporal Devlin and (despite his pleas that he was still sick) Lance-Corporal Wynter had both reported for duty with the 88th Connaught Rangers on the evening of the 4th of November. It was true that Wynter's wound had not completely healed and that he was in a great deal of discomfort, but the regiment was short of healthy men. Wynter was told that though he was not to idle away his time in hospital, he would be on light duties: work that would release a fit man to do duty at the front.

'I expect even if I walked in with no head on me shoulders, they'd have still said I was to be on duty,' he grumbled to Devlin. 'We're heroes, we are. We blew up half the Russian fleet – and see what thanks we get for it!'

'I think that's a small exaggeration. Wynter, but I know what you mean,' sympathised the Irishman.

Shortly after this conversation, Devlin had gone with a companion picquet to spend the night in a 21-gun battery.

He and his comrades employed themselves in trying to keep dry. The incessant rain ceased only in the early light, when the night picquets came back. Then the fog was so thick they could see only a few yards in front of them. Devlin attended an early morning brigade parade, which took place just before daylight, after which four companies of the 88th had gone into the sodden, waterlogged trenches to stand ankle-deep in water.

Once the picquets had been exchanged in Middle Ravine, the rest of the regiment settled down to making breakfast in the damp chesty air, with Wynter assisting the cook who was preparing food for the officers. He was trying to keep alight the miserable fire on which he was making tea, when the sound of musketry came from the hill above the 88th's camp. There followed the call of Alarm, followed quickly by Assembly.

The four companies still in the camp – the Light, the Grenadiers and two centre companies – immediately fell in. Wynter, looking along the lines, could see there were less than three hundred men present. General Buller suddenly appeared, looking as if he had been up all night. Without waiting for the rest of his brigade – the 77th and 18th Foot – he ordered the 88th to march forward in the direction of the firing.

'Christ, what are we coming on to now?' grumbled Wynter. 'Can't even have breakfast without somethin' going on.'

The regiment marched quickly in the direction of an old windmill at the end of Careenage Ravine. On the way they saw the Guards turning out and making ready to march. Some of their picquets had already engaged with a force coming up the ravine into Wellway, almost into their camp. The Guards had driven this probing force back where they came from with some keen enfilading fire down the gully.

'Come on,' said Lieutenant Riley, 'don't let the Guards beat us to the front and get all the glory!'

'They can have it, as far as I'm concerned,' muttered Wynter, 'and they can put it where the monkey puts his nuts.'

Devlin glowered at him and shook his head.

The 88th managed to beat the Guards to the ravine, when General Pennefather rode up and ordered the Rangers forward.

'Keep to the left of the road, men. The picquets of the 2nd Division are hard-pressed out there. I want you to reinforce their numbers . . .'

Just at that moment a cannonball went sailing over the heads of the 88th to land with a thump and bury itself in two feet of mud beyond them. Wynter and a number of others ducked instinctively, even though the round shot had already passed over them. After which they came under even heavier artillery fire, with shells bursting and round shot falling all around.

The Guards Brigade had now come up and took ground to the right of the 88th.

The Rangers moved forward in fours, up the slope of a hill called Home Ridge, north of the 2nd Division's camp. There they formed a battle line, which moved forward into the fog. However, the scrubland over which they were advancing was covered in bushes and dwarf trees. These obstacles impeded the line, which soon broke up into skirmishing parties.

Wynter, Devlin and their party reached a ravine known as Mikriakoff Gully, which led into Careenage Ravine, where they found part of the 2nd Division: the 41st and 47th Foot, who had attacked columns of several thousand Russians, driving the enemy back with the fire from their Miniés. The Russian general had then launched his offensive: ten thousand men were unleashed on the five hundred men of the 41st and a similar number of the 47th. The British fought back furiously at these massed, determined columns of Russians who now came stolidly forward. The 2nd Division were now lying in wait for a fresh attack on their position.

'Where are the Russians?' asked an 88th captain, eagerly. 'Have they now retreated?'

'You jest, captain,' cried the officer commanding the picquets. 'If you keep your eyes on the brow of that hill which keeps wavering through the mist, you will see about six thousand Russians come over it in a very short time.'

'The Light and number Seven companies, follow me,' said

190

the Rangers' captain, running down the slope which then rose at the bottom to sweep up to the point where the Russians were supposed to be. 'Come on, come on!'

Devlin followed the captain, and was reluctantly followed in turn by Wynter, who hated this kind of heroic fighting. To his way of thinking, revealing oneself as a target on the horizon and mocking the enemy with one's silhouette was the action of a would-be suicide. Crossman's *peloton* suited his sneaky ways much better than exposing himself to the fire of six thousand hidden Russians.

'What can we do?' he whined to Devlin. 'We're so few men against a whole Russian army!'

'Quiet back there,' called the captain. 'Keep your mind on your task.'

Suddenly, almost without warning, Wynter found himself clashing bayonets with two grim-faced Russian soldiers who had appeared out of nowhere. When he had escaped from these two and retreated several yards, Wynter turned to see that Russians were pouring down into the ravine in vast numbers. They had forced a passage between the four companies of the Rangers, who were now falling back to a distance of about a hundred and fifty yards.

A man went down with two bayonets penetrating his chest, just to the left of Wynter. Having no time to aim properly, Wynter fired his rifle from the hip and one of the two Russians folded in the middle with a groan. The other grey creature retreated, but by that time the fallen Ranger was already dead.

Then Wynter saw a sergeant-major being overwhelmed by the enemy. There were about eight or nine Russians jabbing at the figure who was lying on the ground, his arms flailing at the enemy muskets with their deadly bladed points. It was as if the unfortunate man were trying to beat away stinging bees with his hands. Again, Wynter was helpless to intervene, there being too many enemy soldiers.

'You bastards!' he yelled. 'How many does it take?'

One of the Russians looked up at the shout and fired, missing Wynter's shoulder by an inch.

Wynter saw that his own Light company was making steady progress ahead, firing into the enemy at will, along with number Seven centre company. It was number Five and the Grenadier companies which had been forced back. Wynter made a quick decision and ran forward to join the Light company again.

'Bloody game this is,' Wynter said to Devlin, breathing heavily as he fell in beside the corporal a moment later. 'We're done for this time, you mark me.'

Nevertheless Wynter kept up with his comrade as they progressed over the rugged ground, pursuing the now retreating Russians. His leg wound felt as if it were on fire and he was limping badly. Wynter exchanged fire with a member of the Russian Rifles. Both men missed and fought to reload before the other. Wynter noticed that the Russian, unlike his line infantry comrades, had one of the old Brunswick rifles. The Ranger knew from experience how difficult it was to ram the oversized bullet down the barrel of a Brunswick. It could take all a man's single-minded strength and the Russian was trying to retreat out of range at the same time as reloading.

'Got you, my lad,' cried Wynter in triumph, as he finished loading while the Russian was still struggling with his ramrod. 'Here it comes.'

Wynter coolly aimed. The Russian glanced up at the last moment and his face took on a look of dismay. The Ranger fired and the Russian swung sideways as the Minié bullet hit him in the right of his breast, spinning him off his feet. He fell to the ground and lay there, his personal war finished. Wynter went past him with barely a glance, knowing the man could not reload now, even if he were still alive and conscious.

In the meantime, Devlin had gone ahead, with over a dozen other men. The Irish regiment vanguard came to a wall about five feet high. Beyond that wall Wynter could see several columns of Russian infantry and masses of artillery. Clearly this was the main enemy force. Some of the Rangers began to climb the wall.

Wynter was horrified by what lay over the other side.

'Don't go over there!' he cried to Devlin, with alarm in his voice. 'Keep this side of the wall, you bloody daft Irishman!'

But whether Devlin was caught up in the heat of the moment, or was so determined to show his worth, Wynter never knew. All he saw was his friend vaulting the wall and running with a few others towards the foe. There was a fleeting moment when Wynter almost ran after Devlin and joined him.

At that precise second however, Wynter heard a Rangers officer yell in pain from not far away. A captain had been bayoneted in the leg and lay on the ground. As Wynter went to assist this man all thought of joining Devlin fled from his mind. There was a large knot of Russians descending on the British officer. Wynter thought the officer, who he now recognised as Captain Crosse, was all but gone. But then suddenly Crosse fired pistol shots into the mob and four of the Russians lay dead or wounded on the ground. The others peeled away warily.

One of these turned and went back again, to try to further bayonet the officer, but the captain struck out with his sword. The blade went skidding along the Russian's musket and into the infantry soldier's hands, severing several fingers. The soldier dropped his firelock with a shout of agony and then retreated, blood pouring from his stumps and down his greatcoat.

When Wynter reached him, the captain held a smoking revolver in one hand and a sword in the other. Despite his wound he looked supremely triumphant.

'That gave the beggars something to think about,' muttered Captain Crosse. 'All right, lad, I'll make it. You see to your duty.'

'Yes, sir,' said Wynter.

Wynter limped back to the wall over which Devlin had gone, and hid behind it with some other soldiers of the 88th. Musket balls were smacking into the wall, sending chips of granite flying through the air with the humming of large insects. Then came the sounds of Retire from a regiment bugle. The Light company began falling back.

Wynter agonized.

'What about them chaps who went over the wall?' he said to a nearby soldier. 'Are we just goin' to leave 'em?'

'I don't think they made it,' replied the soldier, a Private O'Leary. 'I saw Russians all on top of them, so I did. They're not coming back. They're done for.'

Wynter took one last look at the scrubland beyond the wall, now covered in small fires. He could see no sign of Devlin. Then he followed the rest of the Light company to the bottom of the ravine, and back up the slope on the other side. Like his comrades, Wynter fired his rifle as he went. Grey-coated Russians fell and slid down the wet and slippery incline opposite. Some of the 88th were hit. The fighting was scruffy and awkward, with men on both sides shooting on the move from difficult positions.

On reaching the top of the ridge, Wynter dropped his rifle and, bending over, took a look under his leg bandage. The wound was raw and sore. There was nothing he could do for the moment, except tighten the dressing. Then he took off his forage cap and wiped his sweaty face with it. When he straightened again, he saw that there was part of an artillery unit standing ready. Major Maxwell and two lieutenants of the Rangers called for men to rally and defend the guns while the gunners fired into the Russians on the other side of the ravine.

'I'm with you, sir,' cried Wynter, hobbling to assist the officer. Other men came up at the call. The Russians were coming on in even greater numbers. Wynter shot one in the thigh, then engaged with another hand-to-hand. They rolled over in the mud, striking each other with ineffective blows.

Their struggles took them under the wheels of the gun which went off with a crashing, numbing blast in Wynter's ears. Fortunately the explosion startled the soldier with whom he was grappling, as well as himself, and Wynter was able to kick his assailant off.

The Russian scrambled out on the other side of the gun wheels, only to be struck over the head by a gunner with a rammer. Other gunners, including an artillery lieutenant, were fighting the Russians with swords, sponge staves and bare fists, for all the world as if it were a bar-room brawl. The startled attackers, staggered by this furious onslaught from so few, flowed round the battling gunners like a split river taking easier channels.

'Fall back,' ordered Major Maxwell, as the Russians continued to pour up over the edge of the gorge. 'Fall back, 88th.'

Wynter left his rifle behind. He had no time to collect it. Fortunately he came across a Ranger whose head had been blown off his shoulders by a shell. Wynter took this man's ammunition pouch and Minié, joining the rest of the men in retreat. The abandoned guns soon had Russians swarming all over them in great triumph. Frustrated, the men of the 88th wanted to go back in, but now ammunition was in very short supply.

'Where can we get some more ammunition, sir?' asked Major Maxwell after riding over to General Pennefather, who was on his horse nearby. 'We are desperately short.'

'There's none to be had close by,' came the reply. 'Your four companies must stand their ground, give the Russians the bayonet, or be driven into the sea.'

On his way back, Major Maxwell met General Canrobert, the French commander-in-chief whom the British soldiers called 'Bob Can't'. He was with a number of others, some of them British liaison officers.

'What is happening, major?' asked the Frenchman. 'Where are your men?'

'To your front, sir. They are stemming the tide of Russians, but have no ammunition left.'

General Canrobert advanced to the Rangers' forward position to see for himself. There, the 88th were lying down, firing the last of their rounds into the Russians. The French general shook his head and spoke to Colonel Rose, the British chief commissioner with the French.

'Colonel Rose, tell the colonel of that regiment to post his men here, and, if they have no ammunition, let them raise their bayonets about the brushwood, to show the enemy that the passage is guarded. We will send him cartridges.'

The 88th reformed their line after the French general had gone and advanced again upon the guns. These had been abandoned by the enemy, who had more important affairs elsewhere. The ground between the guns and the spot where the Rangers had spoken with the general was covered with Russian dead and wounded. One of them fired at Wynter, missed him, but the round also passed close to a Colonel Jeffreys. Wynter bayoneted the Russian in fury.

'You nearly did for me there, you silly bastard,' he cried. 'Don't you know when it's time to lie still and quiet?'

24

Crossman and the other prisoners could hear the fighting from inside the croft which was being used as a prison. It was clear the situation was serious, for they had not been given breakfast. Indeed, their latrine facilities – two wooden pails – had not been emptied either. They were hungry, thirsty and the place stank of urine and faeces.

'Let us out,' yelled one soldier, hammering on the door. 'Give us some air – we're choking in here.'

The only oxygen they were getting was coming through the cracks around the ill-fitting door. There were no windows and the croft was fashioned of turf and stones which allowed no passage of air.

The soldier put his ear to the door and listened to some low creaking noises passing the croft.

'Either that's a tumbril or they're taking guns up to the front.'

At that moment there were explosions outside and the thumps of heavy objects hitting the ground.

'It sounds like a major assault,' said Crossman, 'and we're all out of it. Just pray we don't get a direct hit from a cannon. This place will come down on our heads with a ton of granite.'

'Cheerful bugger, ain't you, Mr Fancy Jack?' said another prisoner. 'Better you keep your trap shut, sergeant. Your stripes don't mean nothing in 'ere.'

'No, but this does, spud,' said a belligerent Johnson, showing the man a balled fist the size of a melon. 'If you don't get no respect in your voice, you're liable to have it introduced with a bunch of these.'

Crossman was not sure whether he wanted to be guarded by this member of his regiment. It made him feel weak and ineffective, like a child with a protective parent. However, it seemed churlish to reprimand the man. Instead he tried to assert his own authority.

'Whatever Johnson wishes to do or say is his own business, but let me tell you, soldier,' he said, talking to the man who had threatened his authority, 'that I am quite capable of putting a man in his place myself. If you do not believe that, then you had better step over here.'

The soldier glowered at him, but then turned his attention to the noises coming from outside the croft. It sounded as if all hell had broken loose. There were cries and shouts, rifle fire and just about every piece of ordnance seemed to be in use at that moment.

'We'll be overrun and then they'll just come in here and shoot the lot of us,' said a prisoner, gloomily.

'I think our men are made of better mettle than that,' replied Crossman. 'A stray round shot may hit us, but I have every confidence we shall hold the attack.'

There was not much else to say on the matter and they simply sat there and listened to the progress of the war. An hour later Crossman's prediction came true. One moment they were sitting silently, brooding on their misfortunes, and the next a great gaping hole had appeared in the end of the croft. One of the prisoners lay dead under a pile of rubble. A cannonball had indeed struck the croft. The men quickly scrambled through the hole out into the blessed fresh air.

Not a moment too soon, for the croft suddenly collapsed

into a heap of stones and earth. The unfortunate soldier who had been hit was now buried completely. Of the others, one seemed to have a broken arm, but the rest were whole and uninjured.

'I suggest you go off and report to your regiments,' said Crossman. 'It would seem they need all the men they can get. You never know, if you distinguish yourself, it might be taken in mitigation when you come up for trial.'

'Then again,' said a pessimist, 'we might get killed and never have no more worries at all.'

'There is that, too, but don't be faint-hearted, man, go to it with a will.'

Crossman and Johnson made their way through the falling iron to where the 88th, their ammunition replenished, were still firing on the foe. To the left of the Rangers, the French were being pinned down by superior Russian forces. The mist was still too heavy for Crossman to see over the battlefield to the right, but he could sense desperate struggles going on all over the Inkerman Heights. There seemed to be a particular furore coming from the small Kitspur Ridge to the north-east, which was crested by an abandoned sandbag battery.

Crossman found the prone form of Wynter and dropped down beside him. Looking to the front, Crossman could see dead Russians in their yellowy-grey greatcoats littering the gorge, with one or two bodies wearing British uniforms. They were mostly wearing grey greatcoats like the Russians, but a few had removed these before going into the fight, and having been killed lay like blobs of blood amongst lumpy mustard.

There were shattered bodies, without arms, legs or heads, but most of the figures showed evidence of being bayoneted or shot. Some had their innards spilling on to the ground; others were glassy-eyed and seemingly without a mark. A few were in small pieces, beyond recognition as human beings, and their parts were scattered far and wide over the battlefield.

Near to Crossman, stark against the ground, was a Russian boot with its foot still in it. The torn ankle of the boot's owner stood straight up, as if the leg had been snapped from it like a stalk of celery from its root. White bone nestled like a bloated sinister maggot in the middle of bloody flesh.

Russian muffin-shaped hats were scattered over the area, along with muskets and other pieces of equipment. It was as if a whirlwind had passed over and had scattered the men's belongings far and wide. If so, it had been a wind created by the wings of an Angel of Death, as it flew over the battlefield.

Crossman tore his gaze from the appalling scene.

'What's happening, Wynter?'

The battle-weary soldier turned his eyes on his sergeant and shook his head.

'It's been a hell of a fight, sergeant, and it's nowhere near over yet.'

'Where's Devlin?'

Wynter's expression told Crossman the worst.

'And Peterson?'

'Don't know. He went off with Goodlake's sharpshooters, in the early morning. Haven't seen him since.'

'All right, Wynter. How's your leg?'

'It'll bear up, sergeant,' said Wynter, grimacing. 'It's gone this far.'

Lieutenant Howard, looking as tired and muddy as Wynter, came over to Crossman now.

'Where have you been, sergeant?'

'In jail, sir. No time to explain why, but the place was hit and we crawled clear. Myself and Private Johnson here.'

Howard shrugged. 'We'll sort that out later. In the meantime, you two are the freshest men amongst us. We need messengers, to run up and down the lines. Because of this mist communications are almost nonexistent. You and Johnson report to General Buller. He's over there by that spur.'

'Come on then, Johnson,' said Crossman. 'Let's see if you can run as well as fight.'

'Yes, sergeant,' grinned the giant.

General Buller was with Colonel Shirley, the commander of the 88th, when Crossman and Johnson reached them.

Shirley was apprising his general of the current situation as he knew it.

'. . . the Russians have got 24- and 32-pounders on the crest of Shell Hill, sir, perhaps a hundred of them, and they have destroyed many of our guns. All those on the east of the road are gone. My own regiment is depleted and exhausted: many of them came straight from night picquet duty. The 2nd Division is somewhere out in the mist there to our right now, fighting for their lives.'

'Are their rifles serviceable, d'you know?' asked the general with a frown. 'I understand many are useless after yesterday's rain.'

'I've been told that only one rifle in seven is of any use, due to their wet barrels. And ammunition is short. There's no reserves up here on the Heights. We are having to rely on the bayonet. The 2nd Division are going in with blades still wet with blood from the last attack. Colonel Mauleverer led a particularly fierce and valiant charge with two hundred of the 30th Cambridgeshire, and a few 55th Westmoreland picquets, against four battalions of the Borodino Regiment.

'Everywhere small numbers of British soldiers are flinging themselves at solid walls of the enemy. Bunches of the 41st Welch are out there somewhere, and the 47th Lancashire along with the 48th Hertfordshire. It's hand-to-hand over on the Heights . . .'

'Yes, sergeant?' said Buller, turning to Crossman, whom he recognised as one of his spies, 'did you want me?'

Crossman was tempted, but this was not the time to speak of his problems with the major who had locked him up for murder.

'I understood you were in need of messengers, sir.'

'Ah, yes – Lieutenant Howard sent you, did he? And this splendid specimen of manhood with you?' He prodded

Johnson on the chest. 'Good, good. Well here's what I want you to do . . .'

Buller himself was a little distracted. He had been in the thick of the fighting not a short while since. With his ADC, Henry Clifford, and a clutch of 77th soldiers, he had come across a column of Russians who appeared out of the Wellway. This was the same column with which the Guards had had to deal. The shortsighted Buller had been so surprised he did not believe what was happening until Clifford cried, 'In God's name, fix bayonets and charge!' Buller quickly confirmed the order.

There were only twelve Middlesex men with Clifford, who sprang forward with Russian rifles blazing around his head. Miraculously he was not hit. He drew his sword and severed the arm of a soldier who was trying to bayonet him, then killed another with a strike to the back of the neck. Clifford's men had also thrown themselves into the fray. When the Russians finally fell back, six Middlesex men lay dead and three wounded. Fifteen Russians gave themselves up as prisoners to the remainder of the small group, which, with Clifford, now numbered four.

General Buller had seen several of the 77th die, though they went down fighting furiously, blood in their eyes, bayoneting the enemy right, left and centre. Colonel Egerton then led the rest of the 77th forward when he came across two Tomsk battalions. The colonel immediately ordered a volley, and over two hundred and fifty Minié rifles crashed out along the line of grey-coated British soldiers. Minié bullets penetrated the Tomsk tightly-packed battalions to a depth of four men. The dying landed on the dead. The volley was then followed up by a glorious charge, with the 77th yelling their fury at the round white faces milling in front of them.

Just to the left of Egerton's Middlesex men a hundred and eighty-odd men of the 49th had thrown themselves at hordes of Kolivansk. Nearby the 47th were faced by three battalions of Katherineburgers, while to the right, the 30th were engaged with Kolivansk and Tomsk. Some seventeen battalions of Russians were now swarming around Home Ridge and being held by regiments of British, each numbering under three hundred men. These were men who fought as if they were defending their homes against hated bailiffs. They went in with bullet and bayonet, with pistol and sword, with boot and fist, driving swarms of Russians before them like beaters driving game.

The enemy casualties were piled high, many of them from the same bullet which had passed through two or three of their comrades, so powerful was the Minié rifle. Others had been clubbed or stabbed by the men of Middlesex, whose own bodies then added to the mounting corpses across the Heights. A forest of arms and legs protruded from a wall of dead like a grotesque sculpture carved by an artist depicting the horror of war.

The 77th, under Colonel Egerton, had pressed forward, into the heaving multitude of Russian soldiers. They forced their way through the centre of the mass, piling them into the column behind, and spilling others into side gorges. Finally, the 77th were through and under Shell Hill.

There they remained for the time being, drawing needed breath, having fought there through a tide of blood. On the way they had gathered remnants of other regiments. They met up with the 41st Welch, who had also battled and carved a path to Shell Hill with bits and pieces of other regiments.

Among those bits and pieces was a small-statured soldier whose accurate firing had done great service. She was a sharpshooter, a lance-corporal who had been with Goodlake's men, earlier in the battle. This soldier's name was Peterson, of the 88th Connaught Rangers, and her final shot of the action took a magnificent-looking Russian officer out of his saddle, as that unlucky man was falling back with his defeated battalions.

Peterson did not know it, but the man she had killed was General Soimonoff, one of the three top Russian commanders.

25

Crossman and Johnson, striding along the post road, carried a message for General Pennefather. General Buller had sent them out as a pair so that, if they had to go into the thick of the battle, they could watch each other's backs. Both men were now armed with Miniés and they were itching to use them.

Even the post road, behind the lines, was hazardous to negotiate. There was a storm of shell and shot falling from the enemy artillery, which whistled, blasted and thumped around them. Crossman could see allied guns that had been knocked out, lying like broken toys by the road on their backs or sides, some with their wheels spinning. There were bodies and parts of bodies too. A horse had been shot through the head by its rider after it had been broken in two by a round shot.

As the two men passed Home Ridge they saw a great grey tide of Russians flowing towards that very spot, ready to spill over and swamp it. Just then, a battery of three guns arrived. With little ceremony, the gunners proceeded to blast General Soimonoff's oncoming troops with canister – metal containers filled with musket balls – which cut great swathes in their columns. The Russians went down like lanes of wheat in a hailstorm. This appeared to be the final blow to the now dead Soimonoff's push to overrun the Guards Camp and the 2nd Division. His troops retreated from the Saddle in vast numbers.

The cartridgeless picquets were beginning to return now, passing Crossman and Johnson in their ones and twos.

'How was it out there?' asked Johnson, of a fellow who looked about to drop from exhaustion.

The soldier turned his bloodshot eyes on to Johnson.

'It would be all right if the Miniés was not so wet that half of 'em didn't work. It would be all right if we had some cartridges in our pouches. It would be all right if there was any reserve ammunition to be had.'

With this little speech the fellow stumbled off, and Crossman pulled Johnson's sleeve.

'Come on, man, we have to deliver this message.'

The death of Soimonoff had made the Russians pause for breath. The dead general's advance from the direction of Shell Hill had failed, but there were still sixteen battalions of his troops as yet uncommitted to the battle. These were positioned on the West Jut, awaiting orders to move. It was now seven-thirty, an hour and a half since the first assault had taken place. So far sixteen thousand troops had been committed to the battle by Soimonoff and Pauloff, and these had been repulsed by less than three thousand five hundred British soldiers of the 2nd and Light Divisions.

General Dannenberg was at that moment considering his tactics. The mist was still wafting about the Heights. General Gorchakoff's battalions were spreading across the uplands to engage the French. General Dannenberg had now taken command of Soimonoff's and Pauloff's troops and with nearly a hundred guns to back them up. Twelve battalions – Okhotsk, Selenghinsk and Iakoutsk – of fresh troops were now advancing on the British. Dannenberg decided the attack should begin on a disused gun emplacement called the 'sandbag battery' which stood on the Kitspur. This, he decided, would serve as a symbol of victory to Pauloff's columns.

General Cathcart was now approaching the battle area with part of the 4th Division. General Sir George Brown, commander of the Light Division, met Cathcart on the road and they were discussing how best Cathcart's troops should be deployed when the French General, Bosquet, came riding up to them and offered the assistance of two battalions of Zouaves.

Bosquet was a seasoned campaigner from the wars in Africa. Unlike many of the British generals, he knew what he was doing. His suspicions that the Russian attack on the French line was merely a feint to keep the French occupied, while the main purpose of the assault was to force a way through the British lines, had recently settled into conviction. He realised now that the Russians were not going to attack him in force and he could therefore release several battalions to assist the beleaguered 2nd Division of the British Army.

The two British generals, both veterans of wars with the French, haughtily refused any assistance. They were not like Lord Raglan, whose vagueness still caused him to call the enemy 'the French' instead of 'the Russians', thus frequently embarrassing his staff when French officers were present. They were, however, like schoolboys who would rather lose a house cricket match than use members of another house. Except that this was no cricket match, and they were playing with the lives of honest farm boys, who trusted their generals to do what was best to help win the battle, not sit on their hands out of pride.

*

Unable to find General Pennefather up near the road, Crossman and Johnson went out on to the battlefield where they were told he would be. They ran past the Guards on their way to the front. The Scots Fusiliers, the Coldstream and the Grenadiers looked as magnificent as ever in their tall bearskins. They would have been the envy of all the other line regiments, if they were not so arrogant, but this last trait soured their image in the eyes of many of the ordinary foot soldiers.

The air was zipping and whining with musket balls. Crossman saw figures skirmishing in fog amongst stunted oaks. These were men in Rifle Green. Crossman was astonished to see that some of the Rifles had been reduced to throwing rocks at the enemy, their ammunition having been depleted. Crossman guessed this was happening over the whole battlefield, where men had run out of cartridges or whose firelocks were so wet they could not be used without a thorough cleaning and drying of the works.

A group of Russian soldiers suddenly appeared in front of him and Crossman automatically aimed his Minié and fired. Johnson, a little ahead of the sergeant, gave a shout as two Russians came charging at him. He ran his bayonet through the first one, who fell to the earth with a groan. The second suddenly threw his musket away and pleaded for mercy in broken English, saying he was a Romany gypsy who had been forced to fight for the Russians, but did not sympathise with them.

'Please, sir, do not cut off my ears,' cried the soldier. 'I wish you would not cut off my ears.'

Johnson looked astonished. 'Cut off your damn ears, you silly spud? What would I do that for?'

The gypsy explained that the Russian officers told their men it was better to die than to be captured by the British, who were barbarians and capable of the worst kind of torture imaginable.

'They said you would cut off my ears and nose if I was captured. They tell everyone this.'

'Do they, the lying beggars? Well, you have no need to worry, me old spud. Get off of them knees and get you back there behind our lines, with the other prisoners. I guarantee you won't lose so much as a whisker in our hands.'

The grateful soldier then kissed Johnson's hands, much to that pragmatic man's embarrassment, then walked by Crossman, his hands in the air, calling into the mist, 'Don't shoot, please. I am a prisoner . . .'

'Why do they tell 'em such lies, sergeant?' asked Johnson.

'It's a good way to get reluctant men to fight. It's probably quite effective, when you think about it. Better the devil you know than the one you don't.

'Now look, Johnson, we'll never find General Pennefather out in this mist. We'd better go back to the road.'

At that moment the mist began to clear and Crossman found himself on Fore Ridge, immediately south-east of the Kitspur. To his right, the Guards Brigade was advancing on the sandbag battery. Round shot was bouncing all around, occasionally crushing a man or knocking an animal out of action. Already in the fight were the men of the 41st and 48th Foot, facing around four or five battalions of Okhotsk, scrambling up the slopes. Skirmisher lines were clashing and battling it out amongst the bushes.

The smell of powder and blood was in Crossman's nostrils as he went down on one knee. It was his intention to add his fire to the companies of the 41st and 48th. These indomitable troops were firing volley after volley into the Russians coming up the Kitspur, but this time the visibility was good and the Okhotsk battalions could see there were but a few British soldiers in front of them and were determined to break them.

From Fore Ridge, Crossman and Johnson, along with men of the Rifle Brigade, were able to assist the beleaguered few men on the sandbag battery, by picking off their adversaries. It was a futile effort though, for the Russians were as numerous as termites, swarming up the hill. One man here or there made little difference to their massive drive to rid the hill of British uniforms and plant their standards.

Live Russian trampled on dead Russian, clambering over the bodies, to get to the British. Time and again the regimental colours fell on that prominent place, their bearers dead, and time and again they were quickly raised, a new hand on the staff. Guns boomed from behind the two battling armies, shells and cannonballs arced over the struggling masses, forming a moving arch of iron under which the scene played.

Crossman was witnessing a great slaughter, on both sides. It seemed that here was the unstoppable force confronted by the immoveable object. Neither would, or even could, give way. The superior numbers of the Russians came on, while the stubborn British fought with steel and lead. Young officers were battling with their swords, sometimes both opponents spitting each other on the steaming blades, with no positive gain for either side. Infantrymen from both armies were discharging their hot, smoking firelocks, then charging in with bayonets flashing and throats letting out bloodcurdling cries.

Crossman wanted to deliver his message, but he could not see General Pennefather anywhere and he was trapped and locked into the battle now. Reading the scrap of paper he saw that it was a note informing the general that the Light Division had now been supplied with ammunition and could hold their position. It was not a desperate cry for help, nor an offer to give some. It was merely keeping General Pennefather informed of the situation to the left of his 2nd Division's activities.

Down to the south-east of Crossman's position, the 4th Division was coming in: the 21st, the 63rd, the 1st Rifles. The 85th Derbyshire regiment, from the 2nd Division, was also in that area. The most beleaguered regiment in that region seemed to be the 30th, who were desperately trying to stem the flood of Russians at the Barrier.

It was at this point a great cheer went up from the Russians. The Okhotsk regiment and the Sappers had taken the sandbag battery and the elements of the 2nd Division who had been in possession of the battery had been overwhelmed by the sheer weight of enemy numbers. Through the fog of war, the gunsmoke, and the confusion of blasts and explosions, Crossman had difficulty in making out who was who below him. Both armies were in grey greatcoats and niceties such as helmets or forage caps were lost in the mist and smoke.

There was one brigade he could not mistake however, and this particular force of British soldiers was coming up to the front right at this moment. The Guards! First were the Grenadiers, half-a-thousand of them, marching in formed companies with determined step towards the sandbag battery. Round shot began falling amongst the ranks of their seven companies, knocking holes in the line. From where Crossman was standing it was easy to envisage these smart tall men in bearskins, not as live human beings, but as mannequins, automatons. They went down like skittles under a hail of musket and artillery fire, the ranks closing to fill the gaps, those left standing marching resolutely on with grim hard faces.

Behind the Grenadiers was a smaller force of nearly three hundred Scots Fusilier Guards and a similar number of Coldstream Guards. In all, there were less than one thousand five hundred men. There were nine Russian battalions facing them ten times their own number. Crossman watched as the Grenadiers fired a volley into the Okhotsk holding the sandbag battery, then, with a great yell, charged forwards with levelled bayonets.

The blades glinted in the swirling, fleeing mists, their points wicked and threatening. Crossman knew it was one of the hardest things to do in battle: to stand firm against a bayonet charge. A length of sharp steel – many lengths of sharp steel – coming fast and hard at a man makes his courage turn to water in his gut. The Russians fired back, but then retreated before this gritty, resolute attack. Once one man turns, many turn with him, scrambling to be out of the way of those ugly pig-stickers, which went into bodies gleaming silver – and came out smoking red.

The Russians became like children at the seashore's edge, turning and running from the waves, catching each other with their elbows and legs, panic sweeping through them like a quick fever.

The panic did not last for long however. These Okhotsk men were no cowards. They turned and rallied, realising theirs were the greater numbers. The tall men in tall hats looked fearsome, but they were ten times their number. Once they had reformed they came back at the Guards, time and time again, the air full with the cries of the living and the dying.

Some men went down with a groan, a mere rattle in the throat, while others screamed like a factory whistle, or squealed like a farmyard animal in the slaughterhouse. The Guards were in a ragged line now, uneven and bunched in places due to the ground on which they had to fight. Some had wet cartridges and borrowed from others, loading, firing, reloading, firing, into the host of Russians who kept coming and coming, relentless and seemingly without number.

Crossman saw one particular big, bearded Scots Fusilier Guardsman standing on a boulder, his coat torn open and a bloody wound on the side of his face where he had been struck by flying metal. This man was yelling oaths at the enemy in Gaelic, firing into the mass when he could, bayoneting those Russians who tried to rush him and his comrades. He seemed to be made of granite himself, part of the boulder on which he stood, immoveable. Then finally an artillery shell burst above him, his body was flecked with red in a hundred places, and he fell backwards still cursing on to the earth, where he lay like a felled giant.

Crossman added his fire to that of the Guards, picking off men on the edge of the Russian columns. Johnson was doing

211

the same. These two were drawing fire themselves, from Russian skirmishers who kept trying to take Fore Ridge from the 41st Welch, who refused point blank to give it up.

A musket ball clipped Crossman's rifle stock, almost spinning the weapon from his hands. Johnson took a ball through his left calf, but he told Crossman it was nothing: he had suffered worse injuries on the farm.

'. . . but will they ever stop coming?' he said, as they fired yet again into the hordes of grey ghosts coming up over the ridge. 'They be as numberless as ants. You shoot one and five more rush in to fill his place. We'll be here until doomsday, I swear, still working this bloody carnage.'

26

While the battle raged on the Heights, the lieutenant who had locked Crossman up had discovered the destroyed prison croft. He reported this fact to Major Paynte, the officer who had ordered the incarceration. Major Paynte was horrified. A murderer was loose somewhere near or on the battlefield. Not just a murderer, but the killer of one of Her Majesty's commissioned officers.

After a good breakfast of quail's eggs and toast, washed down with India tea, the portly major himself went forth on his mount to seek assistance in order to recover his most valuable prisoner. He saw himself in the role of the knight errant, seeking justice for the world. There was a war on around him, but this was not his personal business. Every man had his duty and if he stuck to that duty instead of interfering with the duty of others, the whole army machine would run more smoothly. That was the philosophy of Major Paynte, who had been given sole responsibility for imprisoning and bringing to trial criminals within the Army of the East.

He went first to Brigadier-General Codrington, commander of the 1st Brigade of the Light Division, who was directing his men from beyond the Lancaster Battery. Not taking note of the fact that the general was busy fighting a campaign, the major explained to the commander what was the matter, and asked for men to help in the search for the missing sergeant and the other prisoners.

'This sergeant is of the 88th Connaught Rangers, a regiment in your own Light Division, sir.'

Codrington's eyebrows shot up in exasperation.

'Are you mad?' cried Codrington, the shell and shot falling all around the pair of them. 'There's a battle going on!'

'I can see that, sir,' replied the major, patiently, 'but this man has murdered one of our own brother officers. He must be found and brought to book. I cannot possibly do it alone, don't you know? He could be anywhere. There's every possibility that he might strike again and murder another officer, and then we would be partly to blame.'

'There are officers dying out there in their tens,' came the reply. 'I'm sure this killer of yours is not going to wait around a battlefield in the hope that one or two officers might leave it alive, so that he may do his dirty work on them. Major, please, get out of my way. The outcome of the war is in jeopardy – and you are worried about a single missing prisoner? We might all be marching to Moscow in chains this evening. Out of my way, sir. You should be in Bedlam!'

With this sharply spoken speech Codrington rode off into the thick of the battle, leaving the major fuming.

'I have my work to do,' muttered Paynte, 'just as generals have theirs.'

He looked about him as if seeking someone to arrest in place of his missing prisoner. In doing so he spied the Duke of Cambridge, seemingly remonstrating with the colonels of two French battalions. The blue uniforms of the French looked rather strange and out of place in British lines. The Duke was of course an aristocrat like himself, and would not approve of rank and file murderers of officers. Major Paynte thought he might enlist the Duke's help in obtaining men for a search.

'Sir,' he began, 'I do beg your pardon, but . . .'

214

Cambridge, relatively young for a divisional commander, silenced him with a wave of his hand.

'Do you speak French, major?' asked Cambridge. 'I do, but these fellows insist on not understanding what I say to them. Perhaps it's something to do with my accent? Would you try to explain to them that we have a gap in the line I can't fill with my Guards, even using men of General Cathcart's 4th Division. We need them to stop the Russians breaking through. Tell these officers that if the Russians do get through, their own forces will be in danger of attack from the rear.'

'I – I – I'm sorry, sir.'

The major's French had never been good. He found languages difficult. He could get by in German, but though he had lived in Paris for three years as a student, he could not communicate in the French language with any success. Cambridge glared at him as if he were a pile of dung in the middle of a parade ground.

Paynte slunk away, before the Duke could request another duty of him which he was unable to perform.

At that moment it occurred to him that he had wandered near to an artillery position and that round shot was raining down all around him. Major Paynte was not a coward – so he told himself – but he always maintained that it was not worth getting killed for nothing. To die of stupidity was a crime in his eyes. It would be really stupid, he told himself, to be blown or blasted to bits near a piece of ordnance, when he had nothing whatsoever to do with the operation of that particular battery.

With this in mind he rode away from the whistling and fizzing of shells, towards Balaclava. All the while his eyes were keenly searching the faces of the men marching up to the front, seeking his lost prisoner. His temper was now such that when he found this Sergeant Crossman, he was likely to shoot him dead himself, without waiting for a trial and firing squad to do the work. An escaped prisoner was after all fair game. If such villains did not want to be shot, they should not escape in the first place.

Not long after these thoughts passed through his mind, and all the time putting the din of cannonade behind him, Major Paynte saw the wife of a quartermaster riding by. It was Mrs Durham, a delightful lady, who enjoyed the breath of battle as much as any man might. Paynte was gratified when Mrs Durham waved to him. He rode over to where she had halted her horse. There he saluted her, smartly.

'G'day to you, ma'am.'

'Why, Major Paynte, what are you doing riding away from the battle area? I myself am just on my way to see what is happening to our boys. Do they need any medical assistance, do you know? What are our casualties thus far?'

Major Paynte felt that his courage was being impugned here and he was called upon to defend himself.

'Ma'am, I am about very important business. You know I am responsible to Lord Raglan himself for all miscreants in the Army of the East. It is my job to see that none escape and all are brought to trial. I'm afraid some have done just that, under the guidance of one particular rogue, and I must find them.'

'Oh, *very* important business, major. You have just come from the front?'

'I was under fire not five minutes ago. Even such a place as the battlefield is not out of my limits when searching for my charges. I am not particular when it comes to my duty and will brave what I must.'

Mrs Durham's mouth twitched at the corners.

'I am sure you are courage itself, Major Paynte. Tell me, how does it go with our fine fellows? Are they showing the Russians their mettle? It sounds very exciting. I have been hearing the clash and clatter of war since dawn.'

Major Paynte felt that here he could regain some of the status he had lost over the few minutes previously. He was informed, he told her, *well* informed, that the Guards had made some magnificent bayonet charges, the 2nd Division were holding the Heights despite great numbers of the enemy, and other regiments and companies were doing their duty to stem the assault by Prince Menshikoffs troops.

'Unfortunately, our men are short of ammunition,' said the major. 'There is not enough at the front and little can be transported to them. Shortage of pack animals I understand, though we are making do and mending.'

Lavinia Durham frowned on hearing this statement.

'There is never enough of anything on this particular expedition,' she said. 'Not enough clothes to keep the men warm, not enough accommodation, not enough bandages, or candles, or blankets. We did not have enough pack animals on arrival in the Crimea because there were not enough ships to transport them from Varna . . .'

Major Paynte knew that Mrs Durham was recalling that the ships were so crammed with men, standing nose to nose with no place to lie down, that the pack animals and many horses had to be left behind at Varna in Bulgaria. Four thousand pack animals and horses had been left to starve to death after the fleet had sailed. It had grieved many in the Army of the East, but not the least Mrs Durham, who loved horses to distraction.

'True, true, I know not where the fault lies.'

Ambulances had been left behind too, and waggons which might have been pulled by men, if not by animals.

'I'm sure the fault lies *somewhere*, major, but it would be unwise of a man of your rank to state its source.'

'It is true the word of a major carries little weight on a campaign where generals are common currency.'

'Weights,' murmured Mrs Durham, with a glazed look in her eye. 'There's another thing they were short of at Varna.'

Again, the major knew that this was a delicate area with Mrs Durham. He was not doing very well at all in his choice of subjects. He knew she was now recalling the fact that the ground had been so hard they could not bury the victims of the dysentery, cholera and heat exhaustion which had carried off many soldiers. Instead, they had weighted the feet of the corpses and thrown them into the sea.

Only there had not been enough weights to sink the bodies, so that when they became decomposed and filled with foul gas, they floated to the top and bobbed head-and-shoulders above the surface of Varna harbour, staring at the activities of the living. Hundreds of ghastly faces, floating about the ships, watching their live comrades board the vessels to sail to the Crimea. It had been a gruesome business.

'Well, ma'am, I must be about my duty,' said the major. 'I have to catch this rogue Crossman, wherever he might be.'

Mrs Durham's head came up sharply. 'Crossman?'

'An unmitigated scoundrel, Mrs Durham. A sergeant in the Connaught Rangers, that Irish regiment which produces rogues by the dozen. You would be well advised to keep a wary eye about you this morning, for the fellow is on the loose.'

'What's he supposed to have done?' asked Mrs Durham, tight-mouthed.

Alas for Major Paynte, he took the narrow lips to mean that Mrs Durham disapproved of such villains so much she had difficulty in controlling her emotions.

'Why, the fellow is very dangerous – a murderer. He killed a commissioned officer, out in the hills somewhere. He'll hang before too long, or my name is not Paynte.'

'Nonsense,' hissed the lady before him, her expression one of fury. 'What utter nonsense. Who told you this drivel?'

'What?' exclaimed the major, reining back his mount from this volcanic outburst. 'What is nonsense?'

'That Sergeant Crossman could murder someone, especially an officer in his own army. I know the man personally, major. He is a gentleman from a fine family . . .'

'Or so he pretends to be.'

'He *is*, major, believe me. I know the family. We are all very well acquainted, I can assure you.'

218

Major Paynte did not want to go into the business of discussing what a gentleman was doing in the ranks. Instead he looked upon Mrs Durham in great misery. It seemed that everything he said to this lady put him in a bad light. He so wanted to appear in a good one.

'I am simply doing my duty, ma'am. The evidence is all against this Sergeant Crossman.'

'Then I suggest you look at the evidence more closely, major, for I am certain he is innocent of any such crime as murder. Sergeant Crossman is not a common criminal. He is a man of honour.'

With that, Mrs Durham spurred her horse forward, riding towards the front.

'Damn me,' murmured the major, wiping his brow with a kerchief. 'Damn me.'

27

During the time that Major Paynte was frantically riding around the countryside, trying to drum up support for his search for prisoners, Crossman managed to deliver his message to General Pennefather. Thereafter he was free to join the battle where he wished. He and Johnson were on the ridge when they saw the only British regiment not wearing grey greatcoats preparing to move against the Russian Selenghinsk regiment.

The 4th Division's 68th Durham Light Infantry were in their red coatees, a splash of colour amongst the dull grey masses on both sides. Crossman raced to join this line, but was waved away by an officer of the 46th South Devon, who saw that he was a Ranger.

'Go and find your own regiment, sergeant,' said the officer, imperiously. 'This is not your line.'

'Sir, there are loose soldiers everywhere, joining with regiments not their own.'

But the 4th Division had just come up to the front line and did not know of the morning's history. This particular officer was fanatically patriotic about the 46th and insisted on its purity. He wanted no outsiders sharing the glory with his men, who were, of course, the best in the army. To his chagrin, however, some 20th East Devon had joined the line while his attention had been on Crossman. There those Devon men stayed and went on down into the battle.

Ahead of Crossman, the Guards were still engaged with the Okhotsk, but they certainly would not approve of an outsider coming into their ranks. At that moment an officer of the Grenadiers leapt over the sandbags, calling for men to follow him in a charge. Several Guardsmen heeded his call and joined the officer, who was almost immediately swamped by Russians. The officer fired his pistol into the face of a Russian soldier, but was in danger of being bayoneted from behind, when a Grenadier private killed the attacker before the officer could be stabbed.

A terrible mêlée then ensued, with several Guardsmen bayoneting enemy soldiers and being bayoneted by others in turn. Fists and boots were flying, as well as blades and bullets. It was a scrap the like of which Crossman had not seen before, and miraculously, several bearskins came out from within this struggling mass alive. There were wounds among them, where bayonets had penetrated their greatcoats, but generally they seemed grimly satisfied with their efforts.

Coming from the Guards' left, a company of the 95th now charged in support of the Guards, even when one of their officers called them back, they continued to lay into the enemy.

Crossman's attention then went back to the 68th and 46th, and he saw that they had progressed to the right of the Guards and were pursuing a running enemy through the bush. The problem with this was that their line was breaking up badly. This put the two regiments in grave danger. Crossman would not have apologised for the fact that he was relieved he was not with them. He saw remnants of them down in the valley beyond, where they were hard-pressed from all sides, their advantage gone.

*

Wynter, still lying with the 88th, firing out towards Shell Hill, heard a regimental cheer to his right. He turned to see the 63rd West Suffolk and a Scottish regiment, the 21st Fusiliers, hurling themselves into the fray. Then he saw a sight which caused him to say to a corporal. 'Well, look who's here – the frogs have arrived at last!'

The corporal looked to his left just as the shrill high notes of French bugles rent the air with the tune *Père Casquette*. The blue-coated *6ième de Ligne* and the *7ième Léger*, led by General Bourbaki, descended on the Russians. The French did not like to go into battle unless supported by artillery. These men were young and inexperienced, and though British and French officers had cajoled and threatened them, they had not marched forward until a French general had arrived to lead them. But now here they were, with all their colour and verve, to the relief of those beleaguered British soldiers still out in the field.

All except xenophobes like Lance-Corporal Wynter of course.

'What did they have to come and spoil everythin' for?' growled the Essex farm labourer. 'We was doin' all right without them here.'

'They must have been asked for by Lord Raglan,' replied the corporal in defence of the French. 'Otherwise they wouldn't be here.'

'That's no bloody recommendation,' answered the impudent Wynter, 'seeing as how his lordship hasn't done much which gets my vote of confidence in this war.'

He watched in distaste as the French charged the Okhotsk's right flank, driving them forward with bayonet and ball, herding the Russians back down into St Clements Ravine like panicking cattle. With sourness in his heart, Wynter continued to pick off Russians, only huddling down when artillery opened up on his particular position, convinced the enemy gunners were out to get him and him alone. Wynter's war was a very personal affair, between him and those out to destroy him, and his every successful shot at them gave him great satisfaction.

Immediately to Wynter's right there were others who had done nothing to earn his distaste, but got it anyway. The Rifles in their dark green were sweeping forwards, driving into the Russian Iakoutsk regiment, which now retreated towards Quarry Ravine. Some of the 88th were asking their officers to lead them in a charge, but Wynter was glad to see this did not reach fruition. He felt the Rangers had done their bit earlier, when they had been out there with uselessly wet rifles and very little ammunition, almost without support

Down at the barrier, the 30th had repulsed the Borodino regiment, only to have before them now four battalions of the Iakoutsk. The 30th were so depleted by their efforts they had to fall back, firing, to safer ground.

Then up over Fore Ridge to plug a gap in the line came the left wing of the 20th, accompanied by the 57th. The 4th Division carried no Miniés, but were still armed with the Brown Bess muskets. These had neither the range nor penetration of the new rifles. Thus regiments like the 20th and 57th were having to fight on Russian terms, but without the backing of Russian numbers. They did it with such fierce pride and determination, underlined with the strange and bloodcurdling 'Minden yell', a battle cry which issued from the throats of the 20th, they sent the Russians back down the ravine in retreat.

All over the battlefield now the British regiments appeared to be in tatters. The Russian Army paused in its deliberations. Though the cost of the last assault had been over a thousand soldiers, there were still sixteen battalions which were untouched and waiting to be thrust into the battle. Over ten thousand men of General Dannenberg's original attacking force still remained. General Gorchakoff had not yet attacked the French in earnest and had twenty-two thousand men ready for the purpose.

On the crest, facing General Dannenberg, were around three thousand scattered allied troops. They were utterly battle-weary, desperately hungry and thirsty, and had very little ammunition in their pouches. It would take a miracle for them to hold out against such odds.

Added to this, the Russians also had over two hundred guns, half of them on Shell Hill, much larger and certainly more numerous than the guns which faced them from the British side. General Dannenberg sent his columns forward again, this time confident of smashing through the British at Home Ridge.

'Here they come again,' croaked Johnson, his throat sore with gunsmoke. 'Come on, sergeant.'

Crossman and Johnson joined with remnants of other regiments to hold the host of Russians back. Crossman's shoulder ached with the recoil of the hot Minié. Like Johnson, he was parched and hungry, his eyes were smarting, and his head was spinning with the noise of cannons and howitzers. Shells were bursting, round shot was falling, all seemed confusion and chaos. Yet, strangely, the situation was quite clear to him. There seemed nothing to stop the Russians overrunning the British and turning the flank of the French.

A soldier near to Crossman suddenly darted forward, into a more dangerous area of fire, and began rifling through the belt pouches of a dead comrade. There were 'travelling gentlemen' watching this battle – men who had come out from Britain to see the war – and they might be forgiven for thinking the dead were being robbed. But this soldier was merely out of ammunition, and was replenishing his own pouch with the contents of his comrade's.

No officer had ordered him to do this – privates, corporals

and sergeants were using their own initiative to rearm themselves – and initiative was something army discipline had not instilled in its men. In fact it spent its time trying to knock it out of them and turn them into controlled automatons. Fighting soldiers were like identical small pins in a machine called a battalion: they were supposed to act together in a highly disciplined, regimented fashion. And then only according to definite orders. Individual resourcefulness and initiative was discouraged, disapproved of, even punished.

Yet here at Inkerman, the British soldier had so held back the Russian Army because he had employed individual enterprise, had thought for himself, had acted on his own when it had been necessary. He took the discipline on the parade ground, he let the army try to knock all sense of individualism out of him, he even saw the sense of the battalion fighting as a single entity, a machine of many parts. But deep in the secret recesses of the heart of every British soldier is a stubborn ember, some small red coal which he never lets die, and which he fans into a blaze in times of adversity. This flame of his self-reliance can never be fully extinguished and will flare up when it is required.

'Where are our bloody generals today?' grumbled Johnson, as his large calloused right hand rammed the conical bullet down the barrel of the Minié. 'I haven't seen hair nor hide.'

Crossman knew this was not quite fair. The divisional commanders were there: General Cathcart was already dead, having disobeyed orders and led his men down into a valley where they were cut to pieces. But the high command had done little to direct operations on the battlefield. Lord Raglan was as ineffectual as he had been at Alma.

'They're coming again,' cried a soldier of the 63rd, and indeed the grey coats of the enemy covered the horizon.

Crossman and the others found themselves being pushed further and further back. Until they were level with three British guns which were still manned on Home Ridge. But even here they could not hold and though they fought

225

desperately to stem the tide of the Russian Army, the guns were soon surrounded. Some of the gunners went back with the infantry, others were killed where they stood. But two men, a private and a sergeant-major, defended their guns with swords until they were stabbed and clubbed to the ground.

Unbelievably, and to the utter relief of Crossman and the rest of the desperately tired soldiers, the Russians halted. They swarmed around these three guns and came no further. It was as if they had found some toys and wanted time to play. These engines of iron were the trophies of war and they wanted to take them home with them. Their own Czar had emphasised the importance of capturing guns when he stipulated that none of the Russian guns should fall into enemy hands.

While Crossman was reloading, a flash of colour caught his eye. A company of French Zouaves had appeared out of the bushes and had fired on the Russians around the three guns.

These Zouaves were General Bosquet's 'children of fire', in their red pantaloons, their lace collars and their blue embroidered jackets and red turbans. There were still some Algerians amongst the Zouaves, but now they were mostly European French, with a smattering of wild-spirited English and Irish. They drove into the Russians with all the élan of a swashbuckling force of men, sure of their own fighting superiority.

At that moment, Crossman envied these colourful, reckless soldiers, who had a reputation for fighting like tigers, against the heaviest odds.

'Go into 'em, go into 'em!' cried Johnson, delighted by the intervention of this small company of around sixty men. 'Plough their faces, you froggie spuds!'

Not only were the French there, but behind this tiny force came what remained of the 21st Royal North British Fusiliers and the 63rd West Suffolk. Between them they routed the Russians around the guns, driving them back off the ridge again. Unfortunately heavy artillery fire from Shell Hill began raining shot on this brave band, and they had to take cover in amongst the stunted trees and bushes of the hillside.

'Look over there,' cried a soldier on Crossman's right, as they continued to fire into the retreating mass of the Russians, 'they've gone and broke through the 55th now!'

True enough, the Russians had come up from further along their line and crashed through the weakened 55th Westmoreland troops, but Crossman was gratified to see the Russians had been too swift for their own gunners. Russian shot began to fall amongst Russian soldiers, probably not visible amongst the scrubland to their own men. Bodies and body parts flew through the air as the unfortunate Russian vanguard was hit several times.

The Russians only faltered for a few minutes however, before coming on through the British gun line. They were faced at this point by the *7ième Léger*, who fell back before the onslaught. Then the 77th arrived to bolster the French, and the two regiments marched forward, firing a fusillade, balls zipping into the enemy ranks. The Russians were still falling victim to their own gunners as they came over the ridge, and were subsequently in some confusion. They turned and retreated before the small force of resolute French and British moving towards them.

28

The respite did not last for long, and by the time Crossman, Johnson and a few other wayward soldiers had run up to join the main area of the battle, the Iakoutsk column was moving forwards again. Crossman found himself amongst the 77th East Middlesex, who were in the same 2nd Brigade of the Light Division as the 88th Connaught Rangers. Crossman almost felt he was among family, he had fought so long with strangers. Johnson had been separated from him now and was nowhere to be seen.

Crossman's mouth was gritty and dry. He had no water of his own. Another soldier could see he was suffering and offered him a drink. Crossman took the proffered water and thanked the soldier profoundly. It was as if the man had given him a share in a kingdom. Once he had taken some swallows of cool water he felt like a new man. It seemed to flow directly into his bloodstream and chase away his sluggishness.

General Pennefather was holding the 77th in reserve. In front was the *7ième Léger* with the 57th to lengthen their line. Skirmishers from the 20th were arriving just ahead of the Russian advance, having been previously left behind. The allied guns were sending shot whistling over the heads of the infantry, hoping to cause chaos and confusion amongst the Russian battalions coming up from behind.

But the Russians came on, hoping to crack the resolve of the French, who were beginning to waver.

The 77th, with Crossman in their ranks, were itching to go forwards and assist the French and the 57th, but no order came for the attack. Instead, they witnessed one of those incredible moments during a war, when a seemingly insignificant action makes a huge impact on the outcome of a battle.

A colonel of the 55th, out on the Russian flank with a tiny band of men, suddenly rushed forwards and plunged into the massed ranks of the Russian column, as if he were diving into a herd of closely-packed cattle. His men followed him – the head of one big fellow in particular could be seen above Russian shoulders – and these foolhardy but courageous soldiers punched and kicked their way across the Russian column at right angles.

This small band of men caused all sorts of confusion in the Russian ranks as they drove across the great heaving mass.

Sometimes it seemed that those few intruders could not even move their arms up from their sides, they were so tightly wedged inside the Russian column. At other times the furious 55th hacked and cut their way through, some of them falling, some of them dying. On occasions onlookers could see the butt of a rifle being swung like a woodman's axe, felling Russian soldiers who scrambled to get out of its way, but more often than not fell victim to its blunt edge. This weapon was being wielded by the big man, one of the last to enter the column.

The effect this small arrowhead of flesh-blood-and-bone had when it pierced the side of the grey enemy thousands was astonishing. Those Russians who felt the movement ripple through their ranks, but could not see what caused it, thought they were under heavy attack from another direction. They began to turn away from the swell. This ripple in turn became a wave, that flowed others off their feet, until a comber of panic rolled through the massed column.

The allies had seen what confusion this was causing in the Russian ranks and gleefully went forward to add to the upset amongst the enemy.

Now the French bugles and drums sounded the charge. The French infantry went forward, Zouaves, 20th and 49th in their ranks. They slammed against the mighty Russian column, smashing it back, driving thousands towards Quarry Ravine. What remained of the 21st and 63rd, out on the left, got up with bayonets at the ready and charged with a great cheer.

Firing was brisk and steady, zipping into the Iakoutsk ranks, felling officer and soldier, leaving bodies in a trail back to the road they had reached. The great many-legged column reeled like a drunken pachyderm, staggering back, fighting a hard rearguard action. Some Guardsmen and Rifles, gathered together remnants of a previous fight, joined with around forty men of the 21st and 63rd, to fire volleys into those diehard Russians who kept trying to regain their lost ground. In the end, the foe could not recover and left the front of the field.

'We've done it again,' said Crossman, in a reverent, sobbing whisper, for the idea was almost incredible, given the few men involved in repelling this latest huge Russian assault. 'Our boys have pushed them back again.'

There were bodies scattered over the landscape, of allied soldiers as well as Russians, and men lay groaning with horrible gaping wounds. There were soldiers without arms or legs, with missing eyes, with crushed skulls. There were men whose bodies had been punctured by a dozen or more bayonets, or had been run through several times by a sword. Horses lay kicking and screaming out in the valleys. Others were so smashed they were unrecognisable as the animals they once were.

A lone gentleman, Rupert Jarrard, walked slowly around

the edge of the battle, occasionally aiming his Colt revolver at
the brain of a dying horse and pulling the trigger. There were
others to deal with injured men, but no one to put the horses
out of their misery. He saw it as a necessary function he could
perform, being a man of the American West, who valued such
creatures highly and hated to see them in pain.

Bandsmen came forward to assist the wounded where they
could, carrying maimed men to the surgeons' tents in the
rear. There the saws and scissors were hard at work, cutting
smashed limbs from the bodies of conscious men. A hand
here, a foot there, a leg, an arm. Men were reduced to the size
of babes, a bloody knot on each corner. One or two lived,
many died. How the surgeons managed to work, amidst the
gouts of blood, the splinters of bone and the terrible ear-
piercing screams, only God and themselves understood.

The women were there too with a word of comfort, with a
trembling hand to bandage a torn or broken man. Some could
only hold a man's fingers and try to keep his soul from
wafting away by sheer persuasion of will. Others, more
practical than their sisters, strapped on splints or wrapped a
man so tightly in a blanket that he thought he was whole
again.

Some simply held the dying until they were dead: others
prayed with those who needed prayer.

Not every helper was behind the front either. A young
drummer boy, not more than ten years of age, was brewing
up some tea within easy reach of Russian musketry. A French
cantinière walked amongst the wounded on the edge of the
battlefield, administering comfort, giving out water. A 'gentleman traveller' appalled by the suffering, went about doing
what he could, finding healing skills he never knew he had
within him.

In the background, behind the British lines, where Lord
Raglan and his staff were situated, mounted officers were
trotting backwards and forwards with messages and on necessary errands. The atmosphere of life at the rear was one of

reasonable calm. Officers took their lead from their commander-in-chief, who appeared unruffled by the battle.

Some were standing around talking, discussing the battle or other subjects in quiet tones, even taking the time to read letters from home. It was as if there were a cricket match going on, which, though the fate of a nation depended upon the outcome, was nonetheless only a game.

It might have seemed that these men did not care what was happening, what might happen, but that would not have been true. They cared with every fibre of their being. The trick was not to show it, to anyone, be they enemy prisoners or friends. And especially not to their French allies.

Lord Raglan had several of his relations on his staff, and these were the last people in the world in front of whom he wanted to reveal any concern for the outcome of the war.

The British commander-in-chief was a little bothered in the next few minutes however, as round shot and shells began to rain down on his staff headquarters. General Strangways, commander of the English artillery, was astride his horse when he was struck by a shell in front of Lord Raglan. One of the general's legs went spinning through the air. Blood spurting from the stump, the silver-haired old gentleman blanched and quietly requested that someone help him from his saddle. He sat there waiting patiently for someone to come to his assistance.

While Raglan was recovering from witnessing this gruesome event, a shell burst underneath the horse being ridden by Colonel Somerset. Pieces of iron ripped open the poor creature's belly. Guts, blood and gore were sprayed over the watching staff officers. White faces were splashed with red flecks. Somerset went down with his mount, a startled look on his face, rolling away from the kicking, convulsing beast as they hit the grass together. His scabbard clattered against his spurs as he gathered himself and got back on his feet. He stared bleakly at his horse, which was now lying still on the ground before him.

Then, almost immediately, Colonel Gordon's charger was blown from under its rider, knocking down others as it fell, domino style. There was confusion and bewilderment as horses struggled to regain their feet. There was a mêlée of legs and arms. Shocked men eventually righted themselves. For a short unguarded period their faces registered their thoughts. But they very quickly became British aristocrats again, and the contents of their heads went back to being secret and unfathomable.

Colonel Somerset was amazed to find himself unhurt. Colonel Gordon too, had only minor injuries. Only the unfortunate artillery commander, now assisted away by a Colonel Ayde, was in a bad way. Ayde shook his head to the other officers out of the old man's sight, to indicate that he thought the general's wounds were mortal. General Strangways was too old to recover from such a terrible injury.

Crossman and a few others made their way down to the Barrier, deep in the heart of the battle and the apex of the defence line. There a Lieutenant-Colonel Haines was holding a beleaguered little force together consisting of some 21st and 63rd with a few skirmishers from the 20th and the Rifles. Crossman joined with Lieutenant John Younghusband, a man he recognised from exercises on Chobham Common. Younghusband, who had been but an ensign in Chobham Common days, gathered about him the odd few men not from the 20th, 21st or 63rd.

The Russians were piling on the pressure at this point, trying to outflank Haines's hard little group, but were being driven back time and time again by these unyielding men.

Crossman joined the pack, most of whom were using muskets. Crossman's Minié, and those of the few other men who had joined him, were welcome amongst the defenders at the Barrier, especially since the 21st and 63rd had but few round balls for their own weapons, having somehow been supplied with conical Minié rounds which they could not use.

'Come on, my brave boys,' said Younghusband, who was not more than nineteen years of age, 'let's take the fight to the enemy.'

With that he leapt over the Barrier and ran towards a Russian column, firing his pistol and waving his sword. After a second's hesitation, Crossman and five others joined him.

Younghusband reached the column and slashed with his sword at throat height, making the front rank of Russians instinctively lean back and drop the points of their bayonets. Then the youth stepped on the bayonets of two men, thus exposing their chests, and ran first one through, then the other. They died still trying to wrest their firelocks from under his feet.

The Russians on either side of these two unlucky souls recovered and one drove his bayonet through Younghusband's left shoulder, rendering his left arm useless. At this point Crossman reached the lieutenant's side. He blew the brains out of the soldier who had wounded Younghusband, the bullet going through two more men behind this one. Then he ran another through the abdomen with his bayonet, having to jerk and twist it to remove it from where it was lodged in his victim's backbone.

Two more British soldiers on the other side of Younghusband were using their bayonets. Then one was shot through the side of the head and fell heavily against the lieutenant, who was knocked off his feet. Younghusband fired two more rounds from his revolver from a supine position. He was rewarded with spatters of blood which flecked his greatcoat and bare face as a Russian fell on top of him. Crossman grabbed the lieutenant's collar and wrenched him clear of the Russian front line, but was not quick enough to stop another Russian bayonet from piercing the youth's lung. Lieutenant Younghusband looked up beseechingly into Crossman's face, then at the man who had killed him, before letting out a low moan and gasping his last.

The Russian soldier withdrew his bayonet and stared at Crossman for a split second. Crossman could see this square-jawed man was even younger than the youth he had killed. His eyes were round with the horror of his last action and he seemed to be trying to turn away from it. However, the thick mass of the column behind him would not allow it, and pressed him forward. Crossman snatched up Younghusband's sword, still running with blood from its last two victims, when a shot from behind passed so close to his cheek he felt the heat. This round went straight between the eyes of the soldier in front of him.

The boy let out a surprised yell, as if he had been stung by a bee, touched the hole in his forehead, then dropped away under the legs of his oncoming comrades, felling three of them like skittles. These were lucky fellows, for Crossman saw that he was now alone and went berserk, laying about him with Younghusband's sword like a madman. It was pure survival instinct mixed with fear and panic. All his soldierly training had been chased away by the sight of that creamy-topped grey sea of uniforms surging forward, ready to drown him.

Crossman flayed them, rather than struck them, with the sharp-edged blade. They raised their muskets over their heads to stop the blows from raining down on their shoulders. The strikes were swift, with short backswings, so they did little damage except frighten the Russians with their fury. It kept them at bay long enough for Crossman's energy to run out, before he dropped back exhausted, sucking breath into his lungs with long painful gasps.

When he recovered his senses enough to see a path back, he began a swift running retreat, shots from both sides humming past his ears. Then somehow he found himself behind the Barrier again, the only survivor of that mad rush at the Russian column. The last thing he did, before a wave of men wearing British uniforms swept past him and propelled him to the rear like the backwash of a wave, was to throw Younghusband's sword point-first into a body of pale-faced Russian soldiers bent on a new assault.

Behind and to the sides of the Barrier, the French were coming into the battleground in larger numbers. More Zouaves had arrived, the *Chasseurs à Pied*, the Algerians and the *Chasseurs d'Afrique*, accompanied by what was left of the British Light Brigade. The Zouaves and Algerians immediately began a great struggle with the Selenghinsk regiment at the sandbag barrier, in which the two sides swayed back and forth. The Coldstream Guards, who admired the Zouaves, threw in their lot alongside these dash-and-verve French troops.

Some long-range guns too had finally appeared on the ridge behind the struggling infantry. Previously the 12-pounders of the Royal Artillery had been outgunned and outdistanced by Russian 32-pounder howitzers on Shell Hill. Now two 18-pounders with long barrels had been brought up from the siege line, to start worrying the Russian gunners. The two guns had had to be manhandled through the mud and clay to the ridge because there were no animals available to pull them.

(Mrs Durham, on seeing the swearing men drag the guns, pushing and heaving, all over the landscape, said, 'So we lack drayhorses now? Perhaps one day the army will be equipped to deal with any contingency, but not today – nor tomorrow I fancy – they shall ever come up short during *this* campaign!')

Once the two 18-pounders were in position they proceeded to wreak havoc amongst the Russian guns, which were crowded together on the distant hill. Their unusually long barrels gave them greater distance and accuracy over the 12-pounders on both sides.

The Russians immediately replied in kind, raining shells and shot on the position where the two guns pounded out their rhythmic message of defiance. Then some French guns, 12-pounders, arrived to support the British ordnance, and a serious artillery battle took place.

If there were two things Crossman did not like they were canister and grapeshot, especially the latter which could take off an arm or leg in the blink of an eye. A limb was lost so quickly, in the heat and confusion of the battle, that sometimes the owner was not aware it was gone. There was so much grapeshot in the air now that it was like iron hail the size of cricket balls whizzing around them.

More than once, Crossman witnessed the horrible sight of a man's arm flying off, while the owner was busy with some small necessary one-handed task. Then the slow realisation when the man sat down in stunned surprise to see that there was no left hand with which to reach inside his ammunition pouch.

Crossman had heard tales of worried, retreating men who had seen an arm somersaulting out in front of them and had felt a momentary pang of pity for the owner of that limb, only to find a little later that the wayward arm was their own.

It was not easy to cauterise a bloody stump out on the battlefield, and sometimes the soldiers walked back to the surgeons' tents themselves, to receive treatment for their ugly wounds. Others were carried back by bandsmen, many of whom were now fit only to drop from exhaustion.

'Here they come again!' cried a bearded sergeant-major. 'Give 'em your best!'

Crossman fired, loaded, fired, loaded, fired, until his hands were red with ramrodding. The gunpowder found its way into the cracks of his hands, where it stung and caused a sore rawness to further irritate him. The sweat ran into his eyes, carrying with it the dust and grit of ridge and ravine. It clotted his nostrils and matted his hair. All this discomfort was only noticed during the brief lulls in the fighting, then, when the Russians came on again, it was forgotten, or at most was an annoyance which he could have well done without.

Two more companies, albeit undermanned and well short of two hundred men, joined those at the Barrier to face the Russian thousands. One of the 77th and one of the 49th. These were welcome new faces, some of them from well behind the lines and fresh to the battle.

'Come on in and join the party,' growled a soldier who had been fighting now for over four hours on an empty stomach and very little sleep, 'we're having a fine old dance here with Mrs Russe!'

'Thank 'ee,' replied one of the fresh faces, 'but I think I left my dancin' shoes at home.'

'You won't need 'em. We're all jigging along fine in our hobnail boots.'

29

Sergeant Crossman had seen a lot of action in his time in the Crimea, but nothing compared with this day, the 5th of November, 1854. He had been fighting now for nearly four hours and his joints felt as if they had been lubricated with sand. And this was only two-thirds of the time some soldiers had been on the battlefield.

He could see men falling to the ground from exhaustion. Others wandering around without a weapon in their hands, numb to the noise of danger and death around them, bemused and beaten by fatigue. Still others dead on their feet, but mechanically loading their rifles, firing at an immediate enemy, which was also weary and close to collapse.

'Here they come again!' came the eternal cry, as the Iakoutsk and Okhotsk formed another attack.

Those British soldiers without a rifle or musket picked up rocks and hurled them at the Russians, who were sometimes so near they could have tweaked each other's noses. Bayonets were used as daggers, sometimes thrown in desperation. Anything which could be employed as a weapon of war was snatched up and either wielded or cast. The lucky ones, those still with a firelock in their hands, clubbed, bayoneted and shot those who tried to get over the Barrier and overwhelm its occupants.

In other parts of the battlefield, British soldiers were wandering around, making up their own lines from what remained of the assorted regiments. There were men without officers and officers without men, sometimes seeking each other, sometimes simply going it alone. Wounded soldiers unable to walk and left on their own were being bayoneted to death by angry or frightened Russians. Some men, hale and whole, hid in bushes trembling with battle fatigue, shocked into a state of bewilderment, or frightened beyond the reach of any call to duty.

Several British generals were already dead: commanders of divisions or brigades.

Crossman was dispirited, both with the fighting and with himself. He knew he had not overly distinguished himself in this battle. He had fought well and hard, but had done nothing extraordinary, like some men. There were those who had risked certain death to save a fallen officer or friend; those who had followed or led where others dared not go; those who had made foolhardy but immensely courageous charges. Crossman had done none of these things, but simply fought steadily. He realised he was not a man to win great medals in a battle.

It must be my selfishness, he thought. *I'm a selfish man.*

But if Lovelace had been there he would have told Crossman there were tasks for the many and tasks for the few. And even tasks for the individual. Crossman was one of those men who worked best on his own or with a small group. He did not suit formation fighting on a large scale. He was a lone wolf.

Crossman jerked himself out of the fatigue zone into which he was slipping. Something important had happened. The two 18-pounders, the long-range field guns, had ceased to fire from the ridge behind. Shell Hill was now no longer under attack from the British guns, and in the distance the Russian

240

gunners were going back to work with zeal. Now that they were not being bombarded, they worked enthusiastically to resume their own barrage.

'What's happened, sir?' Crossman asked a nearby captain. 'Our guns have stopped.'

'Out of ammunition is my guess,' said the officer. 'Lieutenant-Colonel Haines believes we must take Shell Hill ourselves.'

It seemed like work for a group of suicides.

There were still some fourteen thousand Russians facing them, albeit many of them battle-weary and dispirited. Yet another twenty-two thousand Russians were at this moment facing the French, but were reasonably fresh and could easily be turned towards the British. The sixteen Susdal, Uglitz, Vladimir and Bourtirsk battalions had still not been used and were as bright as a new day.

The French had sent some reinforcements to the British, but the majority of the French Army was still waiting for those Russian columns poised to attack its own lines.

Crossman said, 'We'll never make it, sir. Some of the men are without weapons.'

But Crossman had spoken too soon. One of those enterprising NCOs whom Crossman had earlier been admiring, had found a solution to the lack of weapons. A sergeant of the 21st with some other soldiers had just been over the Barrier. They had returned with Russian muskets and had cut ammunition pouches from the enemy dead. Now at least most of the soldiers behind the Barrier had a firelock.

Crossman's heart sank in dismay as he thought of crossing that wasteland to reach Shell Hill. Yet he knew the officer probably felt the same. Not a man there would believe that after surviving the morning's holocaust they were not about to die. But Crossman could see that the attack had to take place. It had to be attempted, even if it cost them all their lives. The guns on Shell Hill must be silenced somehow.

'I want all the men with Miniés to follow me,' cried the

241

officer, speaking firmly. 'Our orders are to harass the gunners on Shell Hill as much as possible. We will advance in skirmishing order using the bushes and trees as cover where possible. Those with smoothbore muskets will remain to man the Barrier.'

Those with Miniés! No time now for the scared ones to throw the weapon away, or exchange it for a musket. The sorting had already begun, men moving back and forth, until there was a small group with Miniés, of which Crossman was one. A similar band was being formed amongst the nearby 77th. It seemed the two groups were to attack Shell Hill separately.

Crossman felt a tap on his shoulder and turned to see a grinning Peterson behind him.

'Together again at last, sergeant. How are you? Have you been hit at all?'

Despite his failing spirit, Crossman smiled at the woman who shamed him with her strength of character.

'No – you?'

'A scratch on the shoulder – and some bully struck me on the head with the stock of his firelock. I was out of the fight for a while, but at least I didn't get bayoneted.'

'What do you think of this?' Crossman indicated the ground ahead, where they were to go next.

Peterson licked her lips, and for the first time showed apprehension in her pale face.

'I'm worried, sergeant. Aren't you?'

'Bloody terrified,' laughed Crossman, almost hysterically. 'Right now I wish I'd stayed with Wynter. He's tucked away with the 88th behind some nice cosy mound, where he can pick off Russians at a distance.'

'Trust Wynter.'

'Right,' said the officer, grabbing their attention once more, 'for those of you not from my regiment, I am Captain Astley. I shall lead you across that stretch of dirt, if you will follow me. I have witnessed your bravery over the last six hours, and I tell you that among the tears of sadness for the fallen there will be fierce tears of pride.

'You men are a credit to your regiments, to your country and to your Queen. I am proud to be called a man amongst you. I do not care what you once were. Even though you were perhaps ditch-diggers or rat-catchers, you are now great warriors. I shall shake your hand after this day and feel honoured to do so. I ask that you will follow me, one more time.

'Lieutenant Acton will be leading his 77th on our left, so make sure you don't mistake them for Russians. I am ready, if you are.'

With that the captain walked off into the brushwood, towards Shell Hill. The men themselves hesitated. Then Crossman and Peterson went out, followed by the rest of them, dodging amongst the bushes and stunted trees, working their way through the scrub. Every so often one of the men, including Crossman, would go down on one knee and fire a shot at the gunners on the hill. Sometimes they would be rewarded by the sight of a man flinging his arms into the air, or slipping down out of sight like a creature suddenly robbed of its bones.

Astley's men drew fire from the Russian infantry, who poured fusillade after fusillade into the bushes. Musket balls zipped into the foliage, clipping leaves, snicking bark. Sometimes the air around Crossman seemed so thick with metal it was like trying to dodge drops of water in a rain shower. Somehow he and Peterson survived where others fell. Then Peterson went down, crashing hard on to the rocky ground.

Crossman knelt beside her. 'Are you hit?' he cried, wildly, as the air still whined and sang around him, sizzling with its deadly insects.

'No, sergeant. I tripped over a body. I'm all right.'

Crossman looked back and saw the corpse, lying on its back, staring sightlessly at the sky. It was a man in an English civilian's brown shooting suit and brown leather shooting boots. The suit was obviously Savile Row and of the kind an aristocrat might wear at a shooting party on some estate or other. In the man's hand was a British officer's sword, held in a death-grip. Someone had gruesomely tried to cut part of the hand away, possibly to take the sword for a trophy, but had probably been interrupted, for three fingers still remained tightly locked around the hilt.

With a sudden jolt, Crossman recognised the face of the dead man. It was Lieutenant Dalton-James. He had at least seven wounds in him, most of them appeared to have been caused by bayonets. He had obviously got up and dressed for a walk in his civilian clothes, as many off-duty officers did, and had had no time to change when called to the battle.

'Good God,' whispered Crossman. 'Brave fellow.'

It was always so different when one of those lumps of flesh lying on the battlefield was someone known to you. This was not an anonymous dead body. This was Dalton-James. Crossman had never liked the man, but he knew him. This fact alone was enough to make him reel, and send concerns for his own mortality rushing through his brain. Then Peterson spoke to him.

'What is it, sergeant?'

'Nothing,' replied Crossman, licking the salt from his upper lip. 'Come on, Peterson. Get up. We have work to do.'

She climbed to her feet without looking back at the body, of which there were many covering the ground. Crossman wondered whether to call her attention to their former superior, but decided against it. She was a hard little woman, packed with sinewy strength, but there was a sentimental streak running through Peterson which she was best without when the situation was still so fraught. Soldiers were dying like cattle, and any lapse of concentration might be fatal.

Bullets still pocked the dust around them. Round shot and shell still hissed over their heads. There was nothing to do but go on towards Captain Astley's beckoning hand. Together they went forward again, through the blizzard of metal, until they reached a point near to Shell Hill where they crouched in the middle of some knee-high boulders.

It was from here that Captain Astley indicated that his men should find cover from which to harass the Russian gunners.

They set themselves down behind this stone barrier and continued to pick off the gunners above them. From behind came some support. There were men in green coming up. The Rifles had sent a few of their number to help the two groups.

Crossman looked across and back at Lieutenant Acton's group, which seemed a little more tardy. There was some trouble there. Acton was on his feet, walking forwards, but his men had stopped, had frozen in the advance. Then finally a private ran out shouting, 'Sir, I'll stand by you.' Then another man joined these two, and finally the rest of the group stirred themselves and went forward. It was yet another example of the kind of courage which had continually emerged from soldiers of all ranks, thus saving a day which should have been lost at dawn.

Incredibly, Lieutenant Acton was urging his men to actually attack Shell Hill, not just harass it with fire from below. Acton's men fanned out in attack formation. The Russian gunners used canister on them, cutting a hole in the line with a swathe of bunched musket balls. Men fell to the ground groaning, hit in a dozen places. Others did not even sigh as they went down, but simply came apart where they stood, cut to pieces.

The case shot did not stop Acton's men however, and Astley now called for his own group to support them. The Rifles came up and joined what was now close to three hundred men storming Shell Hill. At that moment, to Crossman's immense relief, the British 18-pounders opened up again, presumably replenished with ammunition. Shot began falling amongst the Russian gunners above.

The gunners on the hill had had enough. They were being bludgeoned to the ground by the long-range 18-pounders.

They began to limber up, fearful that the infantry coming up the slope would capture their guns. Acton's men were on top first, and when Astley's party reached there too, with Crossman and Peterson still amongst them, they found the guns gone.

Those who had possession of Shell Hill were joined by a few 21st, and from there they had a view over the battlefield.

Despite being ready for such a sight, Crossman was appalled by the carnage. There were not hundreds, but thousands of bodies and parts of bodies lying over the Heights. It was as if a cloud had opened up and rained bloody lumps of flesh. Some of these lumps were still moving, crying out, crawling for . . . they knew not where. There were blind men stumbling around, falling over the remains of their friends. There were dying men looking for their own limbs, in order to be buried whole. There were men whole in physical form, yet dead in their minds forever.

There were also dark shapes, larger than the corpses of men: these were pack animals and horses, many smashed beyond recognition. Here and there were more signs of destruction: a ground pitted and marked by cannonballs; shattered limbers and waggons; equipment and weapons scattered over the area as if by a whirlwind.

'I feel sick,' said Peterson, staring out over the ground clotted with corpses.

'Go ahead and be sick if you wish, Peterson. I don't think there's a man here who would not understand.'

She stood for a moment, pale and lined, before saying, 'I would be, if it was all over, but it isn't.'

This was true. There were still the Russian columns gathered ominously in their great oblongs. There was still a gritty, resistant British line, narrow as a ribbon, but looking determined to hold fast. There was still the depleted British cavalry, anxious to be seen doing their part. There were still the blue ranks of the French, peppered with their more colourful units of infantry and cavalry. Over all this, the blue hazy smoke of war drifted, obscuring one moment, revealing the next.

Guns still pounded from ridge and hill. Rifle and musket fire still clattered out. Men were still dying, losing feet and hands to shot, losing their heads, being ripped to shreds by grapeshot and canister, losing one limb, or two at once.

'It seems as if this day will never end,' Peterson said. 'Will it ever end, sergeant?'

'I'm more worried about the next few minutes, rather than the end of the day,' replied Crossman. 'We're over a thousand yards from assistance of any kind. A mere three hundred, stuck out here in the middle of it all, with thousands of Russian soldiers just a stone's throw away. If one of those Russian columns comes for us now, we do not stand a chance.'

30

A British battalion was made up of eight companies, each of approximately one hundred men, though often as few as sixty. Up there on Shell Hill were the equivalent of *three* companies, each consisting of bits and pieces of several regiments, and even some lone individuals. They had not trained to fight together, had not built up that trust in each other which is essential to the line soldier, they did not know each other's names. They were strangers in a strange place, and just *one* enemy battalion outnumbered them by over three to one.

Mere yards away stood sixteen fresh battalions of Vladimir, Uglitz, Bourtirsk and Susdal regiments.

There were cannons everywhere which could pound them to a pulp in minutes.

Up there on the hill, with the smoke from a hundred Russian guns still hanging in the air above them, Crossman, Peterson and the others waited for the inevitable.

The inevitable proved not to be so. Incredibly, the Russian commander-in-chief, General Dannenberg, finally gave up hope of conquering the Inkerman Heights. His men had fought bravely, the casualties were high, yet his precious guns were still safe in his own hands. He decided to cut his losses.

He began at that moment to withdraw his guns and troops from the Heights.

'They're leaving!' cried Peterson, her voice choked with emotion. 'I can't believe it. They're going.'

The soldier next to her, who had been standing grim and defiant, every inch the unyielding man, suddenly broke down and fell to his knees sobbing. Others collapsed, or simply sat on the ground. Their bodies had been held rigid with determination only, and now that fortitude was no longer required, the framework which had held them tall and steady was gone. They wilted like flowers robbed of bamboo supports, their feelings now strong and terrible.

As they watched however, one Russian commander decided to ignore or disobey the order to retreat. The Vladimir regiment alone suddenly began marching forward, bristling like a porcupine with unblooded bayonets. Perhaps because they had been standing idle for the whole battle, their commander was frustrated and wanted to make his mark on the day. Or perhaps he had misunderstood the message from his superior. Whatever the cause, this regiment seemed prepared to fight on.

They had been seen by the British guns, who now trained their sights on this column alone and began to blow it to pieces. It was a sickening sight, watching shells burst about men's heads, turning them from solid beings into flying bits of rag-covered jelly. Great holes began to appear in the column and the piercing screams of the dying penetrated deep into the ears of those on Shell Hill with a chilling horror. Arms and legs, parts of torsos, whole heads, went spinning through the air, striking the uniforms and faces of the soldiers who marched stolidly on. Finally, the Vladimir commander saw that he was committing his men to a slaughter, and turned them back towards Sebastopol.

*

The aftermath of a battle is in some ways more dispiriting than the battle itself. It is like some sort of purgatory. An unnatural silence, punctuated by the final horrific shrieks of dying men, settles over the land. The smoke seems to draw weight into itself and hangs heavy over the scene in a great gloomy swell, adding to the sombre mood. Those exhausted survivors out on the ridges and in the ravines, begin to wander back towards their camps. At the same time, those from the camps, especially the women, start to wander out amongst the dead and wounded. The two groups pass each other like phantoms of an underworld, neither looking at one another, nor speaking.

Crossman and Peterson walked slowly back to the camps. They passed a young drummer boy and a bugler, struggling to carry a wounded man. His face had been battered to a purple pulp by rifle butts, and he stared out between puffed slits, his tiny eyes glinting their pain at the sergeant and lance-corporal. Crossman went to help, but was waved away irritably by the drummer boy, as if the youngster felt this was a musician's responsibility and the fighting men were to keep to themselves.

'Leave them be, sergeant,' said Peterson, 'they want to do their part too.'

Dark wings fluttered over the battlefield and there was movement amongst the dead. Already the crows and other birds had begun to descend on the bodies. Women tried half-heartedly to shoo them away, but the crows always came back. Crossman reflected that once night fell there would be foxes and various other scavengers. In a few days the corpses would be crawling with maggots. There was new life in the state of death.

Just before roll call with his regiment, the 88th Light Company's colour sergeant stopped Crossman and took him aside.

'One of your men, who is it, Corporal Devlin? He be one of the dead, Sergeant Crossman. I thought you ought to know sooner, better than later. He died a brave man, with some others, who chased after the enemy over a wall, while others held back. We found him and they all heaped together. They put up a spankin' fight by the look . . .'

Crossman's heart sank. So Wynter's premonition had been right. Devlin was gone. He would miss him. The corporal had been the steady one, the mainstay of the *peloton*. There was a wife to tell too: she had accompanied her husband to the Crimea, though she had seen little of him of late. It would not be an easy task, to inform Mrs Devlin that her husband had gone. Though sometimes the women appeared to know before they were told, sensed it somehow, already feeling bereft before they knew for sure.

'Thank you, colour sergeant.'

The man nodded, sympathetically, and was about to go on his way when he suddenly reached into his pocket.

'I nearly forgot. Some mail for you. Arrived yesterday before the battle, but you could not be found.'

'Thank you again, colour sergeant.'

Crossman took the two letters. One of them he knew was from Lisette, who was in France. The other was in a handwriting he did not recognise. This had been addressed to and sent on from his old lodgings in England. It bore his civilian title: *Mr John Crossman, Esquire.* Whoever had posted it did not know Crossman was a sergeant fighting a war in the Crimea.

The style was a neat copperplate, very precise, very even. It looked somehow official, like the hand of a lawyer's clerk, or perhaps that of a debt collector? Crossman decided not to open either letter for the moment. He stuffed them in the pocket of his coatee, to read at a later time.

'Devlin's dead then?' said Peterson, in a sort of wondering way.

'I'm afraid so.'

'Well, I'm sorry for that. He was a good corporal. I liked him as well as any man.'

251

Something occurred to Crossman at this point.

'By the way, Peterson, I'm supposed to be under arrest for murder, so you'd best go on your way until I get something done about it.'

'Sergeant? I could stay with you.'

'I'd rather you did not get involved, Peterson. It will do neither of us any good. Major Lovelace will support me.'

Peterson said, 'If the major is alive.'

This was a point Crossman had not thought of. What if Lovelace were dead, and indeed General Buller? Many men had fallen, generals and majors amongst them. Without one of those two men Crossman would surely hang for the act he had been ordered to carry out. It was one of the dangers of working as an agent. When you operated in secret, you had little support.

After a little more persuasion, Peterson left him alone. Crossman decided not to go back to his usual quarters at Kadikoi for the moment. He was mentally drained and he needed to boost his energy before taking on that self-styled policeman, the major who had had him arrested. Crossman needed sleep before tackling that problem.

Someone was handing out chunks of bread and salt beef. He took some and swallowed it down with nearly two pints of water. Then he crawled under a tumbril and lay back. At first he could not sleep, so he took out the official-looking letter and opened it. It was from a man who called himself Cedric Hodgson.

The Studio,
Rye,
Sussex

Dear Sir,

Knowing, as who does not, the hopeless position of the Artist today, especially one with responsibilities, I beg you to forgive me for introducing some of my work to your notice, in this manner, unorthodox, but

252

owing to the high cost of exhibiting, the only one open to me.

These little Etchings are, of course, my own original work and the lithographs are Artist signed proofs.

I only ask twopence each, though I once received half-a-guinea each, because they are sincere works and, except in price, are in no way cheap.

Should some of them appeal to you, I should be more than grateful, because it would be an expression of an appreciation of my work, which I find my tiny price is apt to deny. I have hundreds of original etchings of places of interest and am always pleased to send on approval, so that a number of any one etching in which you are interested can be ordered and Private Greetings and envelopes can be supplied at a small extra charge.

Though you are under no obligation to even return this packet, I enclose an addressed envelope for your convenience.

Even though my work may not appeal to you, do please forgive me for having had to bother you.

> Yours most faithfully,
> Cedric Hodgson

Crossman looked in the envelope and there were some examples of the humble man's work: a print of Canterbury Cathedral, one of a boy fishing on the Thames, another of a cottage in the country. Crossman did not know whether to laugh or cry. The letter was both poignant and pathetic, yet also quite brave.

Pictures of home. It was a place that seemed so unlikely, so remote at that particular moment, it could only exist in the imagination. Yet here it was, in black-and-white, that mythical land from whence Crossman and these other soldiers had once sprung. They had left its shores and gone out into a nightmare world, where they died like flies from disease, and those who escaped cholera and dysentery were swept away by the engines of war. This was a church! This was a village guildhall! So that was what those strange buildings looked like, yew trees growing around stately granite walls, roses climbing a trellis arch next to a white gazebo. How quaint, how exotic, how foreign. Glimpses of a fabled land brought nearer by a humble artist.

'You shall have half-a-guinea for these few glimpses of home at such a point in my life,' murmured Crossman, 'if I can ever get it to you.'

Crossman woke next morning to the dull screams of men undergoing surgery. Not all of them cried out of course, but many did. There were those who preferred to die, rather than subject themselves to the saw or knife. Piles of pale amputated limbs grew like faggot heaps outside the tents and houses used by each regiment's doctor. Blood ran along trenches and in gutters, filled buckets, was thrown into pits to form small lakes.

The smell of gunsmoke still filled the air, along with the sickly smell of blood and the putrid stench of decay.

Crossman walked out to the battlefield again. He still could not quite believe the slaughter was all over. It was not of course. There was still the occasional musket shot, as some wounded but fearful Russian, hidden by foliage, was approached and put up a resistance to being found.

Two officers passed Crossman's path and he saluted them. They returned his salute perfunctorily. Their minds were on other things. Lisping in the manner of cavalry officers, who affected a certain manner of speech, they spoke of the battle. Crossman overheard a rough estimation of the casualties.

Over ten thousand Russians had been killed or wounded: a quarter of the number who had taken the field.

More than two thousand five hundred British soldiers had

also met the same fate: curiously the same percent of their total number.

French casualties were almost a thousand.

One of the officers realised they were being eavesdropped and turned angrily towards Crossman.

'Did you want thomething, tholdier? What are you looking at? Be off with you!'

Crossman despised this kind of officer, who treated common soldiers with such discourtesy and contempt.

One manner of speech deserved another. Crossman adopted an Irish brogue.

'Sorry surr, begging your honour's pardon, I thought I knew your honour from the battle yesterday. Did I not save your life at some time or another? No? Then it must have been your brother, surr, for you look just like the officer I pulled from underneath a pack o' rascally Russians. I'll be on my way, surr, and sorry to have bothered your honours.'

With that, he left them open-mouthed and incredulous at his audacity, to duck behind some waggons.

As he walked on, Crossman had a vision of white crosses, covering the Inkerman ruins, nearly fourteen thousand of them, like strong white lilies. He strolled out on to the Heights, where others walked, some looking for friends and relatives, others just feeling safe where they had trod in such fear and bloodshed the day before, finding the peaceful nature of the earth strange to the touch and hearing.

One or two officers and travelling gentlemen were painting or sketching the scene as it was, or as they remembered it from the day before. The colours were vivid, the lines stark. These were quiet, studious men, who perhaps yesterday had worn the ugly mask of war, wielded a weapon in terrible anger, but who today had shed both mask and weapon for a thoughtful, intense expression.

Their weapons now were their crayons or paints, as they tried to capture scenes they hoped would never be repeated. A pistol blazed on the canvas held by fingers which now made delicate brush strokes. A pencil was now in the same hand that had yesterday used the cutting edge of a sword.

Crossman walked out to the Barrier. There he found the corpses frozen still in poses of agony. There were three British soldiers in a huddle of Russian bodies. Two men were caught in the act of bayoneting each other and had fallen face-to-face like brothers about to kiss, their hands still grasping their weapons.

One British soldier had a grip on the epaulette of a Russian officer, whose right hand clutched dirt and grass in his slim clenched fingers. There was a pistol in the left hand of the officer, and a bayonet through his throat. Their bulging eyes still stared fiercely into each other's, their facial muscles remained twisted, frozen, revealing the strenuous and deter-mined nature of their conflict.

This tableau was only different from others in its particular poses, but there were many such pairs, sometimes forming just a small part of a group, a testament to the many various desperate hand-to-hand struggles which had taken place all over the battlefield just a few hours before.

Crossman stood and stared out over the windy Heights, seeing the sandbag battery where the Guards, worst hit of all in the casualties, had fought so valiantly, so magnificently. It looked nothing, that small piece of ground, nothing at all. And Shell Hill looked like it was just a hop and a skip away, standing there, appearing so benign: a calm hill amongst other calm hills.

Yesterday the scene of bloody war, today a picnic spot.

31

There were many stories after the battle, of good luck and of bad luck. Some men were wounded many times and survived, others fell dead at the first shot or thrust.

Crossman learned that one soldier was struck on the boot heel by a piece of metal from an exploding shell, lost his balance and tumbled over, to strike his temple on a boulder and thus terminate his life.

Another, a colonel in the 95th and a chieftain of Glencoe, was struck by a musket ball and became entangled in his stirrups. His unfortunate horse dragged the colonel along the ground while the enemy shot him several times. A young soldier ran to free him but was ordered away, it being a dangerous area. The colonel was then bayoneted by Russian soldiers, beaten senseless with rifle butts, and left for dead. He sustained twenty-one wounds in all – and lived to tell the tale over a glass of port.

There was no accounting for luck or life: it chose one man over another whatever the odds.

At first, Crossman had that post-battle depression which most soldiers experience. He was alive, but there were many who were dead, including Devlin. That elated feeling of being soaked with relief after it was all over had now gone, to be replaced by guilt, sorrow and a myriad of negative emotions. Other soldiers he saw walking around, who had been full of camaraderie yesterday, were morose and silent today.

Crossman would have given anything to smoke a chibouque full of tobacco, but his long-stemmed pipe was back at his quarters. It would be stupid to go back there, where the police major had no doubt posted a guard.

In consequence, he spent the whole day after the battle looking for Major Lovelace, and at the same time trying to avoid the police major who was after his blood. At one point he did come across Lavinia Durham, who was riding past. She saw him and a look of relief came over her pretty features.

'Alexander! I am so happy to see you. I thought you might have fallen in the action yesterday.'

'No, as you see, I am very much alive.'

'I'm glad for it, Alexander, but you must be warned! There is this quite horrid major who seems to think you capable of murder. A squat ugly creature with a permanent leering expression. He has been searching for you everywhere and is determined to catch up with you. Please be careful, Alex, for he seems bent on murder himself.'

Crossman smiled at her earnestness.

'Thank you, Lavinia. Do you know the major's name?'

'Yes, it is Paynte – Major Paynte – and he is a little fat man with a greasy upper lip.'

'I know what he looks like, I just did not know his name. He threw me in jail two days ago. Well then, have you seen Major Lovelace, my commanding officer? I need to talk to him urgently, before I see this Paynte.'

Lavinia Durham shook her head, her locks flicking coquettishly.

'No, I have not. There's another thing. Major Lovelace seems to have disappeared. He was listed amongst the missing after the battle yesterday.'

Crossman felt a jolt of panic. Lieutenant Dalton-James was dead, Major Lovelace was missing, and General Buller was nowhere to be found. He had run out of people to vouch for his innocence.

'You have gone pale, Alexander. Do you know of something I do not? It is not about poor Major Lovelace. Is he dead?'

'I certainly hope not, Lavinia, or I am a cooked goose. Where are you going to at this moment?'

'I was on my way to assist Mrs Nell Butler, whose husband is in the 95th. She is helping to care for the wounded. Oh, you should see Balaclava Hospital, Alex! It is dreadful. The wounded are overflowing into the yards. Some do not even survive the journey there from the battlefield, over those bumpy hill tracks. The jolting is often enough to kill them.'

'Are they not being put on board hospital ships, bound for Scutari?'

'Yes, and many will die on them, for they are not fit to carry pigs, those ships. And when they get there, I'm told the wards are running with rats and fleas, that there is no change of clothes for any man, and that they sleep on beds of rough sail canvas. Miss Nightingale was due to arrive at Scutari Hospital on the 5th of November, the very day of the battle, and I hope she makes a difference with her presence there.'

Crossman had been told of the filth and stench of the Scutari wards, where nothing was clean. Where unwashed bandages, still clotted with one man's blood and pus, were used on another once he died. Where open wounds festered and clumps of maggots bred in them, turning them into deep pits. Where the smell of gangrene was so strong it overpowered even the foul odour of raw sewage which flowed in the halls. Once a man entered Scutari he might as well pray for death to come quickly.

If this Miss Nightingale – a lyrical name if ever Crossman had heard one – could make a difference, then it had to be for the good. He feared, however, that she would be one of those insipid females of the upper classes who drifted about in silks and satins and could do little but offer a word of solace or two to a dying man. He had seen such women before, whose intentions were good, but whose skills, and stomach, were weak.

'I think you and Mrs Butler – and Mother Seacole – would make better nurses than this Miss Nightingale. You've seen the horrible wounds men can incur, Lavinia. I fear Miss Nightingale will be too squeamish for such work.'

'Not from what I've heard, Alex. They say she is a no-nonsense lady with firm views on the use of clean bedding and soap. I think she will transform Barrack Hospital Scutari into a proper place for the sick – or die in the attempt.'

'I hope she warrants your faith in her.'

Just at that moment there was a series of explosions just a few yards away. Some soldiers had stupidly thrown a few Russian muskets on to their bonfire to burn them, and one or two of the weapons must have still been loaded. They had gone off and musket balls were whizzing through the air. Men were running, diving and ducking.

Lavinia Durham's horse shied, and Crossman grabbed the bridle to prevent her from falling to the ground. At the same time he saw Brigadier-General Buller riding just a little way off. The general had paused to look at the pyrotechnics. Crossman fought with the horse, trying to bring it under control, while Lavinia Durham strove to stay on its back and calm it with soft words. Just then another voice spoke from behind Crossman.

'Unhand that woman, sergeant, or I shall shoot you dead where you stand!'

Crossman inclined his head to see Major Paynte astride his own horse. He was levelling a revolver at Crossman's chest and his finger was tightening on the trigger. If Crossman let go of the horse's bridle, the beast might bolt. He kept his hand firmly on the leather and told Major Paynte to go to the devil.

'What was that, sir?' screamed the major.

'I said go to blazes, you old fool. Can't you see I'm battling with a mad horse here! Get off that mount and come and help me, before the lady is hurt.'

At that moment Brigadier-General Buller came riding over, accompanied by a colonel. Buller demanded to know what was going on. The major yelled that Crossman was a murderer and that he was using the lady as a shield to prevent arrest.

Crossman by this time had calmed Mrs Durham's hunter. There were no more explosions from the nearby fire, and bystanders were now more interested in the drama surrounding the lady on the horse. Was this major her husband, discovering her in the act of an indiscretion with a common soldier? How was it that a general was involved? It was all most intriguing for the troops, and they gathered at a safe distance to watch further events.

'Major, I know this soldier personally,' said General Buller. 'It seems to me that he was assisting a lady in distress, rather than using her as a shield. We're gathering an audience here. Both of you come to my quarters and we'll investigate this thing further. Put up the pistol, major, there is no necessity for a weapon . . .'

'Sir,' interrupted Paynte, 'this man has escaped from custody once – I do not intend to let it happen again.'

'PUT UP THE PISTOL!' roared the colonel at Buller's side. 'Are you deaf, major, or simply foolish?'

Paynte winced and holstered his weapon.

Crossman took his leave of Mrs Durham and accompanied the officers on foot. Once they were in Buller's room in an old farmhouse, Paynte went into a torrent of accusations. Buller held up his hand for silence, but it was only the warning gleam in the colonel's eye which stopped the flood pouring from the major's mouth.

'Major Paynte,' said the general patiently, pacing the floor with his hands linked behind his back, 'I said I knew the sergeant personally, and I meant it. He is one of my most valued men . . .'

'Moreover,' added the colonel, 'I witnessed this man fighting yesterday at the Barrier. He was with Captain Haines and was one of Captain Astley's party who took Shell Hill. The sergeant fought like a tiger, as did most of those men, I recall. If you have something against him, major, you had better be in a position to substantiate it with firm evidence.'

Major Paynte nodded enthusiastically. 'Yes, yes. I have proof he murdered a British officer. An eyewitness.'

'What do you say to this, sergeant?' asked General Buller. 'Do you have a story?'

'Sir, it might be better that you listen to me in private, for the matter is very involved.'

Crossman said this slowly and carefully, so that General Buller would know it was spy business. Buller's expression showed that he understood. However, he waved down the inferred objection to airing it publicly.

'I do not think secrecy will serve us here, sergeant. The colonel will need to be better informed and the major cannot be silenced it seems. Go on, tell your story.'

'The officer I killed . . .'

'He admits it!' exclaimed a round-eyed Major Paynte. 'The fellow has the audacity . . .'

'Do be quiet, major,' said the colonel, 'or you really will have to leave the room.'

'The officer I killed,' repeated Crossman, 'was a Captain Charles Barker. He was at the time trying to murder myself and Lieutenant Dalton-James of the 2nd Battalion Rifle Brigade. Charles Barker was a traitor. I had been ordered by my superior officer to shoot Captain Barker on sight, but the captain saw us first and opened fire. Lieutenant Dalton-James and I managed to kill this Barker before he killed us.'

'Where did this take place?' asked Buller.

'Out in the hills, east of Mackenzies Farm.'

'So, let me get this straight. Major Lovelace ordered you to kill this Captain Charles Barker . . .'

'It's a little more complicated than that, sir, but you have the core of the matter.'

'Dalton-James and yourself carried out the act, then reported a successful fox hunt to Major Lovelace.'

'Yes, sir. Major Lovelace said he would deal with the body. I considered the whole matter behind me at that point. However, it appears the drama was witnessed by a goat boy, and this is where Major Paynte comes in. He knows where to find the boy. I am telling you all this, sir, in the sure knowledge that you already know the details.'

Crossman's heart was picking up pace here, for the brigadier-general was listening to him with an intent expression on his face. It was as if the general were hearing the story for the first time.

'I'm afraid you're wrong there, sergeant. I know nothing of the matter. If Major Lovelace had discovered a traitor, he did not tell me, probably in order to protect me and my position. Unfortunately Major Lovelace is missing. He was last seen leading some of General Cathcart's men into the gullies to the east of the sandbag battery, during the battle yesterday. You know the general was killed in the fighting? Many soldiers were lost with him, the 4th being out on a limb, swamped as they were by Russian troops.

'You may or may not be aware that Lieutenant Dalton-James was also killed in the fighting yesterday . . .'

Major Paynte could not help but intervene with, 'Which is why he is using a dead man's name.'

General Buller ignored the interruption.

'We are therefore left with no one to substantiate your claim that this was a direct order, sergeant. You took up special duties reluctantly, I seem to remember, when you were taken from your company by Major Lovelace, then a captain. He formed your little group from misfits. Since then you seem to have performed well, and certainly Major Lovelace thinks a great deal of your skills as a spy and saboteur. However, this will not satisfy any court martial of your innocence in the charge brought by Major Paynte here. We must therefore find Major Lovelace.'

Crossman felt as if he were being betrayed by the general.

'What if the major is himself dead?'

'Then I cannot help you. You were warned that this kind of thing might happen.'

It was true that Lovelace had often stressed the point that they – and Lovelace had included himself in this – were working outside the knowledge of Lord Raglan. It followed from this that they were working beyond the rules and regulations of the army. Their group was in fact illegal. Lovelace had said that Buller could not always protect them. Crossman needed Lovelace here to take responsibility for the killing of Captain Barker. Without Lovelace, Crossman could be hung for murder.

'What do you suggest, sir?' he asked General Buller, calmly. 'How shall I defend myself?'

Here the colonel, whose name Crossman did not know, came in with a suggestion.

'General Buller, I know nothing of these affairs as you are aware, but it is obvious from this conversation that such dealings go on under your guidance. We do not know yet if Major Lovelace is alive or dead. No body has yet been found, though there are many still littering the battleground. Might I suggest that the sergeant takes a party to look for the body. If it is not found, then the sergeant will know he has a new duty, to find Major Lovelace, wherever he might be?'

Major Paynte said, 'I cannot agree to that!'

'You, sir,' said General Buller, fiercely rounding on the corpulent major, 'will kindly keep your mouth closed. You have brought something down on our heads which endangers even my position in the army. If you interfere in these matters further, before I give you the word, then you will suffer for it.'

The major blinked rapidly and took a step back.

'I think,' continued Buller in a calmer tone, 'that Colonel Albright has the answer. You will find Major Lovelace, alive or dead, and bring him back. This is your next fox hunt, sergeant, and your own life depends on the outcome.'

'Yes, sir.'

'In the meantime, Major Paynte will not interfere in your business. I don't know where he thinks you can go to escape military law here, except to the other side. The major is not however aware that there is a price on your head. There are several Russian officers who would sell their grandmothers to slavery if it meant they could have you in their clutches. There are Cossack regiments who would *eat* their own grandmothers if they could have you for just one hour.

'You have ten days to find Major Lovelace. Good luck. I hope for all our sakes you are successful.'

The colonel nodded. 'I watched you fight, sergeant. You are a good man, I am sure. I wish you luck.'

Crossman left the room, closely followed by Major Paynte, who hissed in his ear as they parted, 'I don't believe any of this fairy tale. I'll see you dangling from the end of a rope, sergeant, you mark my words. I'll watch the crows picking at your liver and obtain great satisfaction from the sight.'

'Major, you may be right. I may not find Major Lovelace and you will have your satisfaction. You will have the laugh on me then. But, major, it will do you no good whatsoever, for you will still be a squat ugly little toad in the eyes of women like Mrs Durham, and nothing I can think of will ever change that.'

He left the major seething impotently, purple in the face with anger, knowing he had made an enemy for life.

32

Crossman's first job was to find his Bashi-Bazouk, Ali, who knew the Heights well. With some questioning, he managed to locate him amongst his Turkish irregulars. Ali was with a female companion, a busty women Crossman had met before. Like Ali himself she was round and overripe, went everywhere bare-breasted, and she smelled strongly of goats.

She smiled at Crossman with brown teeth when she saw him, and pointed to where Ali was sitting enjoying a pipe. He smiled back at this stocky Tartar woman with her embroidered goat skin coat and long thick hair. She was a strong, handsome female and Ali was very proud of her.

'Ali, I need your help,' said Crossman, squatting beside the Turk. 'We have to find Major Lovelace.'

'Major Lovelace go missing?'

'Yes, he hasn't been seen since the battle started, yesterday.'

Ali nodded. 'We take the men?'

'Peterson and Wynter are exhausted. They fought well in the battle. You would have been pleased with them. Devlin was killed.'

'That's bad,' said the rotund but hard-muscled Bashi-

Bazouk, as he offered Crossman some tobacco. 'He was good man.'

Crossman said no more. He took the tobacco, then realised he had not got his chibouque to put it in. Ali, seeing this, yelled for a pipe from one of his Turkish friends. A black stubby clay pipe was produced from the folds of a deep pocket.

It was much like the clay pipes used by British soldiers. The British infantry had even had them in their mouths, puffing away, as they battled the Russians the day before. This particular pipe was well used and the stem rattled with tobacco juice when Crossman blew down it. He could not afford to be fastidious however, and was soon smoking some of the harshest tobacco he had ever tasted. It made his head spin.

Ali found a sheepskin coat which smelled even more strongly than his mistress, and gave it to Crossman, who put it on. Once wearing the coat, Crossman could have been a Tartar, with his black beard and unkempt hair. No trace of his uniform could be seen, since he was wearing Russian boots and his Oxford trousers were covered with a pair of blue pantaloons. He had not bathed for three days and was probably as high as his coat.

'Dalton-James is dead too,' explained Crossman, as the pair walked away from the Turkish camp. 'I hope to God Lovelace is not, or I'm going to hang for murder. You remember the British officer I was sent to kill? They do not believe he was a traitor. They think I shot him for other reasons.'

'I not let you hang,' Ali said, very soberly. 'I take you into the hills before they hang you. You hide there and then I take you back to Turkey by land. No man can hang my friends. They will not follow. They will lose themselves in these hills.'

'I'm sure you're right, and I thank you from the bottom of my heart, Ali, but I'd rather prove my innocence.'

'Of course. We try to do this. But if we fail, then you still will not hang. I tell you this to keep you from a worry of the rope. They not hang you. They never hang you.'

There was some comfort in the Turk's words. Ali was very sure of himself. Crossman had no doubt Ali would help him escape if it came to the worst.

On the way to the Inkerman Heights they met Rupert Jarrard. He waved them down.

'Where are you two off to in such an almighty hurry? On another fox hunt?'

'You could say that,' replied Crossman, wryly. 'Lovelace has gone missing. I've got to find him to clear up a serious misunderstanding. Ali and I are going out to look amongst the bodies in St Clements Ravine. That's where he was last seen, with Cathcart's men.'

'I heard Cathcart was killed and his men were cut up pretty fiercely. I'll come with you. I haven't been to that area yet. I need to get all the information I can before writing my piece for the *Banner*.'

'You don't have to do this, Rupert.'

'No, no – I do have to do it. I'm a war correspondent. I have to see these things to report on them. Lead the way.'

Above them the sky rolled with dark clouds. It was a grey dismal day. There were people picking amongst the corpses, some of them doing decent and proper things, others perhaps scavenging from the dead. There were all manner and nation of men out there, as well as women. The place had become a ghastly, haunted landscape dotted with figures as numerous as had been the hundreds of picquets the day before, cut off from their comrades and from their line.

The three men went down past the sandbag battery, scene of some of the bitterest fighting the day before. This spot had no particular strategic importance so far as the topography went, but both sides had decided it was a matter of prestige to take it, and retake it, several times, many men dying in the process. Russians and British had been slaughtered on the battery, which had been empty of guns, for no apparent reason, unless it be that the battery was a symbol of victory for both armies.

Now there were arabas, such as could be found, being piled high with corpses. The Russians on one cart, the British on another. Those working were sweating, even though it was a cold day, while others watched in a numbed state of silence. The arms of these men were placed in piles by the battery. Crossman was reminded that he no longer had his German hunting knife and his Tranter 5-shot pistol. He would need to retrieve these from Major Paynte. It would not be a pleasant task.

The three men went down into St Clement Ravine, where Major Lovelace had last been seen. There they searched amongst the bodies, already showing small signs of decomposition. Some were horribly scarred and broken. Others were literally in pieces. Crossman was reminded of a gory history lesson, during which, as a boy of twelve, he had been told by his father of bishops in King Henry VIII's time, who were hung, drawn and then quartered. There were men here whose faces bore the look of a strangled man; who had their entrails hanging out; who had been blown into four pieces and the bits scattered.

They spent several hours scouring the area, finding pockets where men were still alive. Some were Russian, some were British. Jarrard called to other search parties of bandsmen, who were out finding the wounded, directing them to these unfortunates who had probably been lying there for thirty hours or more. The evening began to close in and still they had not found Lovelace's body. This was a good sign, but it was getting Crossman no nearer to the major's whereabouts.

While they were searching, Crossman went into a narrow crevice in the rocks, to come face-to-face with a live Russian.

The man was wedged there in a sitting position. His legs had been broken with the fall from the ridge above and were projecting at peculiar angles. His bloodshot eyes regarded Crossman feverishly. He was an officer and in his right hand he held a pistol which he pointed at Crossman's face.

'Easy, sir,' said Crossman. 'I mean you no harm.'

'I suppose,' said the Russian officer in reasonably good English, 'that the soldier who shot me in the shoulder and knocked me down here meant no harm either.'

Crossman kept his eye on the injured man's trigger finger, to see if it was being tightened. He was ready to leap aside if the other squeezed off a shot. Whether such action would save him or not, Crossman did not stop to think. He only knew that until something definite happened, he should not make any sudden moves.

Ali and Jarrard had heard him talking and were making their way stealthily towards the spot. Jarrard had his Navy Colt in his hand at the ready, but Crossman waved with his fingers, not looking at the American, to caution him not to use the weapon. Jarrard holstered it.

'Who are you signalling to?' gasped the Russian captain in a hollow, strained voice. He was obviously exhausted and in a state of confusion. His pistol hand wavered. 'I do not want to have to kill you.'

'Two friends of mine. We are searching for the body of another friend, a British major. We mean you no harm, captain.'

Finally, the man's arm went down. It seemed he was very weak and that the action had been the result of the sheer weight of his pistol. He sat there looking pathetic. Ali and Jarrard came up now.

'Jammed between the boulders, eh?' murmured Jarrard. 'It's going to hurt him when we pull him out.'

'He speaks English,' warned Crossman.

The captain, who had closed his eyes in pain, opened them again and regarded his rescuers.

'I realise I am not going to escape pain.'

Ali gave the man some water. He drank it down gratefully.

270

Then Crossman and Jarrard each took a side and tried to ease the captain out from the crevice. He screamed at them and clawed their shoulders, but they knew they had to continue. Finally they wrenched him free, just as the captain went into a swoon. They laid him out carefully on a blanket Ali always carried around his shoulders like a bandolier. The captain's poor broken legs hung one over each side of the makeshift litter. It was perhaps a good thing that he remained unconscious while they carried him back to the British lines.

They dropped him off at a staff surgeon's tent and went on to Crossman's quarters. Wynter and Peterson were still asleep when they arrived. Crossman found his chibouque and within minutes was happily puffing away. They discussed the day's failure.

'There's nothing for it but to try again tomorrow,' said Crossman. 'You don't have to be there, Rupert. I'll use those two sluggards now that they've had some rest.'

'Oh, I don't mind. As I said, I need some copy. This makes for an interesting story.'

'What, "Sergeant will hang, if major not found"?'

'Something like that,' grinned the American, ruefully.

The three of them played whist in the dim light of a candle to pass the time, with Ali continually winning.

'We should have pitted Ali against Captain Sterling Campbell,' said Jarrard, sorting through his hand for some non-existent trumps. 'We wouldn't have needed to send him to India then. Ali would have cleaned him out.'

Crossman felt a pang of guilt on remembering Campbell, who was now somewhere on the high seas.

'Just lucky,' said Ali, modestly. 'All the time I lose my goats to my cousin when we play cards. I make him a rich man. My cousin is very good player, not like you, Mr Jarrard.'

'Be careful you don't praise me too highly,' replied Jarrard, sarcastically. 'It might go to my head.'

At that moment a messenger arrived at the hovel asking for Crossman.

'The Russe captain you brought in, sergeant? He wants to speak to you. Says it's urgent.'

Crossman put on a fur cap and went out into the cold night, followed by the other two, who were as curious as he was himself to find out what the captain had to say.

They found the Russian officer lying in a hut. His legs had been straightened and his shoulder wound bandaged, but he looked a ghastly grey colour. He seemed only just on the waking side of consciousness. His hand came out and gripped Crossman's sleeve, when the sergeant knelt beside him.

'Thank you, sergeant, for saving my life. And I thank your friends too. I must speak quickly for my mind is spinning. You spoke of a major? We took a major prisoner. He was not in the uniform of the others. He was a Green Fly.'

Crossman knew that the Russians called the Rifle Brigade 'Green Flies', because of the colour of their uniforms and the way they swarmed about when skirmishing. Like Dalton-James, Lovelace had originally been from the Rifles, before taking up special duties with General Buller. Although in his capacity as a spy he wore a variety of uniforms, Rifle Greens would be the uniform he would choose to fight a battle in.

'Do you know what happened to this major?'

The captain closed his eyes and looked as if he were about to faint away, but he rallied, and came round again.

'They would take such prisoners back to Sebastopol, or march them to Kerch. I think probably he has gone to Kerch, to be taken on a ship to Russia. There was one of our majors who was much interested in your major, if indeed he is the man you seek. His name is Zinski – Major Zinski.'

Crossman knew at once that they were on the right track. Zinski was the major in whose cruel hands Crossman had found himself not so long ago. The major had seen to it that Crossman was tortured and beaten, to try to obtain required information. Wynter and Ali had rescued Crossman from that predicament, but the sergeant carried a hatred of the major, who had almost taken his life. On an attack on a hill,

Crossman had been lucky enough to encounter Major Zinski again. Crossman had tried to kill the man, but had only wounded him.

Zinski would certainly be the officer who would take charge of Major Lovelace, for interrogation purposes.

'Thank you, captain,' Crossman told the injured Russian, 'you have been most helpful.'

But the man had now slipped into unconsciousness. Crossman enquired of the surgeon whether the captain was going to live, and received the expected shrug of the shoulders. The sergeant then turned to his two companions.

'Rupert, Ali and I are going to have to go out on a fox hunt. Thank you for your help. We shall see you when we return.'

'The hell you will. I'm coming too.'

'You're a civilian, Rupert,' said an exasperated Crossman. 'I would get into deep trouble for taking you with me.'

'You're in deep trouble already.'

This was of course true. Crossman sighed. 'All right, but try not to get killed. I must stop off on the way. I have to see another major. The world is full of majors, isn't it? Sergeants like me seem to be a rarity.'

'They are in your line of work,' agreed Jarrard.

Crossman left the other two to make his visit. He walked to the house where he had been taken by the arresting lieutenant. A light was glowing in the window. Without knocking, he threw open the door and marched into the room beyond. Major Paynte was sitting behind a table, writing some reports.

He looked up, startled by the intrusion, thoroughly shaken on seeing a ragamuffin bandit in the room. Before he could recover, Crossman snapped up a salute causing the major to almost fall off his chair in alarm. It was as if he were expecting to be assassinated in his own quarters.

'Sir, I have come for my weapons! They were taken by the lieutenant when I was arrested. A German hunting knife and a Tranter 5-shot pistol. I would be grateful, sir, if they could be returned to my possession. I am going out on a mission to rescue Major Lovelace and I need them.'

Major Paynte, now recognising the intruder, quickly recovered his composure, obviously put out by the fact that he had shown fear to this man.

'Oh, you need them, do you? I seem to recall these weapons were not army issue.'

'Nevertheless, sir, they are mine by right. I purchased them in London. Many officers and men carry weapons not of army issue. I would appreciate their return.'

'By God you have the impudence of a monkey,' snapped the major, going bright red. 'I ought to have you flogged for barging in here like this . . .'

'Sir, you are wasting valuable time,' replied Crossman. 'I came here quickly because it is imperative I have my weapons before going out into the field. You are endangering the life of an officer, a major like yourself, by holding back. General Buller would see it of the utmost importance to go after his captors straight away, without delay – sir. When I return, you may flog me all you like, but I must go now, out into the hills, to rescue Major Lovelace and bring him back.'

Major Paynte crumpled, though his eyes were full of hate. He went to a greasy-looking rickety cupboard which had once stood in a Tartar kitchen. He opened it and took out Crossman's weapons, handing them to him without another word. The sergeant took them and saluted again, smartly, before marching to the door.

'I'm sure Major Lovelace will be the first to thank you for your co-operation on his return,' said Crossman.

'You are just after saving your own skin,' hissed Paynte, 'but I will have you yet, sergeant.'

Crossman turned with his hand on the door handle and looked at the major as if he were a bug crawling in the dirt.

'I am after saving a good friend and a brave officer,' he said, scathingly, 'and I would do the same for you, major. If you ever fall into the hands of the enemy – and I have been there too – you will pray for someone like me to come for you.'

With that he left the room.

33

Crossman next went to see General Buller to request the use of four horses.

'We need to be near Kerch before the prisoners arrive,' Crossman said. 'They should be fast mounts, sir.'

'You will have your horses, sergeant, but listen to what I am about to say. I am ordering you not to try to save any of the other prisoners, if it will jeopardise your mission. The officers and other ranks taken captive will be treated with a certain respect. Major Lovelace, on the other hand, is a spy, and sooner or later he is going to be recognised as such.

'I have no doubt they will torture him and then execute him. He is also privy to information which would harm us if it fell into enemy hands. He is a strong man, but who knows what methods will be used to break him down? You are not to try to save everyone – that is not possible – so you will save no one except Major Lovelace.'

The general clasped his hands behind his back and paced the dirt floor of the room.

'I would like to send a force to Kerch and effect the release of *all* the prisoners, but it would be detected in advance and would be met with at least an equal force. The only way to do this is for two or three men to sneak about unseen. In which case we have to sacrifice the many to obtain the one who is most important to us and our schemes. Finally, if you cannot release Major Lovelace, but have the opportunity to shoot him, you must do so. They will show him no mercy. He would, I know, prefer a quick death.'

Crossman quailed at the thought of killing Lovelace.

'Sir, I do not know whether I can do that.'

'It is an order, sergeant.'

'I was also ordered to kill Captain Barker, yet I stand accused of his murder. It seems to me that if I shoot Major Lovelace out of kindness, I then lay myself open to hanging on two counts, where one would actually be enough.'

'I shall protect you against any accusations regarding the death of Major Lovelace.'

'You might not be able to, sir – begging your pardon, but you might follow the road General Cathcart took.'

Buller stopped pacing and stared at the sergeant.

'You mean I might be dead? It's possible. There may be another battle tomorrow, or the next day, or next week. But then again, you might not survive into the next hour, either. Our lives are always on the line here in the Crimea. It's something we have to live with, the constant threat of death. However, I shall leave a letter for Lord Raglan. Major Paynte will try to have your head, but if I am not here to stand by you, my letter will explain everything to the high command.'

Crossman felt this was all he could ask.

'Thank you, sir. We'll be on our way then.'

'I have every confidence in you, sergeant. It is hoped you will save Major Lovelace and thereby save your own neck. I need both of you even more these days. The enemy is devious and we need to constantly update our information on his disposition.'

'Yes, sir, but by attempting to release Major Lovelace, if he is indeed still alive, I am not merely trying to save my own neck. Nor am I merely doing my duty. Major Lovelace is a personal friend of mine, if rankers can be said to have friends who are commissioned officers. Also, we went to Harrow together and I'm sure you realise what that means.'

Crossman left the general's quarters. He had not dared tell General Buller that he was taking a war correspondent with him – an American at that – or the general would have objected and forbidden it. He waited outside the house until a messenger was sent to fetch the horses. Then he took the beasts by the reins and led them to where Jarrard and Ali were waiting. The three men mounted and then rode out of the camp.

They went immediately towards the Fediukine Hills and then struck out eastwards. It was night, but there was light enough to see by. They were soon in familiar territory, Ali and Crossman having used the tracks before when escaping from the Cossacks. They kept the Woronzoff Road in sight, below them, and saw various Russian camps down there. Any one of these might have been an overnight stop for prisoners on their way to Kerch, but they could not investigate them all. It seemed best to get to Kerch and wait there for developments.

In the early hours of the morning they reached a small village. It was a pretty area, with cork oaks, laurels and cypress growing on its outskirts. There were vineyards stepped into the sides of the hills, and cattle and sheep roamed the lower meadowland slopes. A small white house on the edge of the village had an almond tree growing in its yard. They hitched their horses to this tree and broke their fast, helping themselves to water from well and trough, for man and horse while the occupants of the house slept.

Before daylight arrived they were on their horses again, Ali leading the spare mount, following the goat trails into the hills. The land on the eastern side of the Crimean peninsula is fertile and the climate healthful and mild. There was none of the dampness of Kadikoi and Balaclava harbour. Morning mists were quickly dispelled by the sun, and though a sharp crisp frost bit into their bones, it was not a coldness that encouraged respiratory problems.

They reached a good ambush spot above the road which led to Kerch. There they lay in wait for any movements along the road. Luckily, although there were many troop movements, there were few waggons going into Kerch. Most of the traffic seemed to be going the other way. Crossman was reluctant to go into the town itself. It was one thing to carry out acts of sabotage, but quite another to go in afterwards and see what havoc had been wreaked.

Eventually, after several days of waiting, Ali was on watch when a string of prisoners was herded along the road.

'They come,' he told the other two, waking them just after dawn 'Many prisoners, from the Inkerman fight I think.'

Crossman and Jarrard went with the Turk to a good vantage point and looked down on the road. There beside it, resting, was the line of British and French prisoners. Guarding them was a single half-company from the Koliwan Regiment. There was a captain in charge, a tall, thin and rather pompous-looking fellow who strutted along the line counting the captives. Alongside him walked two lieutenants: the older one seemed utterly bored and kept yawning ferociously behind the captain's back; the other lieutenant was very young, not more than eighteen years of age, smooth-faced, immaculately turned out, keen and sharp.

These three officers would not be the best the Russian Army had to offer, nor would they be men of high breeding. Guarding prisoners of any kind is commonly regarded as rather a lowly occupation, fit only for third-rate officers. That would not make them unwatchful or slack in their duty, for sometimes third-rater men do not know they are the scrapings from the bottom of the barrel. They sometimes believe themselves to be the élite, not yet recognised for being so, but top-notch army material. Occasionally they even convince themselves that the work they are doing is highly important, though clearly the older lieutenant travelled under no such illusions.

Their troops were the usual pale, round-faced peasants who filled the ranks of the Russian Army by the thousand. These would be men who were too poor to bribe the conscription boards: too poor to be able to avoid service. As Crossman had seen in several battles with these small compact men, there was no lack of bravery amongst them. They were expected to fight and die for an aristocracy which gave them very little in return, yet they did so with honour.

Crossman spoke with the other two about a plan.

'It's a day's march to Kerch, but for fresh well-fed men. These look weary to their bones. Some are obviously coping with wounds. They won't make it tonight, which means they'll have to bivouac by the roadside. We'll strike when they stop again to set up camp.'

'Can you see Lovelace amongst them?' asked Jarrard, peering down at the men's faces.

'No, but it would be difficult to recognise anyone from this distance, especially out of that grimy dishevelled group. I have not got a spyglass. I just hope he's there somewhere.'

Some time later, the soldiers and prisoners below were on the march again. Crossman, Ali and Jarrard followed, keeping out of sight in the ridges. It would not matter a great deal if they were seen, since there was nothing about them to distinguish them from Tartars. Indeed, they travelled through cherry and apple orchards, and across vineyards, without being challenged by the local people, who simply stared a little.

Around four in the afternoon, three-quarters of the way to Kerch, the prisoners were halted. They fell on to the grass at the roadside: an exhausted, dispirited crocodile of men.

Crossman judged there to be about fifty of them. It was not going to be easy, to go down there and look for a single major. He remembered his orders. He was to free Lovelace, but to ignore the pleas of the other captives. How difficult that was going to be when he made himself known to them and their hopes rose.

Darkness fell. Crossman and the other two descended from the ridge, down on to the road behind the troops. There he posted Jarrard and Ali in some rocks, one either side of the highway, to cover any rapid retreat he might have to make. He left all the horses with them, travelling the rest of the way on foot. It was not difficult to find his way to his goal: the Russian infantry had lit fires on which to cook.

The last three hundred yards Crossman travelled on his belly, until he was about twenty yards from the outermost sentry. Here he stopped and waited. Eventually, the camp settled down into sleep, leaving only the sentries awake. There were ten of them posted around the camp. Crossman took up a position between two of them and, when the watchfires were low enough, he slithered through the long grass into the camp. The sentries were not much interested in what went on outside the group. They were there to see that none got out, rather than guard against anyone getting in.

He found the line of prisoners and worked his way along until he came to a group of officers. He slid up to the head of one of them, a colonel, and woke him with difficulty, for the man must have been very tired. He lay beside the officer as if he were asleep and one of them. The colonel stared into his eyes, looking very puzzled.

'Don't move or make any loud noises, sir. My name is Sergeant Crossman, from the Connaught Rangers,' he murmured. 'I am not one of the prisoners. I have crept into the camp to speak with you.'

Hope sprang to the colonel immediately. He looked suddenly eager. Crossman winced inside.

'I have not come to effect a wholesale rescue, sir. I'm seeking a Major Lovelace. Do you know if he is here?'

The colonel hissed. 'What do you mean? Why are you interested in just one man?'

'I can't save you all,' admitted Crossman. 'Major Lovelace is important to the high command. He has certain information they require.'

'And we're expendable?'

The colonel's voice was full of bitter disappointment.

'I could sugar it for you if I wished, colonel, but that is basically the argument. To set you all free I would have needed a company, and you can't hide a hundred redcoats in these hills for very long. We would never have reached you. Major Lovelace is on special duties. It is imperative I find him.'

'Your major is not with us. I have acquainted myself with all the officers here and most of the men. There was someone they took aside before the journey began . . .' The colonel described a man he had seen being roughly dragged from the group: a man not in regular uniform. '. . . he looked more like a Turk to me, though he spoke perfect English. I heard him arguing with the Russian officers. Would that have been him?'

'That was he,' whispered Crossman. 'You have described Major Lovelace. Do you know where they took him?'

'I heard the man himself shout something about not wanting to go to Mackenzies Farm.'

'Yes, yes, he was letting you know where they were taking him. Thank you, colonel. I'm sorry I can't do any more for you. I must leave now.'

'Can't you give us a small chance of success?' pleaded the colonel. 'These men will run like the wind once they are rested. Can't you at least create a diversion to occupy the Russians, while we make a quick run for it? Some of us have sneaked through the guards before during the night hours, but of course only one or two at a time, and the Russians have the numbers to hunt us. We are counted every four hours on the dot and they know immediately if anyone has gone missing.'

'I'm surprised you are not in manacles and chains.'

'All spare iron is going to make ammunition for the guns around Sebastopol. In other words, they can't afford to waste potential grapeshot on a bunch of motley captives.' The colonel's face hardened. 'Those who have attempted to escape have all been shot dead. They don't bother with bringing you back in. They hunt you down like an animal and shoot on sight. The penalty for attempted escape is harsh.'

'I see.'

'However, if we break as a much larger group, some of us will surely manage to outwit our pursuers, especially if they are spread that much more thinly. The captain who is in charge of the Russians is not a very bright individual. A mass breakout would have him panicking, thus creating a better chance for the men on the run. What say you, sergeant? Will you at least give us the fire power to put a bit of distance between us and our captors?'

Crossman sighed heavily. 'I am under direct orders not to.'

'I see,' replied the tight-lipped man lying beside him. 'Then of course you must obey your superiors.'

'I'm sorry.'

'I understand you, sergeant, even if I do not understand the situation. I can see in your eyes you would like to help us, but cannot.'

Crossman bit his lip and made a quick decision. It might result in him being flogged, but he could not leave this colonel and his men without doing something.

'Colonel, I am going to disobey orders. It is not long until midnight. I have two good men with me. We will fire down on the Russians at precisely twelve o'clock. You must pass the word amongst your men to be ready to make the break at that time. Run north, for a tree-covered ridge, where we will be hidden amongst the rocks. We will cover your escape as best we can for the first few minutes, then you are on your own.'

The colonel's eyes lit up. 'Bless you, sergeant. You sound like a gentleman, by your voice. You are really a sergeant in the Rangers?'

'Any of my Rangers would have done the same, whether gentleman or no,' replied Crossman. 'It is not breeding which brings forth this decision on my part, but simply a feeling of comradeship with my fellow British soldiers. You realise some may die in the attempt? You will have to take responsibility for any deaths, sir, for I shall not.'

'None will take part who do not wish to undergo the risk, I assure you, sergeant. They will be given the choice.'

'Very well. Good luck, sir. Hopefully I shall see you in the British lines within a few days.'

'Ask for Colonel Davenport – I shall be there – or dead.'

With that, Crossman made his way out of the camp, much the same way as he got in, using the tunnel he had created in the long tall grass. At one point he had the feeling he was being followed and looked back to see a figure in his wake. Someone had not wished to wait for the main break, but had decided to leave the camp on his own. This made Crossman angry, for by jumping his signal the soldier was endangering him, and his whole mission to find Major Lovelace.

34

Once he was far enough away from the Russian guards and hidden amongst rocks, Crossman turned angrily on the man who was following him.

'You are jeopardising the safety of your comrades,' snapped Crossman in undertones. 'Who the hell are you?'

'Don't you recognise me, sergeant?'

The man rose from his belly and stood facing Crossman.

'Private Johnson? You?'

The big man grinned. 'Yes, sergeant. I got took in the battle by some Russe spuds. There was five of 'em. I laid out three with me fists, but the others clonked me on the head with their rifle butts.' His face took on a more serious expression. 'I want to come with you, sergeant.'

Crossman groaned. 'Johnson, what happens when they count the men and find you missing?'

Johnson's face took on a look of alarm.

'Why, they usually double the guard.'

'And they will also be on the alert. Your colonel and I have arranged a breakout at midnight. If they discover you missing before then, you will destroy any chances your comrades might have of escape. You must go back.'

'But I want to come with you, sergeant.'

'You can't come with me. We are on horseback and we have a mission.'

Johnson's face fell. 'Ain't you got no extra horses, sergeant?'

'No. That is, yes, we do have one spare horse, but she is for the man we are seeking. Now, Johnson, I'm ordering you to return to the prisoners. I understand there'll be a count at ten o'clock. You must be in the line before then.'

If Johnson refused, Crossman did not know what he was going to do about it. He could hardly manhandle the man down to the prisoners' line. If Johnson caused any sort of fuss at all, they would be heard by the Russian guards. He could lay Johnson out with a pistol to the head, but that would just leave him with a heavy body at his feet. He waited, apprehensively, for Johnson's reply.

'I might get shot the second time.'

'You might indeed, but you will be caught and shot anyway, without a horse. Once they do the count and the alarm goes up you will be on the run for your life. Without others to spread the searchers thinly, you will stand no chance whatsoever.'

'An' you won't give me a horse?'

'Not a chance, Johnson. General Buller would have me shot if I did. Go back into the line, now.'

Without another word, Johnson turned and went down on his stomach. The last Crossman knew of him was the waving grasses as the big man crawled back towards the camp. He felt sorry for him, but there was no other path to take.

At midnight Crossman, Ali and Jarrard were posted on the edge of a copse about two hundred yards from the line of prisoners. They opened fire all at once – Jarrard blazing away with his Navy Colt, Ali using a Ferguson breech-loader he had stolen, and Crossman with his Tranter. The Russian guards, not knowing where the firing was coming from at first, began to shoot back randomly into the night. There were shouts of alarm and the three Russian officers began to scream out orders.

At that moment, while there was still confusion amongst the Russians who had been sleeping, the prisoners rose up *en masse* and ran into the guards, knocking them down and wresting their weapons from them. The Russian captain began firing into the prisoners as they spread into the night. A single shot from Ali's Ferguson laid the captain low. He did not rise again. Those prisoners with firelocks fired once back into the flustered Russian soldiers, then flung their muskets away. Having no ammunition, the firelock was merely an encumbrance.

Crossman, Ali and Jarrard continued to keep the soldiers pinned down, until one of the officers thought to douse the fires. Once the camp was in complete darkness there was little point in the trio remaining. They ran back fifty yards, mounted their horses, and scrambled down the slopes to a spot further along the road. It was too dangerous to canter over the countryside at night, but they could trot along a white ribbon of a road just visible in the starlight.

Having put some distance between themselves and the Koliwan soldiers, the three slept away the rest of the night until dawn. Then they were back in the saddle again and riding west. It made sense to return to Balaclava and change the horses. It took two days to reach the British lines. By the time they got back the horses were blown.

Once there, Crossman left word with Jock McIntyre of the 93rd, who guarded the pass to Balaclava, that a batch of British prisoners had escaped their captors and would hopefully be coming back, probably in small groups. Jock promised the picquets of the Sutherland Highlanders would be on the watch for them and would assist them.

Crossman did not report to anyone. There was little point and time was growing short. They picked up fresh horses and took Peterson and Wynter with them. The five of them set out for Mackenzies Farm on the morning of the 13th of November. If Crossman returned without Major Lovelace this time, he would be arrested, for the period allotted to him by General Buller would have exhausted itself.

When they finally arrived in the hills above the farm they found a cave to stable the horses. Then they went to the edge of the escarpment, the spot from which Crossman had seen Dalton-James approaching the farm two weeks previously. There they looked down on the house and the outbuildings. They saw that it was guarded by a whole company of infantry. It was not possible at that distance to tell what regiment, even with the spyglass Crossman had now thought to bring with him. There was also a squadron of Hussars camped around a windmill nearby.

There were picquets posted out beyond the farm, but there seemed to be a concentration of sentries around one particular outbuilding, a barn of sorts, from which they saw one or two high-ranking officers emerge and go back to the house later in the day.

'I'll wager he's in there,' said Crossman. 'I'll go down this evening, after dark, and try to reach him. Ali will accompany me. Peterson and Wynter, you have your Miniés and will be best posted here. Rupert, you will come with us as far as the first line of picquets. You may have to assist us to escape. Now everyone get some rest.'

'What happens if you don't come back, sergeant?' asked Wynter, rubbing his leg, which had again festered. 'What do we do then?'

'You make your way back to the British lines.'

'Without you?'

'Yes.'

When darkness fell, Crossman, Ali and Jarrard went down to the plain below. They left Jarrard on the perimeter. Crossman and Ali crept through a vineyard, shielded by the vines, using their long lanes as cover. However, when they reached the end of the lanes they found they were still fifty yards short of their destination. There were far too many sentries around the barn to attempt a quick dash into the shadows at the back of the building.

Crossman left Ali in the vineyard and snaked his way to a water trough close to the barn.

He crouched there behind the trough in frustration, wondering if he would get a chance to proceed later on. But at that point a soldier came out of the barn with a dozen hurricane lamps, hanging them on hooks around the farm area. Crossman rolled under the trough, lying full length beneath it. The man with the lamps passed within two feet of him. Clearly the Russians were taking no chances. It was as if they expected someone to try to spring an escape.

For two hours Crossman waited. From time to time moans of agony came from within the barn. Once, there was a terrible scream, which chilled Crossman's blood. Clearly someone was being subjected to great pain behind those wooden walls.

Then the sergeant had a stroke of luck. The barn door opened and four guards came out with a hobbled prisoner shuffling along in the middle of them. The captive was wearing Turkish pantaloons and a white shirt which had been torn open to reveal his chest. He had been beaten and abused: there was blood on the shirt, his hair was dishevelled, and he limped along as if he were in pain. His head hung low and his shoulders drooped from a bent back. In the light of the lamps Crossman could see purple bruises on his skin. His nose was a bloody, squashed mess in the middle of his face.

Normally this man strode around, tall, straight and square-shouldered.

It was indeed Major Lovelace.

He was escorted to some latrines nearby and allowed to relieve himself, though the guards left the door wide open. Major Lovelace was in the latrine a long time, still using the lavatory, which indicated that his captors had not allowed him to go for quite some time. No doubt this was part of their humiliation technique, the debasing of the victim.

Then another, greatcoated, figure came out of the barn at a leisurely pace. This man looked comfortable and casual, languidly smoking a long cigar. He stood watching Major Lovelace with impassive eyes. When the prisoner was returned to the barn, the man spoke in English to him.

'These interruptions will only prolong your ordeal, major. You must talk to us. The sooner you tell me what I want to know, the quicker we will shoot you. You surely do not wish to extend your period of torture indefinitely? I find that inflicting pain is a distasteful exercise.'

'I doubt that,' came the thickly-spoken reply.

Then the two men and the guards disappeared inside the barn once more. A few moments later the groans were clearly audible in the night air. One of the guards turned and frowned at another one, before glancing at the barn. Then he turned his face out to the night again.

Crossman stayed another three hours, then finally gave up and returned the way he had come.

'He's there all right, but I couldn't reach him,' he told the others. 'There's someone I know with him.'

'Who's that?' asked Jarrard.

'A Major Zinski. The same man who had me tortured when I was a prisoner in Sebastopol. The same man who would have hung me, had not Wynter and Ali managed to set me free. The same man I wounded in the Battle of Balaclava.'

'He appears to be your nemesis,' said Jarrard.

'Perhaps,' said Crossman, through narrowed eyes, 'or I his.'

He explained the position down by the farm.

'If we attack the barn and try to rescue him, we'll be cut down. There are too many firelocks and a squadron of cavalry nearby. For once I haven't the faintest idea what to do next.'

290

'We wait until the morning,' suggested Ali, 'maybe the cavalry go away then?'

'If they don't, we're in very grave trouble. And all the while Major Lovelace is undergoing terrible torture. Perhaps it might be better to post Peterson in a good spot and have him shoot Major Lovelace the next time they take him to the latrine – it would end his terrible agony.'

Peterson paled. 'Shoot Major Lovelace? I – I couldn't do that, sergeant. Don't order me.'

'Would you rather he suffered? They're cutting pieces off him in there. That Major Zinski is an animal.'

'I couldn't do it. Don't make me, please, sergeant.'

'You may have to, Peterson – I'm sorry.'

The rest of the night was spent in uncomfortable circumstances. At least the cries stopped about an hour later.

When Crossman saw Zinski leave the barn he guessed that Major Lovelace had probably fainted and Zinski was going to get some rest. Even torturers need sleep. Hopefully Lovelace would stay unconscious until the morning.

Around six o'clock, a brisk wind sprang up and there was rain in the air. Then a strange silence fell on the land and the awakening sky revealed a colour Crossman had never seen before. It was an eerie sky, a pale yellow, with streaks of cloud like lazy paintbrush strokes. On the horizon was a dark band which seemed to grow with every minute.

'What's happenin', sergeant?' asked Wynter. 'I can smell a bit of rain in the air.'

Wynter was a country boy and was instinctively aware of changes in the weather.

'Looks like some sort of storm coming in,' said Crossman. 'I don't know . . .'

Within an hour they were in the middle of a hurricane. Torrents of rain and sleet fell, hammering into the hillside, causing flood water to gush down to the plain below. Crossman and his men had to cling to the rocks to prevent themselves being blown away, so fierce was the wind. A landslip occurred to the right of them, with mud, shale and rocks tumbling down into the vineyards below. Visibility was down to almost zero at times.

During a clear patch, through a swirling tunnel of light, Crossman saw the sails of the windmill being torn from the tower and sent crashing into the Hussars' camp. The horses down there were panicking and kicking out, while the men fought with the bridles, holding their mounts, trying to calm them in the chaos and confusion. Crossman saw tents ripped from their guys and swept away like ghosts. One of these tents covered a charger, causing it to bolt and drag its owner along the ground.

Crossman realised it was a good thing they had their own mounts stabled in the cave. Wynter was sent back to calm them if they were jittery. The lance-corporal returned to say the animals were restless, but deep enough in the cave to prevent the wind from reaching them. It was only the howling noise across the entrance which bothered them at all.

Part of the farmhouse roof below them was now ripped off, the slates flashing through the air in a deadly fashion, likely to decapitate any unfortunate guard who happened to be in their path. Barrels were being blown around, farm equipment was whisked up into the air and thrown against walls. It was mayhem. Infantry soldiers deserted their posts and sought refuge in nooks and crannies around the farmyard.

After a shrieking and groaning, the tall farmhouse chimney came crashing down, smashing through the roof of the building, shattering slates and timbers. A water tower did the same just a few moments later, breaking its timbers on the yard. Its tank burst and the flood of water carried a soldier off his feet and swept him a hundred yards to leave him pinned against a fence.

The livestock did not escape the wind either. Terrified chickens were snatched up into the air and carried away like flapping pieces of paper. A squealing piglet was blown over the ground like a rolling ball, to end up stuck on the curved spikes of a hay-turning machine. Even waggons were disintegrating, being blown apart, the pieces scattered over the farm area.

'Now,' yelled Crossman, into Jarrard's ear. 'We go down now!'

Jarrard passed the word down the short line of men, who prepared to descend the dangerous muddy slope before them. God had sent them a storm to mask their activities. They would be fools if they did not take this opportunity, no matter how difficult it was going to be. Peterson went first and was almost immediately blown off her feet and carried twenty yards across the face of the hill. The others linked arms and snaked down the escarpment, collecting her on the way.

35

When the five men reached the vineyard, the wind was tearing the vines from their roots. Crossman indicated that they should go straight to the barn, shooting anyone who got in their way. The sleet was coming down thickly now. Visibility was down to a few yards. Wind was screaming around the buildings, tearing at everything it could loosen. Certainly it was doubtful that the cavalry could be summoned to the assistance of those in and around the barn. The noise of the wind would drown any bugle call, any drum beat, and even if a messenger could reach them, the Hussars were in no condition to mount an attack.

Crossman's fingers were freezing and he was having difficulty in keeping on his feet. A guard hunched in the doorway of the farm opposite saw him and evinced surprise. The sentry raised his weapon, but before he could fire Ali had launched himself at the man and pistol-whipped him to the ground. Crossman and Ali then fought their way across the yard to where the barn door was banging and rattling on its hinges.

Before they reached the door, shouts went up to be flung away by the wind. Peterson and Wynter engaged with some of the other guards, who began to emerge from behind stalls and from underneath pigsties. Shots went wild, as the force of the storm destroyed men's ability to aim: their firelocks wavered in the hurricane, their eyes were sore from bearing the brunt of the wind. Sleet destroyed their concentration. Musket balls flew back and forth, but not a single man was hit on either side.

Crossman reached the barn door and, lifting a latch, threw it open. It crashed back against the barn, instantly ripped from its hinges, and flew over the yard to slam against the farmhouse wall. Crossman and Ali ran into the barn. There were three soldiers inside the swaying, creaking building.

The first man reached for a pistol and was shot in the arm by Ali. Sorely wounded, this soldier clutched at a hanging rope to save himself from falling to the ground. He held on there, gritting his teeth against his pain, now unable to reach into his coat for his pistol.

Another young officer drew his sword. Crossman put two rounds in his chest and he was dead before he hit the dirt floor.

The third man's face registered alarm and fear. He threw his arms above his head and shouted something in Russian.

At that moment the barn began to shake violently. While the large doors had been closed, the barn had held together, but now the wind was swelling inside, blasting full-force into the wooden building. The walls flexed and expanded, first sucking in, then bulging out. Finally the whole barn began to rip at the seams. One wall went slapping down in the yard, crushing a sentry.

The roof was ripped away and thrown up into the crashing, whirlwind sky. The young Russian soldier who was holding on to the rope was whipped upwards like a toy into the air. They did not see him come down. Bales of straw and hay were tumbling about now, being blown from the exposed shelves in the barn's roof space, where they had been stored. A cow was standing foursquare in the middle of the floor, its eyes wide with fright.

Lovelace was bound to a harrow at the far end of the barn.

Crossman and Ali rushed to him and cut his bonds. The major was unconscious. Ali heaved the inert body up on to his broad shoulders and then walked with it as a Smithfield market porter walks with a side of beef on his back.

The Turk headed straight for the hills, while Crossman found himself entangled with plough chains, that whipped around his legs. He struggled to get them off as the Russian soldier with his hands in the air ran away, towards the farmhouse, yelling for assistance. Crossman could do nothing to stop him.

While Crossman was trying to disentangle himself, a man came out of the farmhouse, struggling against the force of the wind. He was barely visible in the driving, heavy sleet which had increased in vigour during the last few minutes. As he came closer, Crossman could see he was a bulky man, whose dark hair blew wildly in the raging storm. His angry eyes were fixed on Crossman in a determined way and the sergeant knew that the man had come to kill him.

It was Major Zinski and he had a sword in his hand.

Crossman grappled with the chains around his ankles and at last managed to free himself. Zinski had reached him and stood over him, two hands on the handle of his sword, which was poised to drive down into Crossman's chest. In the swirling sleet and fierce wind the actions of both men were slow and laborious. Even the lifting of an arm took great effort. The two men formed a dark sluggishly-moving scene within the remains of the barn. It was like some ghastly act of two monsters battling it out in primeval ooze.

Crossman aimed his revolver at the major's face and pulled the trigger. A dull click came from the pistol, which made Zinski jerk backwards and blink. Then Zinski smiled wolfishly down at Crossman.

'Misfire,' murmured the major, and he drove the sword hard down.

Crossman rolled aside, but the point of the sword went through the fleshy part of his underarm, pinning him to the mud. Zinski however had overbalanced, slipping in the slush on the ground. He fell heavily on top of Crossman. The sergeant smelt Zinski's breath in his nostrils, an offensive odour of red cabbage and meat. Crossman dropped his pistol and wrenched his German hunting knife from his belt.

Zinski tried to get to his feet, but Crossman had gripped the officer's coat collar with his injured hand. Zinski punched Crossman several times in the face, trying to make him let go of the coat. Crossman held on like grim death.

Finally, there was an opening. Crossman drove the knife blade into Zinski's throat, downwards towards the lungs, opening up the man's chest. Zinski's eyes widened. The Russian major clutched at Crossman, eventually managing to get a hold on Crossman's neck. He pressed down hard with his thick thumbs in the hollow below the Adam's apple, trying to cut off Crossman's oxygen.

Crossman savagely twisted the knife still lodged in the major's throat and chest. He worked it back and forth until the fingers around his neck gradually loosened. The major finally let go and attempted to wrench himself free of the blade. Crossman's response was to force it in further, using both hands. Zinski rattled out a choking sound and rolled away from Crossman, clutching the gushing wound.

As Crossman freed himself from the sword, Zinski staggered away into the wind, choking and gasping. Then the Russian fell full length and face down in the slush. He lay there gargling.

Crossman felt a thump on the shoulder.

He looked up. Peterson had returned for him. There were other shapes in the distance behind her, presumably Russians, like phantoms battling against the storm. She helped Crossman to his feet and the two of them went off into the remains of the vineyard.

Jarrard was waiting for them. The American blazed away with his Colt at the dark shapes following Crossman and Peterson, causing the figures to fade away for cover. Jarrard then went on ahead, while Peterson helped the wounded sergeant up the slope. It was a case of two steps forward, one step back, but they eventually made it to the top. Finally they reached the cave where the horses were corralled. Inside the cave, Jarrard, Wynter and Ali were already discussing a defence.

Such preparations proved to be unnecessary, for the storm did not abate, in fact it increased in intensity. For twenty-four hours the wind and rain raged at the Crimean peninsula. In the cave, five soldiers and a war correspondent waited patiently, ready to ride out when the wind dropped to a safe velocity.

Lovelace slipped in and out of consciousness. Ali was doing his best for the injured man. The Bashi-Bazouk had lit a fire from the charcoal of an old goatherd's fire in the cave. He had wrapped the major in a blanket and was cleaning up the abrasions and cuts on his body.

Crossman knew that if the major died, he too would probably die, but that was not his main reason for hoping that Lovelace lived. He had strong feelings for Major Lovelace – regarded him almost as an older brother – and it would have hurt him deeply to lose that adopted brother.

As Jarrard bandaged Crossman's wounded shoulder, he said, 'You've been punctured so many times now it's a wonder the air doesn't hiss out of you, leaving you a shrivelled balloon!'

Crossman sighed. 'Rupert, I swear your knowledge of science is appalling sometimes.'

'My knowledge of science is far superior to yours, Jack, and well you know it. I can see you're worried about Major Lovelace. I think he will live. But you have no need to worry. We questioned him before you and Peterson got back to the cave. It seems you told the truth about the traitor, Captain Barker. Ali, Wynter and I will testify to that at any court martial. Isn't that so, you men?'

Ali and Wynter gruffly agreed with the American, though

something in their faces made Crossman think it was the first time they had heard of such a thing.

Crossman looked keenly and suspiciously at Jarrard.

'Major Lovelace has not spoken a word, except to groan in pain, the whole time I've been in the cave.'

'Perhaps,' replied Jarrard, now cleaning his Colt revolver in a preoccupied fashion, 'but nevertheless he did speak before you and Peterson arrived back. He told us Barker was a traitor and that he had ordered you and Dalton-James to assassinate him. There,' he looked down the barrel into the glowing fire to see that it was clear and shining, 'you have it on the word of a gentleman. I shall swear it on the Bible at your court martial, Jack, and glaring at me like that will do you no good whatsoever – you can't subvert the truth with dark looks, you know.'

'If it is the truth.'

'You doubt my word? I take affront. However, since you are a close friend, I'll overlook it this time. Next time, beware. I'll challenge you to a duel. And I am a good shot, as you've already witnessed.'

'Rupert, you are an incorrigible rogue.'

'I hope so, for as a Westerner I'm supposed to be rough and tough, though made of good honest dust.'

When the wind finally dropped, the group mounted their horses and rode out. Major Lovelace had to be held in his saddle by Peterson, who shared the same mount. Because of this, progress was a little slow. Eventually they reached the Woronzoff Road and crossed it without running into any Russians. Peterson and Wynter took the major to the small cottage hospital at Kadikoi, while Crossman went to report to General Buller.

As Crossman strode towards the general's quarters, he saw that Major Paynte was waiting outside. It seemed incredible, but it appeared that the major had been waiting for

Crossman's return, loitering daily outside the general's place. When Crossman passed him, Major Paynte looked into Crossman's eyes and saw the answer to his question there. Without another word, the corpulent officer turned on his heel and walked away.

Crossman gave a full report of the *peloton*'s activities to General Buller, saying that they had Major Lovelace safely in hospital.

'He's in a bad way, sir, but hopefully he'll pull through.'

'I'll question him when he's better, but I'm sure it's merely a formality. You would not have returned with the only man who could clear you if you were not innocent of the crime of which you've been accused. I'm sure that's not the only reason you rescued the major, but I am relieved for both of you.'

The general paused in his speech before continuing.

'You disobeyed my orders, regarding the other prisoners, you say? You made it possible for some of them to escape?'

'I hope so, sir. And I know what you're about to say, but I wish to offer a defence. Though I am merely a sergeant here, I am a commander in the field. Therefore the decisions, and the responsibility, are wholly mine. I liken myself to a captain on a ship. I have to use my initiative, sir. I have to gauge the situation at the moment.'

'You liken yourself to a ship's captain, do you?'

'Or the commander-in-chief leading his forces in battle.'

The general's expression was disapproving, as if Crossman had just likened himself to the Pope.

Crossman sought to explain himself.

'I hope that does not sound too audacious, sir, but I must tell you what I mean. On the battlefield, a commander has to make decisions, as events unfold themselves. It is no use a politician in London telling him what he can or cannot do in the heat of the moment, while the battle rages on the Crimean peninsula. That politician is not around to assess the situation first hand. So the commander does what he feels is right, and expects to take responsibility for his actions later.'

300

The general shifted in his chair. 'And I am the politician in this particular case?'

'Yes, sir. I was there. I had to weigh the situation. I did so and could see no reason not to help the other prisoners. It did not jeopardise our mission in any way.'

General Buller stared at the table top for a long time before raising his head once more.

'It seems,' he said, 'that times are changing and I must attempt to change with them. A sergeant used to be simply another man in the line; a private soldier with stripes. Now men like you act on your own initiative, your own resources. You become the commander in the field, as you say, for there is no one else. I accept what you are telling me, but I am an old man, change comes hard to me, sergeant.'

'Yes, sir.'

The general snapped back, 'Don't be so quick to agree with me, when I call myself old.'

'No – no, of course not, sir.'

'That is all.'

'Thank you, sir.'

Before Crossman left the room, the general pointed out, 'Sergeant, there is blood seeping through your coat – are you all right?'

Crossman did feel a little woozy, but he wanted to get this interview out of the way.

'I'm fine, sir.'

The general paused, then added, 'You've done well, sergeant, as always. Very well. Some recognition is called for and I shall certainly recommend you and your men, the Turk especially, for medals. We can do that, since this was not spying or sabotage, but a straightforward rescue. Perhaps it will prove something to Lord Raglan, who believes the Turks to be untrustworthy in battle. He thinks them unreliable and cowardly, after they abandoned the redoubts during Balaclava.'

'A few Turkish gunners against the whole Russian Army?

They only retreated after holding the guns for several hours. What did our commander-in-chief expect of them?'

'I know, I know,' sighed Buller, clearly uncomfortable with criticising a general while speaking with a sergeant. 'But that's Lord Raglan for you. He has other merits. Still, your chap Ali seems to be made of fine mettle.'

'The very best,' said Crossman, fiercely. 'He is a superb fighter, a fearless man who would give his life without hesitation to save any one of us. I can think of no praise too high for him.'

'Good, well, let's hope his Pasha thinks so.'

'Much appreciated, sir. I'm not too concerned about medals myself, sir, but my men might enjoy them.'

'One day I hope to reward you properly for all this undercover work, but while Lord Raglan is commander-in-chief that's not possible. You know what he thinks of spies and saboteurs.' The general paused again, checking any further criticism of Lord Raglan, before continuing. 'I understand you lost two of your men recently.'

'Yes, sir. Private Clancy was drowned and Corporal Devlin was killed on the Inkerman Heights. They were good men and will be sorely missed by those who remain in the *peloton*.'

'I'm sure we can ill afford to lose such boys. I'll make sure they are rewarded posthumously, for all their services to the Queen. We have also lost Lieutenant Dalton-James of course. I know he and you did not always see eye-to-eye.'

'He was my superior officer, sir. If there were any differences, they were of no consequence. I did as he ordered me to do. I am as sorry for his death as everyone else.'

'These feelings do you credit. Regarding the two dead men. Have you any replacements in mind?'

'I may have, sir. Can I speak with you later?'

'By all means. By the way, you say you took an American correspondent on this fox hunt. That won't do, you know. I only want Rangers out there. If you lose a civilian on one of these missions, we'll really be in the soup. You know that, don't you, sergeant?'

'Yes, sir. I couldn't stop him. He's one of these rough-and-ready Americans from the Wild West, full of vinegar. He wants to be where the action is.'

'Tell him to join the army then, but he's not to accompany you again.'

'I understand, sir. Thank you, sir.'

Crossman saluted and left, relieved to get away with just a mild reprimand for taking Jarrard with him. He went first to the hospital, where he was delighted to find the prognosis for Major Lovelace was good. The major was badly injured and it would take time to mend him, but he would not be put on one of the so-called hospital ships and sent to Scutari.

'You will not, I'm afraid, be able to pay court to the admirable Miss Nightingale, sir,' said Crossman, 'nor indulge in the delights of Scutari Barracks.'

Sergeant Crossman then went from the hospital to his quarters in the Kadikoi hovel for a well-earned rest.

36

The storm had wreaked havoc on the Army of the East at Balaclava and indeed all along the front. In all, over twenty British ships had been sunk, many of them thrown against each other in the harbour and smashed to pieces. One large ship, the *Prince*, had gone down with warm clothing in the hold. Quantities of medical supplies and ammunition had also been lost. A total of fifteen cargo ships laden with stores had foundered, as well as warships and smaller vessels. It was a disaster for the men at the front, who were awaiting clothes to replace their rags before the winter really set in, with icy tooth and claw.

For a day or two after the storm, the skies were clear and bright and of an unusually soft colour. Crossman was able to appreciate these. He heard no more from Major Paynte, but did receive a visit from Colonel Davenport, the officer he had helped escape from the Russians outside Kerch. The colonel expressed his thanks, saying that at least thirty captives had escaped and more were coming back in ones and twos by the day.

'I'm sure we lost some of the men,' said the colonel, regretfully, 'but theirs was the choice and many desired to take it. You made that possible, sergeant. Are you sure you would not like me to put you in for a commendation?'

'No, sir.'

'Well, then, we must leave it there. But I shall not forget, believe me, sergeant. There will come a time when I shall be able to repay you, and indeed I shall take that opportunity with pleasure.'

With this, the colonel left Crossman sitting in his quarters pondering on all that had passed around the battle of the soldiers in the mist, reflecting on his feelings over lost comrades and considering the future of his *peloton*. He needed two good replacements for his little band. One would have to be Johnson, of course, if he ever made it back from Kerch. That big man had earned his place in the team.

And the other? Well, he had heard of a soldier out of sorts with the rest of his regiment. A disaffected man from the Australian colonies, good with a knife so it was said, with soft feet and keen eyes. Crossman would have to investigate further, but he sounded the right sort of replacement for Clancy.

This man would have to be knocked into shape of course, but Crossman was becoming used to recruiting wild men and channelling their aggression into more productive areas.

'Private Dan Kelly, is it?' Crossman murmured, reading the missive from General Buller again. 'Well, Mr Kelly, we shall see if you are as tough as you believe to be.'

A shape suddenly appeared in the doorway of the hovel, darkening it, and Crossman looked up to see a lieutenant standing there, the sneer of cold command on his lips.

'Sergeant Crossman,' said the junior officer crisply, 'I am your new immediate superior, Lieutenant Pirce-Smith.'

'Oh, God,' said Crossman, audibly, 'don't they ever come with just a single surname?'

'What was that, sergeant?' snapped the officer. 'It sounded remarkably like insolence to me. I was warned of you by your last superior officer when he was alive. Lieutenant Dalton-James was a particular friend of mine. You can be assured I am not of the same forgiving nature as he.'

'*Oh, and he looked fine, in a coat of claret wine,*' sang a gruff voice, softly, from deep in the recesses of the room, in the country accent of Lance-Corporal Wynter, '*as he marched to the band, with his baton in his hand.*'

A higher yet quieter voice, which Crossman recognised as that of Lance-Corporal Peterson, added to this refrain.

'*A general he would be, if he could leave his mother's knee . . .*'

The lieutenant peered into the darkness, coming to the conclusion that deference, so far as he knew it, was not present in this lowly dwelling, nor in anyone residing there.